THIS EXCLUSIVE EDITION OF

WE ARE UNPREPARED

MEG LITTLE REILLY

HAS BEEN SPECIALLY BOUND
BY THE PUBLISHER

WE

ARE

UNPREPARED

A NOVEL

MEG LITTLE REILLY

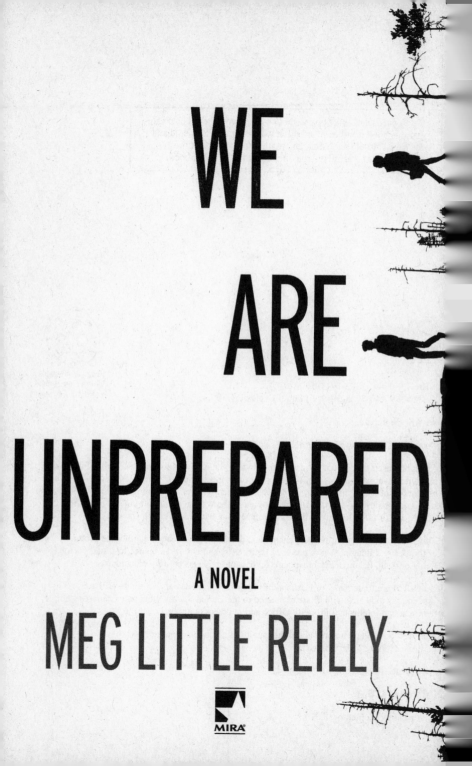

MIRA®

ISBN-13: 978-0-7783-1943-6
ISBN-13: 978-0-7783-3052-3 (Target Exclusive Edition)

We Are Unprepared

Copyright © 2016 by Margaret Reilly

www.MIRABooks.com

Printed in U.S.A.

First printing: September 2016
10 9 8 7 6 5 4 3 2 1

Dear Target Reader,

Thank you for choosing my novel! I'm so honored to join the wonderful selection of titles in the Target Book Club and to share this thrilling story with you.

The idea behind *We Are Unprepared* was hatched in my final year in Washington politics, as I turned my focus to our budding family and my lifelong passion for writing. I grew up in Vermont and always knew that my first novel would take me back there. Even after a decade in our nation's capital, I am a country girl at heart. So that's where my inspiration began: in the wild, enchanting woods of my childhood.

The Northeast Kingdom is a real and beautiful place along the eastern side of the Vermont-Canadian border. It's the sort of breathtaking setting one fantasizes about escaping to. Well, Ash and Pia—the main characters in this story—actually do. They leave behind their fast urban existence in search of a more authentic life. But their dreams are derailed when stark news of an impending storm breaks and they're forced to live with their mounting fear in a remote new place.

I loved this idea of the natural world as offering both an escape and entrapment. It was supposed to be Ash and Pia's salvation, but it threatens to be their undoing in the end. From the very start, I envisioned this fictional rural town of Isole as a central figure in the story, and a complicated one. Growing up in a place where Mother Nature makes the rules will do that to you. But the character who reveals more about who I am than any other is seven-year-old August. He possesses something the adults around him lack: the ability to transcend the hard truths of his life. Despite the darkness descending around him, August finds friendship in woodland animals, pleasure in everyday discoveries and magic in fairy rings. He's not an autobiographical character, but an aspirational one. I'm always working to listen to my inner August.

The novels I've always loved reading, and that I now strive to write, are the ones that help us understand the human experience. At the heart of this story is the universal question of how we live with fear. Some people rise above it. Many do not. Today's storms may be bigger than they've been before, but our responses to fear are timeless. Writing *We Are Unprepared* was an opportunity for me to explore how a modern threat can unravel the most intimate parts of our life—and maybe even make them stronger. As a mother, wife and active member of my community, I grapple with questions like these every day.

It's this tension between the darkness and the light that I love to write about. Fear and courage. Danger and security. In the end, the light always wins for me. *We Are Unprepared* is a frightening story about real-life threats, but there's too much beauty in people like August and places like the Northeast Kingdom for me to believe that darkness is greater.

We may be unprepared, but we're not without hope. Please enjoy.

Meg Little Reilly

This book is dedicated to the wild places worth protecting.
And to Dan, with whom I want to explore them all.

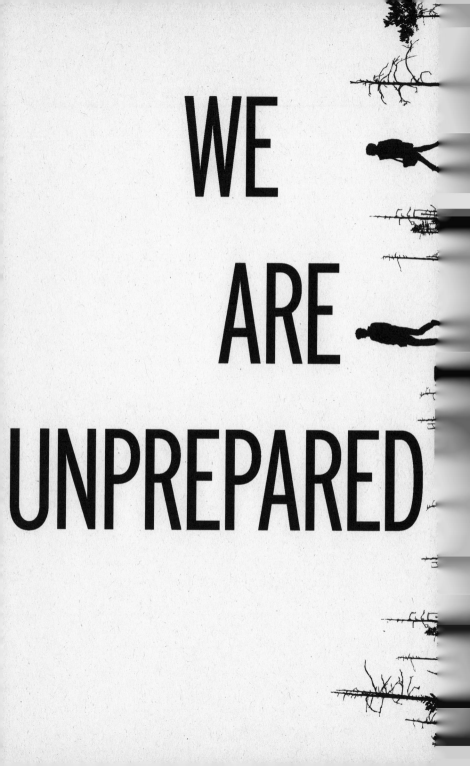

PROLOGUE

Isolé—(French) / EE-zo-LAY / adj.: isolated, remote, lonely.

Isole—(English) / i-sol / n.: rural town in the Northeast Kingdom of Vermont. Population: 6,481.

IT WOULD BE narcissistic to assume that the earth conjured a storm simply to alter the course of my life. More likely, we'd been poisoning this world for years while ignoring the warning signs, and The Storm wasn't so much a cosmic intervention as it was a predictable response to our collectively reckless behavior. Either way, the resulting destruction—to North America and our orderly life in Isole—arrived so quickly that I swear we didn't see it coming.

Looking back, I realize how comforting those months leading up to The Storm had been as we focused on preparing for the disaster. News of the changing weather patterns gave each of our lives a new clarity and direction. It didn't feel enjoyable at the time, but it was a big, concrete distraction in which to pour ourselves, even as other matters could have benefited from our attention. It was urgent, and living in a state of urgency can be invigorating. But the fear can be mistaken for purpose, which is even more dangerous than the threat itself.

PART ONE

I pine, I pine for my woodland home;
I long for the mountain stream
That through the dark ravine flows on
Till it finds the sun's bright beam.
I long to catch once more a breath
Of my own pure mountain air,
And lay me down on the flowery turf
In the dim old forest there.

O, for a gush of the wildwood strain
That the birds sang to me then!
O, for an hour of the fresher life
I knew in that haunted glen!
For my path is now in the stranger's land,
And though I may love full well
Their grand old trees and their flowery meads,
Yet I pine for thee, sweet dell.

I've sat in the homes of the proud and great,
I've gazed on the artist's pride,
Yet never a pencil has painted thee,
Thou rill of the mountain side.
And though bright and fair may be other lands,
And as true their friends and free,
Yet my spirit will ever fondly turn,
Green Mountain Home, to thee.

—"Green Mountain Home" by Miss A. W. Sprague of Plymouth, Vermont.
First published in 1860.

ONE

WE WERE DRIVING east on Route 15 when the world first learned of the coming storms. Pia and I had just met with a fertility specialist in Burlington and we were both staring straight ahead at the road as we digested the information we'd received there. I didn't want to see a doctor about having babies. That was for people who were old or sick or in a rush, and we were none of those things. But it was true that we had sort of been trying on and off for a year, so with little persuasion, I agreed to the appointment. Conceiving a child had become Pia's obsession in the preceding months, and her determination trumped my ambivalence.

We sat completely still in our seats and stared at the empty road as we drove back toward our new home. I gripped the wheel at ten o'clock and two o'clock, focusing on the act of driving to avoid looking over at Pia, who I knew was crying silently. I could feel the steam from the fat tears that rolled down her smooth face. I wanted to comfort her, to make them stop, but I couldn't will myself to.

There had been soft Celtic music playing in the waiting room of the Full Moon Fertility Center and amateurish oil paintings of naked women in various states of pregnancy hanging on the walls, all of which annoyed me immensely for their obviousness. Weeks earlier, blood had been drawn and samples had been submitted, and this was the day Dr. Tan-Face explained to us in a soothing voice that conceiving a child on our own was unlikely. Pia had a hormone imbalance that would require "assistance." It made Pia cry to hear this word, which made me almost as sad to see.

It was a hot September day in Vermont and everything that had been green was beginning to turn brown under the unrelenting sun. It was hotter and drier than it should have been on September 20. We passed roadside produce stands and fellow drivers occasionally but were mostly alone for miles of farmland. Fireweed grew along the edges of the road and, if I squinted, I could see fluffy dandelion heads mingling with drying milkweeds in the fields. There was a group of grazing cows and a carload of children pointing excitedly at the lazy ladies. I was trying to conjure more sympathy for my wife as I took this all in. Species were propagating all around us, but we needed *assistance*. I understood why this news was difficult to hear. Other couples had told us of the heartache of infertility and the shattering of a romantic fantasy for how this milestone is supposed to unfold. I wanted to feel that heartache with her, but any sadness was crowded out by an overwhelming sense of relief—relief that it was her faulty machinery and not mine and, mostly, relief that we had just been given the gift of more time. The doctor had explained that getting pregnant might take a little while, which was all I really wanted to hear him say—that I would have a little more time to live life like the young, happy thirty-five-year-old I believed myself to be.

The air blowing in from our open windows smelled like overheated livestock and corn that had passed its prime. I

MEG LITTLE REILLY

could picture the exact stage of transformation that the kernels on the mature stalks would be entering at that moment. The extreme heat had forced early harvests and they were already losing their plump, yellow corn complexions as the sugars dulled to starch. I knew those smells. I knew that the cut stalks were already so sharp that if you ran through them in your bare feet, they could slice right through the skin. These were passive memories, absorbed unknowingly in childhood and left dormant for the years I'd been away from Vermont. They surprised me in their specificity and sureness, awakened by the smallest triggers. It was as if a whole room in my brain had been locked for a long time, but when it finally reopened, every object was just as I had left it.

When the silent crying and focused driving got to be too much, I reached for the stereo dial on the dashboard of our aging Volvo, permanently set to Vermont Public Radio. It came on too loud, which was awkward at that moment. My hand rushed back to the knob, but as I started to turn it down, Pia grabbed my wrist and said, "Wait, Ash."

A somber, male NPR voice was explaining that the head of the National Oceanic and Atmospheric Administration had just briefed the president of the United States about the latest long-term storm forecast. At first, it didn't sound all that serious. Big storms had already become the norm. Tornados, wildfires, floods, hurricanes—it seemed as though some part of the country was always in a state of emergency. But the tone of the reporter's voice and the odd timing of the report suggested that there was something new here.

"What we know for sure," the reporter said, "is that, due to rapidly rising sea-surface temperatures in the Atlantic and Gulf of Mexico, we are now approaching a period of extreme weather events. NOAA is predicting as many as thirty named tropical storms and hurricanes in the coming months, along with likely heat waves and drought, and even severe blizzards. It's too early to know precisely when or what we're in for, but these water temperatures are unprecedented and the storms they trigger will almost certainly be record breaking. These storms have the potential to be very, very disruptive."

He said *disruptive* with emphasis; we were expected to infer larger things from the restrained word.

"Jesus," I said out loud.

Pia had stopped crying. She was leaning in toward the dashboard as if coaxing the news out of the speakers.

"How firm is this science?" a female interviewer asked the male voice, and I wished that we had heard the report from the beginning.

"Government scientists say the data on rising seawater temperatures and levels are reliable. They are less certain about how these variables will interact with other weather forces. Storm experts that I've spoken with say that there is a plausible worst-case scenario that the government doesn't want to talk about just yet."

"And what's that?"

"If this warm air above the Atlantic collides with a colder pressure system from the west, they could create a sort of superstorm along the eastern seaboard that could be positively devastating. But again, no government officials have made such a warning. All we know for sure right now is that we have several months of extreme weather events ahead. But I believe this is the first time the federal government has issued such an early and emphatic warning of this kind, so it must be dire."

The radio voices went on to discuss global ramifications of extreme weather—food scarcity, political unrest, war—but we had already drifted back into our own minds by then. Moments before, we were fixated on creating new life, and

MEG LITTLE REILLY

now we were confronted with the uncertainty of the life before us. We didn't linger for long on the thought—our babies were as abstract then as the coming storms.

I turned right, toward our house, past the broken mailbox I kept meaning to replace and down the dirt path that served as our driveway. I loved everything about that house. I loved the way the overgrowth of sugar maples and yellow birch trees along the driveway created a sort of enchanted tunnel that spat you out steps from our expansive porch. I really loved the way the porch, crowded with potted plants and mismatched furniture, wrapped all the way around the faded yellow farmhouse. This was our dream home in our dream life and, though we had been there for only three months, it felt as if we were always meant to live there. The yellow farmhouse was the realization of all the fantasies borne from our marriage. To be there, finally, was a victory.

There was a creek that ran through the backyard, threading all of our neighbors and hundreds of spring thaws together. Some of the people in the area kept their yards neatly manicured, but most were like us: they mowed now and then, but they gave the wildflowers a wide berth and relished the sight of a deer or—even better—a brown bear, snacking on the ever-encroaching blackberry bushes. This was where you lived if you wanted not to conquer nature, but to join it. This was the Northeast Kingdom of Vermont and there was nowhere else like it on earth.

I turned off the engine and looked over at Pia, whose expression had turned from sullen to intrigued. Her face had reassembled itself back to its baseline of beauty. Pia was gorgeous. Her thick, wavy blond hair was twisted off over one shoulder, frizzing slightly in the unseasonable heat. She had bright green eyes protected by long lashes that were still wet with tears. She sat back and looked at me with one bare heel up on the car seat, short cutoff shorts nearly disappearing in that position. Her body and her utterly unselfconscious ownership of her body was an invitation—not just to me, but to the world. Pia was that enviable combination of beauty, self-possession and grace that makes people want to be closer. She was magnetic. Not quite fit, but small and smooth in the most perfect ways. She attracted attention, male and female, everywhere we went. Every head tilt and arm stretch seemed effortless, though I knew that they were choreographed for an imaginary camera that followed her around. As an artist, she'd achieved only middling success, but Pia was unmatched for the artfulness with which she inhabited her own skin.

"I think this is serious, Ash," Pia said. Her eyes were wide. "We all knew these storms were coming eventually, and now they're here—not that they would ever admit the *real* cause."

There had been no mention of global warming in the news report, but by then no one needed our reluctant government to confirm what we knew to be true. Pia was reflexively defiant of all authority and she seemed to enjoy the vindication that this weather report was already providing. I reached a hand across the front seat to squeeze her knee, sensing that the mood in the car had shifted. We had been drawn out of our own anxious heads and were feeling unified now by our fear and fascination with the coming storms. A familiar wave of guilty relief washed over me. I suggested that we relax on the back porch with cold beers, which she did not object to.

Pia stretched out on a hammock on the porch while I went inside to grab two Long Trail Ales from the fridge. The sun was low in the sky by then and our house was finally beginning to cool. Even though it was September, the temperature hadn't dropped below eighty-five during the day yet.

I held a wet beer against Pia's thigh, which made her

MEG LITTLE REILLY

squeal. She pulled me into the hammock with her, an un-
steady arrangement, but I was happy to have her body pressed
against mine after a particularly trying couple of days. She
was a virtuoso of affection—both creative and infectious
with her demonstration of love. After years together, I was
still always grateful to receive it.

I ran a finger along the curve of her breast and she closed
her eyes.

"We need to start planning," Pia said. "We need to start
stocking up and fortifying the house and…getting seriously
self-reliant."

We talked about self-reliance in those days as if it was a
state of higher consciousness. It was the explanation we gave
for leaving our jobs in New York and starting a new life in
Vermont. We wanted to grow things and build things, preserve things and pickle things. We wanted to play our own
music and brew our own beer. This, we believed, was how
one lived a *real* life. There was a pious promise in the notion of self-reliance—a promise that we would not only feel
a deep sense of pride and moral superiority, but also that it
would ensure eternal marital bliss. Some of this we were not
wrong about: it was supremely satisfying to eat cucumbers
that we had grown and sit on furniture we had made (two
Adirondack chairs assembled from a kit, technically). Pia
was taking a pottery class in those days and our house was
filled with charmingly lopsided creamers and water pitch-
ers with her initials carved into the underside, like a proud
child's bounty from summer camp. I had taken a weekend-
long seminar on beekeeping and the unopened bee materials that I ordered online were still stacked neatly against the
house. When the news of The Storms broke, we were only
three months into this real-living adventure and we hadn't
learned much at all yet.

Pia and I weren't alone in these aspirations. There were others like us around the country, young(ish) people, intent on living differently. In the aftermath of America's economic crisis, a burst housing bubble and an overheating earth, we were part of an unofficial movement of people who wanted to create a life that wasn't defined by a drive for more stuff. We wanted to spend less time at work and more time with each other. We were smug, sure, but I still believe we were basically right in our quest to find pleasure in simpler pursuits. It wasn't so much a rejection of our parents' choices as it was an admission that those choices weren't available to us. The world was different and we were adapting.

Isole, Vermont, was an answer to those yearnings. It offered a delightful mix of hippies and rednecks, cohabitating in the picturesque valley between two small mountains. You went there only if you knew what you were looking for. There were old farm families and loggers who had been in Isole long enough to remember when it was pronounced in its traditional French way: EE-zo-LAY. But the economic engine of the region came from outside money in our time—reclusive liberals with trust funds, self-employed tech whizzes and socially responsible venture capitalists, all hiding out in a picturesque hamlet that was too far from a city to ever be truly civilized.

I liked to think of myself as a native because I grew up in central Vermont, but the real locals knew us as outsiders. We had come from Brooklyn, where we'd spent the previous twelve years building successful and lucrative careers. Pia had worked in advertising and I was a partner at a graphic design firm. The firm was well established by the time I sold my portion of the business back to my colleagues, but I had been there in the early days, before we had an in-house gym and black-tie holiday parties.

Pia and I fell in love with our Vermont farmhouse on vacation earlier that year. We had taken an extended spring weekend on Crystal Lake. It was too cold to swim, so we took long drives around the Northeast Kingdom, basking in the slowness and serenity. On the last day of our stay, we drove past a perfect yellow farmhouse on a slanted dirt road with a just-posted for-sale sign out front. It was *our* sign, we decided. We had been waiting for it.

Years before, Pia and I had made a pact to live a different sort of life one day. We had only the vaguest plan to escape the city and remake ourselves, but we were sure the details of this plan would present themselves when it was time. So when we found the farmhouse, we recognized it as the natural extension of the dream we had created together. I sold my piece of the firm and stayed on as a long-distance consultant. Two months later, we were unpacking in Vermont. It was such a fast and easy process that we didn't have time to iron out all the wrinkles of our new life. Pia didn't have a new job lined up yet and we hadn't met a soul there.

It sounds reckless in the retelling, but that was an important part of its appeal. Pia was great at embracing the new and unpredictable, but I was far more cautious, so this leap to a new state also felt like a leap toward my wife. We were going to forge a new path together, armed only with years of shared daydreams about a country life.

The hammock rocked gently as the breeze picked up, and I could smell the goldenrod that was being mowed at the farm upwind. Pia was still listing things that would need to be addressed before The Storms came: gutters, faulty wiring in the basement, a stuck bedroom window. I knew she was probably right; if this storm was for real, then we did need to start preparing. But I stroked her hair and suggested that we spend the rest of the now-enjoyable Friday relaxing. We could get to disaster preparations tomorrow.

"Hey, dudes. What are you doing?" said a squeaky voice.

Approaching us was our seven-year-old neighbor, August, whose dilapidated little house sat on the other side of a thick wall of trees and shrubs to the east. His place was invisible from our porch but connected by a short, neat path that I had helped August clear to facilitate easy movement back and forth. I had met August on the first day of our arrival, when he walked through our open front door and began peppering us with questions. He seemed desperate for friends and bubbling with curiosity. Since then, I'd seen him almost every day. He'd come over to kick a soccer ball back and forth or invite me to check out the new fort he'd built in the woods behind our homes. Pia thought August was sweet, but it was I who spent so much time with him. I wondered sometimes about the adults in his life who had left him so hungry for attention, but I didn't ask many questions, mainly because I didn't know what exactly to ask, but also because I enjoyed our time together and wanted to just be with him. And August was helpful. He'd spent his entire short life in those woods and he knew more about self-reliance and country living than Pia and me combined.

"What's up, buddy?" I said, reaching a hand out for a sticky high five.

As usual, August was barefoot, filthy and smiling. The burdock lodged in his curly auburn hair appeared to have taken hold days before.

August wanted to play Frisbee, so we hoisted our bodies out of the hammock and met him on the lawn. The mood had shifted and we were happy to play. That was the way things changed with Pia: she could be crying and sad, but the minute it was over, it was really over. Most of the time,

MEG LITTLE REILLY

this was a relief, though there were times when I knew we probably should have actually worked things through instead of just riding them out. But it was so much easier to just wait for storms to pass, and the highs were so high that we didn't want to look back at the lows once we had escaped them. We just drove forward, secure in the knowledge that we were in love and nothing was worth dwelling on. This unspoken arrangement required a willingness on my part to indulge every emotional whim that Pia wanted to follow. In return, she kept things uncomplicated and asked very few questions. Abiding by the rules of this dynamic felt intimate. It worked for us.

Pia dived theatrically as the Frisbee left August's hands, which made him double over in laughter every time. I laughed along with them but let my eyes wander to the group of flycatchers above. They were migrating south, no doubt, but they were several weeks late. They should have been in Central America by then. These were the details of nature that I never got wrong. I was as passionate about nature as Pia was about art, and I knew bird migratory patterns like the moles on my left arm. I assumed they were just as immovable. But the birds were confused and their travels had changed.

Our backyard was magnificent that day. The enormous sugar maples along the lawn's perimeter swayed cheerfully as the low sun illuminated their drying leaves. It would have been a perfect July day, were it not for the fact that it was late September and there was no shaking the feeling that everything was off. The leaves seemed to be skipping past their most brilliant orange-yellow-red phase and going straight to the browning at the end. We were playing Frisbee in shorts, for Christ's sake.

Weather was the primary topic of discussion in the Northeast Kingdom that summer—even more so than usual—

because it was all so wrong. Everyone was nervous: the farmers, the maple sugarers, the people who relied on ski tourism, the ice fishermen and the hockey fans. Pia talked a lot about a global-warming government cover-up, but I was the one in our household who truly mourned the changing Vermont climate. I had grown up there (technically, I grew up in Rutland, a sturdier, postindustrial town in central Vermont). Every milestone of my life was tied in some way to New England weather; and every romantic vision I had for our new life relied on the weather being right. Some part of me understood this to be unrealistic, but I wasn't ready to accept that.

When the sun finally disappeared and our toes started to chill in our flip-flops, we sent August home and Pia and I went inside to make dinner. I loved making dinner together. It was an activity that could lay the groundwork for hours of sexually charged companionship. It wasn't just sex—though that almost always came later—but also wine and storytelling and laughter and touching. Those nights always felt to me like scenes from a movie. I envisioned someone watching us through a window, not hearing exactly what we were saying, but being impressed by the ease and tenderness of our home life. It was the shade of domesticity that I liked marriage in.

Pia browned fat chunks of bacon in a pan that would soon be joined by split brussels sprouts and a drizzle of maple syrup, an addicting recipe she had acquired from the little girl who ran the farm stand down the road. These were the details we relished but worked hard to seem cool about when we breathlessly relayed them to our friends back in Brooklyn. *We buy our sprouts from a farm girl down the road! That's where we get our eggs, too—you have never eaten eggs until you've had just-laid eggs. I can't believe we ever bought our meat vacuum-sealed at the grocery store. Just-butchered and free-range is the way to go. It's just the way life is here…* The narrative we'd created about our life in Vermont was almost as important as the experience itself.

I massaged salt and pepper into a local sirloin and carried it out the back screen door to place over high flames on the grill. Pia joined me minutes later, slipping a hand around my waist and lifting her pinot noir to my lips. I took a sip before leaning down to kiss her hard. I loved that I was almost a full head taller than her. Being tall and broad was my best physical feature. Without expending much effort on appearance, I projected the illusion of general fitness, even as my stomach softened slightly and my dark, groomed beard sprouted grays. I drew most of my confidence with women from my size, which worked fine for Pia, who liked to be enveloped by someone larger than herself. On cue, she melted into my chest and then pushed me away, darting back inside to tend to her sauté pans.

"I want to change the world," I once said to Pia during a marathon late-night session of drinking, fooling around and philosophizing early in our courtship. We were on our second bottle of wine and both feeling drunk.

"No, you don't." She laughed.

"I do!"

"No, people who want to change the world go on disaster relief missions in Haiti and deliver vaccines to babies in Africa. You just want to be outside and feel like less of a yuppie dick."

I considered this correction as I studied the pattern of the blanket beneath us. We were sitting on the floor in our tiny Brooklyn living room having a sort of indoor picnic.

"It's okay," Pia went on. "I'm the same. I'm too selfish to do something truly good, but I think choosing to live a life that doesn't make the world worse is okay, too."

"Shit, you're right," I conceded. "So how do we not make the world worse?"

"Smaller ecological footprint, conscientious consumerism, freedom from prejudices, that sort of thing. It sounds trite, but I don't think it is. You live a more thoughtful life than your parents did, and you teach your kids those values, and voilà: the human race evolves. That's meaningful."

"I'd rather actually be a good person, but I guess you're right. Maybe that is meaningful," I agreed. "So let's make a pact to live that way. Somehow."

Pia stretched a hand toward me to formalize the agreement. "I love that. It's a deal."

We shook on it.

"I feel like a good person already," I said.

"Not good, just a not-bad person," she corrected.

We set our wineglasses aside and I dived toward her. She enveloped me with her legs and fell back.

Pia was a marvel to me in those early days—as witty and esoteric as she was sexy. It was just nice being together and we never wanted to stop.

Dinner was served on the dirty porch furniture, which looked perfect in the glow of a dozen tea lights that Pia had carefully arranged. We sat across from each other, drinking wine and discussing the superior origins and experiences of the dead animals before us. There would be no mention of her ovulation cycle or my quiet resistance to the project. This was a good night. After some discussion of the strange and beautiful sky, we eventually turned to the most obvious topic.

"So, what are we going to do, love?" Pia asked, more excited than scared. "These storms are just terrifying! We need a plan."

I nodded. "We do need a plan. I can't imagine that our

little landlocked state is in all that much danger, but I guess we should err on the side of caution and get this leaky old house sealed up. I assume that we'd stay here, even if a really big storm came, right?"

"Of course—we have to stay!" Pia said, gulping her wine. "This house is our baby. And where would we go anyhow? Certainly not to your parents' place. And certainly not to mine!"

I was surprised that she hadn't considered the possibility, but it was true that there wasn't really any reason to go to either of our parents' homes in the case of an emergency. We were adults and we were no less equipped to handle disaster than they were, though I felt as though they'd attained a level of adulthood we hadn't yet graduated to.

Pia's parents, both academics, lived in a tony Connecticut suburb outside of New York City, which was where they had raised their one beautiful child. They were aloof and opinionated, but they had always been kind enough to me. Pia spoke of them as if they were monsters. And maybe they were. I once assumed that she liked believing that hers had been a cruel childhood because it made her more interesting and tortured. But I was wrong about all that. Something had been missing from her childhood; there was a chaos inside of her that I couldn't account for.

I didn't like Pia's parents, but not for the reasons she provided. They offended a Yankee sensibility in me that valued industriousness and discipline. I couldn't understand what justified their haughtiness when, as far as I could tell, they hadn't left much of a mark on the world. It wasn't that their pretensions were unfamiliar to me—there was no shortage of artsy liberal affect in the corner of New England I grew up in. I just hated playing along with it. Pia's parents attended the symphony and followed culinary trends and read theater reviews, but they didn't create anything themselves and this bothered me. They seemed to believe that, by virtue of association with greatness, they, too, were great. They told us stories about so-and-so who just produced a one-act play or wrote a book about his trek across Nepal as we nodded with appropriate awe. Visits with them required pretending that we weren't having cocktails with appreciators of great art, but with the artists themselves. All of this was made even more maddening by their undiluted disappointment at the lack of *formal* culture in our lives. That was their term for distinguishing the kind of culture that we enjoyed from the established arts of the aristocracy they believed themselves to be part of.

My family was less complicated in every way, a point that Pia liked to make when she was annoyed with me. My father was a lawyer at a local firm in Rutland, where I grew up with two sisters and a brother. I came second, which secured my rank as neither the most successful nor the most screwed-up of my siblings. My mom stayed at home and I believe Pia disapproved of this, but she never said so aloud. My parents volunteered at our schools and picked up trash on green-up days and supported local theater. Since moving to New York, I hadn't met anyone who cared about their community in the way my parents cared for their struggling town. I like my parents and, although my younger sister's kids and my brother's drug habits had commanded most of their attention in recent years, we were all okay. (My older sister lives in London with her wife. We had always gotten along well, though we've fallen out of touch in recent years.) This is what family looks like to me. It's not always joyful, but it's big and messy and kind of fun some of the time. I expected to have something similar one day, when I was ready.

"Yeah, we have to stay here no matter what," I agreed,

pulling the collar on my sweater a little higher. It was cool outside now and so dark that I could barely see Pia's face floating above the candles.

   She moved our bare plates aside and took a small notebook with a matching pen from the pocket of her bulky sweater. It was list time. Pia loved the idea of being a writer, someone who writes, so she was forever collecting pretty little notebooks to have on hand in case inspiration struck. But inspiration never stayed with her for more than a few minutes, so her notebooks were mostly used for frantic list making, which struck much more frequently. She listed books she planned to read, organic foods she wanted to grow, yoga postures that would heal whatever was ailing her. Her lists were aspirational instructions for a life she wanted to live. They rarely materialized into much but served a constructive role nonetheless, as if the mere act of putting her plans in writing set her on a path to self-improvement. I didn't object to the positivity of it all.

   Pia had begun a shopping list of home supplies we would need for The Storms. She wrote, "canned goods, multivitamins, water filtration system, solar blankets." It read more like a survival list for the apocalypse than a storm-preparation plan.

   "Babe, I was thinking we would just, like, board up the windows and try to seal up the root cellar a bit," I said. "Do you really think we need all that?"

   "It can't hurt to be prepared." Pia shrugged, still writing in the dark. "And if nothing comes of these storm predictions, then we'll have some extra supplies the next time we need them. No harm done."

   Her reasoning was sound, but there was an edge to her voice that surprised me. The coming storms excited her.

   Pia came around to my side of the table and wrapped a

wool blanket around both of our shoulders. It smelled like campfire from a previous summer outing. She put her arms around my chest for a quick squeeze and then turned back to her notebook. I listened to the leaves swaying with the wind and the din of summer insects that were somehow still abundant. Her hair fell all around us. I could smell the natural almond shampoo she had started using since adopting a more country approach to hygiene, which made her hair wilder than it used to be. Pia was getting charged with each new idea she recorded. I loved her like that: present and energized. I knew what my role was at those moments. I would be adoring and attentive, which I really was.

Pia pulled a knee up to her chest and I noticed a new drawing in ballpoint pen on her upper thigh. It was a tree with the face of an old man in its trunk. She must have done it that evening, mindlessly doodling in a moment of boredom. Our lives were filled with these small reminders of Pia's artistic gifts, washable and impermanent, but impressive. She had won awards in college for her oil paintings, and a prominent gallery in Manhattan had offered to show her photography years before. But Pia lacked the discipline to carry out long-term projects and she changed mediums too often to be truly great in any of them. With focus, she could have earned a living doing the kind of art she loved.

"You're going to be great at this," Pia said.

"At what?"

"You know, bracing for these big weather events, finding industrious solutions to things, living without some of our old comforts. You like things a little difficult."

She was complimenting me, but teasing, too. Since we'd started making real money, modern life was feeling a bit squishy for me, all morning espressos and personal trainers. I secretly feared that I was growing too attached to it all. A tiny alarm in the primal recesses of my brain had been going off, warning me to stay sharp and focused in case of future uncertainty. I never told Pia about this growing discomfort, but I should have guessed that she could sense it.

"Fingers crossed for frozen pipes." I smiled.

We stayed outside until nearly eleven, building our plan for The Storms and laughing—flirting even—as we huddled together in solidarity. When I finally convinced Pia that it was time to go to bed, she took my hand and led me upstairs to our bedroom, where she instructed me to sit in a small antique chair to watch her slowly peel off each layer of her clothing.

It would have been comical on a less beautiful woman as she unbuttoned her oversize flannel shirt and pulled off fading green cotton underwear, but it wasn't. My physical response to Pia's naked body hadn't flagged in the years we'd been together. If anything, it had grown more intense as sex tapered off a little. When she was done undressing, she turned and walked her naked body to the bed to wait for me. Her ears and nose were still cold from the evening chill, but the rest of her body was warm, hot even. I attempted restraint at first, but that didn't last, and what followed was the wild, forceful passion that we'd founded our relationship on years ago. Better even. We fucked like two people desperate to occupy one another. It was feral, afraid. Pia was alive, the weather was our common enemy and I was relieved.

As she fell asleep beside me, my mind drifted back to our unconceived baby and the news of The Storms. I wasn't ready for a baby, not then, but I loved Pia's desire for one because it was the embodiment of my favorite things about her: a hunger for new beginnings, adventure and, above all, optimism. Whether there was a place for optimism in the stormy new world we inhabited, I didn't know. And I wondered—for the first time in my life—whether this was still a world that babies wanted to be born into. And how could the answer to that question be anything other than an emphatic yes if we are to go on living wholeheartedly? Is there a moment at which the human race should decide not to perpetuate itself, or will we keep going until the universe decides that for us and just wipes us out? The latter seemed more likely. So I wondered how the universe might kill off our species, whether it would be instantaneous and painless or cruelly slow. Perhaps it was already happening at a pace just slow enough to go undetected. Were we at a beginning or an end?

TWO

WE WOKE UP early the next morning, a clear Saturday that seemed incongruous with the austere task ahead: storm preparations. Pia walked around the bedroom naked for a few minutes, checking her phone, tying her hair up and then taking it down again in front of the mirror. The warm mood of the previous evening still lingered, though daylight had brought a new urgency to our self-assigned task of storm shopping.

I walked downstairs and turned the radio on even before making coffee, hoping for the latest from NPR on the new weather predictions. No one seemed to have any more information, but overnight, countless opinions had been hatched and opposing teams established. A conservative commentator suggested that this was part of a wider liberal scheme to divert public funds to global-warming-research and climate-change "slush funds." Someone from a think tank feared that the president was withholding information and called for a congressional investigation into what the Department of the Environment and NOAA knew. Pia and I drank coffee with sweet local cream while we watched old men on network TV discuss how this might influence the outcome of the upcoming midterm elections. The Storms dominated everything, but they were still only an idea. It was just a Saturday project for us.

We took showers and climbed into the Volvo, bound for the closest family-owned hardware store, twenty-five minutes away. That morning felt like what I thought our Vermont experience would always feel like. We were close, she was smiling and the landscape unfolded before us like a picture painted by a child in crayon: all blue skies and red barns. The windows were down and we talked about how the smell of manure made us feel. Pia said she hated it but couldn't resist taking a few deep breaths. I took a native's pride in sharing that I loved that farm stink. It evoked for me a million childhood experiences, most real and some fabricated in the haze of nostalgia. She leaned across the front seat to kiss my neck and call me a hick as I pulled into Dewey's Hardware.

"You're so country." That was what Pia had said to me when we met nine years earlier. We were at a raucous costume party in Williamsburg and I was fighting my way through a wall of bare male torsos, trying not to touch the smooth, sweaty shoulders standing between me and the keg. The host, a mutual friend, was a professional party thrower and an amateur drug dealer. His events were always predominantly gay and half-naked, but this one was exceptional even by his standards. My chances of talking to a pretty girl seemed better than average, given the demographics, so I took a risk and smiled at Pia, who was still unknown to me then. She immediately grabbed my arm and pulled me through the crowd until we found safety in an unoccupied corner of the room.

"You're not from here, right?" she yelled in my ear.

Her costume was composed entirely of a vine that snaked around her curvy body, with plastic leaves covering all the critical areas. It was held in place with flimsy green tape.

"No one's from here," I said. "This isn't real. It's a costume party within the costume party of Brooklyn. This is a redundant party."

Pia seemed impressed by the profundity of this drunken observation, so I kept going. I explained that I had been living there since I graduated from Amherst, that I was working in graphic design and that I had no intention of staying in Brooklyn forever. "I miss trees," I said, which she liked a lot. When Pia, who had attended Middlebury, learned that I was from Vermont, she touched my arm and told me that she was "madly in love with the dirt there." I told her about a harvest festival near my hometown that she would enjoy, which was when she smiled an amazing smile and decided that I was "very country."

We slept together that night. There was no courtship or pretense. She just took me back to her messy apartment and, without a hint of modesty, pushed my head between her legs as if she was giving me a gift I had been waiting for. For the briefest moment, I considered fainting in the humid, earthy cave of her body, but I didn't. I came alive. Pia didn't exude the soapy perfume of the girls I'd been with before; she was all salt and musk. She was the most animate being I had ever encountered and a switch was flipped inside me. I wanted to consume her and she wanted to be wanted by me, so our frenzied union felt like a perfect fit. I knew from the start that with her passion came a moody and mercurial element, but that was fine with me. Life was so much more fun with her in it. So we built a relationship there, on a lumpy mattress, beneath glittery, draped tapestries, surrounded by stacks of books in unreal Brooklyn.

My confidence in those initial days with Pia can be largely attributed to the recent realization that my specific brand of geekiness was in high demand in that particular corner of the universe at that moment in American culture. I had always been a tall, slightly awkward dork who would rather be reading nature journals or distance running in the woods than mingling at a party. In Brooklyn, this was misinterpreted as sensitive, progressive and cool. Even my accidental wardrobe (workman pants, flannel shirts, hiking boots) seemed to impress. I would have resented the objectification if it didn't work so well with hot hipster girls.

"I knew we should have left earlier," Pia said from the passenger seat as we approached the hardware store.

The parking lot was surprisingly crowded for nine o'clock on a Saturday morning, but we found a spot in the farthest corner, next to a pickup truck with giant, muddy wheels. Two rows down, a woman hurried small children into the backseat of a car filled with shopping bags.

"Whoa" was all I could say when we entered the store. The normally orderly establishment was roaring with people pushing squeaky shopping carts, many holding lists of their own.

A young man wearing a navy Dewey's Hardware polo shirt nodded at us from the entryway. "It's the latest storm report," he said. "Everyone's getting prepared."

I wanted to talk further with this teenager, who probably could have been helpful to us then, but Pia had already claimed a cart and joined the melee. We moved quickly up and down the aisles, most of which had been picked so bare that it was impossible to know which essential items were no longer available to us.

"Tarps have been sold out since seven this morning," one man reported, "and don't even bother trying to find sandbags."

Neither was on our list, but they sounded important all of a sudden.

As whole sections of the store were emptied, shoppers veered to other areas looking for creative uses for seemingly useless items. One man bought all the remaining plastic sleds from the previous winter. I watched him jog to the register with his purchase, satisfied with whatever discovery he thought he'd just made.

It wasn't the bare shelves or the full parking lot that unnerved me that morning; it was the behavior of the patrons. We were in the heart of the Northeast Kingdom with people who had lived through dozens of epic weather events. They had seen ice storms kill harvests, barn roofs collapse under wet snow and heavy winds bring trees down over livestock. They adapted to bad weather with whatever was in the shed or could be borrowed from a neighbor and they never, ever panicked. This wasn't full-blown panic, but it was something close. (We would learn later what real panic looks like.)

Pia crumpled up the list in her hand and stuffed it in the pocket of her jean shorts. We wouldn't find anything on that list. Taking a cue from the shoppers around us, she started just grabbing random items: gardening gloves, a box of large nails and a hammer, three bungee cords, shipping tape. I considered stopping her, but she looked committed, so I stood back. We went around the store like that for a while before finally making our way through the checkout line and out the door, arms full with plastic bags of odd items. As Pia had said the night before, there's no harm in being prepared.

When we stepped outside, fat raindrops hit our faces and the temperature seemed to have dropped dramatically.

"Shoot, the windows," I said, remembering our exposed car.

We broke into a clumsy run toward the Volvo, hoping to beat the rain, but the unexpected storm was much faster than us. The raindrops grew larger and somehow sharper as we ran. I felt one sting my ear and heard Pia shriek from up ahead. When we finally got to the car, we jammed our bags in the backseat, rolled up the windows and huddled in the front, stunned. I blinked the water out of my eyes and realized that it wasn't rain anymore, but hail. Icy golf balls were pelting cars and frantic shoppers. The sky was dark directly above us, but bright and inviting just to the north. On the grassy border in front of the car's bumper, I could see two birds—more flycatchers on their way south—lying dead, their faces frozen in shock or pain. I hoped Pia didn't see them.

"Fucking biblical," she said. Her hair was wet and she was shivering, so I reached into the backseat for a dirty sweatshirt that I'd left there weeks ago. She pulled it on and shook her head in disbelief at the weather change. There was a slight smile on her face.

"Ash, we should keep shopping...track down the stuff on our original list. This isn't going to get less weird, you know?"

I did know. I felt it, too. The sun was already returning, but an uncertainty had stung us with that hail. We needed to start *doing things*. So I steered the car toward Burlington and the big-box stores that would have what we needed and the countless new items that popped into our heads as the distant notion of catastrophe inched closer.

Pia laughed out loud as we gained speed on the highway. "It's kind of fun, isn't it?"

"What?"

"Waiting for disaster. It shouldn't be, but it's kind of fun."

I knew what she was talking about. Candlelit blackouts

and immobilizing snow days always thrilled me. To be briefly thrust into a more primitive lifestyle awakens something in us. But it must be brief and risk-free to be fun. It can't be real. The storm predictions before us sounded more consequential than those fleeting adventures of the past.

"Remember that summer storm in our old place when we lost the power for three days?" she asked.

"It's one of my favorite memories. My sister still talks about it."

Years before, soon after I had proposed to Pia, a hurricane hit New York on its way off the coast, bringing torrential rains, followed by three hot, powerless days. My sister and her girlfriend were visiting from London at the time, and I was already uneasy about their first encounter with Pia. But I needn't have been because Pia was at her best when life went off script.

We spent two boring days playing board games in the dark and finishing all the wine in the apartment. Without air-conditioning, we were grumpy and smelly, just waiting for life to return to normal. Pia was bouncing off the walls and I could tell that she was going to manifest action imminently. Finally, the rain stopped and Pia went outside. She ran to the corner store for a thirty-pack of Miller Lite, turned our speakers out the window toward the wet street and started knocking on neighbors' doors. She had started a block party. People poured out of their apartments, many contributing to the beer tub, calling their friends to bring more. Makeshift barricades of chairs and garbage pails were set up on either side of the block to keep cars out, and someone filled a kiddie pool with fresh water. Within twenty minutes, there were close to a hundred people in the street, shaking off the sweaty cabin fever of the preceding days. It felt organic and spontaneous—the big bang of block parties—and no one remembered later how it began. But it wasn't organic; Pia created it out of nothing. She saw the world for its potential and made interesting things happen. Life with someone like that is limitless.

"She's rad," my sister said later. "Fucking nuts, but rad." That was Pia's effect on people.

We drove along in silence, thinking about that party and the complicated pleasure of doom.

"I saw the birds," Pia said quietly. The sun had reappeared. "The dead ones. It's spooky—the hot weather and the sudden hail. Everything is a little wrong."

I nodded and put a hand on her bare knee. There wasn't much more to say, so I kept driving silently. It was eighty degrees when we woke up, and now the dashboard said sixty. The hail, the birds, the panicked shoppers. It *was* spooky, but I was grateful for the simple, shared task before us.

Forty-five minutes later, we were making our way up and down the aisles of Home Depot, joking about the impending apocalypse and thoroughly enjoying each other's company.

"Of course, the dollar will crash after The Storms come, and we will have to turn to primitive forms of currency," I said with a wide sweep of my arm as we passed the lawn mowers.

"Like spices and fermented cider and stuff?" Pia played along.

"No, much more primitive than that. Blow jobs primarily. Hand jobs also, though they aren't worth nearly as much."

She shrieked with laughter, turning several heads around us. Pia never cared who saw her laugh (or cry). I felt proud to be responsible for delighting this beautiful woman.

We bought a snow shovel and two pairs of work gloves,

caulking and sheets of insulation. We didn't know what we were doing, but it felt proactive. The hurried shoppers around us made small talk about which items were essential in which types of weather events and I studied them closely, eager to pass as an experienced local. We bought what they bought and hoped they were right.

Several hours and hundreds of dollars later, Pia and I were drinking wine on our back porch again, surrounded by bags of items that promised to keep us safe from whatever was coming. The back porch was the best part of that house, looking out on our unkempt backyard that dissolved into dark woods. It was home.

I don't remember the indoors of my childhood. I grew up in a pretty Victorian house, bigger than most of my classmates' homes and lovingly cared for, but I didn't spend much time inside it. My parents were strong believers in the character-building properties of outdoor play, so they hurried us into the woods behind our house as soon as the sun was up each morning. We played until we were shivering, hungry or injured and then slept as if we were dead each night. My siblings eventually resisted this parenting technique, which would undoubtedly classify as some form of neglect today, but I embraced it until high school. The woods were freedom to me: undeveloped; unregulated by grown-ups and infinite in their potential for discovery. There was an order to the woods, but it wasn't dictated by man. I wanted to understand that order, to have dual citizenship in both the natural and human worlds. Passing freely between them seemed the ultimate power. So I became a voracious consumer of science and nature writing. I wanted to know every species of wildlife and the subtle languages with which they spoke to one another. I wanted to be a part of that organism and welcomed by its inhabitants.

With puberty and the new concerns of young adulthood,

my commitment to that mission waned and I eventually left the woods. I went inside. I didn't think much about that departure at the time, but I've come to realize that it came at a cost. The sense of purpose and belonging I'd had in those woods hadn't been replaced by anything in adulthood.

Pia had her head resting in my lap as we swung back and forth on the bench watching the sun set. It was warm again and there was no evidence of the surprise hailstorm that had barged through earlier that day.

"This isn't what September is supposed to look like," I said, shaking my head. I was comfortable with her there in my arms, but unable to relax entirely.

"But this is lovely," Pia said with her eyes closed. Beauty, she believed, had inherent value. "Remind me what September in Vermont is supposed to look like."

I swatted a mosquito from her forehead and thought for a moment.

"I don't know... Colder, quieter... The wind should be louder than the bugs and animals. Do you know that some years on Halloween, we would have to trick-or-treat in the snow? That's only a few weeks away."

Pia opened her eyes and touched my face. "I don't think that's going to happen ever again, my love. It's sad, really. Lots of things are going to be different for our kids."

It was a surprisingly dour observation considering Pia's recent obsession with having children. But I didn't know then that her attention had already shifted away from those hopeful plans.

THREE

"SURFACE WATERS ARE expected to reach eighty-two degrees—maybe even higher—sometime in November. We will also see warm, moist air traveling up the Gulf Coast and very low wind shear."

A familiar NPR storm reporter's voice issued from my desk radio as I stared at the computer screen, attempting to work. It was only a few days since news of The Storms broke and the first day since we moved to Vermont that I deviated from my morning work routine. Normally, I woke up around seven, drank one cup of coffee at the kitchen table with Pia, who was less enthusiastic about mornings, and brought a second cup back upstairs at eight, where I posted up at a large antique desk in our airy bedroom. From my desk chair I could see the backyard over the top of my computer screen and a banged-up thermometer that had been nailed outside the window by a previous owner. If I worked until two—including breaks for more coffee and lunch—I could get more client work done than I ever did in the office. My colleagues back in Manhattan seemed satisfied with the arrangement, so I was careful not to abuse it.

But on that day I couldn't sit still or will myself to turn off the radio. I was already on my third cup of coffee, which was bad pacing. "It could start with a series of nor'easters this winter, each moving up from the southeast and hitting inbound arctic systems from the northwest," the deep radio voice continued. "Everyone from Chicago down to DC and as far north as Maine can expect several feet of total accumulations and high, damaging winds at various times. Those storms alone will be costly and dangerous. But there's another possible scenario that would be worse. The frequency and intensity of this year's hurricane projection makes it likely that a tropical storm caused by the record-breaking ocean temperatures will be gathering around the same time as these snowstorms. Because the water temperatures are higher than we've ever seen, we don't quite know how large any one of these hurricanes might get, but we know they could be enormous. If the arctic air coming in from Canada and the Midwest collides with this warmer air from the Atlantic and the Gulf, we will face the 'frankenstorm' effect that we saw back in 2012. But in this case, that cold air will be moving faster and covering more of the US than we've ever seen before. Here, again, we're in uncharted territory.

"There are so many variables that could determine this winter storm season, but given what we know, it's wise to assume that the eastern side of the US is looking at several hundred square miles of direct contact with at least one massive hurricane and several blizzards, with accompanying flooding and broad wind damage. I'm not even sure *hurricane* and *blizzard* are adequate terms for what could happen here. If any of these storms are as large as the most pessimistic forecast models project, it won't matter if you're in their direct paths because wind and flooding in surrounding regions from storms of this size can be just as damaging as what occurs in the path itself.

"Even in the most optimistic scenario, forecasters are expecting tens of billions of dollars in losses to the US economy and our basic infrastructure. The worst-case scenario is almost unthinkable at this point."

I heard the car door slam outside as Pia drove off in search of groceries and probably a hidden antiques shop or two. She was better with a job, we both knew that, but her motivation to find one seemed to have diminished in recent weeks. As someone who believed in routines, I wanted badly for her to find somewhere to go each day or something to do. She was good about leaving me alone while I worked, though I knew it was hard for her to fill the time. She ran errands and took books out from the library. At the start, she'd spent hours researching possible job leads in area arts organizations, but that wasn't happening anymore. We had enough in savings, for now, as a result of my buyout from the firm, but my income wasn't as high as it used to be and it wasn't a sustainable financial arrangement. She would need to find at least a part-time job by spring if we were to stay afloat. Still, I liked the companionship, hearing her putter around the house planting things and cooking things as the spirit moved her. It felt more like playing house than actual domesticity, as if we were putting on an ironic performance instead of careening toward an inevitable financially precarious rut. Every few days, Pia would find a recipe that inspired her and dance around the kitchen for a few hours until something delicious emerged. Or she would decide that we needed a new accent table and spend the whole afternoon browsing quirky local shops. But we were really only playing; there was no consistency or order to it. Dinner was often organic frozen pizza, and dust gathered in the corners of our beloved home at an alarming rate. We hadn't been playing house long enough to get the act down.

I spent the first hour of my workday looking past my computer screen through the dirty window that framed our backyard. The browning grass was about six inches tall and peppered with old dandelions. Lady ferns spanned the perimeter of the lawn, claiming more of it all the time. I thought I saw the vibrant blue of a closed gentian flower, a comforting sign that autumn was close and nature's clock wasn't entirely out of whack. This day didn't look like the previous one. Darker clouds had moved in and parked right above us, as if daylight had never quite arrived. The thermometer said sixty-eight, so it was moving in the right direction, but still too slowly.

August emerged with a soccer ball from the path in the woods that connected our homes and I watched his little body dribble around imaginary opponents. It was just after eight, so he wouldn't have to leave for school for another half hour. My stiff legs twitched at the sight of August's weightless movement around the yard and couldn't resist joining him. With a few brief words, we were passing the ball back and forth between us. His kicks were usually too far to one side or the other, so I spent a lot of the time chasing after the ball and dribbling back to the center of the yard. After a thoroughly aerobic kickabout, a wild shot to the left planted the ball into a dense blackberry bush.

"This one's all you, buddy," I said, but August was already parting the prickly branches.

I bounced on one foot and then the other, trying to revive the spring I remembered in my feet from youth soccer games.

"Hey, look at that." August pointed to a patch of moist earth beneath him where a perfect footprint had been left by a small animal.

MEG LITTLE REILLY

I leaned in. "A fox maybe? I don't know…" I crouched down to get a closer look as August pulled himself out of the bramble and fastidiously cleaned the soccer ball with his hands.

"When I was a baby fox…" he started.

"What?"

"When I was a baby fox, I liked to run through these woods."

When I was a baby fox. He wasn't talking to me, exactly; just reminiscing to himself. He was in his own head now. He said things like this from time to time, weaving imaginative fantasies with the tangible present. It wasn't the sort of thing that seemed worrisome, not to me anyhow. No, these were precious clues about who August was. This was a small, open door to a brilliant and busy interior life. A vibrant ray of light poured out that door, illuminating a slice of our backyard. I wanted to see more of it. Were all children this amazing and I'd just failed to see it before now, or was there something special about this dirty, neglected little boy who roamed these woods alone whenever he had a chance?

I knew that the neglect was in some part responsible for what made August extraordinary. He hadn't been properly socialized. August was unschooled in the parameters of our adult reality. He was smart—above average at least—but like a baby, he still lived in a world in which you could hear colors and touch sounds and reach back to memories from lives lived before this one. The curtain between real and unreal hadn't yet come down for August. I don't know when it comes down for the rest of us, but tragically, it must be so early in our lives that we retain no recollection of the change. Or perhaps that's an act of mercy committed by our brains because the memory of our former selves would leave us wanting forever. August was still that early self, unmolested by reason and order. I hoped for him to never change. Like a collectable figurine, I imagined boxing him up neatly and preserving him on a shelf. But of course, that impulse was in direct opposition to the conditions that enabled him to grow this way. He needed safety, but not captivity. How a parent maintains such a balance, I couldn't imagine.

We kicked the ball back and forth for another ten minutes before August announced that he needed to catch the bus for school and disappeared into the path that connected our homes. I spent two more hours at my computer before calling it quits and heading out to the shed. I'd been making incremental progress on a maple coffee table for weeks and was itching to get back to work on it. It wasn't real woodworking—I bought each of the raw pieces precut from the lumberyard—but the act of sanding and hammering and staining was no less satisfying. I had a compulsive need to drive each day forward with projects, tangible evidence of progress made. But more than other hobbies I'd flirted with over the years, making furniture felt like the best fit. To be dirty, scraped and physically tired—these were admirable male traits to me. As a child, I most loved my father when he was building things. I can distinctly remember the smell of his sweat mixed with sawdust and the way his thinning T-shirts clung to his skin. Even after years spent in Brooklyn, living among the overeducated creative class, that was what truly stirred admiration in me. It was self-improvement by hammer, and I nearly believed I was building a better version of myself with each swing.

I moved a hand plane slowly back and forth along the underside of the tabletop and thought about August in that small dark house. He was the only child of two reclusive, spaced-out aging hippies. The father never seemed to leave the house and the mother was a part-time cashier at the yarn shop downtown. They were poor, but not hungry. What worried me was their absence from August's life, his un-fettered freedom to roam and their apparent disinterest in his whereabouts. There was something going on inside that run-down little house that wasn't right, but I hadn't put my finger on it yet.

Swish, swish, swish. The plane moved rhythmically with me until it felt like a part of my own hand and the texture of the smoothing wood passed right through it to my finger-tips. I thought about August, the dimming woods behind our house and the enormous changes our lives had undergone in just a few short months.

I must have been out there for several hours because I didn't notice how cool the air had gotten until Pia's voice shook me out of my trance.

"What are you still doing out here, Ash?"

She stood in the doorway of the shed, her keys dangling in one hand and a cloth shopping bag in the other.

"I'm working on the legs to this table. Come take a look. It's really coming together. I need advice on the finish."

I suspected that she wasn't interested in the finish. It was getting dark out, though I guessed it was only about one in the afternoon.

"We need to go inside and start preparing," Pia said, slightly agitated. "Have you looked at the sky? Those snow-storms are coming. This isn't a joke."

Behind Pia's silhouette in the doorway, I could see charcoal clouds moving in. I hadn't noticed the weather change from dim to ominous in the time I'd been working, but something had indeed shifted. Anyhow, I was tired and happy to have her back, so I followed Pia inside to the kitchen table, where she unpacked the contents of her shopping bag. I mentioned that the nor'easters weren't expected for another month or so, but she pretended not to hear me.

"Heirloom seeds are the way to go here," Pia said as if I'd asked. She pulled handfuls of small paper seed envelopes out of a cloth bag and stacked them on the kitchen table. "Hybrid and GMO seeds are going to be useless in the future because they aren't stable, or can't be stored, or something. Apparently, we have to have heirloom."

She was lining the seed envelopes up in rows, according to variety.

"I have black turtle bean, snowball cauliflower, green sprouting broccoli, champion radish, golden acre cabbage," she went on. "Plus I got these moisture-sealed containers, which will protect seeds in even subzero temperatures."

Pia pointed to a cloth shopping bag on the floor that held small hard boxes one might take on an underwater expedition. She stopped to take inventory of her purchases, her finger nervously tapping a bag of radish seeds.

"Wow, you're not kidding about these disaster preparations!" I laughed, assuming she'd appreciate the humor in it all, but she didn't laugh back, so I stopped. "Pia, do you really think our food supply is going to disappear because of a big storm? In the United States?"

She looked up at me, frustrated. "Maybe not right away, but eventually, yes, it could. Ash, you know you have an almost fanatical trust in the system—our government, capitalism, whatever. It's possible that our civilized society is only a few bad storms away from chaos, you know?"

Her humorlessness was a surprise to me, but I got the message: take this seriously. I didn't have any reason to fight with her about it, so I shrugged and walked to the refrigerator to take stock of its sad contents. Should it matter that she was going a little overboard with this disaster planning, I wondered. What was the harm in being prepared? It irked me that she couldn't laugh about it as we had in previous days. But, whatever. The refrigerator housed a slimy bag of scallions, separating cream in a precious glass bottle and a growler of lager. My stomach fluttered.

"Okay, I have no problem with all this, Pia, but don't make this about me." It came out meaner than I intended.

"It *is* about you," she said. "It's about you and me and our life here in the woods. Will you help me get ready for these storms or not?"

I realized that we had already settled into a language for the new weather reality before us. There were *The Storms*: immediate, multiple and unseasonable storms of every variety that we should expect for several months, beginning soon. There was also, further off in the future, *The Storm*: the collision of several atmospheric forces that would create something so historic and violent that we still chose to believe it was a statistical improbability.

Pia went on, "Ash, I'm going to a meeting tonight and I would really like you to come. It's just a group of locals who are brainstorming about storm preparations. I think it's important."

I didn't want to go to a meeting. I wanted to lie on the couch and drink a beer and read a book that had nothing to do with weather or survivalism. But she looked like she needed me.

"I guess it wouldn't hurt to listen." I shrugged.

Pia jumped up to throw her arms around my neck and I was immediately pleased with how I'd handled the situation. I didn't mind being taken on her impromptu adventures and I appreciated the freshness they injected into married life. Freshness was never a problem for us.

★ ★ ★

"Let's memorialize this moment!" That was what Pia had said when we first arrived at our new Vermont home.

It was a brutally hot June day and we'd been driving for seven hours. The air-conditioning in our car had broken in Connecticut, so our clothes were damp with sweat when we finally peeled ourselves out of the seats at the end of our journey. I got out first, sending Dunkin' Donuts cruller crumbs everywhere as I stepped away from the car to relieve myself. Pia wiped her sweating face on her shirt and stretched to touch her toes.

It was just us and our new house on that steamy, overcast day. The movers weren't expected to arrive with our belongings for another two hours and, although we were tired and dirty, it was euphoric to kick our shoes off and feel the grass under our feet. Our grass. Grown by the clean air and rich soil that was ours now, too, free of the pollutants and cynicism we had left behind. We were in Eden.

I walked to Pia and wrapped both my arms around her, squeezing hard, and we held each other silently for a long time, exhaling.

Finally, we walked up the porch stairs to the front door and turned the key. It was just as I remembered the house when we last saw it, but even better now: clean and scrubbed of any evidence of previous lives lived there. We hugged again quickly and then ran from room to room to reacquaint ourselves. After so many years of small urban apartments, it felt obscene to be in possession of so many rooms dedicated to subtly different activities. The kitchen was bright and airy with shiny outdated appliances and plenty of counter space. A stream of blinding light in the living room drew a straight line to the ancient woodstove—the most substantial machine I had ever been responsible for. And the two upstairs bedrooms oozed charm with their countless gables and unfamiliar angles. It was gluttonous to us then, but we hungrily ate it all up.

There wasn't much to do without furniture, so we eventually walked to the back porch and sat side by side.

"We have to do something that we'll never forget to mark the beginning of our new life here. What should we do?"

For once, it came to me first. "Let's go skinny-dipping in the creek."

"Yes, I love it."

We stepped off the porch and began peeling clothing off. The enormous trees around us were lush with leaves by then and we were hidden from the rest of the world on every side.

I'm not a prude, but I've never been the sort of person who's entirely comfortable with nudity in nonsexual, broad-daylight situations. All that pink flesh rubbing and bouncing is a little too much reality for me. But Pia was just the opposite. She was entirely comfortable with her own nudity—which wasn't much of a feat, since she looked fantastic naked—and she also appreciated the naked form on others, marveling at the beauty of human imperfections. She once told me that she saw God's artistry in the way time drags and molds our bodies into new shapes. It was as if she didn't understand shame at all. What a gift that must be.

I was happy to ignore the embarrassed voice inside me as we stripped down and ran toward the creek at the far end of our backyard. Pia let out a celebratory holler and we stepped into the cool woods to look for just the right spot for our swim.

It wasn't swimming, exactly—the creek was only a foot deep in most places—but there was one perfect little basin lined with rough sand where the incoming current pooled and swirled before moving farther down the rocky path. We stepped carefully along mossy rocks and into the pool, startled by how cold the water was. It was almost numbing, but we didn't care. We were hot and happy and so insanely in love at that moment.

"It's incredible to think that almost two hundred years ago, another family was living in this house and probably washing their clothes here in this creek," Pia said as she squatted in a little shivering ball in the water. She had created a romanticized historical narrative of our new location in the weeks before, and I couldn't resist teasing her about it.

"Ah, yes. The Green Mountain Boys probably washed their uniforms in this creek." I smiled and blew bubbles into the dark water.

Pia moved in and wrapped her legs around my lower half. We kissed and laughed in high, frigid octaves, working hard to stay in the icy bath.

When finally it got to be too much, we stepped out of the creek and walked up the bank toward our home. The humid air of our new backyard was a relief as we roamed aimlessly around waiting for the air to dry our bodies. I picked a young green blackberry from its bush and tasted its tart flesh. Pia lay flat on her back in a cluster of red clovers. Our red clovers.

I went to her and lay down on my side, one hand resting on her bare stomach. The new, verdant smells of late spring were all around us, competing for our attention. Wet moss, honeysuckle, stinky trilliums. It was hotter than it should have been in June, but we didn't mind. In those early days, we still thought hundred-degree June temperatures were just flukes, delicious details in our sweet homecoming story.

Pia rolled onto her stomach and kissed me while my hand wandered toward her smooth bottom. I began to inch closer toward her when we heard the sound of a nearby car door slam. We both froze.

　　　　　　　　　　　　　　MEG LITTLE REILLY

A tall twentysomething man appeared in the yard and immediately spun around when he discovered us.

"Put some clothes on, Adam and Eve. Your shit's here."

We erupted into laughter and scrambled to find our clothes while the movers waited safely at the front of the house. We pulled everything on and tugged it all back into place and then broke down once more, this time in a fit of laughter that had us choking and snorting on our knees. It was a perfectly memorable start.

At six o'clock that evening, Pia and I were sitting in folding chairs in the basement of the Elks Club in downtown Isole. There was no signage outside or handouts at the door or anything else that would have signaled that something formal was occurring. I wondered how Pia knew about the meeting. The chairs were arranged in a circle that filled up quickly around us and stragglers had to drag new chairs over to form an outer ring. There were seven men and four women, most of them decades older than us. A bearded fiftysomething man wearing a faded denim vest greeted Pia warmly, as if they had met before, then he walked to a chair at the center that seemed designated for him.

"Thanks for coming everyone," the bearded man said. He rolled up his sleeves and pulled a military dog tag out from beneath his shirt. "My name is Crow. Glad everyone found the place okay. I'm not big on email—because of the surveillance—so we will continue to rely on word-of-mouth for these meetings. Please do your part to let people know about them."

Several people nodded. An elderly woman I recognized from the local ski shop adjusted the position of her chair across the room. Then she patted the hand of a young man to her left who could barely keep his puffy eyes open and I felt a pang of jealousy at his freedom to be so unabashedly stoned.

"We have a lot of ground to cover over the next few weeks," Crow continued, "so we're going to dive right in tonight with a focus on energy. Later we'll get to water safety, food supply, communication technology and, finally, personal protection."

In the corner of my eye, I saw Pia glance at me. This meeting didn't feel as though it was going to be about what she had led me to believe it was about. But what was it?

A middle-aged man in neat khakis and a plaid shirt cleared his throat. "Crow, what's your advice on solar? It's easier to set up than wind, but it's too unreliable if you're planning on unplugging from the grid."

"Good question." Crow nodded. "The key here is to maintain a hybrid system. Ideally that would mean wind, solar and hydro. But you have to tailor that plan to the available natural resources on your land. I know you've got very little wind in your woods, Ron, but you do have that creek, so maybe look into hydro to supplement solar."

An obese woman to my right took frantic notes whenever Crow spoke. I leaned to my other side.

"What is this?" I whispered to Pia.

She pretended not to hear my question and instead jumped into the conversation that Crow and Ron were having. "What about gasifiers? I've been reading about that as a viable option," she said.

What did Pia know about gasifiers? The lady to my other side craned to see who had asked the question.

"Such a good point, Pia," Crow said a little too enthusiastically. "Wood gas is a great option. It can be loud and a bit dirty—and I can't speak to its legality around here—but if all hell breaks loose, that's going to be the least of your problems."

A round of nods ensued. The stoned guy smirked in apparent response to Crow's disdain for the law. What the hell was this, I wondered again. How did they know Pia?

"*When* all hell breaks loose," a crouched older man corrected. He looked like Crow would in twenty more years. "And when hell breaks loose, it will be the preppers who survive."

Preppers. I'd read a *New Yorker* piece about them several months before. These weren't concerned locals who needed advice on how to water-seal their windows. These were deranged weirdos fixated on the apocalypse. As I understood it, they were people like Crow whose minds hadn't recovered from the damage of earlier wars, and antigovernment recluses who trusted no one, and angry bigots who relished the idea of a race war and religious fanatics who thought God was coming to punish the unsaved urban intellectuals. I wasn't one of these people and neither was my wife.

A ten-minute discussion about superior brands of rechargeable batteries ensued (a "no-brainer"), and then we broke for coffee in small disposable cups. I was annoyed and itching to leave.

"Polystyrene cups," I sneered to Pia. "It's almost quaint in its inappropriateness."

She didn't laugh but sighed instead. "I should have known you wouldn't get this. You're too conventional for this kind of thing. I shouldn't have asked you to come."

She was disappointed by my reaction, which I felt bad about, but her disappointment was mean, too. It was a new tone. All of a sudden, I didn't want to accommodate her.

"Let's get out of here," I said. "This is pretty extreme. Can't we just buy a how-to book or something?"

She shook her head in apparent exasperation with my naïveté.

"Let's reconvene, people!" Crow shouted with a few claps.

I felt myself being shuffled back to my chair between Pia and the note taker.

"Before we move on to the next topic," Crow started, "I'd like to say a few things about our little group and…society."

He leaned into the last word and looked around, as if he was using a code that everyone in the room would recognize.

Crow went on, "At times like these—when we're lookin' straight into the eye of disaster—authoritarians will try to wrestle control from the people. Governments and power keepers will do their best to make the public frightened and submissive. They will take away the people's will and make them think they gave it up freely. What we're doing here isn't just helping each other prepare for a life of self-reliance— we're thinking for ourselves and protecting our free will. Let's all just keep that in mind."

Several people nodded their heads, and I noticed the oldest man purse his lips together, angry at the sheer mention of our authoritarian government.

"This isn't my scene," I whispered to Pia. "You can stay as long as you want, but I gotta get out of here."

Wishing that I had made my exit before everyone sat back down, I took a few moments to plan a graceful departure. Finally, I forced a fake cough and walked out quickly to tend to my phony problem. I knew it was a bratty move and that Pia would be angry, but it seemed too late to avoid that now. We didn't fight often, but once a disagreement was sparked, its natural life cycle involved several childish acts by each of us, followed by a passionate recovery. It seemed a worthwhile price for leaving the prepper meeting.

I walked up a flight of stairs and through the front doors

of the old building. A blast of cool, dark air hit my face as I peered down Isole's Main Street, relieved to be outside and alone. I was a five-minute walk from the cluster of downtown establishments that comprised most of our local commerce. The Blue Frog. That was where I would go, I decided. The Blue Frog was a newish bar that catered to people just like me. It had a sophisticated microbrew list, locally sourced chili, and, on most nights of the week, you could find someone singing folk or bluegrass in the corner.

As I walked down the dark street, the only other person I encountered was a shopkeeper locking his bookstore for the night. We exchanged a nod and I noticed that he was roughly my age. Seeing anyone from my own demographic living and working in Isole always puzzled me. How does a thirtysomething guy come to own a bookstore in a small mountain town? This stranger was a reminder that paths other than the one I had taken after college existed. It would never have occurred to me as a younger man to live in my home state and pursue something as parochial as running a small business there. But seeing it now, I wondered if there was any more perfect life than this guy's.

As I approached the door of the Blue Frog, I saw a large group of people five years younger than me laughing around a rustic wood table, and I became suddenly aware of my aloneness. Normally, I wouldn't mind having a beer on my own, but I wasn't up for it at that moment, so I kept walking. When I got to Polly's, the darker, sadder townie bar several doors down, I opened the door.

Polly's smelled like old cigarettes and my feet felt sticky on the worn carpet as I stepped to the bar. There was one other patron in the room—a large, red-faced man at the far end of the bar who was busy circling things in the classified newspaper pages before him.

"What can I getcha?" a petite, female bartender asked me as I took a stool. "We have draft Bud. Everything else is cans and bottles."

She wore a tiny cropped shirt that appeared to be constructed of macramé over a denim miniskirt. It was distracting how much of her body I could see and I was grateful for the curtain of dark hair that hung behind her. How old could she have possibly been—twenty-two, maybe? I couldn't tell.

"Budweiser is fine, thanks," I said. "Are you guys always this quiet on Tuesdays?" I couldn't think of anything more interesting to say than that.

"Yep, until the preppers let out. Then we get another wave."

I tried to look casual in my curiosity. "Oh right, the preppers. So what's the deal with them anyway?"

She handed me my beer and started drying glass mugs, one hip gently leaning against the sink in front of her.

"They're freaks," she said matter-of-factly. "I get some weirdos in here, you know? But these guys are, like, totally paranoid. And they never shut up about it. They come in here all fired up after their meetings and lecture me about how I need some kind of bunker for when the end of the world comes. I tell them, if the apocalypse comes, I'm not sticking around this shitty world anyhow."

"Yeah, they sound really weird." I nodded into my beer.

She stopped drying mugs for a moment and looked up at me. "So what's your deal? You're not our usual type. You hiding from a girlfriend or something?"

"Kind of," I said.

"That's what I figured. Not like it's such a genius guess—most guys are doing that. But you're more of a Frog type," she said, referring to my original destination. "I bet you guys live up the hill in an old house, and you've got a little organic garden and some nice wine in your basement. What's wrong with your life that you gotta hide? Sounds nice to me. Did you cheat?"

It was embarrassing and somehow emasculating to be summed up so neatly by this tough little girl.

"No, I didn't cheat. And we hardly have any nice wine at all!"

I smiled and she tossed her head back to laugh. This was the first time I had spoken with anyone other than Pia in days and the conversation was refreshing.

"I just needed some air, I guess," I said, sipping my beer.

"That's what everyone says when things are going bad."

"Oh, no, things aren't *bad*. I wouldn't say that. Just not good tonight."

"Sounds like the same thing to me, but what the hell do I know?" she said. "I've been living in this town my whole life."

"I love it here."

"Sure, because you don't *have* to be here," the bartender said as she dried one mug after another with great efficiency. "I wouldn't even care if I was in another shitty town, you know? It just wouldn't be the one I grew up in. That's the difference."

I was sure that I didn't know what she meant, but I nodded my head like our problems were all about the same.

"Anyhow," she went on, "I got a friend who runs a fancy bar on Martha's Vineyard, and as soon as I have enough savings, I'm going to meet her there. I figure it will be like a working vacation."

She walked away to check on the other guy and I puzzled over the idea that someone could be stuck, financially marooned in our town. This was a side of Isole I hadn't experienced much of since moving there: the real locals. There are pockets of immense wealth and worldliness in northern Vermont, but the state wasn't built on those people; they're just interlopers in its history. At its core, Vermont is defined by tough, industrious people who live modestly and know the land intimately, even if they no longer make their living from it. They prize independence and privacy over any allegiance to a nation or political identity, and they resent the ceaseless push by outsiders to transform the state to a socialist utopia. (I knew such generalizations made me seem like a patronizing asshole, but the locals had their own generalizations for me, too; it was how we made sense of our cohabitation.) Pia's prepper meeting was a funny mix of the old and new Vermont, I realized, though it wasn't a flattering light for either camp.

The clock above the bar struck eight, so I paid and thanked the bartender for her wisdom, which sounded stupid as soon as I said it out loud. I just wanted to get out of there before the prepper meeting ended, and Pia and her new friends made their way to Polly's. It seemed important that this nameless bartender never find out that I had been at that meeting. Plus I was concerned about how angry Pia might be.

I walked back in the cool air and waited in the car as people streamed out of the Elks Club and said their goodbyes. Some were laughing as they emerged, but there was a seriousness to the whole enterprise. That was perhaps the part that bothered me the most. On its own, preparing for disaster was inarguably a wise thing to do. And if Pia hadn't dragged me to that meeting, I would probably have regarded those people as nonthreatening curiosities. But Pia was always searching for religion. When she was a vegan, she emptied our fridge of all my favorite foods; and when she was a performance artist, she announced that she needed to be surrounded exclusively by creative people; and when she was a political activist, she accused her parents of being fascists.

Then there was the time that she actually did find religion, when she decided that we should be Buddhists. It involved a lot of Tibetan prayer flags in our apartment and mercifully little else. Her zeal was always genuine, but she lacked the conviction to see any of it through. And, inevitably, her avocations failed to deliver on whatever promise she thought they held. I regarded all of these phases as the hobbies of a passionate artist seeking purpose. They gave her focus, briefly, and a frenzied sort of pleasure. It wasn't a placid existence, but it was interesting.

This particular hobby, though, seemed more morbid. Her new friends weren't the ethereal waifs she used to bring home from tantric yoga class. (Weirdos are always harder to spot when they're bendy and beautiful.) No, this was darker and stranger. And maybe I knew it appealed to something frightened inside her, a part of her that I never fully understood. I wanted to believe this was out of character, but somewhere in my brain I knew that wasn't true.

The passenger door opened violently.

"We can go now. Are you happy?" Pia said, dropping into her seat like a child.

I looked at her in disbelief. "No, I'm not happy at all, Pia. I'm annoyed and a little freaked-out about the meeting you just tricked me into. What was that about?"

She shook her head in disbelief. "It was about seeing *the truth*, Ash."

And with that, our fight was under way. I didn't bother trying to reason or even argue; I just drove and let her fume. She pinned her hair up and took it down again, making the faintest huffing sounds to herself. I wouldn't give her the satisfaction of an argument. My plan was to just get home, open a bottle of wine and, after she'd consumed most of it alone on the couch, feel her groggily fall into bed beside me. That was how it was supposed to go.

But when we got home, Pia wasn't interested in wine or the couch. She sat down at the kitchen table and pulled out her little book of lists and nonsense. The handwriting was wild—alternately big and sharp and then small and controlled. She was making notes in the margins in a tiny new cursive style.

"You can go to bed, or do whatever you do," Pia said without looking up.

Whatever I did wasn't such a mystery, really. Unlike my wife, I was predictable, boring even. When it was warm outside, I would drink one or two Otter Creek Ales on the porch with a book until I got tired enough to pad upstairs to our bedroom. Pia would join me outside sometimes and we'd talk about all our plans for life in Vermont. And on the rare night of marital discord, we would just give each other space to ride out our anger privately. It was comforting to know that the parameters of our conflict had been set.

What I wanted to do at that moment was storm into another room and watch cable television loudly, but that wasn't an option. I missed ESPN and the foggy passivity that only mindless TV can enable. But Pia said that it would be "counterproductive" for us to get cable in our Vermont life. And, even though we had it in Brooklyn, thanks to a spliced wire from a neighbor, she felt that we didn't really *have it* have it. We didn't pay for it and, most important, we had an Argentinean tapestry draped over the shameful box when it wasn't in use—like it didn't exist at all! This always struck me as comically pretentious, but in truth, I'd adopted enough of these pretensions by then to go along with her.

MEG LITTLE REILLY

So the tapestry and its dirty secret followed us to Vermont, but our only option on that night was fuzzy network news.

I decided instead to sit on the porch with a wool blanket and a book about bird migrations of North America. The temperature had cooled to the low sixties, finally, but the sounds of summer weren't completely gone yet, which was disorienting. I could hear the unmistakable call of an American bullfrog—a rare treat anytime, but unheard of in late September. When we were little, my older sister and I used to go for walks down our dirt road in bare feet, collecting any living thing we could find in buckets. It was red salamanders mostly, sometimes dozens if we went out on the right day, but wood frogs and bullfrogs on occasion, too. They were hard to contain, so if one of us was lucky enough to capture a bullfrog, we'd stop everything to consult my pocket guide to amphibians before letting the terrified thing go again. I thought about digging around for that old book, but instead I rocked on the porch swing until I couldn't keep my eyes open any longer.

FOUR

"ASH, OPEN UP!" *Bang, bang, bang.* "Are you in there, Ash?"

I pushed my laptop aside and jumped off the couch for the front door. When I opened it, the first thing I saw was August's mother standing before me. She wore a knitted red cap over long gray hair and a terrified look in her eyes. This was the closest I had ever been to her and I could smell something on her that reminded me of dorm-room incense.

"August is missing!" she said. "Do you know where he is?"

My stomach jumped as I worked to take in the scene before me. It was late afternoon on a cool, windy day. August's father stood a few steps behind the mother. I couldn't remember either of their names, so I wasn't sure how to address them. He was thinner and sadder, but they could have been siblings, they looked so much alike to me.

"No, I don't," I sputtered. "How long has he been gone? Wait, let me get my shoes."

I stepped outside again with sneakers and a light jacket. This time I noticed a short, round, middle-aged woman with a nice face standing in the driveway. Despite the cool air, she wore a large T-shirt with a picture of an amusement park on it. She was moving her cell phone around, trying to find a signal. I had a hard time focusing on the scene before me as panic took hold of my body. Pia had left early that morning, still angry about our fight the night before, and I wished that she was there with me.

"What's going on? What happened?" I asked the group.

The new lady put her phone in her pocket and stepped toward me. "August has been gone since last night. He does this—wanders off sometimes—but this is a long one, even for him." She glanced to her left at August's parents and planted a lingering look of disapproval on each of them. "He goes into the woods. We need to get in there and fan out."

"Have you called the cops?" I asked.

August's mother stiffened. She hated that idea.

My stomach turned over and over on itself.

"They're already in there," the lady said, nodding at the woods behind me. "We have to get going, too." She pointed at August's parents now. "You guys go to the east. I'll pair up with Ash and we can go to the west. Go on."

August's parents walked away quickly and obediently. They didn't look confident in their ability to brave the woods alone, but this woman wanted to be alone with me for some reason.

"I'm Bev." She put her hand out for a quick, joyless shake. "I'm the social worker. August says you're his friend, so let's talk."

I nodded and we walked toward the woods with impatient strides.

"I don't understand what's going on," I said.

"As you've probably figured out—" Bev was walking ahead of me and pumping her arms "—August's parents are not up to the job. His father has paralyzing depression, which leaves him near comatose most of the day. And his mother is so panicked about the father that she barely notices the poor kid. I shouldn't be telling you any of this, but I know he looks up to you and I need another set of eyes on him. They abuse prescription drugs in front of him and can't be bothered to keep a damn thing in the fridge. They're not monsters. They love him. But they're selfish and irresponsible and getting worse all the time. I first started coming around here a year ago when August's 'treks' started. That's what he calls it when he goes off into the woods. He always has some important mission or something in mind and just takes off with a backpack. But it's usually just for four to maybe six hours. Once, it was eight. But he has never been out overnight and this is just… These goddamn people… I'm sorry. I'm mostly mad at myself. I should have removed him months ago."

My toe caught on a root and I nearly fell over as I tried to wrap my head around what she was saying. "He's been out here overnight? What could have happened to him? What does he do out here? We'll find him, I'm sure."

"I don't know. I think we will. August is a real adventurer, but he's not stupid. This is really bad, Ash."

"Wait, you said 'remove him.' Are you going to take him away from his parents?"

She shook her head, still walking quickly ahead of me, and said, "Forget that for now. Let's just find him. We have to just find him."

My head was spinning now, on top of my churning stomach. August had been out there all night long. I tried to imagine him smiling, sitting at the base of a tree with a piece of beef jerky in hand, talking to a chipmunk. But I couldn't hold on to the cheerful image. Unwanted pictures kept flashing before me: August, shivering in the dark; August, injured and crying;

MEG LITTLE REILLY

August, facedown in the fall leaves. The feeling was unbearable, like no other concern I'd ever felt. That wasn't even the word for it: *concern.* It was heartsickness and desperation—and I had known August for only a few months. I wondered how his parents were feeling at that moment. Desperation mixed with guilt. Those motherfuckers. I felt guilty now, too, for not seeing it all sooner. All of a sudden, I wanted to find them and push them into the forest floor, make them stay there all night. Whatever happens to them will be deserved, I thought. But August, we have to find August. Stay focused.

"Ash? Ash!" Bev was right beside me, yelling to break through my nightmarish thoughts.

"What?"

"You look pale. Are you okay? I need you to stay with me here."

I rubbed my face with my hands. "Yeah, I'm okay. Should we be shouting his name? Let's do that."

"Yes, okay," Bev said. She seemed at least as frightened as I was, but not as confused. Bev had seen families like this, cases like this, no doubt. She was probably fighting back her own images of what had become of August, but hers would be more vivid and plausible because she'd seen it all before, I imagined.

We watched our feet as we walked along the uneven forest floor, veering close to each other and then back out again. I shouted August's name, loud and hoarse. It hardly sounded like my own voice and I wondered if the boy would recognize me if he heard it from afar. As I walked, I had a strange realization that this was the longest I'd gone in weeks without thinking of The Storms. The weather seemed insignificant all of a sudden. And then it didn't. *What if the weather changed tomorrow, before we find August, and he's trapped out here without a coat? What if the cloud cover gets so bad that he can't use the sun for direction and time?* This was fear compounded by fear.

I wanted to ask Bev how this works. How long do we look and what clues can we search for and where were the police… But we just kept going. Step, step, shout. Step, step, shout. After an hour, I excused myself to pee behind a large tree and check my phone, hoping to see a message from Pia. I wanted to tell her what was going on and ask her to join me. This was too hard without her. She would be a help and a comfort. But she hadn't called. As far as she knew, this was still a normal day in which she could stay mad for hours and wander back when the feeling faded.

I sent her a text: August is missing. Please come home. I'm sorry for everything.

Within seconds, she responded: I can be there in twenty. That's horrible.

I felt a small, unsatisfying flash of relief as I pushed my phone into the back pocket of my jeans, but then I was back in reality, looking for my lost seven-year-old friend. He was my friend. That was the word, I suppose. Or was I his mentor? His surrogate big brother? It wasn't the sort of friendship I'd had before, but I wasn't a parent, so what else could I have been?

I looked up to find Bev talking to August's parents. I wasn't close enough to hear what they were saying, but she was moving her hands around, giving them instructions.

When I approached them, Bev said, "These guys are going to go back to the house in case August shows up there. The police are moving toward us from the far end of this forest. Ash, if you're up for it, you and I can just keep pressing forward until we meet the cops. Hopefully, one of us will find something before that happens."

Find something. It sounded like a compromise in expectations and it made my head hurt.

"Yes, of course. Let's keep going."

I sent Pia one more text explaining that we were too deep into the woods for her to meet us and that I would be back when I could. I wanted to hear her voice, but the reception was too poor for anything more than that. I looked back up at Bev The Social Worker and nodded. Let's keep going.

We walked for another hour. More yelling his name, mixed with feet crunching on branches, but no talking. There was nothing to say. It was starting to get dark and we didn't want to acknowledge what that could mean. I was hungry, or I would have been if I could feel anything other than panic and sickness. We just had to keep going.

"Hello?" a deep man's voice called from somewhere to our left.

"It's Bev and Ash," Bev yelled back.

"We've got him," the voice said.

Bev and I broke into an awkward run toward the voice until a large police officer came into focus. At first, we couldn't see him, but then the officer turned to reveal a tired, dirty August clinging to him piggyback-style. The boy's too-short pant legs wrapped around his torso. A smaller cop stood next to them, holding August's blue backpack and a large water bottle.

When August saw us, he released his hold and dropped to the ground, landing on his feet and sprinting toward us. For a moment, I wasn't sure who he was running to, but it was me. He gave me one quick squeeze around the neck as I crouched down and I wrapped my arms around his little body so hard it made him squirm. He was happy to see me, but a little confused by all the adult dramatics. He seemed fine.

"I made a sweet fort, Ash! But then it got so dark and I

lost my compass and I had to stay in one place. That's an important rule of ranger safety: stay in one place if you're lost."

I smiled. "Yes! Good thinking, buddy. Are you okay? Were you scared?"

August shrugged. "Yeah, I was a little scared."

And that was it. We would get more from him later about where and how he made it through the night, but none of that mattered at that moment. We walked back through the woods in a long line with the officers at the front, followed by Bev The Social Worker, then me with August on my back. It took over an hour and my legs ached, but I was so grateful for the weight of his body and the sound of his soft breath near my ear. I was surprised he let me carry him like that for so long. We had never before touched beyond the occasional high five, but this felt perfectly natural. August fell asleep like that for the final stretch and I wondered what his parents would think when they saw me deliver him to them, his body melting into mine, in all its trusting vulnerability. "Attachment issues" is what Pia once called it. She said August seemed to have some attachment issues with his parents, which may have explained some of his neediness with me. It made more sense now, though I'd thought she was overreacting at the time.

August awoke as we approached his house and I watched his parents run out to make a big show of hugging him in front of us all. They had been terrified, no doubt, and were so grateful to have him back, but I saw them in a new light now and felt them unworthy of his return.

"Let's talk," Bev said, nodding at the path that led to my house.

We thanked the officers and walked back to my home, which was invitingly warm and bright as we stepped into the kitchen. I kissed Pia long and hard and introduced her to the social worker. She put a pot of water on for tea, but Bev said she wasn't staying long.

"I wanted you to know that I'm taking August away," Bev said. "This is the last straw for those two. Strictly between us, the officers searched their home and found illegal pain pills in several places. They're probably high right now. Who knows how long he had been out there before they noticed. He can't stay in that home."

"But where will he go?" I took the kitchen chair opposite Bev and Pia sat down beside me.

"Into the foster care system. We will find a temporary home for him." Bev shook her head. "It's not an easy case. August's parents don't abuse him, but they aren't present either. Neglect is easy to overlook, but it can be life-threatening, particularly because August just keeps wandering off. And who can blame him? It's awful in that house with those two zombies."

I tried to imagine August moving away, into a different family, a different house. It didn't seem right. He would hate to be away from these woods and me and his stupid parents. He loved his parents. But I wasn't sure how to talk about this. I didn't have the language to navigate this world of social workers and foster care.

"What if…" I started. "Can you just wait? Do we have to do this now? What if I kept an eye on him? I could check on him every day, do activities with him. I could even make sure he eats a healthy meal each day."

Bev shook her head. "Ash, you can't look after him *all day*. August is desperate for attention and boundaries right now and he's going to keep pushing limits and taking risks until someone provides him with that. Right now, he needs constant attention. Now, if you wanted to be a formal caregiver, that would be another question…"

Pia's eyes opened wide. "You mean, be his foster family?"

Bev shrugged, leaving the possibility out there on the table.

I raised my eyebrows at Pia. It sounded crazy, but maybe it wasn't crazy. Maybe this could save August; wonderful, weird August. She stared back at me in shock. I knew that look. We needed to talk. Of course I wouldn't commit us to something so big without a lot of discussion between us.

Bev understood. "It's not as simple as this. Any potential foster family needs to be thoroughly vetted. And you would need to be 100 percent on board with this idea. There can be no uncertainty."

"I think we're getting ahead of ourselves," Pia said politely.

"Yes, we need to talk about this," I added. "But what will happen to August for now?"

Bev took a deep breath. She was unsure herself and it struck me just how haphazardly a child's future could be decided. This woman had too much discretion, nice as she was. And none of the answers seemed obvious to a table of adults. I wasn't even sure I understood what the question was.

"I'll let him stay over there for now," Bev said, "on the condition that you promise me to check in with him every morning and evening. I'm going to be calling you for updates."

I nodded.

"But we can't do this for long," she went on. "You've got three months to decide what you want. After that, I'm putting him in a foster family. I don't want him in that house when these storms come. That's not happening."

Pia and I both nodded. We knew that she was serious. And she was right: August's fate needed to be determined before The Storms came.

We sat silently at the kitchen table for a moment, listening to Bev's car drive away. When there was no chance of her return, I put my head into my hands and yelled, then rubbed my face over and over. Pia walked over and wrapped my head in her arms as she stood above.

"I thought he was dead," I said into her body.

"I know."

"I kept seeing these images of him in the woods... It was so bad."

Pia released me and sat in the closest chair. She nodded in sympathy, which was all I needed her to do. There was nothing else to be said about that horrible day. August was okay.

"How could his parents just lose him like that?" I asked. "The social worker's right. He can't stay in that house."

Pia drew a reluctant breath. "You want to take him, don't you?"

"Yes. Don't you?"

She breathed again, then shook her head. "I see what you're doing here and you have to stop."

"What?" I asked.

Her tone was kind, but firmer now. "Don't confuse this situation for a message from the universe about us becoming parents. Don't do that. This isn't serendipity; it's ugly reality. It's a poor kid in a marginally dangerous household. This isn't ours."

"I'm not doing that," I said, shocked. I didn't think I was doing that. I wasn't sure.

Pia looked at me kindly, almost pitifully so. "I love that you want to save him and that you think we can. I love that about you. But it's not black-and-white, Ash. This is so much more complicated than what we're equipped for. It can't be solved with love." She said the last word as one might refer to Santa Claus.

I understood the point she was making, but it seemed irrelevant. "Some of this is perfectly black-and-white, though. He either stays here with us or he goes somewhere else, with people he doesn't know and a million other unknowable variables. There's a deadline and a decision to make. It's not a philosophical difference we're talking about here; it's August's life. He's here or he's somewhere else, probably somewhere worse."

I suspected that Pia thought this sort of reasoning made me simple and naive. I was okay with that. A problem existed and we could offer a solution. It wouldn't be uncomplicated or easy, but how could we leave this helpless young human to such an uncertain future? It was uncertainty multiplied by uncertainty with the storm looming. And I wasn't suggesting it out of a misguided sense of poetry—to have a child that binds us forever—I was suggesting it because it was right.

"This is the right thing to do," I said. "You know that it is. It's not a fashionable reason, but it's just the right fucking thing to do and we will always hate ourselves for doing the wrong thing."

"Oh, don't do that." Pia shook her head. She had shifted back in her chair, away from me. "Don't be *good* because it makes you feel superior to me. The stakes are way too high for that. You're not considering the very real possibility that we would be terrible parents to this kid. With his upbringing, he probably has special behavioral needs that we know nothing about; and maybe he needs special doctors or schools that cost more than we can afford. Maybe we are the bad option for this poor kid. It's arrogant to assume we're not."

She was making perfect sense and gaining speed with her strengthening argument. It was true that we probably weren't equipped to handle a traumatized seven-year-old boy. Was that what this was: trauma? I didn't know. Pia was right about all this, but it still made me sick to imagine him alone in a world of strangers who didn't appreciate his specialness. Or worse, people who confused his specialness with dysfunction,

MEG LITTLE REILLY

something to be fixed and medicated. It got worse and worse as my mind wandered.

"But did you read that think piece, in the *Nation*, I think it was, about how horrible foster care is?" I asked. "All that sexual abuse and fraud. We can't let him go into that."

"I'm sure it's not all like that," Pia said. She paused and then seemed to collect herself after a moment of weakness. "Anyhow, it's not a problem that we can solve. That's the point here. All of these options are bad, including us…especially us."

I stood up and walked to the sink, which was filled with dirty mismatched coffee mugs from the previous three days. A rind of whole wheat crust floated in dirty water. "I don't know. I have to think. We have to decide quickly."

"Also, who would be the primary caregiver?" she asked. "It can't be me. I have to figure out my career."

"Yes, you do," I agreed.

"Well, don't say it with such disdain. It's not a crime to be unemployed and confused."

I had never heard her describe her situation so honestly.

She went on, "You know, we were told our whole childhoods to find something that we love doing. Major in something we love in college and all that. So I did those things, but then the world changed, and now we have to just do anything that pays. I'm sure I sound like a privileged brat, but I haven't adapted to this new world. I don't want to just do something that pays."

It *was* privileged and bratty, but Pia was being honest and she looked ashamed by this admission. I didn't want her to have to do something she hated either. For me, it was different. I didn't have a singular passion like she did for art. I was better when I was working and the work could be more broadly defined. I didn't really know the feeling she was describing, but I knew she was sincere about it.

"I'm sorry, honey," I said. "This is a discussion worth having, but it's a different discussion from the August one."

"Well, maybe not." Her shoulders rose and fell. "It's a discussion about what we want to do with our days. I'm telling you I don't know what I want to do with my days and that's not the right way to be thrust into parenthood."

"Everyone is thrust into parenthood, though." I didn't mean for it to sound so grim. "I mean, it starts abruptly."

"A lot of things feel abrupt lately."

I knew what she meant. We had moved to Vermont only months before with only peaceful daydreams of a more rustic life, and then we learned of The Storms, and now this. Things just kept happening at us.

I stood up and kissed the top of her head. "I hear everything you're saying. Please, just think about this for a few days. I will keep an eye on August for now, but let's keep talking about this, okay?"

"Okay," she agreed, but her thoughts were already elsewhere.

FIVE

BY MID-OCTOBER, insomnia had become a regular occurrence. I had always been an easy sleeper, out by eleven most nights and unmoving until dawn. But everything changed that fall when the fear crept into our lives. At first, it was just a few restless nights—I hardly noticed the change—but soon a pattern emerged. And by the time this particular evening rolled around, October 18, I expected one to two hours of generalized anxiety before I had any chance of sleep. My mind jumped back and forth between present dangers and old memories. I tried to dwell on the old stuff, the good stuff.

"Our kid will be cool," I said. "Or kids, plural."

We were lying on our backs in the grass of our backyard, looking up at the clouds. It was the second day in our new Vermont home.

"Yeah, they'll be cool," Pia agreed. "But not, like, into being cool. They'll just be really great people, but they won't care about the idea of being cool."

"Right. Smart and funny and fearless."

"So fearless," she went on. "They will need to be… The world is changing. Things might be harder for them."

I remember wondering what she meant by that, but I didn't ask.

"Oh, I'm not worried about our imaginary kids," I said. "They've overcome every imaginary obstacle they've faced."

"They're really kicking imaginary ass," Pia agreed. I could feel her smile beside me.

"They are."

We laughed and kissed, so pleased with our wit and drunk on our hopeful fantasies.

I tossed in bed with my gentle memories and emerging concerns. Would the world be different for our kids, I wondered. Of course, it's different for every generation, sometimes easier, occasionally harder. That's just the ebb and flow of humanity, right? Cultural pluralism is winning in America, but California is running out of water. Gay marriage is law, but social mobility is reversing. Is it getting better or worse? And do we have an obligation to consider the conditions our not-yet-conceived children might live under?

Finally, I drifted off, only to be woken again by a clanking. *Bink, bink, bink.* It sounded as though someone was banging on the kitchen sink with a hammer. Oh my God. Pia? She wasn't in bed beside me. Where was she? I reached under the bed for a wood baseball bat that had been signed by Wade Boggs in 1990 and ran downstairs in my boxers. I imagined that someone was breaking in through a window, maybe collecting what little we had of value or, worse, attacking my wife. Though I had been asleep less than a minute before, I could already feel my armpits tingling with sweat and my head pounding audibly. At that moment, only my truest, most elemental feeling about Pia was known to me.

It was the feeling of desperate, protective animal love that a parent might have for a child. I was ready to attack, maybe even *kill* someone at the thought of helpless, beautiful Pia being harmed. It's a thrilling feeling—to know that your primal self has not been dormant for so long that you can't transform into an attack dog when you must.

I thudded downstairs with my arm cocked back, ready to strike with the bat at whatever I encountered. But there was no intruder. Pia stood at the kitchen sink in a long, ratty nightgown with a hammer in one hand and a plastic tube in the other. She obviously heard me but didn't acknowledge my arrival.

"What are you doing?" I huffed, still on a breathless high from the sprint downstairs.

She looked frustrated, close to tears, over whatever project was keeping her up at three o'clock in the morning.

"This, this thing!" She waved the tube in front of her, looking near me but not exactly at me. "I have to get it to fit into that other piece, but it's impossible!"

There was a pile of odd parts on the floor beside her, which, according to the empty box nearby, was supposed to be a hand-crank water sterilizer. I noticed that her feet were filthy, as if she'd been walking around outside. I thought I would find a robber or rapist when I ran downstairs, which now seemed like a much less complicated situation. The obsessive, wired woman before me was more frightening.

"You don't have to do this—not now, love," I said gently. "Let's have a cup of tea and then go to bed."

To my surprise, she nodded and stepped out of the mess of objects into my arms. I led her by the hand to the couch in the living room, as if a stranger might still be lurking around a corner, and threw a blanket over her while I prepared mint tea for each of us. It was cold downstairs. We had turned the woodstove on earlier that week for the first time, but it had burned out hours before. I focused on making the tea, unsure of whether I was angry or frightened.

It wasn't uncommon for Pia to find inspiration at odd hours or obsess over a project for a few frantic days. Those episodes were exciting for her, but never upsetting. And often they really did produce something inspired, like the time Pia made an entire quilt to hang on the wall in our old apartment. She had taken a workshop in abstract quilting and spent hundreds of dollars at the fabric store. Oddly shaped strips of colorful torn fabric shed threads around the living room for days, until one sleepless night, I awoke to find a striking quilt the size of an entire wall draped around her as she trimmed stray ends. The vibrant colors danced together in an explosive design that looked something like a sunrise. It hung in our apartment for two years, until we moved to Vermont. The quilt was a symbol of Pia's exuberance and artistic gifts. I don't know why we hadn't hung it yet in our new home, but I missed it as we drank tea on the couch. The quilt always helped to explain and excuse the erratic aspects of passionate Pia.

We sat quietly for a while, staring forward at the inert television.

"I'm sorry," she finally said. "I don't like this about myself. I wish I could change it."

I hugged her. "I know."

"I'm just…scared. I can't explain why."

I wanted to be entirely there for her, to dedicate myself to conquering the internal and external threats that frightened her. But I was scared, too. The future that we'd planned for had been unmoored by the storm reports, and I wanted comfort now, as well. I didn't know where self-care ended and selfishness began or what my obligation to my wife should

MEG LITTLE REILLY

have been then. I only knew that suddenly I didn't have that selflessness in me. I was afraid, too.

We shivered together under a blanket, each privately fearing the changes afoot.

SIX

"I THINK YOUR joists are rotting," August said with authority. "I've seen this before."

We were on our knees in the backyard examining the underbelly of the porch steps, which appeared to be melting into the earth. This was the sort of handyman challenge that little August excelled at. In all his solo wanderings to neighbors' homes and nearby farms, he'd gleaned useful information about just this sort of thing, so I was happy to have him close by as we tinkered. Plus it was an effortless way to keep an eye on him under the new arrangement.

I squinted to see deeper into the dank cavern. "Do you think we need to rebuild the steps entirely, or can we just replace a few of those pieces?" I asked. I had no idea how to do either of those things.

August stood up and put his finger in the air like a cartoon character signaling that a big idea had hit him. "We should go see Peg! She has a buttload of leftover wood from when she fixed the doors on the stable. It's walnut, which is wicked hard. I'll show you how much it hurts when we punch it."

Lacking any other ideas and curious to meet our neighbor

Peg, who lived just through the woods on the other side, I agreed and followed August's determined march toward the road. Pia was reading a book about candle making inside and seemed happy to have us out of the house, so I didn't bother disturbing her.

It was late Sunday afternoon on November 3 and the autumn cold had finally arrived. I wanted to bundle August up in one of our extra winter coats, but that wasn't the kind of relationship we had; not yet. We both watched the sky as we walked, which was as magnificent as any I had ever seen that time of year. We were entering the part of fall when everything shifts to gray. It's a transitional period between the fiery explosions of foliage and the austerity of winter, and you could miss it if you weren't paying attention—but everyone was paying attention in those days. The sky wasn't steely as it should have been, but speckled pink as if a firecracker was suspended in the clouds. It had something to do with the wild temperature fluctuations and the hurricane that was, on that day, attacking the Carolinas. The effect looked magnificent and felt eerie as we walked along the road.

Although Peg was our immediate neighbor, I'd had very few interactions with her and knew virtually nothing about her life. As far as I could tell, she was a busy sixtysomething woman with a lingering Irish accent and no immediate family nearby. Even August was light on details about her. Some people move to the woods to be left alone and I assumed Peg was one of those people. So it was a surprise when she opened the door with a big smile and personable ease.

We stepped inside to find that Peg was involved in an elaborate applesauce-canning project, which she left unattended to make tea for the three of us. Because of the applesauce, we were surrounded by a heady fairy-tale scent, but hers was not the home of a kindly granny. Everywhere I looked, there were artifacts from different parts of the world—African masks, Chinese vases, tiny Russian dolls swimming in a bowl with stray pennies and paper clips. It was dizzying but beautiful and utterly natural, not the curated gallery of someone looking to impress. This was the cluttered house of a woman who'd lived a full life.

August and I immediately forgot the purpose of our trip and instead drank tea on worn, mismatched furniture in the living room while Peg told us about the objects around us and the circumstances of their acquisition. August had never been inside her house either, and he peppered her with one breathless question after another, which relieved me of the job. She gestured constantly while she spoke, pointing to trinkets and tucking behind her ear the stray gray hair that kept falling from a loose ponytail. I noticed that her clothes looked as if she might be scheduled for a safari later that day. She wore a white linen shirt tucked into those polyester khakis that looked like rain would slide right off them. They had multiple pockets of varying sizes that I assumed were intended for compasses and jackknives.

Peg was a botanist and a professor at Lyndon State College. She had published two books on the reproductive patterns of conifers and lived in several countries, which she would drop into the conversation like afterthoughts ("that was when I was in the Philippines, which has a sensational culture but disappointing food…"). She never married, but there were pictures of a younger Peg with tanned men in adventurous settings displayed around her home. August inquired about a large instrument that occupied the corner of the living room and she explained that she played the cello in a local ensemble "not terribly well."

I loved Peg immediately. She was expressive and a little kooky but obviously smart and accomplished. I wondered

MEG LITTLE REILLY

about the men who appeared in her pictures. She seemed like the type who might casually refer to them as having been *lovers*, a word that made me shudder but seemed completely natural on her. I also liked that Peg had made her way from Ireland, around most of the globe, to Isole—and that she seemed to think it was as wonderful as I did.

"And what about you, Ash?" Peg asked, picking up her teacup after a summary of her time spent studying shrubs in Senegal. "What brings you here?"

I wished I had something less conventional to tell Peg than the fact that I was returning to my home state to eat organic food with my lovely wife, who'd been acting strange lately. Instead, I gave her a version of the truth that emphasized my love of nature and new furniture-making hobby, which I thought might make me seem slightly less boring.

"You didn't like New York?" she asked.

"Oh, no, I love New York," I replied. "The energy and the culture… I know it's a cliché, but all the things people say are great about New York really are great. I will definitely miss it."

"Then why did you leave?"

"Well, Pia and I had always dreamed of starting a new adventure somewhere, living a little more mindfully and simply…something like that."

Our reasoning sounded obnoxious as I said it aloud and I made a mental note to prepare a better explanation for future conversations.

"So why Vermont?" Peg probed. "You could have gone anywhere, but you're back in your home state."

I took a breath and started slowly. "I guess for me it was more like I needed to get back to my natural habitat."

I waited to see if this was enough for Peg, but she didn't appear satisfied, so I went on. "It's like everyone is born with a certain constitution, you know? And you can enjoy all kinds of places, but there's only one place that you feel absolutely at home in. That's how I feel about the woods of Vermont. I could never envision myself growing old in a different environment. I don't know, maybe that sounds insane."

Peg nodded and smiled slightly. She appeared to understand.

August pushed off his chair and announced that he was bored.

"What do you want to talk about, buddy?" I said.

"I want to know what Peg—who is a *scientist*—thinks about The Storms that are coming."

August said *scientist* with great emphasis and I made a mental note to nurture this interest in him.

Peg set her teacup down and picked a piece of lint off her safari pants before looking back up at August and me. She was serious all of a sudden.

"August, the most important thing for you to remember is that everything is going to be fine. You've got a house and two parents and me and Ash, and we're all going to make sure you're safe."

August didn't look particularly distressed to me, but Peg gave me a firm look suggesting that I needed to play a role in this lesson.

"She's right, buddy," I said. "It's just weather. We'll make it an adventure!"

It felt strange to speak that way, and I realized that perhaps I had no idea how I was supposed to speak to children.

August shrugged and looked bored again. "Okay. Can I feed carrots to the horses?"

Peg sent August to the stable with a small, dirty tote bag of carrots and sat back down across from me. Then we had a very adult conversation about August's parents' negligence and how we could help provide him with a sense of safety in the coming months. I was reminded again that there was a lot I didn't know about looking after a child.

"And The Storms?" I said. "Do you think they will be as bad as the predictions?"

Peg looked into her tea. "I do. I think they will be much worse, in fact."

"But how can you know that?" Her certainty shook me.

"Governments are conservative about such things. They have reason to be—every storm report has the potential to move markets and set into motion a series of events at a global level. It's not willful deception, exactly. It's more like a compulsory downplaying. If the US government panics, everyone panics. So yes, I think The Storms are going to be much worse than they are predicting."

It seemed as though Peg had more to say on the topic, so I waited.

"And these predictions ring true to me as someone who has studied the earth for most of my life," she went on. "In the field and through a microscope, I've been watching things change for years. I've been waiting for The Storms, in a way. And it's not just *these* storms; it's the dramatic changes that are about to start happening regularly. This is the real lie that our government is telling: they are leading Americans to believe that this winter is an anomaly, a freak event for the history books, but it's not. There could be something bigger right behind it, and then another after that."

Still I said nothing. Peg seemed to need to tell me this story.

"Of course, it's not just the United States. It's also the governments of China, India, most of Europe—the rest of the world is doing the same thing. They know that their own big storms are coming, though they will be different everywhere."

I thought of a movie that Pia and I had seen in the theater about an earthquake in the Pacific Ocean that triggered a tsunami in China, which sent global oil prices into turmoil, causing war to break out across the Middle East and parts of Africa. After the movie, we'd laughed about how improbable it was.

I must have looked concerned because Peg held up her hands and said, "I'm not a climatologist, and any good scientist knows that there's so much more we *don't* know, so I suppose anything could happen, Ash."

Peg said my name quietly to herself twice more, and she seemed to move on to a different thought.

"Do you know about the ash tree?" she asked. "It's very important in Celtic mythology."

I raised my eyebrows, trying to follow the turn in conversation. "I had no idea. I guess I don't really know why that's my name."

"It's considered one of the most powerful of all the trees," Peg said without a hint of jest in her voice. "Actually, in parts of Europe, they used to use it to make spears and the handles of weapons. It's associated with enchantment and healing. The pagans considered it positively holy! There's a lot going on with the ash tree. Were your parents druids or hippies?"

"Ha." I laughed. "No, not to my knowledge. My grandfather was a logger, though. I don't know; that's the only tree connection I can think of."

Peg nodded. "That's probably it. He knew the trees and ash is an important tree. It's very fitting for you."

I suddenly felt self-conscious about the conversation and wanted to move on.

"So, you're into mythology?" I asked.

"Of course!" she said. "You can't study nature and ignore mythology."

"What do you mean?"

Peg looked serious again. "Ash, you're smart—not a black-and-white thinker. I can see that. So don't allow yourself to be seduced by the blacks and whites of science. There are other ways of knowing things, too, ways that rely on instinct and emotion. Life is fuller when you leave room for all of it."

Peg stopped there, apparently satisfied with this answer and maybe even enjoying my confusion a little. The discussion had taken an unexpected turn, but I was more intrigued by Peg than ever now.

August ran in at that moment and announced that he was out of carrots and hungry, so I thanked Peg for the tea and helped her carry the chipped china to the sink. She handed August a sleeve of crackers that he stuffed into a back pocket.

"Oh, August," Peg said as we opened the back door to leave. "Be sure to check out the fairy ring just past the barn. The fungi won't be there much longer!"

"Got it," August replied in his most serious voice.

We walked into the cold and I asked August what a fairy ring was.

He sighed impatiently and explained that it was an enchanted circle of toadstools and "any dummy knows that humans are never supposed to enter a fairy ring."

I smiled, feeling a surge of love at that moment for August and the Northeast Kingdom of Vermont, where the scientists make room for the metaphysical.

We observed the circle of mushrooms from a safe, reverent distance.

SEVEN

I WAS HALF-ASLEEP in bed on a Wednesday night in mid-November, thinking about windows. An old man at the coffee shop told me earlier that week that I needed to start "getting the storms in." I didn't know the man and I had only the most vague understanding of what he was talking about, but his instruction sent a wave of panic through me. It was another reminder that I needed to figure out quickly how to be an adult homeowner in the country. Extreme weather was on its way, and I owned a big, leaky house and I wasn't even sure if we had storm windows or how to install them. I repeated the old man's advice to myself, practicing his confidence. *Of course, you have to get those storms in before it's too cold. You wouldn't want to wait too long.* I imagined saying it to someone else in the same knowing tone, after my storms were safely in. What a relief it would be to be the guy with the rural know-how.

Despite the gulf growing between Pia and me, she recognized my panic as I tossed about in bed, thinking of the windows. She rolled over and put a hand on my forehead, an uncharacteristically maternal gesture that I appreciated. I hadn't spoken to her about the windows or any of the other chores and light construction that needed to get done. Her head was full enough.

It had been almost two months since Pia's first prepper meeting and she was more engrossed in the mission than ever. She knew not to bother me about it, but I could see that it was occupying a growing role in her life. I found cryptic notes around the house, written to herself about preparations she needed to tend to. She still had no job or real obligations, but she hurried around all day, then stayed up late into the night and drank wine: sometimes a bottle or more. But I did, too, now, so I chose to look past the modest increase in recyclables that we brought to the redemption center each week. That was the puzzle: distinguishing Pia's unraveling from the rest of our fraying nerves. Everyone's mental health was diminishing. Life moved forward mostly undisturbed, but we were all having a third glass to trick ourselves into sleep.

The Storms were with us all the time but only detectable if you were looking for them. They were ghosts that we were beginning to grow comfortable with because we had no other choice. What else could we do? Across the country, bills still had to be paid and grass had to be mowed and children had to be raised. Life was still grinding forward.

The Storms were affecting things beyond the walls of our little life, too. The lines that divide Americans—the ones we like to believe are always softening—were beginning to sharpen. Just that week, a group of young men had held up a mosque at gunpoint in New Jersey, yelling about how they didn't want to share the country with outsiders anymore. A few days later, a renegade group of civilians in Texas launched their own border security operation, killing two Mexican immigrants before Homeland Security shut it down. And the state of Colorado had just passed a law requiring that classrooms start each day with the Lord's Prayer "to ward off evil in the face of uncertainty."

It was impossible to know what the coming threats would look like and how our lives might be upended. In the absence of clarity, we used our imagination, which for many morphed into paranoia.

Congressional members from the West Coast were forming bipartisan alliances to enact legislation that put caps on disaster relief funding, apparently unable to envision a time when a superdisaster might strike their side of the country (and it would). These were just the early signs, the small things that signaled bigger injustices ahead. For instance, we didn't know then that a group of hackers would break into the Department of Homeland Security's computer system and reveal that the government had willfully ignored evidence of The Storms for over a year before warning the public. I guess I thought it would take more for our trusted institutions to abandon us, but I was wrong.

Pia and I learned all this and shook our heads, saddened for our country, but also vindicated in our decision to hide out in a corner of America that didn't identify much with the rest of the country.

In response to the growing tensions, the government plastered the airwaves with a public service campaign that featured a multiracial group of washed-up celebrities smiling and embracing. "Safer Together" it was called and it had a catchy theme song that was obviously intended to sound something like U2. Sometimes August hummed it to himself, though I doubt it had much effect on its target demographic of hate groups and antigovernment protesters.

All of this was too much for my anxious 1:00 a.m. mind to ponder, so I thought about storm windows instead. Pia thought about water-filtration systems and I thought about storm windows, and we both drank a bit too much wine and the world still felt almost manageable this way.

I could feel Pia inch closer to me in bed, pressing her warm breasts against my shoulder. Bed was the best place for us, disarmed in the pitch-black. Our bodies hadn't changed, so we could pretend while we were there that nothing had. She slid a hand into my boxers and began working gently.

With so little provocation, I was out of my nervous head and back in my body. She was still Pia and we were still *us*, and it felt as electric as the first night she took me home and spread unabashedly before me. I kissed her neck, her shoulder; I pulled her hair. She gasped and dug the fingernails of her free hand into my thigh. I climbed on top of her and, with great force, did my best to push the unknowable demons out of her wild body. But of course, the demons were part of the electricity.

We were alternately fucking and making love, holding on for dear life and then punishing each other for something unnamed. The change was subtle, but it was a more selfish, individual style of sex than we were used to. When she came, she cried out and then bit my shoulder so hard I thought she'd draw blood. It was part of her performance, I knew, but I appreciated the effort. And I was grateful for the pain, which made the blood in my body pump with frightening force.

When we were lying still again, exhausted and self-satisfied, Pia put her head on my chest and whispered, "I think our family is just right the way it is."

She was talking about August, of course, but maybe also about the possibility of conceiving our own children. She had slowly and inexplicably been drifting away from the idea of children in the preceding two months. I could feel her moving on to other things. Until very recently, this would have been a relief, but it wasn't any longer.

It had always seemed a great privilege to me, to be two

adults in love and unbound by children or even pets. Everything about our life was intentional, chosen by each of us every morning because we wanted it that way. We were forging close-but-distinct parallel paths, and we were light enough and lean enough to veer off into any direction we wanted together. The people I saw with children seemed carried along by the momentum of all their freight. They looked helpless. But lately—even before August disappeared—our freedom was feeling unnervingly light, as if we might both float away from each other and this earth, disappearing into the cosmos forever. I wanted the weight now. I needed a life that felt more substantial. Was it wrong to want August to tether me to the ground? What are the right reasons to want children if not that? Sometimes it seemed we had waited so long and thought so thoroughly about *why* to have children that any primal instinct for it had been smothered by theory.

Maybe we need a pet, I thought, as we lay naked beside each other.

We had a cat once. Burt. He belonged to the elderly woman across the hall from us in Brooklyn, but after six months she declared the cat "a real asshole" and offered him up to Pia. Without consulting me, Pia agreed to take Burt and he was there when I arrived home from work one night.

I tried to be open-minded about Burt, given his orphaned state, but it wasn't easy. He was anxious and in the habit of pulling out large chunks of his fur when life got to be too much. And his moods were so unpredictable that he could curl up in your lap at breakfast and attack you when you arrived home that night. After Burt drew blood from me for the third time, I lost patience.

"He's got to go, Pia," I demanded. "He really is a little shit."

"He can't go," she cried. "Don't you see it? This cat is me! He needs to live here."

"What?"

"He's me. It's uncanny. He was deprived of affection as a kitten and now he's acting out through aggression and self-harm."

I took a deep breath. "That's a little dramatic."

"Not if it's true." She folded her arms across her chest. "I'm keeping Burt. We need each other."

Argument seemed futile at that point and I didn't hate Burt enough to declare war over him, so I conceded. And I couldn't help but admit that Pia's emotional resemblance to Burt—as described by her—was real. I will never know if Pia's parents were cruel or simply cold or if the difference matters to a small child, but something about her early life left her wanting. Beneath her wit and allure, there was always a simmering reservoir of needy energy that could bubble over as anger or excitement. I didn't understand it, but I knew by then that it predated our relationship and I had no power over it. So Burt stayed.

Maybe Burt could have helped, but we never had the chance to know. He sneaked out one night during a dinner party and we never saw him again.

Pia curled into me and kissed my shoulder, bringing me back to the present.

"I love that," I said, in reference to the sex we'd just had.

"Mmm, me, too," she murmured. "We'll be grateful to have it when everything else is gone."

EIGHT

BY THE LAST week in November, everyone was a weather expert. Strangers in the checkout line exchanged pleasantries about tropical storm masses and air density. We watched the White House Weather Briefing every Saturday morning—a recent invention intended to tamp down panic and convey the impression of control—and we searched new terms as they were introduced. Were the chilly temperatures part of a simple cold front or an occluded front, we wondered. Was this wind just a brief disturbance or should we expect sustained gales? Having a language for this new reality made it feel manageable, mundane even. And though we had private moments of fear, The Storms were folding into our lives.

"They used to think the crazy weather was caused by El Niño," I heard a boy say to his younger brother at the Winter Farmers' Market. "But now they think it's something new that we don't even know about."

I was roaming around the barn at the edge of town that hosted contra dancing on Fridays, Quaker services on Sundays and the Winter Farmers' Market on Saturdays. I had picked out a knitted hat for August and was browsing the rest of the precious offerings—goats' milk moisturizer, artisanal sausage, purple potatoes. When I stopped to eavesdrop on their conversation, the older boy was stacking handmade beeswax candles while his younger brother looked on, impressed.

"Yup," he went on, "there's going to be a hurricane…and a blizzard…and maybe a tornado, too!"

The little brother raised his eyebrows at this frightening and flawed information. "All at once?" he asked.

"Yeah, they're all going to crash into each other at the same time!"

To emphasize this point, the boy picked up two delicate honeycomb candles and smashed them together like colliding vehicles until the candle vendor shooed them away.

Even I knew that we should have been working harder to shield children from the incessant chatter of catastrophe, but it must have been impossible for parents. It wasn't just the dominant topic of conversation among all the adults living east of the Mississippi River; it was also blaring from talk radio and cable news. New conspiracies and outlandish scenarios could travel across social media before anyone's teacher had time to explain their hollow, and sometimes sinister, origins.

August wanted to talk of nothing else, but I tried to repeat Peg's message of safety whenever we kicked a soccer ball back and forth or tackled new home-improvement projects together. Whether he believed my false confidence, I couldn't tell.

When I worked at my desk, I consumed a steady stream of media chatter about the weather. I knew the distraction was impeding my productivity, but I couldn't stop. The official government forecast was growing more specific and ominous each week, with the latest prediction calling for a series of smaller storms in December and January, followed by one very large superstorm. We didn't know precisely what this superstorm might look like or just how super it might get, but that part of the forecast had emerged as the focus of our anxieties. The worst-case scenario had gone from a faint possibility to a likely outcome, and fear was increasing accordingly. Taking a cue from the public, news outlets began calling it "The Storm," which sounded more terrifying for its supremacy over every storm that had come before it. It was also cinematic, which none of us could resist. We developed a detached fascination with The Storm as if we were waiting for the opening of a blockbuster movie. We didn't know how it would end or just how gruesome the destruction would be, but we tingled with impatient anticipation of its release. When The Storm would hit was still a matter of dispute among experts, so every dip in temperature set off a new wave of public speculation, reigniting our fears and our morbid excitement.

Even those of us who were impervious to hype and over-reaction realized eventually that we would need to make preparations. *Something* was going to happen. On the first Friday of December, the sky turned an unfamiliar shade of pinkish gray and the town of Isole snapped into action.

This Wednesday: all townspeople are welcome at the Isole town hall meeting. Memorial High School gymnasium at 7:00 p.m. Baked goods appreciated.

A poster bearing this message was plastered around town, announced after church services and passed along by reliable gossips until it seemed everyone was planning on attending. It was understood that this would be the meeting in which town leaders elaborated on emergency plans and decided how to allocate finite resources. Apart from her prepper meetings, Pia and I hadn't involved ourselves in local matters since moving to Isole, but the idea seemed pleasingly quaint to me. I was itching to meet more people in our new town and for excuses to get out of the house.

When we entered the high school gymnasium that Wednesday night for the big meeting, it looked to Pia and me like the set of a movie—too wholesome and charming to be real. About a third of the faces in the full room looked familiar, though I could count on one hand the number of people whose names I actually knew. The man from the bookstore was standing at a table overflowing with donated baked goods and talking to an older guy in muddy work boots who I'd seen riding a tractor up and down our road. The goth girl who worked at the coffee shop was standing by herself, clearly annoyed to have been dragged there by a parent. Dozens of others were milling around, exchanging pleasantries. The range in age struck me immediately—from the newly born to the nearly dead—which was not a characteristic of my former life. Everyone in our Brooklyn neighborhood was between twenty-two and forty-five, all self-consciously cool and wearing the disinterested expression of an impertinent teenager. This room held an entirely self-contained ecosystem of humanity.

To my relief, I saw Peg at the far end of the gym and gave a too-enthusiastic wave to get her attention.

"Hi, neighbors," she said warmly as we approached, putting a hand out to formally introduce herself to Pia.

Peg wasn't wearing her safari gear this time but flowy layers of earth tones—the New England uniform of sophisticated aging hippies. I assumed she had come from teaching at the college. Pia seemed surprised at the familiarity with which Peg greeted me and I was proud to have a secret friend to unveil before her.

"Let's take our seats, please," yelled a woman in the bossy tone of an elementary school teacher. A child standing nearby clanked a cowbell to punctuate the instruction.

"A cowbell!" Pia whispered in my ear, surely dying to tell our Brooklyn friends of this adorable detail.

I smiled back. We had been pleasant with one another ever since the night of ferocious sex, but I was wary. Pia's behavior had been growing more erratic with each day. Her obsession with the weather had become all-consuming, and it worried me. In response, I'd been spending most of my afternoons with August. We talked less and less.

"Seats, *please!*" the woman yelled again. "Thank you."

The hum of Yankee mumbles and boots scuffing the gymnasium floor tapered off as attendees took their positions. There was a ring of seats around the edge of the room for the elderly and pregnant, but most of us stood in a herd in the center, facing forward. A middle-aged man with a fit build and bald head took the microphone at the front of the room. People smiled at seeing him. Two young girls chased each other through the sea of adult legs and the man waited for their parents to wrangle them before speaking.

"Thanks, everyone, for joining us tonight. My name is John Salting—everyone knows me as Salty—and I'm the chairman of the Isole select board. I'm happy to see such a robust crowd here today. I think everyone appreciates the need for this meeting and I expect that it will be very productive. Instead of going through our usual formal select board process, we want to open discussion up to the whole room at the start. This is a bit of an experiment, but sometimes things need to be done a little differently to account for new challenges."

I knew of Salty from a recent story in the paper about locals working to repair the covered bridge in the west end.

He was a lawyer and part-time judge from a third-generation dairy-farm family. It was clear from the newspaper story that Salty was a member of Isole's unofficial group of elder statesmen. The elder statesmen (my term, not theirs) are a critical demographic in any small New England town. They're the civically engaged, financially successful fathers of the town. They raise money for the good causes and sit on the boards and help run the festivals. They serve as both the institutional knowledge keepers and the moral compass of each little hamlet. The elder statesmen of Isole held some of the offices in the town, but that was not where they derived their authority from; it came from a more intangible *clout* built on years of hometown loyalty, commitment and levelheadedness. I didn't realize it when I was growing up, but my father was an elder statesman. On any Tuesday morning, he could be found eating an early breakfast at the diner with five other professional men, discussing hockey scores, who was going to college where and how to attract small business to our flagging Main Street. They could always be relied upon to donate their time or relative resources to any efforts of *betterment*. I mistakenly thought that all fathers were like mine in this way.

"We are all here tonight to make some decisions about how to best prepare Isole for the coming superstorm," Salty continued, hands on his trim hips. He wasn't a big man— maybe five feet ten inches—but his presence was commanding and his pleasantly weathered face made him seem familiar. "We have a long to-do list, so I suggest we just dig in. For the first order of business, I will hand things over to my colleague on the select board, Hannah Altman. Hannah?"

A middle-aged woman came to the podium to discuss the challenges facing the volunteer fire-and-rescue departments. They would need significantly more people on call for when The Storm hit—a grim concern I'd never thought of before that moment. Two local doctors raised their hands to donate their time and someone else said he could tune up the rescue vehicles for free. Next was a discussion of whether the lone fire truck needed chains on its tires and how much damage chains would do to the roads. Several people had detailed opinions about chained tires and the corresponding havoc they usually wreak.

I shifted my weight back and forth, feeling bored and guilty about it. Pia gave me an eye roll that I hoped no one saw and wandered over to the table of baked goods. I watched her touch three brownies with M&M's pressed into their tops before selecting just the right one for the occasion. No one else would have noticed, but I could tell from her body language that she was checked out. It annoyed me that she wasn't giving the meeting a fair chance.

"What about the plowing?" someone shouted.

"Plowing is later on the agenda," the woman at the podium said, nodding toward a row of other select board members seated at the front.

I noticed that Peg was among the select board members and taking notes on a clipboard. Peg was everywhere.

"Let's talk about the plowing," the same agitated voice said again. It was coming from a man standing a few feet ahead of me. As the people around him stepped back, I could see the distressed look on his face. It was an expression I recognized from before my brother got sober.

A sweet-looking woman put her arm around the man and gently tried to direct him outside, but he shook her off. People exchanged knowing glances with one another; I got the feeling they had seen this before.

"I want to know whose street is going to get plowed first after the big storm," he went on, "because I've gotta get plowed early. I need to get out to make the deliveries early and every one of you knows it!"

The woman trying to speak yielded the podium back to Salty, who said kindly, "Roger, we know you'll have to get out and get to work. Everyone has to get to work. Part of our job tonight is to find the most efficient and fair way to make that happen. Will you work with us on this?"

The angry man stared at Salty, unsure of what to do next. When he finally appeared to drop the issue, Salty took the opportunity to move on.

"Okay, let's talk about flood prevention," he started. "If the ground isn't too hard, we should start digging a few more water runoff routes around Main Street now. Better drainage could prevent a lot of damage to local businesses. As you recall, we commissioned a few studies last year that demonstrated that east-west routes are—"

An older gentleman had raised his hand. "Actually, Salty, I would like to discuss the snowplow plan now, too. We could get a big dump any day now and it's the reason a lot of us are here."

A few others in the crowd nodded in agreement. There was more tension in the room than I'd realized.

"We know the snowplow plan is all politics!" a shrill woman's voice yelled from behind me. She said *all politics* as if it was a meeting of Tammany Hall, but I didn't laugh when I saw the anger on her face. People were scared.

A prudish old woman at the front put her hands on her hips to scold the hecklers, "Now, let's please remain civil and wait our turns to speak. Salty says that's later on the agenda, so we'll tend to it shortly."

From across the room, I saw Pia roll her eyes again at this call for obedience.

Salty nodded and tried to return to his agenda when a

noisy crowd began forming around the angry man who had spoken up first. The man was equidistant between the podium and me, but it was difficult to see what exactly was going on. An elderly man pushed past me and hurried to the door just as someone said, "There's no need to get worked up, Roger."

I moved toward the crowd and saw between the bodies that Angry Roger was hunched, rifling frantically through a backpack. He was pulling things out at a rapid pace, obviously in a hurry to get to whatever it was he was really after. A dirty towel came out, followed by a tattered magazine about off-road vehicles.

Salty took the opportunity to look through his notes at the podium while the disruption ensued and the row of select board members behind him whispered distractedly.

Suddenly, a woman cried out and Roger's arm shot up toward the ceiling holding a cocked handgun. Everyone in the room was watching now and they let out a collective gasp at the sight. Roger's angry face was transformed by a demented smile, eyes wide at the realization of the new power he wielded. The rest of the select board sat frozen, as if the slightest movement might detonate the weapon remotely.

"Roger, do…not…move," Salty said, taking slow-motion steps toward the man.

Roger waved his arm around, causing another wave of gasps. Some people dropped to the floor.

"Don't test me, man," Roger said. "I've been saying this for a while, but *no one listens*. I gotta get out there to do the deliveries early. I gotta get plowed. *We are unprepared* for this shit, man."

I saw that look again, the one that reminded me of my brother when he was high.

Salty continued to make a slow catwalk toward Roger as

everyone looked on. Suddenly—*Bam! Bam!* The gun went off twice, sending a puff of ceiling plaster down around us. As our ears rang, there was a split second of stunned disbelief in the room and then everyone sprang on their most immediate impulse. Salty leaped at Roger, knocking him onto his stomach, but losing control of his body as soon as they hit the ground together. A large man about my age dived into the melee and sat on Roger's backside, pinning his flailing body to the ground. That was when I burst forward, shoving several people aside to get to his arms and the hand with the gun.

He was skinny but possessed by the superhuman strength that only drugs or madness can inspire. As soon as I had Roger's forearm in my grasp, I dropped my knees down on top of it with enough force to make him yelp in pain and loosen his grip on the gun. I pulled the weapon from his hand like someone who actually knew how to hold a loaded gun, which I did not.

The room was buzzing around me. From the corner of my eye, I saw a young woman with long red hair scoop two small children up and carry them into a nearby janitors' closet. I heard later that Peg had hustled a pregnant woman into the closet right behind them, before pulling out her phone to call for help. As for the rest of the crowd, most pushed their way to the doors at the back of the gym (Pia was among them) or simply dropped to the floor with their hands over their heads.

It all happened in a matter of seconds, before we had time to decide who we wanted to be in a crisis. I was most surprised by my own response; I don't remember *deciding* to do anything. I was like one of those people who wake up from sleepwalking to find that they are already making a sandwich or driving a car. That was what it felt like, except that I wasn't making a sandwich, I was wrestling a gun from a maniac.

Someone took the gun from me—Salty, I think—because it made its way to the authorities. By the time the police arrived, Roger had stopped resisting. He knew that his powers had been revoked, and he was once again a pitiable local man, now with new legal troubles. Two police officers handcuffed him and took him away while everyone else straightened their coats and dusted off their dirty knees, which had been pressed into the cold floor moments before. I noticed that Pia was in the corner, twisting her long blond hair into a bun on top of her head, over and over as if the precision of that particular bun mattered immensely. I was relieved she was safe, but I didn't go to her.

At first, it seemed that we might try to just pick things up where we'd left them before the fracas began—discussing where to build the water runoff routes and which trees needed pruning in the parking lot and how much more money was available to salt the roads… But as Salty stood at the podium and readjusted the microphone volume, it became clear that too much had happened. Competing whispered conversations were taking place around the room as everyone worked to piece together what had happened. A toddler clung to her mother's torso while the crying mother thanked the pretty redhead for acting so quickly. I saw another woman say something angrily to her husband and storm out through a back door. Something had changed. We were no longer a civilized group of locals discussing mundane municipal concerns. We had been forced to take a fleeting glimpse into each other's souls and we didn't like everything we'd seen.

One of the police officers stayed behind to interview witnesses, memorializing the role that each of us had played. I noticed that some of the people looked sheepish and sad as they relayed their own reactions to the scene. Others were boasting, lying really, about their heroics. I enjoyed sharing my version of the story with a polite, young officer. Without any exaggeration, I could proudly explain my role in disarming the man. I had never done anything like that before. It felt strange and wonderful to know I had such valiance. I suspected it had something to do with August; he was changing me somehow.

When Salty finally announced that the meeting would have to be postponed, someone shouted, "So, what, the ten of you will just make all these decisions for us, without our say?"

"Yeah, what about the goddamn plow plan?" someone else said. "We still haven't figured that out."

Salty tried to respond into the microphone, but his words were inaudible over the yelling. The bossy lady from earlier was shushing people, which seemed to be doing more harm than good. Order had been lost. Still, most of the people in the room were watching in silence or quietly pulling on their coats and heading for the door.

"This isn't a productive environment," Salty shouted into the microphone. "I don't see how we can move forward tonight."

A large, middle-aged woman in a chunky sweater responded, "I think you and the rest of the select board are happy Roger acted out, so you could cancel this little democratic show. Screw the regular people when the big storm comes, right?"

A few people nodded, but most just kept their eyes on Salty, waiting for his response.

It seemed outrageous to me that anyone could have seen a conspiracy in that room. Mostly, it seemed unbelievable that this group of people whom I had been regarding as a monolithic demographic saw such dramatic divides among themselves. In that small gymnasium, there were rule makers and rule followers, the untrusting and the marginalized.

Angry Roger had dissolved the thin veneer of civility that had held things together only twenty minutes earlier. I had the overwhelming urge to rescue Salty, a man I had never met before, from this awkward moment. In the time it took to wrestle the gun from Roger, I had become part of Isole. I felt entitled to join the group.

"Salty's right," I said. "We can't do this tonight." The sound of my voice was strange at that volume.

Now everyone was looking at me, some with approval, most just curious. I could see in the corner of my eye Pia taking two steps back, embarrassed perhaps. She looked over at the chunky-sweater lady, who was visibly unhappy with my comment.

"Okay, well, the authoritarians have spoken, so I guess that's that," the woman said sarcastically. Then she looked directly at me and pointed her finger. "Don't try to intimidate me, big guy. I don't go quietly."

Intimidating anyone hadn't occurred to me and, in fact, I was quite terrified of this woman, but the lines had been drawn, so I wasn't backing down. And I didn't entirely hate being Intimidating Big Guy.

Salty cleared his throat and said unconvincingly, "We will pick another date and let everyone know about it. Thanks for coming tonight."

Salty and the rest of the select board hustled out quickly. I looked at Pia, who was near me but not recognizably *with* me. We both moved toward the door when someone grabbed my arm and I spun around. It was Salty.

"Thanks for the backup there," he said. "I'm Salty, and you are?" His voice was low.

"Ash," I said.

"Listen, we're putting together a sort of subcommittee to

address a bunch of these issues and we'd be happy to have you join if you have the time."

"Different from these meetings?" I asked, though I knew I would join whatever he was inviting me to.

"Yeah, it's a smaller group," he said, glancing at Pia, who I could tell was straining to hear. "We need something more efficient than this. It's…additive… It will help move things along. Time is not on our side, as you know."

I took Salty's number and told him that I would be in touch.

When we got to the car, Pia was furious with me, which I was not prepared for. She had heard enough of the last conversation to get the gist and accused me of "joining the authoritarians." Apparently, her prepper friends had warned her about the possibility of this happening, but she hadn't expected that I would be so eager to join them, the shadow government. Those were the words she used: *shadow government*. I knew I shouldn't, but I laughed out loud. This, of course, made her more angry and I thought for a moment she might try to dive out of our moving car.

I remember everything about that ride home because I felt charged in a way that I hadn't in a long time. Pia was mad at me, but I didn't feel desperate for her to forgive me. She was beautiful, I remember that, too. Her cheeks were pink from the cold air and her little blue cargo coat—the one I teased her about looking like Paddington Bear in—fit neatly around her body. At one point, I stopped listening to what she was saying and just stared at the road, thinking about whether or not she might let me touch her that night. I still felt high from the adrenaline of the scuffle, and I wanted to fuck something.

But sex would not be in the cards. Pia was angry, and not in a hot-angry-sex kind of way, which we were no strangers to.

She was angry in her new paranoid way, which was a solitary state with no room for me.

I needed to bridge this growing gap between us somehow. I felt confident that this particular fight would come and go, but I was more worried about this drifting trend in our household. I wanted her back, not only for me, but for the fantasy of a family that I envisioned with August. The three of us would be great. The Storm would pass and we'd start anew together. If only I could keep her attention with me and her growing fears at bay.

NINE

THE SNOW MUST have started right after we'd gone to bed because there was almost a foot on the ground by the time we woke the next morning. Still, roads were plowed neatly and schools were open. It takes more than ten inches of powder to keep Vermonters home. I was home, of course. I pushed through three hours of client work at my computer and made two unnecessary calls to colleagues in an attempt to obscure my eroding attention to work.

At eleven, I walked back downstairs for coffee to find that I was alone in the house, but there was a small piece of paper, the size and weight of a playing card, placed next to the coffee press. It was from Pia, who must have left quietly while I was working. On the card was a fine, intricate pencil rendering of the backseat of our car, as seen from the front. It looked exactly as I remembered leaving the backseat the day before: there was a small pile of dirty clothes on the left side of the bench seat, two dog-eared books behind the headrest to the right and a shoe box on the floor. "I'm sorry" was written in tiny letters along the spine of one of the books. It was an apology. It was also a call for our old selves. Years before, when one of us stumbled financially or professionally, we would remind each other that all we really needed was what we could fit in the backseat of our car, and each other. "The backseat" became shorthand for our ability to handle anything and keep things simple. I appreciated the gesture. We hadn't spoken since our fight after the town hall meeting the night before, so this was a nice turn, but surely she knew as I did that we needed to talk face-to-face. Time was moving quickly and we needed to come to an agreement about August. I considered that perhaps the backseat drawing was another subtle argument against taking more into our life but decided to give her the benefit of the doubt and just accept the little apology picture. I slid it into my wallet and made coffee.

I thought of my father, who would be puttering around outside on mornings like this, and I decided that my first order of business would be to shovel snow. The roof over the back porch was already bowing dangerously and the snow showed no signs of slowing down. So I left my coffee and pulled on long underwear, ski pants, a flannel shirt, boots, a hat and a puffy coat and went out to inspect my project.

With an enormous broom that the previous owners had left behind, I reached awkwardly above my head toward the porch roof and tried to sweep the accumulating snow toward me. Several clumps fell—some down the back of my neck—but most of it resisted my efforts. I jumped a few times, hoping to get a better glimpse of what I was working with. All I could see was an undisturbed blanket of heavy snow that threatened to collapse my porch. There did seem to be something else on the roof, farther toward the center of the house and out of my view. I pointed the broom in that direction and attempted to pull some more snow away to get a clearer picture. When I jumped again, I saw the perfect silhouette

MEG LITTLE REILLY

of two birds that lay dead on the roof, their wings splayed out as if in midflight. They weren't flycatchers, the fallen birds I'd seen during the hailstorm earlier in the fall. These were much bigger; I might have even guessed that they were broad-winged hawks if it wasn't far too late in the season for them to be around. Then again, the strange weather could have disrupted hawk migration. Broad-wings are particularly sensitive to changing weather patterns because they need predictable waves of warm air to migrate south. I remembered reading that rising thermal air lifts them and then they follow the warm bands away for the winter. It seemed cruel to me that a species' survival should depend upon something as fickle as bubbles of warm air passing at just the right time. It was an arrangement too delicate to last in this new world.

I had forgotten for a moment that this wasn't just the first snowfall, an event that still thrilled me as an adult. It was a foreshadowing, a possible threat of greater things to come. We didn't know whether it was the start of The Storm itself or just the first of many strange, not-right weather events, but we knew it wasn't an innocent first snow because there was no such thing anymore.

I heard our phone ring inside and knew it would be Bev The Social Worker. She had been calling every few days to make sure I was still watching August closely and to see if we had come to a decision about taking him in. I didn't want to have the conversation that morning. We needed more time, so I let it ring.

Even with the eerie threat it posed, the Northeast Kingdom of Vermont was breathtaking before me. The sky was silver through the fast-falling precipitation and there was an absence of sound. Our backyard had the warm, insolated feeling I knew so well, like standing in an infinite blanket of soft down.

I pushed the sight of the dead hawks, and Bev's call, out of my mind and tried to focus again on removing the snow from the porch roof. It was clear that I would need better tools if I was to prevent the roof from collapsing, so I tromped through the pristine woods bound for Peg's house on the other side of the trees, where I knew I would find whatever specialty item could handle the job.

I walked slowly toward her house, enjoying the neat impressions my boots left in the snow—the only human interruption in an otherwise undisturbed tableau. It didn't occur to me until that moment that Peg would likely be out in the world doing her work like a normal person on a weekday.

"Ash, perfect timing!" Peg said from the doorway, as if she'd been expecting me. "I've got Salty in here and we're talking about next steps for the Subcommittee and need help managing the politics of it all. Not my area, thank God."

As Peg led me into her kitchen, I saw Salty sitting in front of a steaming mug of black coffee. He looked up from his notes to greet me.

"Ash, good to see you," he said. "Great cover out there, isn't it? I love the first snow. Hate to be inside on a day like today, but there's work to do."

"Ah, yeah, great cover," I agreed, making a mental note to adopt the term.

Apparently, this was the group Salty had been referring to at the town hall meeting the night before. I explained the reason for my visit while I pulled off my boots. Peg assured me she had the right tool and hurried me to the table with the others. "Here's the deal," Salty said, anticipating my confusion. "We don't have time to have a dozen town hall meetings and endless votes on all the minutiae. The Storms are coming." He waved an arm toward the window dismissively. "This is probably just a flurry, but the big one—that's

MEG LITTLE REILLY

the one we have to be ready for. It's going to be hell on our land and drain town resources, and we need smart systems in place if we're to have any chance of ever recovering."

I hoped that Salty was right that this wasn't the big one.

Peg put a mug of coffee down in front of me, which I could have hugged her for. It was such a tiny gesture, but I realized I hadn't been on the receiving end of it in a long time.

"It's not that we're trying to circumvent the formal process," she jumped in. "It's just that we can't indulge every wacky idea and bout of hysteria. The select board is big and slow and those meetings are open to the public. So we're creating this little group to just start ticking through the list of things that must get done quickly. There are a couple other guys from around town we've already approached about this. There will be five of us, including you."

"Why me?"

"Because we need someone young and smart and a little… detached." Salty smiled. "You haven't been here long enough to be entrenched in the inertia that tends to slow things down. You hardly know anyone, which is a great asset in this case. You'll see things more clearly."

"I'm not offended at all," I joked.

They both nodded, not quite getting my humor, which hadn't been tested on other humans in a while.

"Also," Salty went on more slowly, "our main priority is the flood runoff plan we've been working on. We'll explain further, but let's just say it's controversial, and we need one of the affected property owners on our side. It will be easier to make our case."

I nodded at the still inscrutable explanation. In truth, I didn't really care why they wanted me; I was happy to be a part of something.

"And we like you!" Peg said. "So, will you do this with us?"

"Sure, yes." I nodded. "So are we *allowed* to do this, form a subcommittee?"

Peg waved off my question. "We don't know. Probably not, but everyone will be glad we did when the flooding starts and there are enough sandbags to keep the library from turning into a swimming pool."

This all made sense to me. I had seen the town hall meeting; it was a disaster. Not only because of the gun incident, but also because too many people were there with too many disparate concerns. Nothing would ever get done. Plus I trusted Peg and Salty—the worldly intellectual and the wholesome leader. They were good people adapting to new challenges for a place they loved.

We sat at the kitchen table for two hours, creating a list of the most immediate municipal needs that would be addressed by the Subcommittee in the coming weeks. We would need to find a location for an emergency operations center, determine who the points of contact would be for all communications with the governor's office and the Federal Emergency Management Agency, allocate money for repairing fire-and-rescue vehicles, create a plan for reaching out to local media and the public when the power went out and much more. I had little practical advice to contribute, but my project management and communications experience was useful. The town of Isole didn't know how to prepare for a threat of this size and scale—no one did, we would learn later—but it felt right to try.

When we neared the end of Salty's exhaustive list, he looked up at Peg and said, "Okay, so what about the runoff analysis?"

Peg took a sip of coffee and looked at me to indicate that she would start at the beginning. This was the real reason they needed me on the Subcommittee.

"Ash, the runoff analysis is a statewide study examining the waterways that we know are going to be a problem during a large storm. A number of small tributaries in the Northeast Kingdom have become regular flood zones during spring thaws and every heavy rainstorm. We need to start addressing the problem either way, but we really need to do it before the superstorm…if it's not too late already."

Salty jumped in. "We're particularly concerned about the Isole Creek because it runs through dozens of folks' properties and crosses Main Street. A catastrophic flood could wipe out the whole downtown. We need a runoff routing system, which in this case means that we need to widen the creek itself and dig some new routes that will draw water away from our homes and businesses. It's a construction-heavy project."

"Is the state involved?" I asked. "This seems like a big undertaking."

"They are," Peg said with hesitation, "but they are moving too slowly. The governor's office has given unofficial permission to townships that want to move forward with their piece of the flood runoff plan. We get some state funding for it, but it will cost us some money, too. Doing nothing would be more expensive."

"So what's our job here?" I asked, still unsure of why we were discussing it at Peg's kitchen table.

"We need to convince everybody affected that it's in their best interest to consent to the changes," Peg said. "For instance, your property, Ash: we are going to need your permission to widen the portion of the creek that runs through your backyard, which would mean encroaching on your yard by a few feet. We will need to have that conversation with eighteen other owners in Isole."

"But what about the snow?" I asked, looking outside.

Salty sighed. "It's a problem, for sure. But the ground isn't frozen yet, not down deep anyway, so as long as we can get another warm spell, we'll have time to start digging. There are crews from out of state that have said they are ready to go as soon as we are and can get it done within a week. All we need now is to get consent from each of the landowners in the flood zone. That way, when it's warm enough, we can begin digging immediately."

"Which is why we need to skip the town hall debate over this and just start knocking on doors?" I asked.

"Right."

"Exactly."

"I'm happy to help in any way that I can," I said, and I was.

Salty and Peg nodded, apparently already counting on my participation and ready to move forward with the plan.

We decided that the Subcommittee, as it would cryptically be known, would break for the day and reconvene early next week. Salty had to get to the office and we all had driveways to clear. I followed Peg and Salty out to the porch, where a long-handled tool designed for rooftop snow removal was waiting for me. Peg shook both of our hands and left us alone on the porch steps. The snow was still coming down in fat chunks that sparkled under a dim sky.

"I'm sure I don't have to tell you that we should keep talk of the Subcommittee to a minimum," Salty said as he wiggled into the bindings of enormous wooden snowshoes.

I nodded.

He finished strapping in and looked up. Salty was significantly shorter than me, but his presence was substantial.

"Ash, I love this town. Isole is a civilized place. But fear makes people behave strangely. It dissolves the glue. We're not trying to undermine a tradition of participatory democracy. We would never want that. We're just trying to protect

MEG LITTLE REILLY

everyone. The Storm isn't going to wait for democracy. You get it, right?"

I nodded.

"Then I'll see you Tuesday."

Salty took deliberate moonwalking steps away from me and into Peg's apple orchard, leaving giant snowshoe prints in his wake. His family farm was nearby, though it seemed a long distance on foot.

I remembered that Pia and I had snowshoes, somewhere, from a vacation we'd taken in Stowe three years earlier. We had rented a luxury condo with two other couples. It was supposed to be a ski trip, but it had been unseasonably warm and rainy, so we spent the whole week drinking, playing board games and shopping in overpriced alpine stores. It was one of the best trips we ever took together, and I think that was when we realized how badly we wanted to be in Vermont. We bought snowshoes, of course, because that was what all the natives seemed to be doing, along with expensive, unfussy outdoor gear that we thought would camouflage our glaring outsiderness. We wanted to be windburned and fit and *real* like the locals. We wanted to bottle it all up and drink it, whatever it was that they had. Salty certainly had it.

"Oh good, you're back!" Pia said as I opened the front door. I was soaked from an awkward trek home from Peg's, which required forging my own path through the snow and dragging the enormous borrowed tool behind me.

Pia was in long thermal underwear that were dotted with tiny flowers, the sort a young girl might wear, and drinking red wine from a mason jar. It was a surprisingly upbeat greeting given the shaky new energy between us, but I could see that she had moved on to other concerns. She hurried me into the living room, where things seemed to be happening.

"I need help dumping these buckets into this tub," she said.

Our sparse living room furniture had been pushed aside to make room for an enormous wooden box, about the size of a coffin. Propped up around the coffin-like container were four plastic sacks of soil and two large buckets labeled *Eisenia fetida.*

"What is this, Pia?" I asked. "How did you get this stuff in here?"

"Calm down," she said, sure that I would be pleased once I heard her explanation. "They're red wigglers—compost worms. We just *have to* compost, Ash! We've been talking about it for so long now, but we can't wait any longer. Who knows what things are going to be like after The Storm! I'm not even talking about *this* storm; I'm talking about, like, the future in general. We are going to need to start growing more of our own food, so we're going to need fertilizer. Plus there's the reduction in waste and sustainability and everything."

Her talking points were improvised and thin, but I knew nothing good would come of pointing that out.

"But right now?" I asked. "The snow is two feet deep out there. What are we going to do with worms in December? Why are there worms in our living room in December?"

"They'll die outside, Ash." She looked at me like I was a monster. "They *have to* stay inside for winter. That will give them time to get comfortable and breed and grow and be ready for spring. I thought you'd be happy about my foresight! You always say I'm too impulsive, but this is an investment in our future. God, can I do nothing right by you?"

The last part was a dramatic flourish that we both knew to be untrue. I recognized it as a warning for the direction the conversation was taking.

I should have fought her. I should have put my foot down about the fucking worms in the living room, but I didn't know then that every time I would see our worm farm thereafter,

I would be reminded of how different our worldviews had become. I didn't know that it would make me feel as though she'd recruited an army of writhing allies to be on her side, opposing me. They would outnumber me in my own house and make me question which one of us was on the right side of sanity. But at the time it just seemed like a fight worth avoiding because I wanted my own mason jar of wine and an evening of peace.

So the worms stayed. Of course they did. My acquiescence was a temporary Band-Aid on a growing wound, which was fine with both of us. For a while, I even considered that she was right. I *did* want to compost. Or rather, I wanted to be the type of person who composted. So I agreed to the idea of worms breeding in the warmth of our home. Maybe, I thought, this was just the kind of sacrifice one had to make to be a compost-type person. I could see the humor in it, too. I imagined making jokes about it to our old friends. *Sometimes we go out for a long snowshoe hike and come back to find the worms watching TV or making a sandwich in the kitchen. They're just part of the family now!*

The larger problem wasn't over whether we should or should not have purchased five hundred worms. There was a change occurring in our marriage that had been triggered by The Storm. Our most fearful inner selves had been driven to the surface and were beginning to run our lives. And those selves, Pia's and mine, weren't as alike as I once thought. That was what the worms made me think of, every day when I looked at them in the living room.

The truth was that Pia had always been impulsive. I worked hard to see her as a passionate free spirit, but I knew she had a tenuous grasp on sanity most of the time. I didn't wish her any other way because with that impulsivity came creativity and joyful spontaneity. She was just as she was supposed to be and I loved her. But then the storm report came and Pia's compulsions began multiplying, feeding on the bad news like our growing worms. And instead of driving her toward me for support and stability, The Storm was pulling her away. It was also—and this was the most shameful part—it was also repelling me. A seed of resentment was growing inside of me for her selfish ability to make The Storm all about her with no regard for how I might be coping. It probably makes me a truly awful person to be repelled by someone who may have qualified for a mental illness diagnosis, but that's the effect that her unhinging had on me. My only defense is that I was scared and selfish then, too. Wasn't I allowed to be?

If only we had something positive to focus on together, something that required we both stay sane and unselfish, we could get past The Storm. That was what I believed. August could be that purpose.

"Have you thought about August?" I asked.

She turned away from the worms to face me. "I have." She sighed. "And I think what I'm most worried about is passing all this fear on to him. There's so much of it between us and it's toxic."

Pia was sincere. I could see the concern in her eyes, unclouded by the judgment and criticism that was there when I first proposed the idea. I stepped toward her and wrapped my arms around her shoulders, stooping down to bury my face in the pile of hair at her neck. She softened and let me stay there for a moment before standing back up straight.

She was right. But the fear wasn't just between us; it was everywhere. Everyone I encountered was like us, breathing fear onto each other like a deadly contagion. Fear hormones were coursing through our bodies and oozing out our pores, staining our clothes and seeping into the water supply. Our food tasted like fear and it raced through our nervous intestines. I didn't want to give fear to August either, but he was going to get it one way or another.

I wondered if maybe we should see a therapist or a marriage counselor to help sort through these concerns. That sounded like a mature way to handle such a decision. But I knew that I wouldn't suggest it; and if I did, Pia wouldn't agree to it. The fear that she was talking about wasn't the paranoia of a delusional sick person. It was, to some degree, a natural and logical response to the threat before us. The Storm was coming and no shrink could change that.

Pia used to see a therapist, years ago. She was having trouble sleeping and we both thought it would help with her anxiety, so we found a fatherly man in our neighborhood who took our insurance. At first, it seemed like the therapy was helping. She was calmer and more even-keeled, which made her seem saner to me. I realized later that wasn't it at all. The calm faded and eventually it just seemed as if the only thing she was getting out of her sessions was a new vocabulary for explaining her occasionally erratic behavior. It was possible that she just had a bad therapist, but I suspected that she was charming him the way she did me, by making us feel like her attention was the sweetest gift anyone could receive. Pia was fascinated by the idea of introspection, but impervious to the benefits of psychotherapy. After six months of it, she got bored and enrolled in an interpretive dance class, which had roughly the same effect as therapy.

In truth, I was the one who could have benefited from therapy in New York. Pia was living relatively well with her quirks, but I lacked the same self-awareness. I behaved like a happy person, which isn't the same thing as being happy. I had grown bored and detached, letting friendships fade along with hobbies and interests. But that was changing in

Vermont. Ever since we found August in the woods and particularly since I wrestled the gun from Angry Roger at the town hall meeting, things started feeling right for me in a new way. Every part of me was present in Isole, mentoring children and joining secret committees and managing snow-removal projects. I was engaged and emboldened. All of this would have been great if it hadn't contributed to the growing gulf between my wife and me. My world was getting bigger while hers seemed to be closing in.

It's impossible to know just how much of the change in our marriage could be attributed to The Storm, but I suspect it was a lot. We all found out who we were very quickly because of the fear. I guess that was happening in marriages and towns across the country in the months before The Storm, but we didn't have such perspective at the time. It felt as if Pia and I, and the people of Isole, were the only ones falling apart, dividing into factions and turning on one another.

TEN

"THE STORM WILL take your home, your equity, your livelihood and maybe even your loved ones. Do not underestimate the power of nature, which is to say, do not underestimate God's power. Something much bigger than us is coming. The Storm will rearrange our lives and test our faith. It will wash away thousands of square miles of North America and change this country. Will you wash away with it? That's a choice you can make now. You can prepare for this."

This was the new voice of the fear: Rodney Riggins, evangelical meteorologist.

Rodney Riggins—a Canadian-born atheist who had already reinvented himself several times before striking gold with his final act as a man of God—was the most brilliant variety of opportunist. His vaguely Judeo-Christian message was free of bible verse but heavy on folk wisdom. He studied the crowd and tailored his message accordingly, adopting a Creole patois in New Orleans, fronting his vowels in Baltimore and faking a Yankee mumble with enough subtlety to pass at the Isole diner counter. Riggins's message was accessible and within our reach: you don't need organized religion in the face of this threat; you need to commune directly with God, respect the earth's power and prepare yourself ("Pray, Props, Prepare!"). For the people of Isole, his message focused on pragmatism, with a dash of personal integrity, and just enough fear to sell it. What he was selling, of course, wasn't just God. Rodney Riggins had an endorsement contract with a growing company that produced disaster preparedness kits. This part of the pitch came later, after the groundwork had been laid.

Vermont was Riggins's first stop on his tour down the East Coast, so no one had heard of him when he came to speak to a few hundred people in nearby St. Johnsbury on the first Friday in December. His presentation was billed as "Meteorology and Spirituality: How We Can Be Ready," and although the tickets started at twelve dollars each (fourteen for the front section), it sold out so quickly that additional shows were added for Saturday and Sunday. The event was hosted by God's Kingdom Congregational Church, an inclusive and well-regarded staple of the St. Johnsbury community. God's Kingdom was known throughout the region for its volunteerism and civic commitment. Nearly all the revenue it took in was reinvested in after-school programs for low-income youth. And after decades of selflessness, the church facilities were in such disrepair that they were at risk of being condemned. For the small favor of hosting his speeches, Rodney Riggins made a sizable donation toward church renovations. It was an easy agreement.

I think people were starved for more information about the future. We were getting almost nothing from the federal government in the useless weekly storm reports and we were desperate to do something that would make us feel in control again. It wasn't just our little town or state or region; it was everywhere. Rodney Riggins had something—anything—to say at just the right time.

He knew nothing about meteorology or religion, but Riggins was smart enough to know not to sound like a preacher in New England. His two-hour debut sermon was more of a training session for surviving the end of the world. He started with the devastation, a grisly, detailed description of the horrors that likely awaited us when The Storm came: loss of home, civic disintegration, panic, death. It was cinematic and gripping. From there, he got existential. "Why is this storm happening to us and how do we make sense of it?" he asked, a placid expression washing over his unblemished face. "Maybe we won't ever understand why Mother Earth punishes us. Let's all agree to be okay with that. Asking why is a futile exercise and Yankees don't waste time! We need to focus our energy on the opportunity before us: the opportunity to live more purposefully. This means appreciating the amazing gift of community that we—you—have been given and doing what's within our humble power to take care of each other. This storm is coming, folks. Let's face it with grace, love and good planning!"

The crowd responded with as much emotion as a group of Vermonters in a congregational church would allow themselves, with knowing nods and polite claps. Riggins had them.

I wasn't there for his first performance in St. Johnsbury—most of Isole wasn't. But the text of the speech was printed in its entirety as part of a paid ad in the Isole paper that Sunday, and before long, it was as if we had all been in the church for its original delivery. So when Riggins began leaving flyers around town, offering free home preparedness consultations and exclusive deals on "bugout bags," we were primed.

The next town hall meeting was held a few days after

Riggins's presentation. It was the first meeting after the gun fiasco and, though attendance by the general public was normally sparse, the gymnasium was packed on that day. I was there as both a member of the public and a covert observer on behalf of the Subcommittee. Salty's plan for the meeting was to tick through all the minutiae, let the discussion wander and bog down, and adjourn on time with most points unresolved. This was apparently the natural tendency of every public meeting, so Salty felt liberated from his role of trying to squeeze productivity out of an untenable system. The Subcommittee would fix the real problems later.

Things began in their normal, cordial manner and then quickly devolved just as Salty had predicted. He looked a little too happy to me as he sat at the front of the room and watched a group of locals in the audience argue over whether there should be restrictions on which days manure was laid. I leaned up against the wall in the back while August practiced card tricks on the floor beside my feet. I loved his willingness to come along on whatever strange adventure I proposed. Pia was at a prepper meeting and I was grateful for her absence.

People quarreled respectfully and spent too long on topics that I couldn't will myself to care about yet. My thoughts drifted until an older man in a neat flannel shirt raised his hand politely. "I'd like to suggest something that's not on the agenda," he said as heads all turned his way. "This will be a bit out of the ordinary for our fair town, but I think we should consider having Mr. Rodney Riggins host one of his workshops in Isole. It won't cost us anything; we just need permission to use this gymnasium. Whether you're interested in a higher power or not, I think we could all benefit from his message right now."

Following his successful weekend sermons in St. Johnsbury, Riggins had been leaving glossy flyers around town

MEG LITTLE REILLY

advertising his "Facing Fear" workshops, which promised to prepare people of all faiths for "the storms in life." I had never seen him in person, but I was sure that I hated Riggins, who seemed little more to me than a carpetbag salesman.

"No way," yelled the chunky-sweater lady from the last public meeting. She put her hands on her hips and looked at the gentle old man without sympathy. "Religion has no role in our civic concerns, Artie. You and your church friends can pray all day long if you like, but not in our public buildings."

A few others nodded their heads, reluctant to disappoint this kindly man, but firm believers in the church-state separation the woman was invoking.

"It's not really religion," the older man replied, still smiling and polite. "It's just a philosophy, really. I know of a number of people who would welcome it. It's a philosophy, like you and your prepper friends' belief about how the government is out to get you, or whatever it is. We would let you guys use public space if you needed to."

A few people giggled, but most were quiet.

The chunky-sweater lady was not amused. "That is a gross misrepresentation of the prepper movement. We're the only people in this town who can see things clearly. You think these sheep are going to save you when all our systems break down?" She gestured to the select board members at the front of the room, who had been conspicuously silent.

A middle-aged man holding a baby shouted up at them, "This is unproductive. Salty, let's get some order in here! What do you think about this idea?"

I knew that Salty thought Rodney Riggins was a sleazy huckster, so I was surprised to hear him say, "Let's leave this one to a vote. If the people of Isole want to use public resources such as an auditorium to host a religiously affiliated event, I think that's their choice. We can schedule a vote for next week."

"This is outrageous," the sweater lady said. She was pulling her big coat on and gathering her things. "I don't know why I still come to these meetings. They're a sham. If there are any other adults in this room who want to face reality, you're welcome at our prepper meetings on Tuesdays."

She stormed out and let the heavy door bang behind her.

When it was quiet again, the older man she'd been arguing with said, "Thank God for small miracles," and everyone laughed uneasily, some more than others.

Isole wasn't used to open combat, but that wasn't the only reason for their discomfort. It was the mounting pressure to pick a side in this new war. Where Isole had once been a town of old farm families, yuppie transplants and rednecks, we were now paranoid preppers, religious fanatics and government tools. Looking around the room, you could already tell which team many had chosen. Others still looked baffled by this development, unaware that they would eventually pick a side, too.

"You're one of the tools, obviously," Pia said to me later that night when I explained what had happened at the meeting. She was smiling as if it was a joke, but we both knew it wasn't. "I'm surprised you have to ask." She had her legs curled under her on the couch and was highlighting sections of a book about canning. I was quite sure I would never see canned produce stacked in our cupboards, but I liked the idea of it under normal circumstances. "Ever since you joined that secret committee, you sealed your fate as a government operative." She took a gulp of red wine from her mason jar.

I walked to the refrigerator to get a beer. I should not have done this—dug in for a fight—but I couldn't resist on that

MEG LITTLE REILLY

night. "Well, then I guess we both know what you are," I said from the kitchen.

She threw her book down. "Does it make you feel sane to call me crazy?" Pia said. "Will it comfort you to believe that you're one of the rational ones after everything falls apart and we have to rely on ourselves? Are you still going to be tuning in for the president's fucking weather briefings and attending your little planning sessions when all this is washed away?"

I pounded my beer and set it down loudly before responding. "I'm not allowed to be crazy like you, Pia. Someone has to maintain order in this relationship. Does it comfort me to pay the bills and take out the trash and make sure we have flood insurance and snow tires and all the other mundane bullshit that you won't bother with? Yeah, it does kind of comfort me to know that our lives still work. Sorry for boring you with my prosaicness."

Pia's face tensed as angry tears began to stream down her face. "What's going on with us? I feel like you hate me."

I shook my head, confused. "I don't know. You're my wife, Pia. I married you and hoped to have a family with you and a long, happy life together. *I love you.*" I wanted to stay calm, but there was a shriek in my voice. "But we can't have that life together from a subterranean bunker in your postapocalyptic future."

She watched me, her eyes filling with tears. I don't know why I kept stoking the fire, but I went on, "You don't want children, Pia, because you are a child yourself."

Pia threw her canning book across the room, where it hit the wall and landed on the worm box. She stomped out to the kitchen. I could hear her uncork another bottle and cry quietly, but with just enough volume to drive her point home. She wanted me to know that I was cruel. She wasn't crying because of a weakness in her, but an aggression in me. That was the message. I hated this conflict so much, but I wasn't ready to end it. We hadn't spoken of conceiving a child in months and it was making me nervous. She was moving away from that fantasy as I inched toward it.

I put my coat on and took a cold Long Trail out to the front porch while Pia stayed inside to cry. I wouldn't give her the satisfaction of remaining in her audience.

Christmas was one week away and we had over a foot of fluffy snow on the ground. Pia and I didn't have a Christmas tree or any presents or anything that would have indicated that a family that celebrates Christmas lived there. For the first time ever, we just didn't bother. Even August's screwed-up parents had twinkle lights draped over their crab-apple tree, which sparkled through the thick woods that separated our homes. All of a sudden, this seemed unbearably sad to me and I started to cry.

The porch swing felt cold on my backside and I could see clouds of condensing breath in the soft glow of the bulb that hung above. It was too dark to observe much of anything but the sky. In the warmer months, I could sit on that swing and watch the silhouettes of the brown bats lurk above me, but they were gone, winding down for hibernation. There was nothing left outside to make me feel less alone.

Both of us were crying, hating the situation, but not quite hating each other. I wasn't lying when I said I loved her; I did. But being together was hard now. She was isolating herself from me and I was hungrier than ever for human connection. Something about being in Isole—making friends and caring for August—made me realize how alone I had been. I suddenly felt sad for my former self—the one who had tolerated loneliness for so long.

ELEVEN

I ONLY INTENDED to close my eyes for a few minutes, to let the beer warm my brain and let Pia go to bed inside. But I must have drifted off for over an hour because my back was aching from the porch swing and my nose as frigid as the air when I startled awake to the sound of a distant screen door. It was the slow, cautious closing of someone who didn't want to be found. It would have been inaudible to anyone else, but I had heard the distinct screech of August's back screen door so many times by then that I caught it on the first note. It was the dead of night in December and August was taking off into the woods.

I jumped up and off the porch, realizing that I couldn't see my footing and would need to go just slow enough not to fall. I didn't yell for August. I wanted to catch him quietly before we woke parents and wives and the rest of the world.

It took a moment to find the head of the footpath that connected our houses and I started to panic as I waved my arms ahead of me in the dark. Finally, there was a gap and I dived through it, running with arms out and night eyes wide-open. I saw a flash of something ahead and ran faster.

When I emerged from the woods, a small body ten feet ahead stopped, sensing my presence.

"Ash?" August whispered, frightened.

"Yeah, it's me, buddy." I walked to him now and grabbed his backpack, then his head for a quick hug. "What are you doing? This is so dangerous. You know you can't do this anymore. Why are you out here?"

"I needed to check on my fort, to make sure it's still good in case one of the animals needs it for hibernation."

August said this calmly, as if it was the most obvious explanation for his behavior, but I searched his eyes for a deeper answer. If one existed, he couldn't seem to access it. So I walked him back to my house with one hand safely on his blue backpack. He may not have been escaping something horrific, but he was left alone to follow the whims of his imagination right out the back door and into the dark woods at night—undetected—and that was horrific enough. What if I hadn't been outside to hear him? I couldn't entertain the fantasies of how that night might have ended.

I led August through the front door and into the living room, where he made himself comfortable on the couch. He talked sleepily to me about the structural weaknesses of his fort that needed to be bolstered while I assembled a peanut butter sandwich in the kitchen. Apparently, there was still a patch of the fort roof that needed evergreen boughs for cover and the pine needle bed hadn't been completed… Something about a secret door…

When I returned moments later with the sandwich, he was already slumped over, asleep.

I sat down in front of the couch on the oval rug with once-bright woven rings of color. It wasn't soft beneath me, but I didn't want to leave. I didn't want to be an inch farther from August's small body than I needed to be. So I sat and thought about what was ahead. Tomorrow, I would feed him breakfast and make sure his parents took him to school, but I wouldn't tell the social worker about this. Her response couldn't be predicted, and I needed more time to convince Pia that we should take August. I needed just enough time, I figured, to explain to her how frightened I had been seeing his dark shape almost disappear into the cold woods. Surely she would be moved by this. The events of that evening seemed proof to me that August didn't just need *anyone* to rescue him from his negligent home, he needed someone who knew the sound of his feet on fallen leaves in the dark, someone who understood what pulled him into the woods and which animals were his friends. I was that person and I needed him, too.

I stretched out on the woven rug, my head on the sweatshirt that August had shed minutes before. With one hand around an ankle that hung over the couch, I slept.

TWELVE

WALKING THROUGH THE halls of the Isole courthouse
to meet the Subcommittee in Salty's office made me feel like
a young intern, self-consciously pretending to believe that
I fit in. That feeling was probably the result of the nagging
guilt I felt about my real job, which I wasn't devoting nearly
enough hours of the day to. It was six o'clock in the evening
on the first Wednesday of January and there was almost no
one left in the courthouse. In Salty's large but modest office I first saw Peg at the table, wearing neutral colors and a
warm smile. Beside her sat Bill and Bob, the other two secret recruits for the Subcommittee. Bill was an accountant
(and the town treasurer); Bob owned the outdoor sporting
goods store on Main Street. I gathered that they had been
best friends for most of their lives, starting careers, raising
children and taking vacations together. I hadn't had a male
friendship like that since college, before Pia and I started dat-
ing. It looked a little goofy—the way Bill and Bob seemed
to anticipate each other's thoughts—but I envied them. Both
wore "work flannels"—a category of dress that I had only
recently discovered, which involved the same flannel shirts

and rugged boots that one might wear on the weekend, but neatly pressed and free of visible wear.

The five of us sat around a circular table in Salty's austere office, drinking decaf coffee from a pot in the corner. Salty was the unofficial leader of our gang, but Peg seemed to have all the answers. In the eight years she'd lived in Isole, she had learned everyone's name and developed a comprehensive understanding of municipal operations. "I've been joining the natives for years," she said in her Irish brogue. Peg was a botanist; she was supposed to be studying the plants, but it seemed that she had been studying the people all along.

We moved through each issue with great efficiency. Isole Public High School was to be the emergency shelter when The Storm came, with the post office serving as backup. Both buildings would have generators installed and boarding for the windows cut within the week. As treasurer, Bill could authorize spending with town money, and since we decided at the outset that we would consult with no one about how to spend it, decisions were made quickly. We would ask for permission (or forgiveness) later. It was undemocratic and satisfyingly productive.

"Next up," Peg said, "the flood runoff plan. The snow from the last storm is starting to melt and the ground is only frozen a few inches down, so we need to act fast if we're going to get in before the next storm. Let's take a look at the plan and divide up the outreach."

She spread a large map out in front of us that showed the current path of the Isole Creek and the runoff routes that would need to be created to divert water away from down-town and toward an uninhabitable marsh on the edge of Isole. Along the runoff routes, tiny cartoon houses had been drawn with the surnames of the families that lived there scrawled above—those were the people whose consent we needed.

The five of us were quiet as we read the names, most of which I didn't recognize.

"This should be no problem," Salty said, making a pencil checkmark beside a house that was apparently occupied by reasonable people. "I'll give Carl a call tonight and get his permission…and the Girards…and the LeChamps…and the Kellys…they will all understand."

Salty stepped back and circled several more houses.

"These are the people I'm anticipating we may have some problems with," he said. "I think we need to pay them a visit and make a strong case that the town is counting on them. I don't know how this is going to go."

"Ash, you've met a few of these characters," Peg said.

"I have?"

"Yes, this guy—" she pointed to a house that sat at the intersection of Isole Creek and a runoff route "—he's one of your wife's prepper friends."

I had no idea how Peg knew about Pia's hobbies or the preppers, but I was beginning to realize that secrets were meaningless in a town of our size.

She went on, "He's kind of the ringleader."

I knew who she was talking about immediately. "Crow?"

"Yes, Crow," she said. "Just our luck that his shack sits right on this lot. He's not going to go for this."

"And to be fair," Salty interjected, "we need a pretty significant chunk of his backyard to get this done. It's not a small ask. So yeah, he'll make a stink."

"Bob and I will take this stretch here," Bill said, pointing to another prong along the drainage route. "They all fall between our two houses and we know almost everybody."

"Good, perfect," Peg said, tapping her finger nervously on the map. "Let's get as many people as we can in the next forty-eight hours. That way, we'll be ready when the warm front comes through. Salty, do you want to take some of these houses on the east side, near your farm? I'll take Crow and some of these other challenging ones. Ash, you're coming with me."

"Now?"

"Yes, now!" Peg laughed. "It's not going to get any easier."

With our respective assignments, everyone piled into their cars in the parking lot of the courthouse and drove in separate directions. I sat in the passenger seat of Peg's Subaru and listened as she explained the legality of the project.

"We could probably force this endeavor through with an eminent domain argument," she said as we pulled onto the main road. "Certainly the town or state can make a strong case to that end and that was the state's original plan. But it would be so adversarial and costly...it would probably take years to go through the condemnation proceedings. Plus that could involve compensation to the property owners that Isole doesn't have to spend. It's just not an option right now, not with The Storm pressing down on us. If this runoff plan is going to do any good, we need to get it done fast. And getting everyone's consent is the only other legal way to make that happen. If you had asked me six months ago, I would have told you that this would be fairly easy to do. The people of Isole are reasonable. But I'm not so sure now; everyone's wary of their neighbors all of a sudden. We have different ideas about how we're supposed to be preparing for this disaster...and what our responsibility to the land is."

"I never really thought about that. What do *you* think our responsibility to the land is?" I asked.

Peg turned off the main road and onto a bumpy dirt one that was as black as pitch, even with the snow cover.

"I think it's to remember that we're just temporary tenants," she said. "The land can't ever really belong to any of us, so our actions should consider a future when we're not here."

I thought about this point as the woods closed in around us.

"This is it," Peg said and turned off the engine.

It was so dark when the headlights went off that I couldn't tell whether we were in a driveway or just a treeless ditch on the side of the road. We both got out and took a moment to let our eyes adjust in the cold night. Through a wall of pine, I could see a sagging trailer illuminated by several naked lightbulbs that hung from the edge of the roof. There were two cars parked in front that appeared to be disintegrating into the earth and the handle of a push mower stuck out through the snow nearby. Crow's country existence bore little resemblance to my own: it was isolated and run-down, with none of the middle-class signifiers like ski racks and greenhouses that decorated my road. Crow was poor. A dog barked from inside a shed behind the trailer and I felt myself jump as I realized that I had no idea what my role was to be on this visit. I may have been a native Vermonter, but I was surely an outsider here.

"Just hang back at the beginning and I will get things started," Peg said, sensing my hesitation. "He's actually kind of a lovable guy."

We walked through the deep, melting snow until we were close enough to see into two small front windows that had been partially obscured by threadbare towels. It was light inside, but I didn't see any other signs of life.

"What do you want?" someone yelled from the side of the house.

I jerked my head to the left and jumped like a dope.

The man I had met earlier that fall at the prepper meeting was standing beside the house with a large shovel in one hand and a headlamp glowing above his eyes. He looked just as I remembered him, wearing the same faded denim vest over a hooded sweatshirt. Shaggy graying hair fell around his thin face.

"Hi, Crow!" Peg yelled cheerfully. "It's me, Peg. I was hoping we could have a few minutes of your time."

"And who's that?" he asked, pointing the rusting metal shovel in my direction. I was grateful that he didn't recognize me from our first brief meeting.

"This is Ash. He's a friend of mine helping out with some town matters. This is a friendly visit, Crow. Can we come in?"

"All right, all right," Crow said, stepping past us to unlock the front door and watch closely as we entered. "Shoes off!"

We tugged off our winter boots and draped our coats on a nearby rocking chair. The space was small, with only enough room for a ratty couch and two chairs. To our right was a kitchen the size of a bathroom, which led to a bathroom the size of a closet. The decor was tattered, but not dirty. The floors were well swept and the surfaces almost shiny. I noticed a stack of overstuffed cardboard boxes in the corner that were all neatly labeled in marker—books, tools, extension cords. There was a very particular order to the cramped space.

Crow took a seat at the edge of one of the chairs and looked at us expectantly.

"Well, get on with it," he said.

Peg snapped into gear, swiftly laying a small map of the plans out on the coffee table and launching into an overview of the devastation the flood would wreak. I don't think she was exaggerating, but it was clear that she was describing a worst-case scenario, with a focus on Crow's property and little mention of the threat to downtown or even his neighbors. He sat still, listening without interruption, but not encouraging her in any way. When Peg finally took a breath, Crow jumped in.

"Let me spare you, Peg." He put one hand up as a stop signal. "This isn't going to happen, not on my property. You can dig as many holes as you want in the Fabers' land next door, but there's no way in hell that I'm going to let a group of strangers, beholden to God knows who, come onto my property and start tearing it up. Not gonna happen."

Peg nodded. She had been ready for this reaction. "I totally understand, Crow. Really, I do. But if I could just—"

"Does ownership mean nothing to you people?" he asked, louder than before.

"Oh, c'mon, Crow. I'm not 'you people,'" she said. "You know that. And I'm telling you that this is as straightforward as it sounds. There are no political motives in this. Your little house will be floating down the Isole Creek if you don't do anything! Lot of good ownership will do you then."

Peg was more heated than I had ever seen her, but I was impressed by her ability to not be intimidated by Crow. I hadn't spoken a word yet.

"Oh, I'm not so attached to this place," Crow said, looking around his home. A smile crept across his face. "You wanna see something cool?"

I didn't want to see something cool, which I imagined could only involve taxidermy, combat scars or an arsenal.

"Sure," Peg said, recognizing an opportunity to recalibrate her approach.

"This way." Crow motioned for us to follow as he opened the front door.

We tugged on our boots and coats and went back into the dark night where Crow would have been invisible up ahead if his headlamp had not illuminated the path. It occurred to me that if he wanted to kill us, it would have been a fairly easy job. There were no houses within shouting distance and nothing for us to run to. We were entirely at his mercy. I thought about what a strange twist of fate it would be for Pia if I died at the hands of her friend Crow. At least I would be vindicated for calling him crazy.

"It's just up here!" Crow yelled from up ahead as he approached the shed I had heard the dog bark from before.

"Jesus Christ," I whispered to Peg, "he's taking us to his shed. Should we be following him?"

"It's fine…probably," Peg said, with less confidence than before.

The wind blew against my face and I became aware of the sweat that was accumulating on my forehead. I could hear trees rustle around me, but it was so cloudy that even their silhouettes against the sky were missing that night. I could smell the sweet, festive scent of balsam fir and thought I saw white spruce pinecones littered at my feet. It comforted me to be able to piece together my surroundings and made the dark seem less foreboding. Crow lived deep in the boreal forest, which was always dark. The canopy of evergreen above kept light out all year long. And aside from some twinflower and wintergreen, little could grow through the decomposing pine needles on the moist, acidic floor. If I hadn't been so scared, I would have appreciated the beauty of it all.

We met Crow at the door to the shed, where he wrestled with a key and a heavy-duty padlock. Peg and I exchanged a glance of shared panic. But if we were considering abandoning this plan, it was too late because the lock opened easily and Crow pulled the wooden door back with ease. The dog we heard earlier slipped past us and ran toward the house.

Before us was not the interior of Crow's murder shed, but a wall of sheet metal that followed the interior curves of the shed itself, leaving only a few inches between the two structures. It was a shelter inside a shelter. Crow dragged his fingers along a jagged edge of the metal until he found a latch that held a small combination lock. We watched as he entered a set of numbers and then opened the door to the interior shelter.

"Welcome to my backup plan," he proclaimed.

A light flickered on and our eyes took a moment to adjust to what we were looking at. In the space that couldn't have been more than eighty square feet, there was a living room–like area with an old couch and a chair set up around a milk-crate coffee table. A large camp stove was open nearby next to a bucket that attached to a water pump system, which I gathered served as a kitchen. In the corner of the makeshift kitchen, a curtain hung, behind which I could see part of a tiny camp toilet. There were no windows, but a framed watercolor painting of a man in a canoe hung above the little couch. It was like a dollhouse or, more accurately, a clubhouse for a young boy. I couldn't believe the ingenuity that had gone into it.

"What *is* this?" I heard myself ask.

"It's where I go when The Storm comes," Crow bragged. "C'mon, man, let me show you what it can really do."

He waved me into the space, which could barely hold the three of us. I squeezed in behind Crow as he reached up to a latch behind the living room chair and pulled down a small bed that had been folded into the wall. It was wrapped neatly in sheets and an army blanket and had the faint smell of mothballs. I inspected the makeshift Murphy bed and its expert hinges with great admiration. It was a pretty clever use of space.

"And that's nothing!" Crow was getting excited.

He stepped into the kitchen area and pulled something from the wall facing the bucket sink. With a few quick motions, the object unfolded into a small table that fit neatly in

MEG LITTLE REILLY

the space. Next, Crow reached past me to pull out a small bench that was tucked beside the sink and provided seating to accompany the table.

"Did you make all this?" I asked. I had forgotten entirely about my fears and the purpose of our visit.

"Most of it I made, and some of it I found online. It's not rocket science, but I've been workin' on it for a while and I'm damn proud of it. It's insulated, flood-proof and fully stocked. If The Storm came tomorrow, I would have everything I need in here."

Peg had been silent since we entered the bunker and seemed to be waiting for the right moment to revisit the topic at hand.

"Crow, this is very impressive," she started, "and it's very smart. You're a man of great foresight, no doubt. So what do you care if we dig a little hole in your backyard while you're living in here?"

"Well, *hopefully*," Crow said, annoyed, "I won't have to live in this thing. This is an emergency option. I'm not looking forward to a catastrophe."

I wasn't so sure about his last point.

He went on, "This is about principles, Peg. It's easy to abandon your principles in moments of crisis, but that's when we need them the most. I'm not going to surrender all my rights to the state because you think this *might* save some land."

"No one's surrendering any rights here," she replied. "We're simply asking you to consider the consequences of not digging extra drainage. Even if you don't give a hoot about the rest of this town, it could drown your entire property. Do it for yourself."

"That's a risk I'm willing to take."

"Crow, this is selfish!" Peg was losing her composure. "Lots of people could suffer because of your goddamn principles. If we can't redirect the flooding, the entire downtown of Isole could be destroyed. How will you be able to live with yourself if that happens?"

"I doubt I'm the only person in Isole who is putting my foot down," he said.

"You might be!"

"Not likely." He shook his head. "Anyhow, I think I'd do greater harm to our society by giving in to this. Now is the time to stand up for our rights."

I felt awkward, standing between the two of them as they argued in the small space, and I wished we could go back to exploring Crow's secret hideout. But I was there on behalf of the Subcommittee and I needed to say something.

"This affects my property, too, Crow, and I think this plan is in all of our best interests," I said weakly.

Crow turned to me. "That's for me to decide."

We stood there silently for a minute until Crow said, "You two should go."

He seemed hurt that the unveiling of his creation had been overshadowed by conflict. I felt it, too, somehow. I liked Crow. He was thoughtful and smart, even funny in his own way. And maybe he wasn't as crazy as I had originally thought.

Peg gave me a stern nod and I swept my eyes over the secret hideout, taking it all in for what would likely be the last time. I noticed that there were plastic storage containers suspended from the ceiling above the couch. They had drawers that pulled out and could have held a small wardrobe for one person. Brilliant. I was also curious about the bathroom, but now was not the time to explore it. A generator-powered refrigerator sat across from the tiny toilet and I wondered what foods might be in there.

MEG LITTLE REILLY

Peg and I walked silently across the dark property, using our cell phones to light the way. When we arrived at the car, she let out a deep sigh and sank into the driver's seat.

"This isn't going to be easy," she said. "I like Crow, but he's a damn fool."

I nodded. "I like him, too. He's kind of a surprise, you know?"

"And yet, he's also just the angry recluse you'd expect." Peg shook her head in frustration. "We have to keep trying. I'm going to wear him down."

I felt bad that I couldn't help Peg, or Isole, and vowed then to commit myself more to the business of convincing doubters that they needed to get on board with the runoff plan. But what would convince someone who had no concern for their town or neighbors, I wondered. I remembered that Pia had no idea we were a part of the drainage plan. Our own backyard would be changed by it. I guessed that she would put up a symbolic fight, on the grounds of personal freedom or whatever talking points she had been fed by the preppers, and then go along with it because ultimately she'd lose interest in the banal matters of home and property maintenance. No matter what, she could never know that I had gone to Crow's house or, worse, that the guy impressed me. For some reason, I needed to keep that to myself.

Peg and I didn't speak on the long drive back to my car. It was nine o'clock and there was hardly anyone else on the road. She turned the radio on and we heard the tail end of a weather report about another snowstorm that was expected to start the following afternoon. I wasn't listening closely.

As Peg pulled into the courthouse lot, an alarming thought occurred to me and I turned to her, "Do you think other people in Isole are building bunkers like Crow's?"

"I don't think so," she said, "but I guess it's not the craziest idea in the world."

"It's not, no... Do you think we should all be doing things like that?" I asked. Seeing Crow in a new, rational light was confusing.

Peg put the car in Park and turned toward me.

"No, Ash. Once you go there, you're already living in a state of emergency. You're praying for the reckoning just to make all your efforts worthwhile. It's a fine line between being prepared and letting the fear run your life, but you have to respect the line."

"Even if it means being unprepared when something bad really does happen?" I asked.

"Yes, most definitely."

I nodded and thanked her for the ride, closing the car door gently behind me. Seeing Crow's bunker and hearing his utterly rational explanation for his actions had rattled my understanding of what we were all supposed to be doing then...of what sane behavior looked like. It had been easier to dismiss Crow as a laughable, rural caricature. Considering that he was right was more complicated.

THIRTEEN

OUR LIVING ROOM smelled like old gym clothes by the second Saturday in January because of the worms. Pia checked on them regularly to make sure their movement was lively and the soil temperature within the appropriate range. Her care for the worms looked almost parental at times, though she could forget to check them for days on end. Sometimes when I was home alone, I would pull the top off and watch them writhe around in their moist box. They were fascinating, but I hated them intensely. Once, I even carried a single worm out the front door and dropped it in the snow. It moved around for a minute and then just stopped. Murdering that worm was a quiet, disturbing act of protest that I kept to myself. The violence of it surprised me. They were like roommates by then—roommates I resented but never wished any real harm upon.

"I'm going to a meeting," Pia said, keys in hand. It had started to snow.

I looked up from my computer at the kitchen table. "Wait, we really need to talk about August."

She sighed. We hadn't had a chance to discuss August's

near-disappearance into the woods, but Bev The Social Worker would be calling any day now to announce that time was up: he would need to be placed in a home.

"Pia, I really want this and I think it could be good for us," I pleaded. "I don't know what else to say. I really want this."

The expression on her face was soft and sympathetic, but I could see that she wasn't going to change her mind. "I'm sorry, Ash. I love you and I would like to make you happy, but this is bigger than us. It's another life. Maybe you can handle this, but I'm telling you that I can't."

She pulled on her coat and walked out the door.

I watched Pia drive off into the first stage of a snowstorm. The roads were unpredictable then, as we oscillated between blizzards and warm fronts. Accumulation from the previous snow had finally melted, but the temperature was dropping fast again. There was already eight new inches on our front lawn and the sky had turned to a dark charcoal gray even though it was two o'clock. I sat at the kitchen table in front of a drafty window. My laptop was open in front of me in an attempt to catch up on work, but nothing had materialized. I watched the falling snow for a long time. It was hypnotic: the wall of white puffs falling against a gray sky—more like a spooky digital loop that I could have programmed than anything I'd ever seen in nature. The sound, or lack thereof, was strange, too. Maybe I'd lived in the city for too long and forgotten what snow sounded like, but it seemed as if the low hum of life that was always outside had been turned down.

"The entire Northeast and parts of the Mid-Atlantic will get snow. Everyone from western New York to the coast of Maine and down to Pennsylvania should be prepared," the radio voice explained. "Northern New England can expect eighteen to thirty inches, with less as you move south. The southeastern part of the country can expect damaging rains.

The heaviest snow will hit the Northeast in about thirty-six hours. At the same time, we have a tropical storm forming off the Gulf Coast. As long as that dissipates before it makes landfall, this snowstorm will simply be a nor'easter—a big, snowy nor'easter, but not a superstorm as many fear. But if that tropical storm speeds up and they collide, we will be faced with a challenge."

I looked back at my computer, trying to think about anything other than the conversation I'd just had with Pia. That was it; August would be taken away. And I'd be left there, with my panicked wife, as the deadly weather approached.

An email appeared on the screen before me. It was from Salty:

There's no way to know if this is going to be The Storm, so we have to keep moving forward with the runoff plan. It's possible that we will get a reprieve after this snow and still have some time to get into the ground and start digging. I made great progress yesterday with a portion of our affected landowners. Heard you guys hit a wall, but we can't get discouraged. We have to press forward with this. Good luck riding out this storm. Hope for the best.

I tried to focus on the words in front of me but couldn't stop thinking about August. When would he leave and where would he go?

I got up from the table to look at the snow outside, which was piling up shockingly fast. I knew that I needed to clear the driveway for when Pia got home with the car. If I didn't do it soon, it would be too late and she'd have to park it on the road, where it would be buried under a pile of snow after the town plow went by. I didn't feel like doing this for her, plowing obstacles out of Pia's way. I considered leaving the driveway untouched as a gesture of selfishness to match her own. But eventually, I did what I knew I would do all along and I pulled on all my outdoor gear and stepped outside into the cold. The work would be good for me, I decided, maybe hard and exerting enough to keep down the rising tide of sadness in my stomach.

I hadn't used a snowblower in years—not since my dad taught me as a kid—and it took a while to figure out how to turn it on. It was one of those massive push snowblowers, just like my dad's, but rusting in several places. The previous owners of our house sold it to us for two hundred dollars, and it hadn't occurred to me at the time to make sure it was operational. Mercifully, it turned on after a few attempts and I awkwardly worked to steer it from the shed to the driveway. I was grateful no one could see me for this project. My plan was to drive a straight line out to the road and back again, three, maybe four times, until there was a wide enough lane for our car to drive through. Our driveway was long, so it wouldn't be easy, but it wouldn't be impossible either.

At first, things seemed to work pretty well. I loved the razor-sharp cut that the machine made through the snow, revealing distinct layers from each storm we'd had, like a sliced geode. The problem was traction. I had big, warm snow boots on that kept slipping out from under me as I worked to push the heavy rig forward. I wished I'd thought to buy crampons or even just dig up some old soccer cleats. To compensate for my lack of torque, I had to rock the machine back and forth when it stopped to propel it forward again. This worked until I'd nearly reached the road, the section where our driveway tilted up at a slight angle. In the car, it was just a little bump, but it was too much for me to push the snowblower over. I stood there, gripping the handles of the roaring blower while I looked around

MEG LITTLE REILLY

for a solution. Snow was falling in a dense curtain before my eyes, leaving flakes to melt on my lashes and cheeks. Finally, I saw a small log, nearly covered in snow, just to my right. I left the blower in place while I retrieved the log and pressed it into the ground at my feet. I was going to use the log to press my boot against it while I pushed the blower up and over the hump. After a few stomps, the log was secure and I prepared to heave the machine forward. With a forceful thrust, the snowblower took a satisfying leap and it seemed for a moment that we might crest the bump. But just as the snowblower neared the top, I ran out of strength. My muscles quivered in overexertion. The machine stopped moving and then began rolling back toward me. There was no time to think. I stepped back, hoping to find the log with my toe, but it wasn't there. Before I could pull my body entirely out of the way, the blower was rolling into my chest. It jammed one long handle into a lung, knocked the wind out of me and ran directly over my left foot.

I fell onto my back, stunned at first, and then overwhelmed by a hot, rushing pain in my foot. It hurt too much to move, so I craned my neck around to see that the blower had rolled past me and tipped over into the snowbank. The whirring and clanking of its ancient motor was trailing off as the stalled beast went back to its dormant state. I was safe from it, but in excruciating pain. I moaned and then gasped as it occurred to me that not only was my foot likely broken, but my cell was inside and there was no one around to help me. I could die there in my driveway, so close to my warm, glowing house. I let my head fall back into the snow and watched the cold flakes rush toward me.

For a fleeting instant, it seemed more comfortable to just let death wash over me. But as my thoughts came into focus, I realized that I wasn't likely going to die from a broken foot—not immediately anyhow—and I needed a plan. I rolled onto my stomach and began to crawl along my neatly sheared path toward the house. The flat walls of snow on either side kept me hidden from the rest of the world; I was an animal burrowing back to my cave. At the rate I was going, it would have taken about ten painful minutes to crawl back to the house. My foot was throbbing, but pain was now also coming from my wet, freezing knees that were doing all the work.

I hadn't gotten very far when I saw car lights reflecting against the trees ahead. Instinctively, I pulled myself up onto my working right foot, spun around and waved my hands wildly like someone stranded on a desert island. A red pickup whizzed down the hill and then stopped just past my driveway. The scruffy young man behind the wheel rolled down his window and lifted his chin, as if that alone asked the question.

"I'm hurt," I yelled, which sounded pathetic, but it was all I could summon. "Can you take me to the hospital?"

"Hop in," the man said.

I hobbled a few steps down the driveway, pushing through the portion of snow that the blower never reached and wincing all the way. The guy in the truck watched for a while and finally jumped out of the driver's seat to reluctantly help me in. He was matter-of-fact about the operation, and so I did my best not to seem too wimpy, but Jesus Christ, it hurt. Once we were moving again, I nervously told him the story of what had happened, vaguely sensing that later, when the pain subsided, I would feel deep embarrassment at my inability to execute a small snow-removal task. But I had no energy for embarrassment then.

The man, who must have been in his early twenties, didn't seem terribly interested in my injury. He explained that he'd

MEG LITTLE REILLY

been working on a big second-home construction up the hill when the contractor finally let them go for the day. Now he needed to get back to his girlfriend's house in time to get snowed in with her instead of his own parents.

"This snow's too deep for that old piece of shit, you know," he said. Apparently, he had taken notice of the snowblower I left on its side. "You gotta get a bigger rig or find someone with a truck plow for your driveway. I'm surprised that thing's even running still. I haven't seen one of those in years."

This information made me feel slightly less incompetent. I asked him what kind of snowblower I should buy and nodded my head as he gave me incredibly specific advice about motors and tire gauge options. He was just killing time, in a hurry to get rid of this weird injured guy before getting trapped inside with his girlfriend. I imagined that this girlfriend was new to him, based on his urgency. She was probably pretty enough, but also tough in the way country girls can be. My foot was throbbing and, over the course of the ten-minute drive, I thought I might pass out. I wanted this guy to keep talking, to tell me about snowplows and girlfriends and whatever else he was saying while I tried to focus on his words and ignore the pain.

Finally, he pulled up to the very small medical facility that served as a hospital for people who couldn't or wouldn't drive to the closest real hospital ninety minutes away. It looked like a giant cinder block and, on that night, the cinder block appeared to be closed.

"Okay, man, good luck," my driver said.

I sat there for a moment, confused about what to do. There was still no sign of life from inside the hospital and this guy wanted to leave me on the doorstep. It was dark now and snow was falling even faster than before. I don't know what I was envisioning for the drop-off, but I had at least hoped that he would help me wobble inside. Instead of freezing to death in my driveway, it appeared that I would freeze to death on the sad front steps of this building. Maybe this guy *knew* that the hospital was closed, I considered, and he just wanted to dump me somewhere as part of a cruel trick. I sat silently in the cab of the truck for another moment.

Finally, a middle-aged woman in an old-fashioned nurse's cap peered out one of the windows and turned on a light. I let out a sigh of relief and opened the car door, now eager to flee the truck. I slammed the door behind me and mumbled a thank-you after it was too late for him to hear. The front door of the hospital swung open and the nurse and an older man came to meet me. They were wearing scrubs on top, with jeans and snow boots below. As they helped me inside and into a wheelchair, I felt an overwhelming wave of gratitude wash over me. Lights flicked on around us as we wheeled down a hall toward an examination room that could just as well have been for farm animals.

I don't remember most of what happened in that room until the moment at which the pain medication kicked in and my head cleared. Both people (doctors? nurses? I didn't know) were down near my bare foot with a glaring light above them. They murmured and nodded to one another until finally standing up straight and looking at me. By this point, I was sure amputation was inevitable.

"You're looking at several stress fractures in your forefoot and toes," the man said casually.

"Stress fractures?" I asked, disappointed by the mild sound of the term. "There's nothing broken? It really hurts."

"Breaks, fractures—same thing in this case," he said. "These small foot breaks can hurt like hell, but there isn't much we can do. You will get some swelling and probably bruising...definitely more pain."

The woman put her hand on my arm. "We're going to give you a walking boot, one that you can take on and off, and we'll tape some of your toes together. Can you stay off your feet for a couple weeks?"

I shrugged.

"Good," the man said. "And we'll give you two days' worth of the painkillers, but that will suffice."

"Um, okay," I said. "So it will stop hurting soon?"

The doctor shook his head. "No, it will probably hurt for a while. You just have to be patient. Our bodies are very good at healing themselves if we give them the time and rest they need."

I don't know what I was hoping for, but a little more alarm over the suffering I had just endured would have been validating. I was familiar with this Yankee tough-it-out approach to first aid from my childhood, and I didn't miss it one bit.

"Do you have someone you can call to come and get you?" the woman asked as she taped my toes.

And with that, a new wave of panic swept over me. I could probably get ahold of Pia, but whether she would come get me seemed an open question. There was almost two feet of fresh snow on the ground now, too, making it a logistical challenge. I had left the snowblower in our driveway, so I imagined a pissed-off Pia parking the car on the side of the road and walking along my skinny, plowed lane to the house. It hadn't occurred to me that she might actually be worried.

The female doctor rolled my wheelchair up to a flesh-colored rotary phone and I dialed Pia's cell. It rang three times before her voice-mail message came on. I don't know why I didn't leave a message, but the sound of her voice mail sent me into such a fury that I couldn't bear to. Either she was still out with her prepper friends, or she had returned to the disturbing driveway scene. Either way, she hadn't thought to leave her fucking cell phone on in the middle of a blizzard. I returned the receiver to the phone and looked up at the two nice people standing in front of me. Perhaps they were in a rush to get to their girlfriends' houses, too. My head still felt foggy with pain and pills.

"I don't really have anyone to call," I said. "I recently moved here and my wife is unavailable. I don't know... I don't know what people do in this situation...when they need someone to come...but there isn't anyone."

I knew how sad it all sounded, but I didn't have the will to pretend not to be melancholy. I didn't have anyone to call. My wife was too busy with her new obsessions to wonder where I'd been and, while I certainly had acquaintances in Isole, I didn't have any close friends. I didn't know what their lives were like and certainly didn't feel comfortable calling them and asking them to drive into a storm to get me.

My shoulders slumped. I opened my palms out on my thighs as if to surrender to these perfectly nice doctor-like people who had succeeded at making me feel like the most alone person on earth.

"We all need to get home fast, before there's too much snow," the man said. "Libby and I are going west on sixteen, which doesn't do you any good, Ash." I wondered how he knew my name and my address. He went on, "But my daughter lives right up the road from you, and she's on her way home from work now. I'll see if she can swing by here to give you a lift."

I sat in my wheelchair while calls were made and someone's daughter was instructed to pick me up. The man and woman bustled around, turning off lights and returning medical instruments to drawers. It was called a hospital, but it filled a uniquely rural role that was more like urgent care. These doctors were here to tend to what could be fixed on-site

MEG LITTLE REILLY

and send the serious problems to Dartmouth or Burlington. They braved the snow as necessary, and the entire enterprise relied on their judgment and tire treads. It's a startling deficiency to someone unfamiliar with rural America, but you forget that with time. I was still alarmed by the idea as I sat helpless with my bright blue medical boot in my wheelchair.

It occurred to me that I hadn't been in a hospital or even seen a doctor in years. Weren't adults supposed to have things checked and measured now and then? It sounded right, but I hadn't gotten around to such maintenance. I grew up in a household that stressed the curative powers of fresh air and a stiff upper lip; if you weren't vomiting or registering a fatal temperature, you were going to school. I carried that toughness with me into adulthood and it had, thus far, served me well. But as I sat in that lonely closing hospital, I realized what a luxury it was just to *know* that people are available to care for you at any moment, even if you never avail yourself of their services.

Finally, a set of headlights appeared in the turnabout and the three of us exited the building, me hobbling in my air cast and holding a plastic bag of pills and pamphlets. The man and woman helped me to the passenger side of a sporty old Saab, then said their goodbyes and hustled to their cars. I felt like an unwanted child being passed around from one adult to the next. I had no choice but to trust that this new grown-up would make sure I got home safely.

"Hi, I'm Maggie," my driver said.

The interior car light was on just long enough for me to know that I found Maggie very attractive. She had reddish long hair peeking out of a colorful knitted hat. My mind was still jumbled from the pain of the accident and the strangeness of the day, but she seemed familiar to me.

"I'm Ash," I said, thinking I should make some gesture of gratitude, but not doing so.

Maggie pulled the car onto the empty road and followed the tire marks of whoever drove ahead of us. It was difficult to see where we were going, but she had the confidence of someone who had memorized the curves of that route. She turned the high beams on and then off again when it was clear that they were no use in the dense snowfall.

"I remember you, Ash," she said. "You're the new guy from the town hall scuffle. So what did you do this time—wrestle a bear in the woods?"

Was that flirtatiousness? I couldn't tell, but I did my best to muster some charm.

"Close," I said. "A snowblower attacked me. It was a menace to the neighborhood and it had to be put down—but not without a nasty fight. I'm disfigured now, but it's a small price to pay for future generations."

She smiled and I felt pleased with myself.

Maggie took a cautious turn onto an even darker road and pulled her hat off. Then I remembered: she was the woman who'd carried the toddlers into the janitors' closet after the gunshots. I hadn't thought about her since then, but I remembered being impressed by her decisiveness. I also remembered how pretty she was. Maggie was probably in her early thirties, thin and sporty in that pink-cheeked unfussy way that outdoorsy New England girls are. It was a type that had always driven me wild, different from Pia's overpowering sexiness, but bursting with optimism and confidence.

"How far up the hill do you live, Ash?" Maggie asked.

She couldn't take her eyes from the snowy road, so I used the opportunity to take in her lightly freckled face and the long fingers that gripped the wheel. She was wearing snow pants and a cream-colored fisherman's sweater. They could have been men's clothes, the way they draped over her small chest and firm legs, and I didn't mind the mystery of that at all.

"About two miles up," I said, wishing she'd slow down to stretch out the drive. "I remember you, too, you know, from the town hall."

Maggie nodded and smiled a little.

"So what do you do?" I asked.

"I teach math at the high school," she said, "and I coach the downhill ski team."

I didn't know anyone who did things like that. Our friends from New York all worked in the arts or media or public relations. We talked knowingly over brunch about font trends. Maggie's was a world I knew nothing about.

She shrugged. "It's not as sexy as graphic design, but I really love it. And it gives me time to write."

She's a writer! Suddenly, I wanted to ask her a thousand questions, but I tried to stay cool. I wondered, too, how she knew so much about me.

"So this snow must be great news to a ski coach," I said.

Maggie sighed. "This snow? No. This is more than we need. The visibility is too low and we can't keep up with the grooming. It feels weird to say, but this really is too much. This whole season, it's been too much or too little. Very strange."

"Yeah, it is weird," I said, looking out the window. There was no one else on the road at seven o'clock. I wondered how Maggie would get home after she dropped me off.

Anticipating my concern, she said, "We probably shouldn't be on the roads right now, but I live about a half mile up the hill from you, so this isn't out of my way."

She looked down at my foot. "Do you have someone who can take care of you while you recover?"

"Um, yeah, my wife," I said, remembering Pia. "She's there, so I will have some help."

This was a hopeful lie, but it sounded nice to me.

"Good. You really shouldn't try to do too much with that cast." Maggie was all business now. The flirtatious tone in her voice had vanished with the mention of Pia. "One minute it will feel like you can hop around on it no problem, and the next minute it will be throbbing. Just stay off it."

She spoke like someone who had sustained a lot of injuries, which impressed me. I broke my arm when I fell off a jungle gym in fourth grade, but aside from that, my only injuries had been the long-term stresses of distance running in high school, which lacked the drama of ski collisions.

"I'm just up the way, in the little cape around the bend," Maggie said. "It's me and my dog, Badger. He loves a snowstorm."

She looked wistful about the idea of being snowed in with her dog. I imagined them snuggling in front of a crackling fire, Badger sleeping while she read a fat novel. I wished that I could join them instead of returning to my stinky, worm-infested house with my unpredictable wife.

This was it. The snow was still coming down heavily. Maybe this really was *the* big snowstorm, and Pia and I would be trapped together for days. Did we have enough food? Probably not. Neither of us had bothered to think that piece through, which meant that we'd be eating canned soup and whatever else we could find. We had enough wine. I knew that Pia would have been diligent about the wine. We were about to be trapped together, arguing about August or avoiding the subject altogether, and fearing what the storm might portend. This drop-off could be my last interaction with the civilized world, I thought to myself. Worse, it could be my last interaction with Maggie.

My foot started to throb and I reached down to itch a portion of my shin that was now encased and unreachable. Damn, it hurt. Suddenly, it was all too much. I felt the hot tears burn in my eyes first. I looked out my window to the right, working hard to quietly halt a wellspring of sadness, but it was too late. I let out a burst of sound—a cry that I tried to mask as a cough, which just made it sound tortured and strange. I could feel Maggie looking at me. There was no going back now. I put my face in my hands and took five seconds to collect myself before wiping my eyes and looking up.

"I'm so sorry," I said, trying to sound more baffled than apologetic. "It must be these drugs. I feel crazy. I'm just not myself. This is embarrassing."

I had cried more in those past two weeks than in the previous five years combined.

Maggie was unflappable, "Ash, I get it. This is a lot."

She pulled gently up to the edge of my impassable driveway and stopped the car. We both sat there for a moment.

I didn't want to get out of the car, not only because I liked Maggie, but also because the logistical question of how exactly I would get to my house was too humiliating to consider. Would Maggie help drag me past the overturned snowblower, along the plowed path and up the front steps to my wife? The last piece was the scariest because it was becoming more and more difficult to anticipate the mood I might find Pia in.

"It's just snow," Maggie said after a silence. "It seems so scary right now—because of the superstorm predictions—but it melts. It's nature's most temporary creation. That's what I tell my kids at school. It's temporary."

I appreciated her effort, but I wasn't afraid of the snow. I was afraid of the aloneness…the aloneness of finding myself mauled by a snowblower with no one to call, and the aloneness of being left unwanted at an empty hospital and the aloneness of being stuck inside my own house with someone I understood less and less each day. But the snow was our captor, so I guess, in a way, I was scared of the snow.

I looked at Maggie and smiled. There was nothing at all left to say. I was married and it was snowing so hard that we couldn't see the hood of her car. I needed to get out.

"Thank you," I said. "Please be safe getting home. Maybe I'll see you after the snow."

"I hope so," Maggie said.

As I reached for the handle, the door swung away, revealing Pia standing before me. She was shivering in long johns, oversize boots and a parka. She had a relieved look on her face that seemed only half-genuine.

"Are you okay?" she shrieked and leaned into the car to hug me, noticing the cast.

I was startled and embarrassed.

"Thank you *so much* for getting him home," Pia said to Maggie.

She was working to pull my much larger body out to lean on her, which I knew would never work. Everything about the situation felt awkward and needed to end fast. I steadied myself in the snow and smiled again at Maggie. Pia slammed the door without another word and we waited in silence as the car drove away.

"So what the hell happened?" Pia said. She was referring to the accident, but maybe also to the pretty woman who had driven me home.

I started hobbling along the narrow path and ignored her questioning. The snowblower peeked out from under a mound of snow to our left. Despite my throbbing foot, it felt like a very long time ago that I had been run over. Since then, I had dramatically increased the number of people I could count as Isole acquaintances and developed an intense crush on the woman up the road. She lives *just over the hill*, I thought to myself, so torturously close.

It took nearly five minutes for Pia and me to drag my gimpy body back to our house and, although I was relieved to sit, I found no comfort in my arrival. The wet worm smell was creeping into the kitchen and our breakfast dishes were still stacked in the sink. Pia hadn't washed a dish in weeks. She hadn't eaten a proper meal in about that time either, so it was mostly just small plates littered with toast crumbs, coffee mugs and glassware of every size stamped with the dried remains of red wine. I noticed that she was growing thinner, which made her large eyes and full lips bulge disturbingly.

We hadn't spoken as I stumbled to the house. I didn't have the energy to limp and argue simultaneously, but her strange greeting suggested that we were already in a fight. Once I was lying horizontal on the couch, with my bad foot elevated and a beer on the floor beside me, I decided to engage again with Pia. I felt the same tingling, alive sensation that had been passing over me more and more recently, and I wanted a release from the tension.

"I'll tell you 'what the hell,' Pia," I said, looking directly at her across the room. She had one hand on her cocked hip over tight long underwear. "I broke my foot in a million places and you weren't there for me. Apparently, you weren't even nervous about where I'd been or why there was an overturned piece of machinery in our driveway. Does that seem like normal marriage behavior to you?" I was just picking up steam, finding an anger that went much deeper than the day's accident. "A perfect stranger had to drive me home while I made up some bullshit about why my own wife couldn't do it. I should have told everyone the truth: that you were probably out with the other paranoid doomsdayers, that you are too busy indulging your many neuroses and that you don't care about anyone other than yourself. That's what I should have said!"

Pia started pacing in front of me, twisting and tugging her long blond hair with both hands.

"You like me like this!" she shrieked. "You want me to be a little damaged because it keeps me needy and you love needy."

There may have been a grain of truth to this once, but not now.

She went on, "Don't blame my compulsive tendencies for your naïveté and your unwillingness to address the threat we're facing. This is about The Storm. Everything is. You and your orderly little friends can try to control how this goes, but it's not a controllable situation. When The Storm comes, all we'll have are our own preparations. We're all alone when The Storm comes."

That moment should have been a clarion answer to the question of my aloneness, a therapeutic breakthrough. There it was: Pia operated as one. She liked me a lot, but she didn't need me the way I wanted to be needed; the way I needed her. And I don't think she had ever intentionally misled me on this point. But I had been working hard not to see it because I wanted to believe in the parity of our neediness. Our physical desire may have been matched, but not our emotional desire. Need it be? Maybe not, I considered. I was devastated, but confused, too.

I sat up and nodded, which she misinterpreted as assent, but I didn't care. There was no argument left in me. She must have recognized that her point had been adequately made because she didn't pursue it any further. We were silent. I felt an overwhelming urge to walk to the front door, step out into the cold air and run. I hadn't been running since we'd moved to Isole, but I imagined striding effortlessly over the snow for miles and miles, along snowy farms and fields, until the choking tightness in my chest was replaced by sweet exhaustion. But my foot was in a cast, and the snow was becoming dangerously deep. I had no choice but to stay there, with her, for as long as nature decided to keep us.

FOURTEEN

AFTER A LONG sleep and another foot of accumulation, the snow stopped and Pia and I were contrite. We were both still mad, but also aware of our own unreasonable behavior. Without ever saying it, we agreed to just move on. I was devastated about August, but working to forgive her. I couldn't force someone to want a child. A storm was coming—or *The Storm*—and it didn't feel right to be at war with each other as a shared enemy approached.

I had spoken to Bev The Social Worker earlier that morning, explaining why we couldn't take August. She seemed genuinely disappointed but said that she had another family in mind just a few miles away. It was going to take a few more weeks to finalize the paperwork for his move, so we would have some more time together. I was confused about the process but couldn't form the proper questions while I had Bev on the line.

As I sat across the kitchen table from Pia, watching her spread peach-cardamom jam slowly on toast, I wondered how much of this had been explained to August. I was confident that he didn't—and wouldn't ever—know that I had passed on the chance to take him in. The possibility of his knowing this felt like a knife in my chest. But what *did* he know? I dreaded the idea of helplessly discussing the coming changes with August, trying to be upbeat and optimistic. I didn't have that in me.

Everything in the immediate future seemed fucking terrible all of a sudden.

"Let's build a snowman!" Pia exclaimed, drawing my attention back to the present.

I looked up at her and shrugged. "Sure."

It hurt to walk, but I could hobble in the interest of domestic peace. And why the hell not? I was out of ideas and this was an idea. It was also vintage Pia: a spontaneous break from reality, which I needed desperately. We ate the last of our breakfasts without a word and got up to put on hats, coats and mittens. I wrapped a garbage bag around the medical boot on my left foot and took my morning painkiller. It was dumb, but this snowman could be just what the doctor ordered, we thought to ourselves.

When I limped out the front door, the cold air shot up my nostrils and into my eyes. It was clarifying, medicinal even. I was proud to feel my winter toughness returning after years away from mountain winds.

"Over here," Pia said, pointing to a flat location for our snowman.

I packed a hard ball between my hands, then added snow around it until it was large enough to roll along the ground in front of me. Pia did the same a few feet away. We were both crouched, pushing our little growing balls along the snow as they gained volume. We weren't talking, but there was a sweetness in our silence. Each of us wanted to feel the way we used to. We were trying, and I loved her for that.

When finally my ball seemed large and heavy enough to serve as the body, I rolled it back to the spot Pia had picked and went over to help her with her ball. We stopped before it got too large and then hoisted it together atop the first one.

"I'll work on the head," I said, "if you find some eyes for this guy."

Pia looked around thoughtfully, searching for makeshift features. Finally, she walked to the porch and began selecting large rocks from under the stairs. She made a neat pile with them and then ducked inside while I mounted the faceless head.

When the door swung open again, Pia smiled and held up an old scarf and a hat from our basket of mismatched winter gear.

I created a face with the rocks while she wrapped a blue tartan scarf around where his neck should be. Pia had worn that scarf daily for one entire winter back in the city, but I hadn't seen it since. I wondered if it still smelled like the lavender perfume she was wearing in those days. Next she pulled a French beret from under her arm—a misguided Christmas present from my mother from years before—and placed it at a jaunty angle on his round head.

We stepped back to appreciate our creation. At four feet tall, he was more of a snow boy than a snow man. He had a little of each of us in him but bore no resemblance. The beret made him look particularly cartoonish.

"He's French?" I asked.

"Quebecois," Pia corrected.

"Ah, *oui*."

I put my arm around Pia's shoulders and pulled her in. She rested her head on my chest for three seconds, then started back toward the door.

It wasn't there. We were trying, with our little French snow boy and our forced witty banter, but it wasn't there. And our cute creation couldn't fix that. I followed her slowly to the door and we left him outside where he belonged. The snow had started up again.

MEG LITTLE REILLY

FIFTEEN

IT SNOWED ON and off for four straight days, accumulating faster than even the fearless snowplowers of Vermont's Northeast Kingdom could keep up with. Commerce from Montreal to Manhattan came to a halt and millions of people had no choice but to stay inside, nervously consuming television news and social media gossip for something concrete about their fates. At first, we just wanted to know if this was the start of The Storm, the big one. That was the real fear. No one felt ready for that; we all needed one more trip to the picked-over grocery store and a few more batteries and another jug of water. There were also all the things we didn't want to tell each other we were afraid of going without: things like beer and porn and pills. This storm had come too quickly for us to feel *ready*, which was something we still believed was attainable.

When the last snowflake finally fell, there was almost seven feet of snow lying on the ground. Weather experts told us this wouldn't be The Storm, but it didn't matter anymore. That amount of snow inflicted such immediate and costly damage that we couldn't concern ourselves with what came next. It was like something out of a science fiction movie—an endless, blinding cloud that threatened to suffocate us all. It blocked our front doors and came up over our first-floor windows. The child in me was awed.

At Salty's recommendation, I hobbled outside with my long-handled snow shovel a couple times a day to clear a small path around our house and help the heavy sheets of snow slide off our slanted roof. It wasn't an elegant system, but our home was intact in the end, even as many others were not.

Country people fared better in the blizzard: we knew how to stay ahead of the accumulations, improvise tools and anticipate problems. Certainly old barns collapsed, trees fell on cars and a handful of helpless people had to move into shelters after their aging homes became uninhabitable. But most of us in the country were okay. Some of our luck was purely a virtue of space and population density. Weather was granted a wide berth in the Northeast Kingdom. By contrast, in New York and Boston, cars were crushed under falling snow; stubborn fools who refused to begin their afternoon commutes early on the first snowy day found themselves stuck in tunnels and on bridges for hours; and a few people with health problems froze to death waiting to be rescued. Rolling power outages across the Northeast claimed the lives of several dozen elderly and sick people who couldn't live without heat for long.

Still, the flooding was worse than the snow. "It always is," Salty had said to me as an undisputable fact the week before. Almost as soon as The Storm stopped, the sun appeared and our brilliant, glistening world dissolved into an unstoppable puddle the size of a state. The puddle seeped into our basements and our cars. It caused electrical problems and toxic mold. There were pictures in the *Burlington*

MEG LITTLE REILLY

Free Press—when delivery finally resumed—of multimillion-dollar homes on Lake Champlain that had begun sliding into the water with the runoff. And it was dirty. Manure, pesticides, long-dormant materials in industrial buildings across the region were pouring into our water table. Every region had its own set of problems: oceanside communities had been washed away, urban ghettos went without fresh food or trash pickup for days and the rural poor were forgotten entirely.

In all, seventy-six people died and the US economy lost three hundred billion dollars. But those statistics didn't mean as much to us as they used to. We weren't relying on the national news to define our experiences any longer—it had come to our doorsteps. So while it was sad that seventy-six people had died, I could only be upset about the losses before me: August's bike had been crushed by a falling sheet of ice, and my useless foot that was healing too slow. I no longer cared about our tanking stock market or the GDP. Those once-revered measures of progress seemed utterly irrelevant in the more primal existence we'd been thrust into. A simpler life, just like we wanted, in Vermont!

Throughout the storm and the subsequent melting, Pia and I kept our distance. She buzzed around the house, tending to her preparations, always with a sloshing glass of wine in one hand. I, in turn, became part of the furniture. I could get around okay, but my injury was an excuse for immobility. I was moping. I watched television until the reception was lost, then listened to my imaginary friends at Vermont Public Radio and drank beer after beer. Eventually, I stopped noticing the smell of the worms and the dankness and the film of dirt that had begun accumulating on our floors. It was disgusting, but I didn't care enough to change it.

When the flooding finally subsided and we emerged from

our homes to start the rebuilding, there was a shared sense of relief. So much damage was around us that it was easy to believe the universe couldn't possibly muster something bigger and meaner. Surely the gods weren't that cruel. Perhaps, we thought, we'd been spared the big storm. The damage before us was bad, but it wasn't catastrophic. We were cautiously hopeful.

Among the Subcommittee members, there was measured excitement. The melting snow meant that we had been given another chance to move forward with our runoff route plans. The Isole Creek had flooded just enough to demonstrate the urgent point we were trying to make, and it compelled several more affected landowners to consent to the plan. We were very close to getting agreement from everyone, which meant there was a possibility that digging could start by the time the waters dried. The remaining holdouts were Crow, two other preppers and an unoccupied estate that was managed through a trust in Connecticut. Salty was in charge of navigating the legal labyrinth of the estate, while Peg and I were tasked with turning the preppers.

As soon as the roads seemed passable again, I called Peg to ask when we would resume our home visits.

"Does tomorrow at four work for you?" she said, sounding distracted. "I've got a full day of classes to teach and I'm afraid I can't find time before that."

"Yes, that works fine. See you then!" I was looking for a reason to leave my house at that very moment, but it would have to wait. The people around me had full, busy lives.

What I should have been doing was the work I was still being paid for, but that wasn't going to happen. Over the previous week, my work performance had gone from barely passable to obviously inadequate. My coworkers in New York had lived through the storm and subsequent flooding, too, but they all seemed to bounce right back into productivity when the office reopened. Not me. When I opened my laptop that morning and tried to write a memo for a new ad campaign, nothing came. The job itself felt futile. No, it felt stupid—utterly meaningless. I was beginning to hate myself for having worked for so long at something so insignificant. I knew how dangerous this thinking was to our survival and tried to talk myself out of it, but logic was losing out to my fatalism.

On the last day of January, I stepped out into a bright, warm sun to see the water on our lawn still four inches deep. It was uninviting, but I needed to get out, so I put on one rain boot and a fresh plastic bag over the medical boot and hobbled through the path in the woods to August's house. We hadn't seen each other in two days and I was eager to hear his voice.

"Hey, buddy," I said as he opened the door in soccer shorts. "Put some clothes on and we'll go exploring."

August looked nervously over his shoulder to where his mother sat reading at the kitchen table. She was wearing a bathrobe and a colorful turban of vaguely ethnic origin wrapped around her head.

"I can't," August whispered.

His mother stood up and walked toward us in the doorway. Liz, that was her name. I remembered it now.

"Hello, Ash," she said coldly. "How'd you guys fare in the storm?"

It was a neighborly question, though she didn't seem interested in my answer.

"Look—" she put her hand out to interrupt me and went on "—I know you think you're doing a good thing here by looking after August, but we're just fine. And I don't like what I'm hearing about these aggressive government tactics that you're involved with."

"What?" I asked. I was dumbfounded.

"You think you can take my son away and dig trenches through everyone's backyard. You and John Salting and the rest of them think you know what's best for everyone, don't you."

It wasn't a question. At first, I didn't understand why she was conflating August with the runoff plan, but it came to me slowly: she thought I was the enemy. The Storm was drawing lines through the community and I had been assigned to a different faction. She was an individualist and I was a paternalist. No one could be trusted.

She began to close the front door, edging me back out to the stoop. August's eyes watched me for as long as they could before he was sealed off inside with his terrible parents. But he didn't really know they were terrible. They were his parents and he was seven, so they defined reality for him. It made me sick to think that August may have believed what they said about me.

I waded back along the submerged path to our house and down the driveway toward our car, confused and fuming. I needed to get out, to go somewhere and get my mind off what had just happened. I couldn't discuss it with Pia.

I needed a distraction but dreaded seeing what damage might have been done to our car over the course of the recent storm. On the night the snow began, while I was at the hospital, Pia had pulled the car off to the side of the road to be buried and possibly ruined by town plows, fallen trees and any number of variables she hadn't bothered to consider. It had become a new source of simmering rage I suppressed, like the worms but more financially consequential.

To my great surprise, the Volvo seemed to be okay. The

floor had flooded and its wet odor would later turn into a moldy, immutable stench, but for now it smelled like freedom. I turned the key in the ignition, considering too late the possibility that I might be electrocuted. Mercifully, I was not. It ignited and with a few aggressive thrusts to the gas pedal, I pulled the car out of our ditch and onto the muddy, wrecked dirt road. I had heard all the radio reports of stuck cars and knew that going out was probably ill-advised. But staying in that house was not an option. I was anxious and angry after the confrontation with August's mother.

When I finally reached the main, paved road, I realized that I had no particular destination in mind, so I headed toward downtown and decided that my first task would be grocery shopping. Few vehicles were on the road and most looked significantly more equipped for treacherous terrain than mine. We raised our hands from our steering wheels to say gracious hellos and crept past one another. Despite the efforts of state highway crews, which were out in full force, large branches were scattered across the road, along with the occasional car part. I nearly drove into an oncoming truck to avoid a dismembered bumper at the crest of one hill. A grim obstacle course juxtaposed the cheery blue sky. Strangest of all were the dead animals: a fisher, two white-tailed deer and something so small that it may have been a field mouse. It wasn't roadkill; there were no signs of collision. These were just dead animals lying in and around the road. After the first two, I worked to avert my gaze from their eyes. They looked stunned, terrified. I thought of the birds, fallen dead on our roof in the previous snowstorm. They'd had the same expression on their tiny bird faces. All the wildlife around me seemed confused, afraid. I considered that this was a fabrication of my own mind, projecting anxieties onto thoughtless creatures. But did it matter either way? This *was* terrifying, whether they knew it or not.

As I turned the corner for the main road, I passed the run-down old church that sat on the corner. I had never seen anyone come or go from that church, but they must have had a congregation of some size because there was a large sign out front—the kind that cheap steak houses use to advertise specials—with a message that changed regularly. I noticed that there was a new message blaring at me in uppercase letters on that day: THE *REAL* STORM IS COMING. WE HAVE NOT FELT HIS FULL WRATH YET. This was, more or less, what the meteorologists on the radio were saying, too.

When I pulled into the food co-op, I saw the rusty BMW always parked there along with a few other cars. I was grateful to return to all the familiar and ordinary aspects of my daily life. I also realized that I was hungry—really, really hungry. Maybe they'd have the lemon blueberry scones, I thought. I could forget about August and the dead animals and focus on the scones.

I always felt a swell of affection when I walked into the crowded little co-op with its funky smell and aloof earth-girl cashiers. This was why we lived here! I pulled back the creaky door to find that the floor was still wet there, too. It was disgusting, but everything was kind of disgusting that week as North America dried out. Reggaeton music was playing faintly in the background and a few other people milled around. Most of the shelves had yet to be replenished, but there was plenty to choose from for someone with no particular needs. Lucky for me, the baker had arrived that morning and a sensuous pile of nubby muffins and scones was stacked on the counter. I took a few pastries and then walked around slowly with no place to be. I gathered almond milk, cereal, tortilla chips and salsa. Nonperishables were better because you never know.

I stood in front of the frozen-food case for a while, considering which variety of microwave burrito was worth investing in when I heard a muffled sniffle. A woman was crying behind me. I didn't turn around, but I could see her reflection in the glass case in front of me. She looked about fifty, petite in knee-high rain boots and a purple windbreaker. She was crying into a tissue in front of the frozen edamame and broccoli florets. If she noticed me, she didn't show it.

"Frozen peas. Green beans. Who cares?" she said to herself. "Why am I still pretending like any of this still matters?"

I didn't move.

She heaved out loud in a full-body sob, this time attracting the attention of someone else in the store, a young woman who peered around the corner of the aisle.

"Does this still matter," the woman yelled again, not as a question, but a statement.

The bereft woman opened the glass door and began throwing bags of frozen vegetables at her feet. They stacked neatly until a sack of sliced carrots exploded and the other woman who had been watching ran over. She put her arms around the crying older one and shushed her in a manner that seemed condescending to me, but worked. I was facing them now and had that expectant look on my face that people have when they wish to appear helpful but secretly hope someone else does the helping.

"*Shushhh,*" the young woman said again while the older one let out one final sob into the shoulder of this apparent stranger.

I just stood there. I wanted the whole episode to be over, not only because it was awkward, but also because it was frightening. This woman didn't seem crazy or drunk. She seemed like a nice motherly lady who was terrified, and that terrified me. I needed all the nice mothers of the world to be brave and optimistic then. I thought about my own mother, the inventor of motherly bravery and optimism, and vowed to call her soon. Or should she be calling me? Why doesn't she call me more? No doubt, she's completely preoccupied with my needy brother and my sister's kids, I thought. I resented my siblings for the distance that had grown between me and my parents, knowing full well that the distance was a product of my own inaction.

The woman stopped crying and I bent down to help them pick up the vegetables. Another man about my age who had wandered over during the commotion joined us on the floor. His curly blond hair was pulled back into a bun, which looked surprisingly cool on such a masculine guy. I envied the effortless wear on his fleece jacket and imagined that he rock climbed in his spare time. We looked up at each other briefly, saying nothing, and it was clear that he had been rattled by the episode, as well. Had he been crying, too? His eyes were red and his face puffy.

When most of the carrots had been collected, I stood up quickly and nearly ran for the door. Waiting in line behind the crying woman or bun man to pay for my groceries seemed too much at that moment. I needed air. So I left my half-filled basket in the aisle and walked out.

It felt as if I might hyperventilate as I climbed into my car, unsure of where to go next. Why did the man in the store look so scared? I knew why. He was scared because that woman was crying, and she was crying for the same reason we all wanted to. We couldn't live in this perpetual state of fearful anticipation that The Storm suspended us in. It wasn't healthy or sustainable. Our nerves would break before It even arrived.

Breathe in. Breathe out. Breath in. Breathe out.

I turned the key in the ignition and pulled out of the parking lot slowly, unsure of my destination. A few more cars were on the road by then and it was noticeably warmer than it had been twenty minutes before. *Everything is fine*, I reminded myself. I rolled past a bustling gas station and the firehouse. *Everything is fine.*

As I neared the high school, I fell in line behind a row of cars all waiting to turn left into the parking lot. I couldn't imagine what so many people would be doing there—schools hadn't reopened yet since the last storm—so I craned my head around to get a look. A group was gathering around the front doors, but it was too far away for me to discern what they were doing. With nowhere else to go, I followed the cars in front of me and pulled into the lot. Massive piles of melting snow were heaped around the perimeter, where the plows had pushed the excess. It created a sort of coliseum.

As I drew closer, I could see that a few people were holding handmade signs and chanting.

"Hope in God! Hope in God!" they yelled.

I left the car and walked as quickly as I could with a bum foot toward the action to get a better look. A group of people, old and young, surrounded the front doors of the high school. They were dressed shabbily in camouflage and hunters orange. I imagined that most were from once-thriving small farms that had slowly dried up, leaving the remaining generations with few resources and much anger. I felt sympathy for these Vermonters—even a pang of jealousy at their utter *real*ness—but I didn't know any of them personally. At the center of their circle was Roger, crazy Roger, the one who pulled out the gun at the meeting and was escorted off in handcuffs. He was again in handcuffs, but this time they were attached to the front doors of the school. He was a protester and these were his supporters. I could see their signs now; the smaller ones all repeated their "hope in God" mantra. One very large banner required a handler at each end and had a bible verse on it: "Out of the south cometh the whirlwind: and a cold out of the north." —*Job* 37:9. It was a pretty uncanny fit for the actual superstorm forecast.

A police officer whom I recognized from the town hall meeting stood nearby.

"What is this?" I asked.

"Rodney Riggins," he said. "You know, that evangelist or whatever he is. There was a town vote over whether he should be allowed to host one of his talks here at the school, and the Riggins people lost, so they've decided to make a federal case out of it."

The crowd was growing bigger as we talked; apparently word of the kerfuffle was spreading around town. I saw a local newspaper reporter waving a microphone; he looked about sixteen.

"I'm just keeping an eye on things," the officer went on. "They aren't breaking any laws at the moment."

I nodded. It was difficult to imagine any civil disobedience in Isole that rose to the level of police force, but stranger things had been happening lately.

"We need a voice!" one woman shouted. "Who represents the God-fearing people of Isole?"

"Government should be by the people, for the people," a man shouted. "We need more God in government—now more than ever."

The reporter put his microphone in front of the man's face and asked, "What exactly are you protesting here? Is this about the vote to host Rodney Riggins?"

"Heck, yes, it's about the vote," the man said. "The vote was rigged! Where are our rights?"

I stood watching for another moment before an oncoming roar shifted my attention. An enormous pickup truck pulled into the parking lot, jacked up high over wheels as tall as an adult human and splattered with mud. It was blasting a power ballad out the front windows. When the truck got dangerously close, it slammed on the brakes and cranked the music up even further. There was a dramatic electric guitar swell, and then—*bam*—with a crash of drums, a smiling man popped to his feet from the back of the truck and the protest crowd broke into applause.

It was Rodney Riggins. He wore work pants, a neat-fitting blue sweater and hiking boots. His lustrous coif, parted on the left side, gleamed in the sun as he turned and waved to the crowd like a rock star about to start his set. Despite the filthy appearance of the truck that carried him, Riggins looked dewy fresh.

He knocked on the glass window of his driver's cab to signal for him to kill the music. When it stopped, Riggins shook his head in false modesty and waited for the rowdy crowd of protesters and onlookers below to quiet.

"I apologize for the dramatic entry!" he yelled, climbing down from the truck. "I was getting a tour of the damages from the storm. It's hell out there…but this is nothing compared with what's ahead."

Riggins walked toward the crowd. "Were you scared? I was. The suddenness of the storm…the uncertainty…it's frightening. But I'll tell you, it's not so bad when you've got the Big Man on your side."

He stopped just a few feet from me and I thought I could smell cologne on his repellent body.

"You've heard that God helps those who help themselves, right? That's all we're doing here in Isole," Riggins said, briefly locking eyes with me. "We're getting prepared and we're putting a little faith in God that he's going to reward us for our smarts when the superstorm strikes."

The policeman stepped forward and cut in, "Sir, we've got no problems with God. I just want all these good folks to go home. Is all this your doing?"

Riggins ignored the question. "Let's open up these school doors!" he boomed. "Let's open up the doors in our hearts and start preparing ourselves for this test we're about to face. We'll be okay, and the great town of Isole will be okay, with a little hope in God!"

The protest group, which had doubled in size by then, began chanting, "Hope in God! Hope in God!" and Riggins smiled his big perfect smile.

The onlookers had increased in number, as well. I saw Salty and several of the town elders standing nearby. One of them said quietly, "Maybe it's less disruptive if we just allow this nonsense… Surely the school district will let them have the auditorium for a night or two."

"I don't think we should do it," Salty responded. "They lost the vote. It's undemocratic."

I recognized the recent inconsistencies in Salty's approach to democracy but didn't feel particularly disturbed by them. Maybe I should have. I knew that it wasn't quite right to be making municipal decisions in secret as the Subcommittee was, but the old rules didn't seem to apply anymore.

A rowdier group of spectators on the far side from us had begun arguing with the protesters. I couldn't tell what they were saying, but I recognized three of the people from Pia's prepper meeting. They were hollering at one another now and the energy level in the crowd was escalating.

"Your God isn't worth shit!" one of the male preppers yelled, provoking a crazy-eyed protester to break from the

MEG LITTLE REILLY

circle and shove the man, who took a few stumbling steps and fell hard on his backside.

This caused the entire crowd to begin yelling, with some calling for the police to help and others, aroused by the violence, looking for their own opportunity to join in. The lone police officer on-site called for backup and stepped into the ring to intimidate the aggressive characters. As soon as this happened, the flash of a professional camera went off: one, two, three. The reporter was getting his story.

"You don't scare me!" the prepper yelled at the cop. "That badge isn't going to be worth anything when all hell breaks loose! Enjoy your power now, fat man!"

This wasn't just a pejorative cliché, but a statement of fact. The policeman was enormous, which made it seem all the meaner. I wanted to jump in and help the officer, but it wasn't clear who the aggressors were.

"All right, then," Riggins said calmly, as if his voice alone would be a cooling sedative to the crowd. "Let's keep it neighborly."

Rodney Riggins was a fast study, and there was no doubt that he had mastered the look and accent of the locals. But he had a slow swagger about him that gave him away as an outsider. It astounded me that anyone could see anything other than a phony, a desperate actor, when they looked at him in his unscuffed boots. But he filled a void at that moment in Isole and he'd made allies.

"You're not Jesus!" someone yelled at Riggins and I stifled a laugh at the assertion. It didn't come from one of the preppers, but one of the unaffiliated onlookers. "Go back to where you came from! We don't need you here."

Several others hollered and clapped in agreement and I saw a look flash across the officer's face as he realized that the scene might become too much for one cop to handle.

Just then, another police cruiser pulled in and three more cops jumped out, slamming their doors forcefully.

An officer raised a piece of paper to the air and said, "Shut it down. He's in violation of parole."

She was referring to Crazy Roger, who maybe was a drug addict but didn't actually seem crazy at all at that moment. He was one of the few in the crowd who, although chained to the door, seemed peaceful as he observed the chaos around him.

"No, no, no, no, no!" Roger shouted. He was angrier now but seemed to recognize the inevitability of his arrest.

"'Fraid so, Rogg," the cop said while she and the larger one worked to break his handcuffs with a wrench.

Several protesters tried to stop them, but they submitted after being held back, uncommitted to the idea of assaulting a police officer.

The onlookers wandered back to their cars and drove away as the excitement abated. In the corner of my eye, I saw a flashbulb catch Salty wiping sweat from his forehead, and I was struck by how deeply he felt everything that happened to Isole.

Two officers pushed Roger to the ground while another called something in on the radio. Roger kicked one of the officers in the stomach and the man doubled over, losing his grip on Roger and leaving the first officer alone to deal with him. I was only a few strides away and hobbled over to help.

Roger kicked some more, until I squatted down beside him and he saw my face. He stopped moving.

"Hey, it's you," Roger said. "Mr. Hero-New-Guy. What the fuck do you want from this place anyhow?"

I was so startled by his recognition of me that I couldn't think of an answer.

"I...I don't want anything. I live here," I said.

"Why'd you do this, Roger?" the cop asked, now with

compassion in her voice. It was clear that he was well-known by the local force.

"Gotta believe in something at the end," Roger said. "It ain't gonna be me. And it ain't gonna be government. So maybe it's God."

Roger turned back to me. He was sitting calmly on the ground now. His clothes smelled like stale cigarettes and urine.

"I hate it here, man," Roger went on. "I don't know why anyone would want to come here. If I could get out, find a job, I would. You nice, do-gooder types want to try to control the chaos that's going to break out when The Storm comes…make this place nice again after it all blows up. It's not so nice."

One of the cops opened the cruiser door nearby and gestured for us to hoist him inside. I was relieved to be freed of that moment, looking at Roger, smelling his rank clothes and imagining what Isole was like from his perspective. My fantasy hamlet was his vacuum of opportunity. He went into the car easily and waved to the crowd who were enjoying a brief moment of fame before whatever consequences awaited him.

With Roger's exit, the crowd thinned quickly. I saw Riggins giving a pep talk to his followers, vowing not to give up on their important cause and promising more opportunities to make their case to the town. Eventually, even the protesters started to say their goodbyes and migrate toward their cars. I just stood there watching it all, in no hurry to leave but no longer serving any purpose. Salty paced nearby, talking quietly into his cell phone. Roger was right about "do-gooder types" working to control the chaos; that was Salty. But what else was there to do?

Suddenly, I felt a hand on my shoulder and spun around. It was Riggins, smiling as if we knew each other.

"Hey there, friend," he said. The word had never sounded so malevolent. "You're Salty's buddy, right? No reason we can't all work together on this. We all just want the best for Isole."

"You shouldn't be here, manipulating these people," I said.

"I'm here because they want me here," Riggins replied calmly. "*These people* are smarter than you give them credit for. They don't need your protection. Let them choose."

He was a little right, which made me hate him even more.

"You're using an invented religion to sell them something," I said. "You're an opportunist, a snake-oil salesman. You don't care about anything here and we both know it."

I was surprised by my own venom.

"Look, Ash… It's Ash, right?" Riggins had dropped the pretense of a fake Yankee accent and seemed entirely himself now. "I'm using a spiritual philosophy to sell them something they need. How could that be bad? It's not altruism, but it's not a crime either. What are you offering them?"

Salty walked over to us and I could feel Riggins reapply his man-of-God face. He said goodbye as though we'd been having a good-natured chat and walked off before there was time to say more.

"Isole doesn't need this, not now," Salty said. "We can't be dividing up at a time when we need to be banding together. I don't understand what's happening. I didn't see this coming."

Salty shook his head back and forth. He was talking to no one in particular and didn't need a response. There was nothing for me to say, but I vowed silently to continue to help Salty in whatever way I could. I had never committed to anything the way he was committed to his community and I was beginning to appreciate why it mattered. Salty had a full life. It was full in the way my father's life was full, full of things that I mistook for provincial clutter instead of real texture. Family, neighbors he cared about, land he'd grown up on. He loved it all, and it loved him back, which didn't happen without some heartache.

"Well, I should get back to work." Salty sighed. "At least all this is over."

He looked at the school, which was again quiet. The day's drama was over, but we both knew nothing—nothing—had been resolved.

SIXTEEN

"AND THEN, I swear to God, the guy pops up out of the back of a monster truck!" I took a gulp of Scotch through my laughter and slammed the glass down dramatically.

I was sitting at Peg's kitchen table around five, the day after the incident at the high school, drinking my third glass of Scotch and laughing harder than I had in many months. We had gone to visit one of the holdouts on our flood plan earlier that night, which was entirely unproductive. The wife refused to let us in the house and the husband threatened to get his shotgun, so we had no choice but to leave. Instead, we went back to Peg's house for deer jerky and drinks, which was just fine with me. I still had no idea what I was contributing to the operation and dreaded the confrontations with the homeowners. Peg's patience was running low, too. I didn't know her well, but she seemed sadder and more detached than the Peg I had met a few months before. I couldn't put my finger on it, but there was a change.

As soon as I sat down at her kitchen table, I launched into a detailed description of the entire scene that had unfolded at the high school with Rodney Riggins. She listened with rapt attention, laughing and nodding along at all the right parts.

"These are exceptional times in Isole," she said when I was through. "Such histrionics are not common around here. I think everyone's on edge."

Peg looked out the open window as she said this, toward the naked oak branches. It was February 1, but in my whole life I'd never seen a February that looked like this. The snow had all melted and the flooding was mostly dried up. The silence of winter was still there, but the temperature reached fifty-two that day. The most reliable seasonal identifiers had abandoned us. It was a lull between the last storm and the next one.

"This Riggins guy is bad news," I said.

Peg waved a hand to dismiss him. "Oh, I think he'll be gone before The Storm is over. I'm sure there are more profitable places for him to move on to."

I hoped she was right.

"And what about you, Ash? Do you have a god for when the reckoning comes?"

I thought for a moment. "No, not really. I grew up going to church on Christmas, and sometimes Easter, but that was it. I never really had religion, so it wasn't something I ever missed. But I guess I believe in God, whatever that means. You?"

"Well, I'm a Catholic, technically," Peg said in an exaggerated Irish brogue.

"Technically?"

"Yes, technically. But my spirituality is more complicated than that; it goes back further in history."

Peg looked out the window and paused. She might have been a little drunk, too. She went on, "The earth, the trees, the fae…"

I couldn't tell how serious she was. "Is this an Irish thing?" I joked.

"Yes, kind of," she said, unoffended. "Before the church came into Ireland, the Irish lived in close connection with the earth and its spirits. Since then we've all just been pretending not to be pagan witches and descendants of fairies."

I raised my eyebrows. "A scientist who believes in fairies?"

"Don't get distracted by the word. I'm talking about a belief in the earth's innate power. It always felt true to me." Peg shrugged. "And it isn't an opposing theory to science. I'm a scientist *because* of the fairies. I grew up in the country, spent all of my time alone in the woods or on the shore. I knew the natural world like a close friend—and because we lived in such a remote area, I didn't have many of those. Ash, I became a scientist because I have always felt a sort of supernatural connection with the earth. I wanted to study it and know it. But I'll always remember that there are unknowable things about nature. That's the supernatural part. Science only takes you so far and I love that."

Peg let out a long, labored sigh and took another sip of Scotch.

"That's why I live here," she went on, sadder. "I moved to Isole because it was the closest I had ever come to feeling that vibration of nature around me, the one I grew up with. But it's not going to last."

"Why?" I asked. "Because of The Storm?"

"Yes, this storm, and all the storms that come after. It's changing, Ash." A tear streamed down Peg's face as she took another sip and forced a smile. "Don't worry about me," she said. "I'm fine. I get sad sometimes lately...when I think about it all. It makes me feel...alone."

I didn't feel equipped to understand her entirely, but I knew about feeling alone.

Peg wiped her eyes, poured a little more Scotch for both of us and raised her glass.

"To the fairies!" she said.

"To the fairies."

I wandered home soon after that final toast, thinking about everything Peg had said. The vibration she reportedly felt in nature was a startling concept that stayed with me. I think my younger self, the one who spent an entire childhood exploring the woods around my house and diving deep into the science of our wilderness, knew what she was talking about. Grown-up me had a more difficult time with it.

I wondered, too, if all this was why Peg had never married or had children: because she was in love with the land. Can that possibly be an adequate substitute for human relationships? I knew enough to know that I wasn't fit to make that judgment. Peg seemed like one of the most fulfilled and complete people I had ever met. It occurred to me then that she never asked about my marriage. I think she suspected that things were complicated with Pia and that I needed a friend. I imagined that she and I could talk about these things one day.

I felt deeply grateful to Peg as I hobbled home in the slushy warmth, feeling as though we'd shared a secret. It was a sad sort of secret, but Peg had revealed something to me and I was grateful for the closeness it intimated.

When I got home, Pia surprised me by having cooked a proper meal. I was greeted at the front door by a familiar waft of greasy deliciousness: truffle mac and cheese. It was a go-to of Pia's from when we used to host dinner parties in Brooklyn, designed to seem both casual and refined. She would serve it in large, oozing blocks, with a handful of lightly dressed arugula piled on top. We were extra in love on those nights, with Pia shining as the star of the domestic show, our friends around us and aspirations still unmet.

"The social worker called," she said as I opened the fridge for a beer. She appeared to be focusing closely on setting silverware around the table. "Everything's all set for August with that other family. They're going to move him on Wednesday."

This was why Pia had made me dinner. I wasn't hungry anymore, but I appreciated her effort.

We ate quietly and politely, forks clinking against plates and throats choking down sips. All the sounds of the room seemed magnified. The cheese was too leaden for my stomach, but I swallowed most of what I had been served. When finally it was over, Pia suggested we leave the dishes and just go relax in the living room. It occurred to me how quickly we had adjusted to this once-impossible luxury of having a living space large enough to just leave messes intact in other rooms. You just walk away from the dirty dishes, to a place where you can't see or smell them, and it's like they don't exist at all. How had this become so normal so quickly, I wondered.

Pia was stretched long on the couch with her eyes closed when I met her in the living room. She looked so pretty lying there in loungewear and rumpled hair. Her cheeks were pink from being outside and her lashes long. It seemed remarkable that I could still feel so attracted to someone I had such knotty feelings about, but I did. I wanted to peel her tight pants off her body and see if we could still be together in the way that we used to. We hadn't had sex in over a month and I'd been left to my own devices for too long. I didn't want to talk to her; I just wanted to be with her body. I wanted the closeness of anyone that night.

Just then her eyes opened and I had the distinct sensation that she had been reading my mind. She smiled and I smiled back. Yes, maybe this is happening, I thought. I took a risk and went to her on the couch, leaning down to kiss her. She accepted my kiss, so I slid on top of her, slowly as if she might ignite at any moment and I would need to spring to safety. We didn't linger long on the kiss—that's for people who enjoy one another's company. Instead, our mouths wandered hungrily. My body came to attention and, right on cue, her hand slid down to measure my lust.

We began tugging out of our clothes, wasting little effort on seduction, just taking care of our own layers and meeting back on the lumpy couch, naked. I liked sex like this. It was savage and impatient. We were good at it. Maybe, I thought, we hadn't drifted so far from each other after all. Maybe it was all still there; we just needed to work harder. I could work harder. I was still a little drunk from the Scotch, but it wasn't just the Scotch. I needed to believe that when disaster struck, I would weather The Storm with my wife. We were in this together and we'd be stronger on the other side. My survival depended on that belief.

She was riding wildly on top of me, her perfect breasts moving rhythmically with her, when I pulled her face down to mine and, without thinking, whispered, "I love you, Pia. Let's start our own family."

It was the last hopeful card I still held: making children, children that were new and uncomplicated and ours. We could go back to the fertility clinic and start making some babies and living this dream out as planned.

She pulled her face away from mine and I saw that she looked horrified.

"Oh my God, what's wrong with you?" Pia said, dismounting and curling up in a ball at the foot of the couch. "We can't have children! How can we bring children into this world? It's poisoned. The air, the water, the soil, the fucking weather. How can you not see that?"

I considered reaching for my pants, but I wasn't prepared to admit that the moment had ended.

"I thought that's what you wanted, Pia," I said, working to sound calm.

She shook her head. "I thought that's what I wanted, too—six months ago. But that may as well have been a million years ago, before any of us knew how messed up things were. I need to focus now on getting prepared, taking care of us. I thought you understood that!"

She was angry.

"I don't understand anything—obviously!" I screamed, jumping up to pull my boxers on. "You've lost your fucking mind with all of the end-of-the-world shit! There are worms living in my house, for Christ's sake!"

She rolled her eyes, "Don't start again with the worms. I thought you liked the worms."

"I like the worms more than those paranoid lunatics you hang out with in your prepper meetings! So yes, I guess the worms are my favorite of all your current associates!"

Pia jumped off the couch, stark naked, and walked over to the giant worm box at the other side of the living room. It had become a piece of furniture, accumulating books, catalogs and an old water glass. She used her forearm to push everything off the edge, breaking the glass on the floor. She unlatched the lid and pulled it open, releasing a fresh waft of earthy stink. With one hand, Pia reached in and pulled out a mound of dark, writhing dirt. Worms were sliding around her fingers and dropping to her feet, but she didn't seem to notice. She walked past me and opened a window with her free hand. With a slight windup, Pia threw the handful of worm dirt out the window, then went back for another, and another.

I watched as she threw handfuls of worms out into the

MEG LITTLE REILLY

yard, leaving a messy path of moist soil between the worm box and the window. And that was the point: it was a show for me. It meant that I was cruel for hating her worms; or maybe it meant that she felt misunderstood; or maybe it just meant that she really had lost her mind. I wanted her to stop, but I wouldn't break so easily. I even felt a pang of guilt for the worms she'd banished to the outdoors. They hadn't asked to join our broken household. But I wasn't going to let her win.

After a few more dramatic trips to the window, I calmly wrestled her away from the worm box and closed the lid. I hoped that she'd cry, just crumple into a puddle and end the scene, but instead she stood before me, quiet and wide-eyed. We looked at each other for a moment, me towering over her naked body. Then she brought her hands up in front of her—they were coated in the nutrient-dense worm soil—and slowly dragged them down the front of my bare chest, leaving two cold trails of black dirt on my body.

We both contemplated our next move, and then Pia just walked out of the room. I heard her pad upstairs and slam a door. It sounded like a satisfied door slam, the slam of someone who'd just made her point assertively and creatively. Though I was shivering and filthy, I wouldn't give her the satisfaction of a big response. I walked to the kitchen and quietly wiped my bare chest with a dirty dish towel. Then, taking another beer from the fridge, I sat down at the table and chugged it. Having already been drunk and sober again on that day, the beer wasn't particularly pleasurable, but I was way past any expectation of pleasure.

When the bottle was empty, I hoisted my healing foot up onto the table for an inspection. It didn't hurt much anymore, but I had become preoccupied with its progress nonetheless. The area below my ankle was turning from purple to a sickly yellow and some of the tenderness around my toes seemed to be diminishing. But it didn't feel as though my foot was getting any stronger. Instead, it seemed as if I was slowly losing all feeling and control. Maybe it would be best to remove the dead appendage and replace it with a prosthetic, I considered. I certainly couldn't walk around with a dead foot. What if the death spread up my leg, or farther? It seemed a possibility and not one worth risking a useless foot on. I decided to make a return visit to the hospital sometime soon for a follow-up discussion about what was to become of the dead foot.

I waited twenty minutes before taking a shower and slipping into bed beside my sleeping wife. It seems strange to me now that we slept beside each other at the end of those contentious days, but sleeping apart would have been an admission of real change, an official shift in our marriage, and I wasn't ready for that. There was so much change still ahead that I wanted desperately to maintain sameness wherever possible. We had no idea then what a silly impulse that would prove to be.

SEVENTEEN

"GOOD MORNING. It's the ninth day of February and this is your weekly White House Weather Briefing. We begin today with some very promising news for the eastern seaboard…"

It was Saturday morning and I was sitting at the kitchen table, drinking coffee and listening to public radio. Pia sat quietly in the living room doing the same. It had been more than a week since our last fight, the last time we physically touched, the last discussion of the worms that continued to stink up the house. Isole's sky had been dark and drizzly for that time, pressing down on the whole region with a humid hopelessness.

It was work to avoid feeling as depressed as the weather and my circumstances demanded. When I wasn't at my computer, I was walking, trying to strengthen my foot, which was recovering albeit slowly. I replaced the medical boot with a smaller Ace bandage, and the only shoes that fit over it were my snow boots, which were hot in that weather. I took hour-long walks through the woods, across neighbors' property, down logging roads that led to nowhere. Sometimes

I would be out until dark and find myself guided only by the glow of the cloudy sky. Those walks were cathartic, but unsettling, too. I was afraid of reinjuring myself and being left to die alone in the woods.

Scarier than that was the absence of life. There were no birds or small mammals, only insects. Despite the fact that it was February, the temperature hovered around sixty. The mosquitoes seemed to be multiplying and growing in size. Apparently, that was happening everywhere. I had read about an outbreak of dengue fever in Bangladesh, spread by mosquitoes. I studied the magazine image of the *Aedes aegypti* mosquito closely, memorizing the white markings on its legs and the spot on its thorax, just in case I might happen upon one in northern Vermont. It wasn't an outrageous theory—freaky things were happening around the world in those days.

An outbreak of malaria in Florida killed a handful of people quickly, and the incidents of Lyme disease in the Northeast had skyrocketed, which was unheard of this time of year. Insects were thriving in the new climate; they were the only winners at the expense of every other living thing. I wore netting around my head and waded through the swampy land trying hard not to think about why it was so damn swampy in February in Vermont.

August would have enjoyed those walks, but he was gone. Bev The Social Worker had driven him three miles down the road to the McGregor house, where he was to stay indefinitely. August cried and he fought her as she wrestled him into the car the previous week. It was the worst thing I had ever seen, almost worse than the images in my head when we thought he was dead in the woods. As he fought and cursed to stay with his terrible parents—who were high as fucking kites as they kissed him goodbye—I felt as if I was watching the extraordinary dreamer child I had grown to love transform into a hard, angry kid in the system. It was a death of its own kind, except that this time, we'd been the ones to kill him, all of us.

I turned up the radio to drown out my thoughts and sat down at the kitchen table. Pia was drinking coffee in the living room.

"With some new information we've received, we're revising our storm forecast," the nation's chief climatologist went on. His voice had become that of a familiar authority figure—we reviled him but remained utterly at his mercy. "It appears that things may not be as dire as our long-range forecast originally suggested. The current warming—be it natural or driven by humans—may work in our favor. You see, the tropical storm that is expected to gather off the gulf is still on track to become a hurricane at landfall. But the arctic air that we expected around the same time from Canada and the Midwest now looks like it won't be quite so cold. It could warm and dissipate by the time it reaches New England, sparing us the devastating storm collision we had originally feared. We've probably still got a fairly large hurricane on the way, which could do some harm from the Carolinas all the way up to New Jersey. But in the face of what we expected, this is a dramatic upgrade. All of this is forecast to occur in about six days. Things are changing rapidly and we strongly encourage Americans to continue to take the necessary precautions. But this is generally good news."

"The Storm isn't coming," I said aloud. "This is our reprieve. The sun will come out and our drowning land will dry out and we will get back to normal." This means, I thought, the storm could release its hold on my wife and we could begin to rebuild things between us. My heart was racing. The coffee was too strong and my head throbbed from the previous night's beers, all of which heightened the weightlessness I was suddenly feeling.

"That's a lot of bullshit," Pia said as she walked into the kitchen, dropping her mug in the sink. "They're just worried about the markets crashing and people freaking out. They're trying to get a handle on things. It's bullshit and it probably means that The Storm is going to be even worse."

It was the first time she had spoken directly to me in days, but I could barely hear her. And at that moment, I felt too optimistic to argue. Of course she didn't believe this new information. She *needed* The Storm. Her guiding purpose in life had become preparation for The Storm. Her identity had been refashioned in relationship to it. The Storm explained away all of her obsessive behavior. Without The Storm, those obsessions were syndromes, things with labels in the DSM and cleverly named designer drugs. A more attentive me, one from months before, would have worried terribly about this behavior. But I wasn't that husband any longer. She was sick, but she was also an asshole, and I was tired of using one to excuse the other. The thrilling thought occurred to me for the very first time that maybe we should end this. *We could both start over.* It was only a fleeting idea and I didn't allow myself to dwell on it, but it flashed before me, leaving a faint puff of hope before disappearing entirely. We would never do that.

I ignored Pia and walked upstairs to pull on gym shorts and a T-shirt. I had arranged to pick August up that morning to play basketball at the high school gym, and I wasn't going to be late. It felt strange to make a formal date to see him, but these were the new terms and I still held on to a distant dream of having a more formal role in his life one day, improbable as it seemed. I worried a lot about August disappearing again, too. This new foster family couldn't possibly anticipate when he was about to go missing. They wouldn't recognize the look in his eye when he needed to retreat into the woods. And he didn't know the woods by their house like he knew ours; he was more vulnerable there. I thought about him wearing his little blue backpack alone in the dark a lot in those days.

When I knocked on the McGregors' door ten minutes later, August opened it instantly, as if he'd been standing behind it all morning.

"Did you hear?" August asked. "The Storm's not going to come and everything's going to go back to normal!"

I wasn't sure what he meant, but he was happy, and so was I.

"Sounds like that might be right, buddy," I said. "Hey, I missed you."

"Yeah, me, too."

He was pulling the front door closed behind him, so I shouted "thank you!" through the open space, grateful not to have to meet his new fake parents.

"Your car smells gross," August said when we pulled onto the main road.

He was right. Ever since the big flood, it reeked of algae and old sneakers. Everything felt surprisingly normal.

"So how's it going at this new place?" I asked.

He shrugged. "They have a lot of food. And a trampoline. The older sister is weird. It's okay, I guess."

He didn't want to talk about it, so I didn't press him.

"Hey, did you hear?" he went on. "They're doing the Isole Festival this year! The Isole Festival is the best. You gotta come."

I had been reading about the controversy surrounding the festival in the *Isole Gazette*. Apparently, it was always held on the third Saturday in February, which was one week away, but it had been canceled that year after much debate. I had been mostly ignoring the headlines and local chatter about whether or not this was the right decision. No doubt the Isole Festival was an important day in the lives of its people, but it had no special meaning to me. It was just one sad story line among so many during that period. I couldn't muster the will to care.

But now, it was on. As if on cue, the sun had begun to peek through the low clouds above us, creating a sort of pink glow that was unsettling, but pretty. I decided to see it only as a sign of promise. The sun was coming out, and festivals were on again, and I was bumping along our ravaged roads with August!

"So, what's the deal with this festival, August? Why is it so fun?" I asked.

"Well," he said, annoyed by my ignorance, "there's a parade with music and floats, and a cross-country ski race and a big outside party where they serve sugar-on-snow and hot chocolate and stuff like that. It's only, like, the most important day here!"

His sarcasm made me smile.

"Sounds really cool. Maybe we could go together?"

"Sorry, I'm already going with Noah," he said, as if I should have expected that he would already have plans for this big day.

When we got to the high school, there were a few other cars parked near the gymnasium entrance, but I didn't see anyone around. As I pulled an old duffel bag filled with sneakers, a basketball and some water bottles out of the trunk, I heard someone run up behind me.

"Hi there!"

I spun around to find Maggie standing before me—Maggie, my startlingly pretty neighbor. It was only about

MEG LITTLE REILLY

fifty degrees outside, but she was wearing running shorts and a faded T-shirt with a reference to a road race from 2008 on it. Her red hair was pulled back in a loose ponytail and sweaty wisps had broken free around her face.

"Oh, hi! What are you doing here?" I didn't mean for it to sound so rude. I was excited.

"I just had to get out of the house after all the rain and darkness. The track is one of the only dry places in town, so I'm trying to burn off some energy. What about you? How's your foot?"

Maggie's face—her whole body, really—was radiating an energy that I wanted to bask in. It wasn't just fitness, which I envied so much at that moment, but also something more exuberant. It was uncomplicated and fresh.

"It's getting better," I said, opting not to tell her about my dead-foot theory. "Good enough to hobble through a few games of around the world."

"Fun!" Maggie said, looking at August now, who was growing impatient with the conversation that had nothing at all to do with him. "And how are you, August?"

August mumbled a greeting in return. I didn't know how they knew one another, but teachers have a talent for knowing everyone in their small town regardless of age and grade.

"You're welcome to join," I blurted out, feeling immediately stupid. I wondered if it was a strange invitation or insulting in some way.

"Sure, why not?" she said with a casual shrug.

"Whatever. Let's *go*," August pleaded.

She's coming, she's coming, she's coming. I didn't know quite how to behave, so I was grateful when August dragged us inside and bossily explained the rules of the game.

It was amazing to me, the way Maggie managed to be so buoyant and easygoing but not without depth. She was smart and interesting, too. She just seemed free of the angst I had come to associate with smart and interesting people. Angst was impressing me less and less by then. I was also intrigued by Maggie's unabashed *gladness* at such a gloomy time; it was a quiet protest against the doom and I wondered how she maintained it.

We played basketball for what felt like a long time. I was good, but not great—only slightly more skilled than Maggie, but enough not to feel as though I'd humiliated myself. She was a natural athlete, but not at all competitive. And she was so at ease that it was impossible not to feel the same way in her presence. At one point, we bumped into each other and I got a faint whiff of her sweating body, which I bottled up in my brain for later uncorking.

When we came to the end of the game, I racked my mind for a reason to linger, but August announced that he was hungry. I remembered that the outing was for his benefit, so the three of us walked back to the parking lot. At Maggie's car, I stopped and began bouncing the basketball, unsure of what to do with my body. A handshake seemed wrong, but so, too, was a hug.

"Thanks for playing a round with us," I said, opting to keep my hands on the ball. "We'll have to do it again sometime."

"Thanks for having me." She smiled. "Maybe next time I'll get you out on the slopes."

Out on the slopes. It was the sort of phrase that I could never have said without sounding like a jerk, but it sounded utterly cool coming from Maggie's lips.

"Definitely!" Did that sound too eager? I couldn't tell.

"Come *on*," August whined, saving us from another potentially awkward moment.

I waved and smiled one last time and hobble-jogged off behind August.

When we pulled onto the main road, he surprised me with a question: "Are you married?"

"You know that I am," I said.

August looked confused. "Is Miss Chase married?"

"No, I don't think so," I said, hating whatever it was that was happening.

"Are you allowed to talk to her?" he asked.

"I'm not sure what you mean, but I'm allowed to *talk* to anyone I want," I said, unable to hide my annoyance. "Talking is always okay between anyone. You know that, August."

"Okay, whatever," he said, looking out the window. His interest in the topic had already expired, the little imp.

We drove in silence along the dirt road until both of us were shaken abruptly out of our thoughts at the sight of what was ahead.

"Whoa, look!" August shouted as I slammed on the brakes, causing us to slide sideways in the mud for several feet.

It was a black bear cub, about the size of a large sheepdog, lumbering slowly across the road. It showed no recognition of our presence. We watched it stop, move in one direction and then another, seemingly looking for something. And then we saw it: with a few great strides the mother bear was right behind. She batted the cub's head and it rolled over joyfully before her. They were playing just a few feet from us! We sat perfectly still, both mesmerized by the scene. I had spotted bears a few times in my childhood, but never been granted such an extended and close view. They were incredible—at once life-size cuddle-toys and ferocious predators.

After a minute, I grew nervous for the exposed animals. We needed to get them off to the woods, before a car came barreling down from the other direction. I explained this to August and he nodded sternly, appreciating the gravity of the responsibility. So we honked, loud and long. Both bears got the message, glancing briefly at us and then disappearing into the woods.

"That was so awesome!" August yelled when they were gone. "I've never seen one up close!"

"Incredible, really incredible. We're so lucky."

"But, Ash," he said, "they should be hibernating, right?"

"It's technically a state of semi-hibernation," I said slowly, "but you're right that they do usually hibernate this time of year." I didn't want to tell him the truth. Our weather patterns are broken and the bears are confused because it's warm outside and their caves are flooded and their habitat may never be the same again. It's happening to bears all over the world, actually.

I lied instead. "Maybe those particular bears woke up for a few days but are going back to sleep soon."

"Oh, maybe," August considered.

The Northeast Kingdom was densely populated with black bears. Its vast, mostly undisturbed forest made it an ideal place for females to bring cubs into the world. They shouldn't be out here, I thought, as August and I continued on our drive. But nature's signals were getting scrambled. The bears were responding to the warmer weather as they always had—as years of evolution had programmed them to—and changes were afoot that they couldn't have prepared for. Who among them would survive those changes was still to be determined. I didn't want to think too hard about why the bears weren't hibernating or the hopeful fib I had just told August. I wanted that day to be a good one. The Storm had been canceled and the sun was returning.

My time with August was almost up, so I drove toward the home of his new foster family. Like the bears, he was a nomad now. I promised to come back the following week and reminded him that he could call me anytime. He hesitated for a moment as I parked the car in the lumpy mud driveway, and then he was out and the door was shut again. August's walk to the front steps was slow and joyless in a new way.

"Everything good?" Pia asked as I walked back into our house. She didn't really want to know. She was growing bored with the August drama.

"Fine, thank you. Where are you going?"

A battered gray duffel bag sat near the door.

"I'm going to Connecticut. There's a thing in Bridgeport this weekend."

I noticed a folded pamphlet peeking from the pocket of her coat. The little icon in the corner was familiar to me: a clenched fist that glowed like an industrial flashlight.

"It's a prepper thing?" I asked.

"Fine, yes, it's a convention. People are just going to exchange ideas. I can stay at my parents' place at night so it won't cost us anything."

Cost was a strange argument at that moment. Everything we said and did to each other seemed to have a cost, always growing our deficit, never reducing it.

"There's no storm, though. How long will you be gone?"

She sighed, ignoring the former point. "The convention is three days, but I will probably just stay for the week, since my parents are still in Italy."

How had we become the sort of people who go away without each other for days at a time with no notice? This seemed like a meaningful change, and one that I had no say in.

"No, don't, Pia." As soon as I said it, I knew I had lost. My tone was too mild; the expression on my face unchanged. Maybe I didn't want her to stay.

Pia cocked her head, giving me a moment to try again, which I did not do. It occurred to me that this might be a welcome respite. With an empty house and The Storm's threat gone, I could do anything I wanted! Not that I wanted to do anything out of the ordinary. On the contrary, I wanted to do completely ordinary things without my wife's anxious presence.

So I made a choice to accept what was about to happen, just as I understood it. Pia provided me with no additional details on her whereabouts and I asked no questions. I chose not to go down a rabbit hole of worry about whether this long-distance trip to meet with a group of disturbed strangers still worried about a canceled storm signaled the end of her sanity or the end of something else. (And was she even going there? Was there really a convention?) For exactly two seconds, I closed my eyes and saw a wall of flashing neon questions that demanded answers. They were all scrolling at once, multiplying themselves on my eyelids. But then I opened my eyes and, miraculously, they disappeared. So I chose to ignore the questions and move on with the information I had. I would enjoy an ignorant peace, however forced.

Pia leaned in for a perfunctory kiss that never actually landed on my face and walked out to the car without any further fanfare. Being carless for several days would present a number of problems, but ignoring those logistical questions was a necessary part of my response. And it was worth it. Pretending to be cool about it all provided a satisfying shot of power. Maybe this was an important insight about how to live with Pia: ignore the flashing questions. I decided to revisit the idea later, when I was thinking about things again. For now, I poured myself a small bourbon on the rocks and went to the back porch to take in the view.

The bright sun was making fast progress at drying our waterlogged land and patches of earth were beginning to poke through the puddles. It was winter, technically, and the maples that normally shaded our lawn were entirely bare.

But there were signs of life, too. I saw the bright white petals of diapensia developing in a cluster on a boulder in the far corner. I loved that flower. Diapensia and its alpine plant peers like bilberry and Labrador tea were Vermont's hardiest creatures, capable of surviving months of arctic temperatures and unshielded wind exposure, with little rain to sustain them. The species had been around for ten thousand years, watching its more delicate plant cousins at lower altitudes disappear with each frost. Such resilience was a testament to nature's persistence and a reminder of its strength in the face of adversity. I had only ever seen diapensia at the top of Camel's Hump and along the gnarly rock cliffs of Mount Mansfield. It wasn't known to grow so low. To see it now in my backyard seemed, like the black bears frolicking in the road, a pleasant glitch. But how many of these deviations could our natural world endure before the norm was lost altogether? That question cast a dark shadow on every warm winter day and unseasonable flower bloom. We couldn't really enjoy the glitches.

I reminded myself that The Storm was (probably) not coming and I could let go of the panic that had settled in my chest months ago. This was not the end; it was a return to normalcy. The asteroid headed toward us had reversed course, waters were drying and I had played basketball with a beautiful woman on that day.

Ah, Maggie. My mind drifted back to her. Was this a violation of the marital code? No, no, no, I reassured myself. I had hardly any friends in Isole and the day's activities were innocent. They were chaperoned by a seven-year-old! It would be difficult to envision a more appropriate date with a woman who happened to not be my wife. Still, it felt dangerous. It was an afternoon I would never speak of with Pia, not ever. I remembered the look she'd given Maggie when I came home from the hospital, a jealous mammal reclaiming her mate. I could never let her know of the basketball and I could never do that—whatever it was—again.

I wondered what Maggie was doing at that very moment. Was she always engaged in such constructive activities as teaching, physical fitness and creative writing? Yes, I imagined she was, but not because she didn't know how to have fun. Maggie seemed like a doer. That was something she and Pia would have in common, though for very different reasons. Where Pia was driven by compulsion, I imagined that Maggie was the sort of Vermonter driven by a hardwired belief in the value of staying busy and being productive. Maybe that was a compulsion, too, but it's a respected proclivity in New England. Leisure has to hurt a little to be fun here. I had lost some of that intensity since moving away, but I knew it when I saw it and I was still impressed by it. I reminded myself that I didn't know Maggie at all and may have been projecting my romantic feelings about Vermont onto a perfect stranger.

I sat back on the porch swing and closed my eyes, trying to direct my bourbon-buzzing thoughts away from Maggie and toward my drying backyard. All I could hear were mosquitoes. I worked not to be annoyed by their ceaseless drone.

Suddenly, I had the urge to do something myself. I had too much energy coursing through me to just sit there. I decided that, since the ground was drying up, I should revisit the flood runoff plan. We had hit a wall with the prepper holdouts and I knew that the only way to get the rest of them would be to change Crow's mind. I would try again with the old coot.

I took out my cell phone and called Peg. I explained that Pia had taken the car and I would need to borrow hers. She sounded so relieved at the thought of me going to see Crow on my own that she heartily agreed.

Within twenty minutes, I was bobbing along the ravaged roads in her Subaru, squinting through the windshield as I searched for Crow's foreboding driveway entrance. He lived four miles from me, but the only time I had ever been on that road was the last trip we took to his house. It had been so dark then that I hardly recognized anything now at dusk. I passed several battered mailboxes and a broken metal bedframe that had been abandoned in the culvert along the side of the road. Two trucks clanked past me without the friendly nod that I had come to expect. Like much of the Northeast Kingdom, sprawling, pastoral estates were situated beside dilapidated trailers. It wasn't the place to insulate oneself from other classes. But as I neared Crow's driveway, the signs of unemployment and rural poverty outnumbered any trace of affluence. I wondered how Crow had arrived at this place in life and how long he'd been there.

I recognized his driveway by the absence of a mailbox or marker and turned slowly onto the dirt entrance, unsure of how far Peg's car might take me. I drove a few feet and then met a puddle of indeterminate depth, so I turned off the ignition and walked the rest of the way. I was grateful for the last glow of daylight before the sun disappeared entirely. I watched my footing carefully.

Crow's house was set in a lush, dense enclave of what may very well have been old-growth forest. I knew that the Northeast Kingdom was home to some of the continent's remaining old-growth forest, but I hadn't encountered much of it yet and wasn't entirely sure that was the real thing. It had the right characteristics: a thick, mature canopy of hardwoods above, sheltering tiers of trees at various stages—some that would eventually become the tallest in the forest and others that had already peaked and were beginning their descent back into the earth. Even without the summer's leaves, I could hardly see the sky. The ground under my feet was dark and rich enough to feed a host of native wildflowers in warmer months and I made a mental note to come back to see what grew in the summer. This was the land that we couldn't afford to lose to development or pollution or a changing climate. This was where Vermont's memory lived.

Knock, knock. "Crow, you in there? It's Ash."

I held my ear to his front door for a few seconds before banging again, trying to sound confident, but still polite.

After thirty seconds, Crow's face appeared in a nearby window and then before me as he cracked the door.

"You again. What now? I'm not changing my mind," he said.

"That's fine. I just want to chat. I told Peg I would come out here, but I don't care what we talk about."

Once again, I found myself at Crow's house without a plan.

To my surprise, he unlatched the chain and stepped outside. It was possible that he just appreciated the companionship of a visitor, though the expression on his face didn't reveal as much.

"Could I see your bunker again?" I asked, sensing that flattery might be the right appeal.

He softened visibly at the suggestion.

"All right, c'mon," Crow said as he walked past me toward the shed.

I had to jog to keep up with his long strides and felt a familiar pang of unease as we approached his secret hideout.

Once we were inside, I took a seat on the couch and drank in all the details from a new angle. I noticed that one of the chairs was actually a weathered barrel, the kind Pia might buy for an exorbitant price at an antiques shop.

"It's rye whiskey," Crow said, noticing my interest. "I've got a buddy downstate who does some small distilling and we made a batch together last year. It's not the smoothest drink you've ever tasted, but she gets better the longer she sits there."

"That's so cool." I wished I could taste some of it.

We sat there quietly, each admiring our surroundings and unsure of the purpose of the visit. I hadn't brought up the runoff plan and Crow seemed to be growing comfortable around me.

"Hey, man," Crow finally said. "You smoke?"

He pulled a battered tin box out of a drawer and began rolling a joint from the chair facing me.

"Yeah, sure."

I wanted to sound casual, but the truth was that I hadn't smoked pot since I moved to Vermont. I didn't have anyone to buy it from and had lost that sixth sense of youth that enables one to detect a weed dealer from a great distance. It was decriminalized in most states, so it wouldn't have been particularly difficult or risky to find it; I just hadn't been sufficiently motivated to do so.

Crow passed me a skinny little twig of a joint and I took a long hit.

"Thanks," I said.

He nodded silently. There was a reverent, almost ceremonial air in the bunker, as if we were engaging in a religious sacrament. I waited for Crow to break the silence out of respect for whatever was going on.

"Nobody understands pot anymore," he said finally.

"Yeah," I agreed. "How do you mean?"

He was leaning back in his chair now, pensively watching the smoke that swirled around his face.

"What I mean is, nobody smokes pot for the right reasons

anymore. I see these kids walking around town, high off their asses, but they're just playing video games and talking on their phones. That's not how you appreciate pot. It's a gift from Mother Nature, man. It should be smoked out here in the woods. That's where the vibration really hits you. That's what it's about."

I thought of the vibrations Peg had spoken of. This was a surprising dissertation coming from Crow, who seemed driven by such cynical, practical concerns.

"Nature is the only true order," he went on. "All the rest of this is nonsense. But we're trying to rape and murder nature as best we can while we're here—that's for sure."

I nodded. It was a strong sentiment, but difficult to disagree with. We passed the joint back and forth for another silent moment.

"You know why I got those rifles?" Crow pointed to three long hunting rifles mounted on the ceiling above the makeshift sink. I hadn't noticed them before.

"It's not for hunting," he said. "I have no stomach for hunting. Can live on rice and beans if I have to. I got 'em because I don't trust the people. Nature makes sense to me; I can trust it. But not the people."

I wasn't sure if the turn in our conversation should disturb me, but I decided to steer things away from weaponry.

"So is all this because you can't trust anyone?" I asked, waving my arm around the bunker.

"No, man." Crow shook his head. "This is because it feels good to be in control. Shit's out of control and the only antidote to that is self-reliance. It feels good to be able to rely on your own hard work, and smarts. And what else are you going to do—just wait around for the end? No way; you gotta do something just to stay sane."

This seemed an utterly rational explanation for an end-of-days bunker and I nodded emphatically as Crow preached.

"Plus it's awesome," I added, feeling very stoned all of a sudden.

"It *is* awesome!"

The visit had taken such a pleasant turn that my high brain never wanted to leave. I wanted to sit on Crow's couch and talk about the meaning of things for hours. I didn't want to bring up the dredging that was planned for his backyard or the devastating flooding that he could be responsible for if he didn't consent to it. Still, I knew I couldn't leave without saying something about it.

"That's kind of what the runoff plan is all about," I ventured. "We can't really control what's going to happen to us, but it's a proactive thing to focus on, and something that will seriously minimize the pain. So why not, right?"

Crow considered this argument while he sucked on the remaining stub of the joint. He nodded slightly. "I'll think about it."

I raised my eyebrows.

"I don't know, but I'll think about it," Crow said again.

This development was more than enough for me, so I smiled and left all talk of the runoff plan behind us. There wasn't anything else I could possibly say in my altered state that would improve the progress already made.

Feeling festive, Crow took out his little tin box again and rolled another joint, which he was forced to smoke on his own as I was pressing up against the outer limits of my own tolerance. We drank water from a plastic jug and Crow told me about the nearby spring he got all his drinking water from ("not yet poisoned by humans"). It really did taste like the most delicious water I had ever had.

I wanted to know more about the little shelter we were

in, so I asked Crow to walk me through the logistics. He explained the challenges associated with building one's own outhouse; I interrupted regularly with technical questions that he was happy to address. We talked about ventilation and insulation and waste disposal. Then we discussed possibilities for enhanced security and long-term food storage. Crow's mind worked like my own; he dived deep into the science, clinging to the known facts and exiting with new information. We were two happy, stoned nerds.

I don't know how long I was at Crow's house, but it was late enough to fall into bed as soon as I got home. I was tired and satisfied with the progress I had made in bringing Crow to our side. I was also a little giddy about our budding friendship. I never doubted that his new openness to the runoff plan was sincere.

EIGHTEEN

"I THINK HE'S going to come around," I explained to Peg, Salty, Bill and Bob as we sat around the table in Salty's office the following Monday.

The Subcommittee had begun meeting on an almost daily basis in an effort to capitalize on the warm weather and wrap up our runoff plan quickly, before anyone changed their mind again. (We were all still under the impression then that The Storm might not come at all.) Thanks to the aggressive lobbying of the other members, including bribes of Bob's wife's apple cake and cords of wood, we had collected nearly all of the necessary signatures to begin digging. The only holdouts were Crow and one of his prepper acquaintances down the road. Crow still hadn't committed to the plan and seemed to be avoiding my calls. During the one conversation we did have by phone, he said that he needed more time.

"Can you pay him another visit tonight?" Peg asked.

I pressed my lips together. "I don't want to pressure him," I said. "That will have the reverse effect. I think he's trying to demonstrate that it's his decision to make. He can't feel strong-armed. He needs to come to this himself."

"I don't think we've got time for that," Salty said.

Everyone at the table was looking at me, waiting for me to fix it. Without all the signatures, nothing could get done.

I nodded. "I will call him tomorrow. I'll get his temperature on the whole thing, and if there's a way to nudge him along, I'll do it."

I didn't understand what the holdup was. Crow seemed genuinely open to the plan during my visit. I was embarrassed to have not brought this across the finish line yet for my fellow Subcommittee members, but I was also a little hurt for being misled by Crow. It really seemed as though we had connected during my visit.

Still, the group seemed satisfied by my promise and moved on to other business.

"Salty, anything you need from us on the Isole Festival?" Bill asked.

"Right, the festival," Salty said, turning to a new set of notes. "As you all know, the Isole Festival is scheduled for this Saturday and I think it's going to be exactly what this town needs. I'm running the Festival Committee and we've got a great lineup of vendors, performers and activities. We had to make some tweaks this year to account for the unseasonably warm weather. So, instead of the youth cross-country ski races, we'll be doing potato sack races, though it might be a little muddy. And we'll have pony rides instead of sleigh rides. I'll need some extra trucks for hauling chairs, cones, that sort of thing in advance. So, Bill and Bob—if you don't mind donating your time for that, it would be much appreciated. Peg, I know you've got a school obligation that day; we'll miss you, but it's no problem. And, Ash, I was wondering if you might be able to donate a few spare hours to designing signage for the festival. We need banners for Main Street and the floats, signs for the ice sculpture competition and flyers to paste around town. I can handle all the printing—we just need your creative skills for the image itself. Would you mind?"

"Of course not," I said. Since Pia went to Connecticut two days before, I had reclaimed my routine. I was catching up with work responsibilities and eager for new challenges.

"Great, thank you. I think this is really what Isole needs," Salty repeated. "It will be a huge boost to morale and, of course, to the local economy. Things will really get back to normal after this."

It was as if the decision to hold the festival had negated any chance of a superstorm. There was no longer a doubt in the minds of Isole's optimists: the festival was on and The Storm was off. There was still doubt elsewhere, though. For one thing, the official prediction from the National Weather Service had the likelihood of no superstorm at 70 percent, which were good odds, but not great. And there were plenty of others around town, like Pia, who simply didn't believe anything that came from the authorities. At the food co-op the day before, a young man ahead of me in line explained that this was part of a right-wing political conspiracy to "keep the people afraid," and that as soon as we got complacent again, "they" would invent a new fake storm to rally around. Still, most of us were so relieved by the news that life would return to normal that we simply chose to believe it. I was among those people.

With the improved weather projections, I realized that I had been mistaken in thinking we were divided by our approach to catastrophe preparation. That wasn't what divided us. It was our attachment to the promise of catastrophe that divided us. Some, like Pia, clung to that promise. They wanted The Storm to be real. I once heard a Hollywood producer talking about why we love end-of-days predictions— the rapture, the Mayan calendar's end, zombie apocalypse and the like. He said that it gives us permission to enjoy life more if we think it's ending soon. We might work less, love more, eat dessert—that sort of thing. But he couldn't have been more wrong. That's not at all what people do in the face of a real threat. Instead, they cling to the values that have dictated their lives all along; they dig in. The worriers obsess, and the workaholics drown themselves in work to avoid thinking, and the racists blame everything on a different tribe and the elitists cling tighter to the stuff that sets them apart from the masses. No one gets better or reaches a higher state of consciousness. We're not capable as a species of that sort of transformation. I will never understand the allure of the apocalypse. Nothing seemed improved under its threat; everyone became a worse version of themselves.

Do Not Be Lulled into a False Sense of Safety.

That was the warning printed across a flyer that sat on my doorstep that evening. It was the newsletter of The Survivalists & Preppers of the Northeast Kingdom, and it came each month, hand delivered, not mailed or emailed, but delivered door-to-door by a nice lady in a beat-up minivan with two children strapped in the backseat. Pia was still away, so the prepper mom left it that day under a small rock on our welcome mat. I was reminded that we hadn't spoken by phone since Pia left, which was new for us. Still, I didn't feel eager to call.

I picked up the tri-fold and sat down under the porch light and clear sky. Its layout was impressive, neatly organized on glossy stock with professional photos. According to the address on the back corner, it was produced at some sort of prepper association headquarters in Michigan. There was a brief article about the militarization of our domestic police forces. Beside that was an instructional for canning your own tuna. It had the breezy commercial tone of a brochure one might see stacked at a coffee shop advertising a nearby community college or local tourist attraction. Folded within it was a cheap printout from the Northeast Kingdom affiliate group. Apparently, a meeting was scheduled for that night in the basement of the Elks Club.

I swatted a mosquito from my ankle and stared at the hand-drawn map of the meeting location. It was starting in fifteen minutes. I could be there in twenty if I ran to Peg's to ask for her car and drove fast. I didn't want to attend another prepper meeting, but it would be a chance to corner Crow and get an answer out of him about the runoff plan. He would be on his own turf and maybe my presence would suggest a spirit of mutual compromise, I reasoned. Plus it would be my only opportunity to do it without Pia around. It was her turf, too.

With nothing to lose, I ran inside to grab a sweater and two granola bars before jogging down the road to knock on Peg's door. She agreed immediately, impressed by my commitment to the project.

"Maybe you'll learn something!" she joked as I sprang down her porch stairs toward the car.

I drove quickly, arriving ten minutes late. When I walked in through the heavy doors, the group was already sitting in a circle of chairs. Several people turned to look at me, and I nodded as if it was the most natural thing in the world for me to be there. Three times as many people as I'd seen at the last meeting were there, and the crowd looked more like the general population of Isole than the small collection of misfits from before. There was a young couple I recognized as regulars from the Blue Frog bar, the pregnant woman who lived up the road, August's parents and many others I didn't know who appeared to be perfectly normal locals. It looked like Isole itself, which seemed significant.

Crow was once again at the center of the circle. He was speaking authoritatively on the merits of natural insulation methods as I found a seat. My chair scraped the floor disruptively and Crow looked up. We locked eyes briefly without any acknowledgment of each other before he went on with his point about clay-coated straw. I knew he had been avoiding me, but this was colder than I'd expected. Still, I reminded myself that he was busy. Maybe it meant nothing at all.

When Crow concluded, he introduced a new face to the group as "a professor of history and a friend of our work."

A neat man in his early sixties stood and greeted the crowd with a warm smile. He wore an expensive sweater-vest over a soft midsection, trim khakis and brown leather shoes. His well-groomed beard reminded me that I had been neglecting my own scruffy beard in recent weeks. The group watched patiently as he rolled up his shirtsleeves and thanked Crow for the introduction.

"Great to be here, Crow," he said. "My name is Gabe Brownstein, and I'm a history professor at the University of Vermont with a focus on the Great Depression. I'm here today to talk about the lessons we learned—or should have learned—from hard times, and some of the relevant parallels for our lives today. In this era of economic uncertainty and threatening weather events, now is a good time to revisit our history."

Several people nodded in agreement. The crowd was intrigued; I was, too. I leaned forward, resting my elbows on my knees and straining to catch everything the professor said as he turned back and forth to engage the entire room.

"It's not hyperbole to suggest that our economy today is as fragile as it was in the late 1920s," the professor began. "It's certainly more volatile, more leveraged and more top-heavy. Indeed, one could argue that it's *more* fragile than it was then. Now, I'm not saying that it's all going to crash tomorrow and you should start stashing your savings under the mattress. But there are ways for individuals and communities to boost their financial resilience in the face of such fragility."

The room was rapt. To my great surprise, this prepper meeting really was useful.

Professor Brownstein put a finger in the air to indicate that an important point was coming. "Rule number one—get off credit. Debt is the enemy of financial resilience and the surest way to find yourself at the mercy of other people and institutions. If you're paying for your life with credit now, stop doing that. If you've got debt weighing you down, make paying it off a priority. It's the hardest but most important thing you will learn here today. When the last great depression hit, credit was unavailable to most people, so our entire society had to learn to live on whatever they could afford with the money they already had. It's a foreign concept to us now, but we should get reacquainted with it... Are there any questions so far?"

An older man in the front row raised his hand.

"Yes, sir?"

"What does this have to do with being a survivalist?"

The professor smiled patiently. "It's a great question," he said, "and it has everything to do with being a survivalist. You want to rely on yourself? You need to start by getting financially independent. Maybe you want to get off the grid? Bug out? Great, you'll need to disentangle yourself from financial obligations first."

The man with the question looked at Crow now. "I

thought we were going to talk about ammunition storage tonight," he said.

Several people shook their heads in frustration.

The younger woman I recognized jumped in. "I want to hear what Professor Gabe has to say. I thought we had settled this: we're not a militia group."

Three or four others nodded in agreement and the professor looked around the room for a sign that he should go on.

"Well, what kind of group are we, then?" the first questioner asked.

"We're just here to share ideas," Crow said. "We're just here to help each other out in our preparations."

He looked around for a response. Crow had seemed so antisocial to me when we first met, but it was becoming clear that he had an astute ability to manage a range of personalities. He was a leader.

"No, it's more than that," the husband of the young woman said. "I think we're a political organization." Several people grumbled as he went on, "Not like Republicans or Democrats. I mean, we're here to organize around some principles that deserve protecting; things like the right to privacy and the need to resist the encroachment of government into our lives."

"Sounds like libertarianism," someone said.

"I'm not a libertarian!" another shouted.

"Call it whatever you want," the man went on. "I think this is a place to rally around a cause. We need to talk more about protecting our families in spite of government inaction and protecting them *from* government action…like organizing to say 'no' to letting the town of Isole dig holes through our backyards. We can't just be about water purification and food storage. We should have a guiding purpose."

That set off a spirited discussion about the identity of the group, but I didn't hear any of it. They've talked about the runoff plan, I thought to myself. That was what the young man was referring to. They were banding together to rally against it. It didn't make any sense to me. I smoked with Crow in his bunker in a spirit of mutual respect. It really seemed as though we were getting somewhere. But maybe he never had any intention of agreeing to the digging. He was just saying those things so we could have a pleasant night and a friendly smoke. And, as I was learning, he knew how to manage people.

I felt prematurely embarrassed about having to tell the Subcommittee that we'd lost Crow. They would be devastated. What would this mean for the town when the next big storm did eventually hit? I sat and stewed for another ten minutes while the group continued to discuss their guiding purpose or lack thereof. Finally, Crow called for a break and everyone migrated toward a folding table that held coffee carafes and store-bought doughnuts.

I walked straight up to Crow, who was standing in the now-empty circle of chairs, talking to Professor Brownstein.

"What the hell, man? I thought you were going to consider it," I said, louder than I had intended.

The professor excused himself for coffee.

Crow cleared his throat but said nothing. He looked sheepish.

"You're really putting the town at risk by taking this position," I went on. "It's not just about you."

Crow shook his head. "I can't do it. It might make sense in this particular situation, but it opens the door to bigger compromises down the road. It's important that I take a stand. I've got an example to set." He looked around the room at the attendees who were chatting genially.

Crow thinks he's the goddamn savior of these weirdos, I thought to myself. It seemed incongruous that a group defined by its desire to separate from society should be unified on any issue or led by any oddly charismatic individual. They were supposed to be loners.

"This is a huge disappointment," I said. I was running out of ideas for where to take the conversation.

"I'm sorry." Crow did seem genuinely sorry. He opened the palms of his hands in a gesture of surrender, but of course, he had won.

I shook my head and delivered a stern look that was intended to convey my deep disappointment, from which I suspect he recovered quickly. There was nothing left for me there, so I walked through the crowd and out the back door. I saw August's parents on my way out and avoided eye contact.

As I drove home in Peg's car, my anger grew, thinking about how selfish Crow and his cohorts were being. It seemed impossible to me that seemingly intelligent people could willfully put the rest of the community in danger. It was contrary to everything I believed about Isole. I knew it was The Storm—fearful people were clinging to what was theirs—but that didn't excuse it. And The Storm was off, indefinitely postponed by Mother Nature, so why did it still have a hold on people?

The strangest thing of all was how closely the preppers flirted with rationality. For most of that meeting, the discussion careened back and forth between reasonable information and total paranoia. I felt myself agreeing with them more often than I was comfortable. They were *this close* to being the smartest people in Isole.

Peg answered the door with a hopeful grin. "So?"

"It's not happening," I said, handing her the car keys.

Her face dropped, but she nodded as if she had expected that outcome.

"He's just not going to budge." I put my hands up. "I

MEG LITTLE REILLY

tried, Peg. I'm so sorry. I don't know what's wrong with these people."

"I know it's frustrating, but I believe that you did your best. Do you want to come in for a cup of tea?"

I shook my head. "No, I'm not feeling social anymore tonight. Thanks, though."

I walked down the porch steps, toward the dark road.

"Ash," she said as I walked away, "unfortunately, sometimes people just need to see the damage to believe it. It's not your fault."

I nodded and began my walk home in the dark woods. After a long shower and a neat bourbon, I curled up in bed with the latest *National Geographic*. I was trying to read an article about displaced bears on the other side of the world, but my mind kept drifting back to the lecture I'd heard at the prepper meeting. The professor was urging us to learn from the past. Americans have faced hardships before and successive generations have learned from them. Life goes on, people make babies and those babies are a little smarter than their parents had been. *Voilà: the human race evolves.* That was what Pia had said to me years ago as we sat on the living room floor, pledging to live a not-bad life. It's the most optimistic of ideas, the belief that the world is always improving incrementally. But in recent months, Pia had abandoned that optimism. She came to believe that the mistakes we'd made on this earth—and *to* this earth—were beyond redemption. Future generations can't fix it and shouldn't be asked to endure it.

I didn't know what I believed. I was discouraged, but not yet ready to give up hope for the human race. I thought about calling Pia; instead, I fell asleep.

NINETEEN

UPON INVITATION FROM the town, spring arrived early for the Isole Festival. It was fifty-three degrees outside, but a warmish fifty-three of the sort that beckons short-sleeve shirts, Frisbee tosses and girls in flowy, shapeless dresses with bare legs and free breasts beneath. (Fifty-three on the latter side of winter always feels so different from autumn's blustery fifty-three.) While technically a winter celebration, no one objected to the unseasonable and unabashedly cheerful weather. The tyranny of The Storm's threat had been lifted and we were positively giddy.

At most, we would see another round of rain and flooding the following day, but that was probably going to be the extent of it. The possibility of a superstorm was still present in the weather forecasts, but I was among those who chose not to hear it. All I heard was hope.

I had spent my week of solitude leading up to the festival reclaiming my home and righting the parts of my life that had fallen out of balance. I had worked hard, first on the clients I had been neglecting and then on the design for an Isole Festival logo. Making good on both of those promises felt right and created a pleasurable momentum inside me. When I was done with those tasks, I cleaned. I straightened and swept and vacuumed and mopped. I washed sheets and scrubbed dishes. Even the worm smell was improved with the open windows and cool breeze. It was hard not to indulge my anger at Crow for refusing to listen to reason, or at Pia for helping to leave the house in such squalor.

But when I was through, I was too pleased to be angry with anyone. The house looked like ours—the one we had fallen in love with when we first visited Isole and decided it would be our home. Light streamed in through the old windowpanes and illuminated the historic wide-board floors. I especially loved how the kitchen appliances, which were unintentionally retro because we didn't have the money to replace them, gleamed in chrome and white. Everything around me seemed animate again. Even the maple tree that grew right outside the kitchen window was blossoming, pushing its fertile green buds against the glass. (It was months away from the proper growing season, but who could argue with those buds.) All of this had dulled in the months before under the suffocating effects of the dark rains and growing marital discord. To see everything glistening again reawakened an irrational hope inside of me that life with Pia could still unfold as I once imagined it. Second chances abounded. We spoke once while she was away; the conversation was short and polite enough to leave room for possibility.

Peg dropped me off at the festival early Saturday morning and I was happy to be there. The base camp was a large village green at the foot of Main Street, where the parade was scheduled to deposit all the revelers. I was proud of the art I had created for the festival and had offered to help lead the team of volunteers who were tasked with hanging it all. The design was unlike my usual work—uncomplicated and exuberant as our mood. The basic logo, which appeared on everything, was of a sun rising behind Isole's distinct eastern mountain ridge. Bright rays shot out and projecting from the tip of each ray was a twinkling letter, which together spelled *Isole* in a perfect arc overhead. The ridge itself was spotted in snow, which I intended to portray the transition from winter to spring, but could have just as easily been interpreted as the perpetual state of seasonal ambivalence we lived in then. It was artfully executed but simple. A child could have conceived of it.

"I didn't know you had this in you," Peg had said over the phone when I sent her an early draft. She laughed a little and told me she liked it, which I took as a compliment and my signal to stop tinkering. "You love it here, Ash," she concluded.

I was immensely proud to have my design displayed around Isole that day. It was on signs, bandannas, tote bags—whatever we could have printed quickly at the last minute. Locals can still be spotted wearing old T-shirts from that festival or drinking from chipped coffee mugs with the image. That design made me an inextricable part of Isole's fabric.

"Raise it a little on the left and then—right there, that's perfect!" I yelled to a young female volunteer with pink hair at the top of a stepladder. We were securing the last of the signage, a grand banner that arched over the entrance to the village green. It was just us and the vendors setting up, but soon the place would be packed.

I wandered around, feeling a sense of ownership over the event. A space where kids could pet cows, horses and llamas from local farms was set up next to a crafting area where tables stood and all things knitted and felted were for sale. Beyond that, a table of local Vermont cheeses were available for sampling. And at the far end of the green, a folk band unpacked their van beside the beer tent. It was indescribably wholesome, but only "country" in that way that appeals to Northeastern sophisticates: a kind of staged country experience, rural but not provincial. There was political art to be purchased and green energy petitions to be signed and macrobiotic food to be eaten. To be sure, the *New York Times* and the *Wall Street Journal* could be found at select gas stations nearby. Isole's brand of "country" was marketable and safe to the urban tourist.

I missed Pia, but I felt relieved that she wasn't there for the festival. She would have loved the scene and the retelling of it to our old friends in the city, but it seemed as if she had grown incapable of truly enjoying anything by then. Without her, I was unencumbered and free to immerse myself in the experience. I had gone to so many events like this in my childhood and was excited to reacquaint myself with a beloved old feeling.

I could hear the cowbells—rung by a team of first-graders at the head of the parade as they turned the corner toward the green. I wanted to catch the end of the parade and the scene on Main Street, so I ran toward the commotion and found an empty space beside a row of families with strollers. The street was lined thick with people, waiting for the procession that grew louder as it neared. First came the high school band. That was followed by a group of adults wearing elfin costumes and bells around their ankles, dancing to lute music. Our lone fire truck rolled slowly by with Salty at the wheel, waving like a seasoned politician, and Isole's hockey team walked alongside in their jerseys. Prepubescent ballerinas from the dance school threw candy from the next float, followed by the members of the local Democratic Party office and the slightly more rumpled Progressive Party office staff behind them.

Parades aren't a representative sample of any town, and

certainly not Isole. Neither the methadone clinic at the edge of town nor the Veterans Affairs office that had been all but forgotten by the federal government were represented. The local dog shelter had a float, but not the battered women's shelter that sat next to it along the highway. I don't know why I thought of this as the contra dancers spun past—maybe it was what Crazy Roger had said to me by the side of the police car about this place not being so nice after all. It was incongruous with my life, but I knew he wasn't wrong.

The onlookers were a handsome mix of pink-cheeked local families and well-dressed tourists from Connecticut, New York and Montreal. A woman snapping pictures beside me had the thin, taut severity of a Manhattan resident. Her husband stole regular glances at the stock ticker that scrolled across the phone in his hand. I imagined that they had a second home in Manchester or Stowe. The Isole Festival would be one of their annual trips. She would buy cheeses and a handmade cutting board in the shape of a cow and they would drive back to the city calmer, but relieved to return to their luxurious life.

My attention to the onlookers was broken when a loud voice sang out from the parade line: "There's still time, Isole! Let's come together in hope and faith while there's still time!"

It was Rodney Riggins. He was yelling into a megaphone from the back of the same monster truck that facilitated his last grand entrance at the high school parking lot. The truck was waxed and sparkling this time and Riggins wore a spiffy new flannel shirt rolled up to the elbows.

"Our prayers have bought us time—let's use that time wisely, Isole!"

It was a convenient adaptation in message: Riggins's followers had thwarted the superstorm through prayer, but his services were needed more than ever now. Brilliant.

MEG LITTLE REILLY

Most of the spectators smiled politely, unaware of who Rodney Riggins was, but small pockets of watchers cheered in solidarity. It wasn't the place for jeers, but I could see plenty of dissenters in the crowd, too. As the truck rolled by and Riggins scanned the faces looking up at him, we locked eyes for the briefest moment, and I thought I saw him smirk a little, taunting me.

Riggins had been visibly active in Isole throughout the week, organizing prayer sessions in outdoor parks and handing out flyers downtown. He never was allowed to use the high school for one of his talks, but that only strengthened the resolve of his followers to work harder to get the word of God/Riggins out. They were a small antagonistic group and an awkward fit for a culture organically wary of overt religiosity. The unofficial strategy of Riggins-doubters like myself was to wait it out. Riggins was there to capitalize on The Storm's threat, so once that was gone, we expected he would disappear, too. For now, most of the locals just avoided him on the street and averted their eyes when his disciples made a scene.

"Don't give him another thought," a voice said nearby.

I spun around to see Maggie grinning behind me while she wrestled with a large shaggy dog on a leash that I assumed to be Badger. She looked characteristically casual in a purple sweatshirt and snug jeans that hugged her impressive legs. Her long strawberry hair fell everywhere as she straddled the enormous dog.

"Hi!" I said with unabashed enthusiasm. "Do you need some help?"

"Uh, maybe," she said as Badger attempted to chase an alpaca parading down Main Street. "This was a terrible idea. I'm in denial about what a bad dog he is."

I grabbed Badger's collar and held it firmly until he relaxed a little. "Nah, he's just enthusiastic."

Maggie laughed and organized her wild hair into a twist to one side. "Are you busy? I'm starving. Let's get a falafel wrap before the green is too crowded."

The idea of getting falafels with Maggie sounded perfect, but I worked to keep my eagerness in check. "Yeah, I think I'm off duty now. Let's do it."

"Oh, were you working?" she asked.

"Yeah, actually, I designed the festival logo and all this stuff."

I tried to sound casual as I waved my arm toward a cluster of balloons that bore my design.

"Oh wow, that's so cool! I will have to get a T-shirt."

Her guileless support disarmed me. I wanted more of her and I wanted to be more like her.

We walked up Main Street, weaving through children and noisy groups of tourists with the excitable Badger, dropping thank-yous and sorrys along the way as necessary. The sun was high above us by then and it was starting to feel downright hot outside. Maggie handed me the leash so she could peel off her sweatshirt, revealing a taut, muscly torso in a faded gray T-shirt. I tried my best to take in as much of her body as I could in the flash of one glance. Everything about her seemed to spring forth with movement. I imagined that her muscle fibers were made of something different from the rest of us, a superhuman material that mortals weren't privy to.

Most of the parade spectators were migrating toward the green by then, which was filling up quickly. Badger and I followed Maggie's lead toward the falafel truck, but when we got there, the vendor told us that he wouldn't be set up for another hour. We decided to roam around for a while in the interest of wearing Badger out.

We started at the circus-arts tent, where children no older than August swung and dangled from ribbons suspended high above with astounding grace. I was hypnotized, but Badger lasted only as long as it took for a squirrel to bound by. We let him lead the way, sniffing horses and small children, eating fallen cider doughnuts and puddles of handcrafted soda. I couldn't have been happier. There were hundreds of smiling people around us, enjoying the incredible festival in our incredible town. And I was with incredible Maggie.

"I still can't believe you designed all of these," Maggie said, looking up at an enormous banner above. "You're really talented, Ash."

"It's not as impressive as shaping young minds," I said. I tried to sound modest, but I enjoyed the compliment.

Maggie looked back down at Badger, who was gleefully shredding a popsicle stick. "What are we going to do with him?"

We. I loved the sound of *we.* The Badger situation had become our problem to solve and we would need to really put our heads together about it. I considered my next move.

"I know!" Maggie said before I could speak. "Come this way."

I followed her through the happy crowd until we got to the beer tent at the other end of the green. Mellow clusters of people laughed over microbrews and listened to the old white guys playing blues music nearby. Maggie tied Badger's leash to a fat metal tent pole and gestured toward a folding chair.

"Let's drink!" she said, as if there was no other option with her unruly animal.

I bought two draft Long Trail Ales and a bottle of water for Badger's bowl and we set up at a tipsy plastic table. With the dog tethered, we could relax and watch the party unfold before us. I was my most charming self as I made lighthearted jokes about the characters walking by. We still hadn't eaten and the warm wave that washed over me with each sip of beer felt calming. Maggie seemed as relaxed as me, maybe more so. She laughed easily, throwing her head back for my better jokes and running an absentminded hand through her soft hair. I was enamored with everything about her, but mostly her ability to be completely forthcoming and at the same time uninterested in talking about herself. Conversation wasn't a maze to navigate, but an effortless ride.

Over our second beer, I learned that Maggie had grown up in Waitsfield, near Camel's Hump. She was the first of three and the only girl. Her brothers both worked in finance in New York and couldn't believe that she had decided to come back to Vermont after Berkeley. She said she "always knew exactly what she wanted her life to look like, so deciding where to live after college was easy." It was baffling to me that anyone could have so much clarity at that age, but I believed that she did. It was as if she'd skipped over the requisite years of bumbling pretense before getting to the good part, the self-awareness. I was only getting there now.

"That's also my biggest weakness," she said, "hardheadedness. Once I made my mind up, I refused to consider any other path for myself."

She said this as an unapologetic matter of fact and it was a relief to hear that she was flawed at all. Normally, I would have found such false modesty irritating, but I was happy to forgive that, too. She was becoming fuller, more real, before me.

"And let me guess," Maggie said, taking a sip of beer before decoding me. "You're the country-boy-turned-urban-hipster, right? You probably grew heirloom tomatoes from

MEG LITTLE REILLY

a rooftop in Brooklyn and played in a bluegrass band before you moved here."

"I *have* always wanted to play the banjo!"

"Of course you have." She laughed.

"No," I said. "I was more of a country-boy-barely-passing-as-an-urban-hipster. My heart wasn't in the act. But luckily, the same basic uniform is required for both roles, so it wasn't much of a sartorial challenge."

Maggie laughed and slid back in her chair. "That *is* convenient."

The wind blew hard and we looked around lazily, feeling no pressure to fill each space with conversation. It was still sunny and warm outside, but the wind had picked up noticeably, causing some of the festival tents to billow. Maybe it was the cold front coming from the west? This was the way we were conditioned to think by then—that each raindrop and gust of wind was part of a weather event and each weather event was a new threat. Still, I was too happy and relaxed to let weather disrupt our afternoon.

"I thought I might find you here!" I heard a voice from behind me shout.

I turned around to find Salty jogging toward us. He looked as if he had been running around for hours, but he wore a big smile.

"Hi!" I said, stiffening straight up. Was it okay that I was seen having drinks with Maggie? I wasn't supposed to be here. "We're just giving Badger here a little break."

"Do you want to join us?" Maggie asked.

I wished I had thought of that.

"No, actually, I was hoping to round up a few more adults to help with the potato sack races. You guys interested?"

We looked at each other and shrugged.

"Great," Salty said. "You can leave Badger here. I'll have Al keep an eye on him."

Salty spoke with the scruffy guy at the beer taps, who agreed to watch the dog, and we all tromped off toward the section of the green that had been designated for kids' games.

A dodgeball set was just finishing up as we arrived and I saw August run toward me.

"Hey, buddy!" I said.

He wore the same suspicious face I had seen the last time Maggie was around, but he was too engaged in the activities at hand to be distracted for long.

"Ash, I won twice!"

I rumpled his hair with an extra dose of paternal affection and one eye on Maggie. My love for August was genuine, but for some reason I felt the need to play it up around her as evidence of my good-guy status.

Salty pulled us aside to explain our roles. We were to stand at opposite sides of the course, helping kids who fell and working to avoid collisions. (Apparently, local potato sack races had resulted in serious head trauma in the past.) Salty and several other adults with loud voices herded the competitors to the starting line and blew the whistle, which kicked off a melee of thrashing bodies, some laughing and some dead serious. Maggie and I cheered at the top of our lungs. We ran onto the course to help the fallen competitors off to the side and only had to carry one crying girl off to the medic tent for special attention. It was surprisingly fun, not only for the fleeting smiles I stole from Maggie.

I was particularly proud of August's performance on the potato sack field. He wasn't exceptionally athletic, but he had a scrappiness that I hadn't noticed before. It was the first time I'd seen August around his peers, and I was relieved to see that he fit in about as well as any of them. He was quirky and shabbily dressed, but Vermont was uniquely forgiving about such traits. I thought of my own dorky existence in grammar school, which was largely enjoyable. Pia once explained to me that "boys are allowed to be clueless freaks for much longer than girls are in our culture," which may have explained this experience. I wished the same for August.

Maggie and I performed our duties through two more races and an informal medal ceremony at the gelato tent nearby. By then, I was exhausted and starving.

"C'mon," Maggie said, tugging on my shirt to follow her before we could be recruited for anything else.

We walked along the edge of the green, where the festivities met the dark woods. To our left was the bustling festival and to our right was a thick patch of forest I had never noticed before. The afternoon sun streaked through tall conifers, dappling a floor cushioned with pine needles.

I had the sudden urge to do something—anything—to draw out the pleasurable moment. I had forgotten entirely about my earlier vow to avoid Maggie and could only think now of how badly I wanted her. She was two steps ahead of me, so I leaped forward and grabbed her hand, startling her slightly. Maggie looked back and, in an instant, I pulled her toward me and kissed her. She was still flush from the races and I could smell her around me as she held the kiss. At first, the effort was all mine, and then she kissed back softly. We both tasted metallic, from old beer and empty stomachs. It was dizzying.

Maggie stopped abruptly and pulled me several steps into the forest, out of the light and away from the crowd. It was all so careless of me, not to consider where we were and who might be watching, but none of that mattered to me then. All I cared about was that she let me kiss her again, there in the dark of the woods. And she did! She did, she did, she did. We pressed into each other for five more seconds before she pulled back and looked down. The freckles on her nose were blurry constellations just inches from my face.

"We can't do this." I said it first, beating her to it and knowing that I was the one breaking rules. *I* was married.

Maggie nodded in agreement and stepped back.

We both stared at our feet at first, then I put my hand around the top of her arm. I liked the way my entire hand fit neatly around that part of her body.

We walked silently out of the woods, maintaining a few feet between us. Suddenly, I was acutely aware of who may have been looking and what rightful judgment they had for me. I was not a cheater. I didn't cheat, never had and never felt compelled to—not in any real way. There had been times, of course, when I'd gotten too drunk and fantasized about women I knew or looked a few too many times at Pia's hot friends, but that wasn't real. In fact, I always secretly believed that any infidelity in my marriage would be committed by Pia; I believed her moral compass was weaker. But *I* was the one who had committed this infraction, so apparently I had been wrong about that.

I walked behind Maggie toward the beer tent, where I supposed we would pretend to check on Badger or something, but we never made it that far.

"Hey, Ash!" August said as he ran toward us. "Did you hear about The Storm? It's coming, Ash!"

I looked around, unsure of what to make of this news. An older gentleman passing by in a hurry nodded wordlessly, confirming August's report.

Maggie jumped in. "August, where did you hear this?" She sounded like a teacher all of a sudden.

"I heard some people talking about it over there."

He pointed to an old truck filled with melting snow that

had been rented from a nearby ski resort for the grand tradition of sugar-on-snow. There was a camp stove parked beside it, heating dark amber syrup. Huddled around the dashboard in the cab was a group of old men chatting excitedly. Something was indeed happening.

"August, I have a serious job for you," I said.

His eyes widened.

"I need you to go watch over Badger to make sure he's okay for another minute while I talk to those men."

August nodded solemnly and walked to his post near the sleeping dog. I was eager to hear the latest news on The Storm, but I knew enough to give August a filtered version of the truth later. As for Maggie, I wasn't sure what to say next. She was still standing beside me and I was still feeling guilty, but also desperate to keep her close. Luckily, she didn't wait for an invitation and followed me to the truck, which floated in an ambrosial maple cloud.

"What's the latest?" I asked, doing my best impression of an old native.

"Storm's back," one of the men in the group said. True to dialect, he dropped the *r* in storm and dragged the *a* for miles. "It's comin' haaader than they predicted."

There was little useful information in this report, but I could see enough concern on their normally stoic faces to get the message. Salty was jogging toward us now, too.

"Keep your voice down," he said before we could speak, the three of us huddled together. "I don't want anyone to panic. Nothing is happening this instant and there's no need to send this crowd running."

Maggie spoke calmly. "So what *is* happening?"

"Well, it seems..." Salty started, looking around cautiously as if he was the only person in Isole privy to this information. "It seems the hurricane that just made landfall in North

Carolina is still gaining in size and speed. It's expected to be a category five by the time it gets to the Jersey shore and the estimated footprint is just mind-boggling. They are predicting this one is already set to break historic records." Salty was rambling in a voice I didn't recognize. "That's going to be a disaster in itself. But the real problem is that the cold front coming from the west that we thought would dissipate is gaining in force. Thanks to the sheer size of this hurricane, they are going to collide over New England. There's cold air coming down from Canada, too, in an unrelated event. When all this cold air hits the warm, wet air from the south, the pressure is going to crash and…the big storm is coming. And they had it wrong. It's coming and it's going to be like nothing we've ever seen."

All the wrinkles on Salty's normally pleasant face seemed tensed and exaggerated at that moment. It was unnerving to see him so rattled. We wanted badly for that reprieve from The Storm—that perfect day at the Isole Festival—to be real, but it was just a mirage. We had been given one last, memorable day of brightness to hold on to before everything changed forever.

"When is this happening?" I asked in a low voice.

"Twenty-four, maybe thirty-six hours," Salty said. "Word is spreading fast and people are going to start clearing out of here soon to get back to wherever they came from. You guys should probably do the same."

"What about the festival?" I asked.

"The vendors can wrap up quickly and don't worry about the rest. Safety is our top priority for now. Ash, did you ever get that plywood I stacked up for you?"

Salty had ordered giant sheets of plywood weeks earlier for boarding up his own windows and, sensing that I wasn't an expert at such domestic matters, urged me to take a stack. I had been putting off that chore for weeks, which I felt stupid about now. With Pia gone, I had no car and no way of preparing us for this storm. And would Pia come back in light of this forecast? I didn't know now.

"We'll stop by my place, then throw it in the truck before I drop you off," Salty concluded, reading the panic on my face. "Meet me back here in ten minutes."

With that, he jogged off to tend to whatever countless other responsibilities he had assigned himself at the event, leaving Maggie and me alone together.

"I should get Badger," she said quietly.

"Yeah."

We stood there another moment, looking around. The mood was shifting fast as people checked their phones and gathered their kids. Even the perfect blue sky above us had darkened as clouds moved in and the wind picked up. The festival was over. In case there was any question about that, one of the enormous banners above us—my banner—had come untethered at one end and flapped wildly. I could feel my heart quicken at the realization that I had to part with Maggie indefinitely. That day had been perfect. Even the kiss. Especially the kiss. I felt guilty and angry with myself for the kiss, but incapable of stepping away from her. And it seemed possible that she felt something similar. Why else was she still there?

She looked up at me and shrugged sweetly. "One kiss for the end of the world."

I nodded. It didn't seem like such a transgression when she put it that way and made me want more. I hadn't had nearly enough of Maggie. I grabbed her hands and squeezed them harder than I probably should have. I think she squeezed back. If anyone had noticed us, it wouldn't have looked quite right for two platonic friends, but it was the most restrained thing I could do while wanting her with my whole body.

The moment didn't last.

As I held Maggie's hands and looked into her eyes, I saw a fuzzy object marching toward us from the distance over her shoulder. It was Pia.

PART TWO

All day had the snow come down,—all day
As it never came down before,
And over the hills, at sunset, lay
Some two or three feet, or more;
The fence was lost and the wall of stone,
The windows blocked and the well-curbs gone,—
The haystack had grown to a mountain lift,
And the wood-pile looked like a monster drift
As it lay by the farmer's door.

The night sets in on a world of snow,
While the air grows sharp and chill,
And the warning roar of a fearful blow
Is heard on the distant hill;
And the Norther, see! on the mountain peak
In his breath how the old trees writhe and shriek!

He shouts on the plain, ho-ho! ho-ho!
He drives from his nostrils the blinding snow,
And growls with a savage will.

—Excerpted from "A Snow-Storm: Scene in a Vermont Winter"
by Charles G. Eastman of Montpelier, Vermont.

First published in 1848.

TWENTY

I CLIMBED DOWN from a rickety ladder leaning precariously against our house and wiped the sweat dripping from my face with a quivering arm. I was only halfway through my task of nailing sheets of plywood over our windows and it felt like all the muscles in my body were going to give way. It had been almost a full day since we learned at the Isole Festival that The Storm was on its way and everything had changed since then. The sky was the darkest blue I had ever seen while still technically being daylight and the wind was so unrelenting that trees were beginning to fall already. The wind was loud, too, screaming like a banshee foretelling doom. It was impossible to forget for even a moment that The Storm was approaching.

While we all tended to our most immediate tasks of grocery shopping, boarding the windows, charging batteries and bringing wood in, we also consumed news. The hurricane coming from the Gulf Coast had made landfall and was at that moment approaching New York City. My internet connection was still working then, so I set up two computers on our kitchen table where cable news anchors could be seen yelling through torrential rains up and down the coast. Millions of people had already lost power in the Mid-Atlantic and the White House was declaring one state after another in an official state of emergency. There were rumors that congressional offices in DC were beginning to flood with people trapped inside. It was impossible to keep track of the horror stories suffered at hospitals, nursing homes and homeless shelters, and already, lists of names of missing people were circulating online, growing by the hour. At first, the fear felt familiar. Hurricanes Katrina, Sandy and Irene had brought varying degrees of terror to the East Coast in previous years and we knew what to expect. But that feeling of familiarity vanished quickly as every weather record was broken and it became clear that the devastation ahead was greater than anything we'd ever lived through. Our fears were no longer borne out of memory, but of imagination, which was limitless and terrifying.

I walked inside to get a glass of water and answer the ringing phone. It was our landline and I barely recognized its alarming trill at first. Cell phone networks were so jammed up that I had retired my smartphone to a drawer and told our families to use the house number. I knew it would be my parents calling and one of my last chances to talk to them before the storm arrived.

"Hi, Mom," I said into the receiver, working to sound cheerful.

"Ash? Hi, honey. How is everything there?"

It was a relief to hear my mother's familiar, concerned voice, and I had the overwhelming urge to burst into tears and let her lavish me with maternal care, but I resisted. Like any parent of several children, my mother's energy was divided, but the division had become increasingly more unbalanced since my brother's addiction recovery in those years.

I knew without asking that he would be staying with them for The Storm and I resented him for it. Maybe I should have resented her for it, too, but I didn't, and we weren't close enough in those days to have the luxury of fighting. I wanted more of her than she could give and keeping a distance made it easier to manage that desire. How much should a grown man need his mother, I wondered. What about in extraordinary circumstances?

"I'm okay, Mom, thanks. We're just battening down the hatches. What about you guys?"

"Oh, Dad is buzzing around fixing this and that. I don't know what on earth he's doing, but I suppose it's good to be prepared."

She sounded distracted. "Never mind about us, Ash," she went on. "Are you and Pia okay up there? Once The Storm starts, you're going to be really far from everything. Do you want to come down and stay with us?"

It wasn't a real offer, but I liked to hear it.

"Thanks, but we're fine, Mom. I don't think there's anywhere to hide from it now. We probably all should have taken a European vacation this week instead of sticking around."

"Oh, I could never have done that," she said. "This is our home, Ash. It wouldn't feel right to just run away. I guess I sound like one of those crazy people you see on TV who refuse to leave the beach right before a hurricane or something. But maybe they aren't so crazy."

"Everyone's crazy now," I said.

"So we're all the same—that's nice."

The conversation wasn't going quite as I expected. I assumed my mother would be clearheaded about The Storm, offering sound advice and parental comfort, but she was somewhere else. There was a distant falseness to her voice that I didn't know or like.

"Mom, the phone lines are probably going to go out for a long time and we won't be able to contact each other. Let's promise not to freak out when that happens. I will be in touch as soon as I can after that, so just assume that all is well."

"Okay," she said quietly. "That's a good idea."

Silence for a moment.

"Honey, things are all going to be fine," she said. "They always overreact about weather and I'm sure this one will just blow past us like the rest of them."

It was unclear whether she believed this or not, but it seemed an important theory to her. This was how my mother talked: "they" were the nonspecific authorities somewhere else that overreacted about everything, and the rest of us just waited for things to "blow past." My parents were incapable of outsize reactions, a helpful quality for making young children feel safe and secure, but an utterly irrational one on that day. This compulsory need to believe in the absolute resilience of life as we knew it bothered me immensely as I held the receiver to my ear. It didn't apply any longer and I expected her to know that.

"Mom, this storm is going to be bad. You should take the forecast seriously. Do you guys have everything you need?"

"Oh, you know us," she said. I could feel her waving me off through the phone. "We don't need much."

This was true. But all of her stalwart bromides were meaningless then, reckless even, in the face of real danger. I wanted to reach through the phone and shake her by her small shoulders, tell her to wake up. But I didn't have anything to offer her that would make her safer or more prepared. We were too far apart, and I was as helpless as she was.

"Um, okay. Anyhow, I love you and Dad. Be safe."

"I love you, too, honey."

And that was it, until the next time I would hear or not hear from my parents after The Storm. I knew I should call my siblings, too, but the conversation with my mother had been exhausting enough, so I decided to put that chore off for the time being. What were other families doing at that moment, I wondered. Was this the sort of situation in which extended families all came together for a big communal survival experience? No, not likely, I concluded. Maybe in other parts of the world, but not in America. We hunker down on our own here.

"I'm going back out for peanut butter. I think we need to have as much peanut butter as possible," Pia said as she walked past me in the kitchen without a glance.

Ever since she had found me at the Isole Festival with Maggie's hands in mine, Pia had been icy. We hadn't talked about what she'd seen or her prepper convention. I supposed neither of us wanted to know. It was all business at our house and, for once, I was relieved to receive her laundry list of disaster preparation chores. She gave me orders and I executed them. This was a new strategy for Pia, one that required more restraint than I knew she was capable of and that frightened me all the more. Was there an enormous blowup in our future? Some cruel form of retaliation? My feelings on this were so jumbled that I worked to stay busy to avoid thinking hard about the state of things between us. To acknowledge it would have opened doors I wasn't prepared to step through—sadness, rage or, worst of all, maybe relief. I didn't want to know. I wanted peace and survival for the immediate future.

"Okay, thanks," I yelled after her before the front door shut. "Maybe some more black beans, too."

I watched her hustle quickly to the car and realized it had started raining. Shit, the windows. I needed to get those done. I went back outside and repositioned the ladder beneath another bedroom window. My body felt weak as I hauled a new sheet of plywood up the ladder, nail gun holstered around my waist. I hadn't done anything that physical for that long in months and it was approaching excruciating. Still, I relished the feeling of fear mixed with urgency. It seemed so purposeful and managed to displace all other nagging emotions. I vowed to take on more home improvement projects after all this was over—a thought that I knew to be ludicrous even then, as if things would be pretty much the same on the other side of The Storm.

The rain was coming harder now as I finished one window and set the ladder up under another. My strategy was to hold the plywood against the window with my left knee and hand while I shot nails through to the outer border of the sill with my right. It seemed to hold okay, with lots and lots of nails, but because the plywood sheets were perfect squares, two inches of uncovered window still peeked out at the top and bottom. I couldn't gauge how much of a problem I should consider this, but I had no other options and it was raining hard, so my system had to suffice.

It must have taken me a long time to finish the last window because Pia pulled into the driveway just as I dismounted the ladder and ran to get out of the rain. She was right behind me with bulging canvas bags of whatever could still be found at the food co-op. I stood in the entryway and peeled each piece of soaked clothing off my shivering body until only my boxer briefs remained, though they were soaked, too.

"Do you think we should start a fire?" Pia asked through wet shivers.

"Let's wait," I said. "We should save the cut wood until we really need it. I'm going to take a hot shower."

She nodded and began putting groceries away, and I could

see that this was the answer she was hoping for. It was not the time for luxuries like crackling fires. No discussion needed— not that either of us wanted discussion. Anyhow, the rain was coming down so hard that we would have had to raise our voices if there was more to be said.

The wind had begun to make a fierce whistling sound outside. We could hear it pick up the raindrops and send them hammering against one side of the house, and then briefly release its hold, only to swirl around again until another wall of rain slammed into a different side of the house. If there was a pattern to it, we couldn't tell, which produced a menacing sense that we were being enveloped. Like Dorothy's in *The Wizard of Oz*, our home felt as if it could be picked up and whirled around, then dropped someplace else altogether. This effect was compounded by the fact that our windows were now boarded up, so aside from the uncovered strips of dim light peeking through the tops and bottoms of the windows, we couldn't see outside.

I jogged upstairs into the frigid bathroom and let the water run until it was scalding. Thunder roared outside. Was it true that you shouldn't bathe during thunderstorms or was that an old wives' tale? I couldn't remember, but it seemed best to get in and out before the weather deteriorated further. This was it; this was The Storm, I thought to myself. We had gone through so many false starts in those months, but we recognized the real thing when it arrived. The sky was darker and the rain was more forceful. Most notably, the authorities were unambivalent: it's here and it's worse than we thought, they told us. The Storm is upon us.

I let the hot water pour over my scalp until the chill was gone and my head started to feel fuzzy. In the days that followed, I would think of that shower, re-creating the sensation in my mind when the stink and the cold got to be too much. What an underappreciated luxury it is to shower at one's will. I was unburdened then by the cost of such a luxury, which we all mistook for a right. As I stepped out of the bathroom, in my soft, silly sweatpants and an oversize flannel shirt, I had already moved on.

When I went back downstairs, Pia had poured two mason jars of cabernet and was sautéing vegetables on the stove top. I knew better than to mistake this as a gesture of peace—we needed to eat the overripe vegetables in the fridge before they went bad. Still, it was a welcome scene. I took one of the jars and moved to the living room, where the smell of worms had become so familiar that I almost didn't notice it. (Years later, the smell of wet soil would always send me back to that house in those months.) I turned on the radio and stared at the muted television as if, together, they might give me the full story of what was ahead. But instead of the familiar grave tones of nameless experts, John Coltrane's "A Love Supreme" skittered from the speakers, which I'd always loved, with its gentle precision that managed to somehow sound like a new and improvised journey every time. You had to pay attention to appreciate each little step and I was happy for the distraction. Apparently, there was nothing left to be said about the approaching storm. There was only waiting.

I turned the volume up and walked over to a window. With my knees folded beneath me on the cold floor, I could look out to the backyard through the unobscured strip at the bottom. The naked trees thrashed against one another, creating a wet bed of branches and debris beneath. Beside a cluster of evergreens, I could look right through the leafless deciduous trees. At the corner of my view was Peg's house looking small and sweet. Smoke puffed out the chimney. It was oddly comforting to know that she was there, maybe grading papers or reading a novel about a far-off place. The truth was that I didn't have any idea what she would be doing because Peg remained a mystery to me. I didn't even know if she was prepared for The Storm, which seemed a dire oversight now. We had become fast friends only months before, but as The Storm approached, something in her seemed to be changing. I suddenly wished that I had asked her more questions about her own life before The Storm began.

The wind picked up and splattered rain so forcefully against the window that for a moment I couldn't see anything at all. Then it slowed again and, through the dripping pane, I watched the base of an enormous maple begin to disappear in a growing pool of accumulating water. I thought of the bear and her cub that we had seen less than two weeks before and wondered what treacherous hiding place they might be huddled in now. There would be no surviving this, not for the bears or any of the other confused animals that had emerged from hibernation prematurely, looking for spring's bounty.

As I considered the lives that might be extinguished in the coming days—human and animal—my eyes caught something moving far away. It was near Peg's house, in the woods between us. I couldn't make out the form, but the bright primary colors of winter clothing were unmistakable. It moved a little and then got still, repeating the pattern twice.

"Pia, there's someone out here!" I yelled from the living room.

"What? No. Who would be out there?" she said as she hurried over to join me at my lookout post on the floor.

"It's Peg," she said through squinting eyes.

"How can you tell?"

"She wears a blue-and-red coat. I'm pretty sure it's her."

Pia got up and walked back to the kitchen, where she was throwing pieces of a shriveled red pepper into her pasta sauce.

"And you think *my* friends are crazy, Ash?" she yelled from the other room. "That's a strange bird out there."

Sure enough, the longer I watched the form, the more it came into focus. It *was* Peg. Was she walking toward us? No. She seemed to be moving from tree to tree, though she was too far away for me to know for sure. She would have to be completely soaked and freezing. No normal person had outdoor apparel to match this rain. She was apparently just walking around outside, likely catching hypothermia, communing with the trees.

I needed to talk to her.

"Some people lose their grip on reality in times of crisis," Pia said knowingly from the kitchen.

"Thanks, doctor," I mumbled.

I sat and watched the figure for another five minutes, quietly urging it to go back inside and get warm. Peg was older than my mother, but heartier than August and certainly more knowledgeable about nature's power than any of us. That was what made her behavior seem so reckless and strange, as if she wanted The Storm to take her. She stood mostly still out in the rain, but I never considered looking away. Finally, her figure disappeared into its safe cottage. I wanted to call her, to ask why she was out there and hear her rational explanation. She would tell me that she was gathering wood or some other ordinary task and we would laugh about the little scare she'd given me.

"Food's done," Pia announced.

I could hear a drink being refilled and her fork already moving around on the plate. I pushed up onto my good leg and went to meet her in the kitchen. Nothing else to do, really.

TWENTY-ONE

PIA AND I sat at the kitchen table drinking tea after dinner and looking past each other at the boarded windows that promised protection from The Storm. It felt like the middle of the night, but it was probably only about seven. We rarely did that—sat at the dinner table like contented partners with nowhere else to be. It was the sort of small but critical ritual that I wanted more of in our marriage, one of the things I didn't think I needed at the start. Pia wasn't as attached to such conventions; I'd always known that. And I liked that she wanted to rewrite the rules of domesticity. Still, I sometimes longed for some of the rituals of our parents.

In my childhood home, the kitchen table served as the nucleus for all familial activity. It was where we ate all of our meals but also where we carved Halloween pumpkins and colored Easter eggs. It never moved or changed, just acquired new blemishes that enhanced its familiarity. For all I knew, that gently treated pine table hadn't been delivered to our home from a nearby furniture store years before, but had grown straight up through the floorboards. That was how rooted it was in our lives.

No such stability was present as Pia and I sat across from one another that night. She was jumpy and excited.

"Are you happy to be here with me?" I asked. I wasn't looking for a fight, but some evidence of closeness that I could hold on to as The Storm gained momentum.

"I'm not *happy* about any of this, Ash." She sounded annoyed, but her eyes twinkled. She was crackling with energy in anticipation of potential catastrophe. She could barely suppress her enthusiasm.

"Not *happy*," I corrected myself. "I mean, are you grateful that we have each other? That it's me you're trapped inside with?"

"Sure. Yes."

"What do you think other people are doing in their houses right now?" It was a dumb question, but I needed a new angle to break through to her. She wasn't there with me.

"Jesus, Ash, I don't know! What does it matter?"

Pia looked around impatiently and I knew it would only be a matter of minutes before dinnertime ended. That brief silence was interrupted by the sharp crack of a small tree breaking outside. She jumped slightly at the sound.

"I was just wondering," I said. It felt pathetic, to ramble on while Pia stared at me silently. I wanted desperately to hold on to her attention while I had her there, but I knew deep down that I didn't have her at all. She was looking through me, waiting for the conversation to end. The weather made me feel needier than ever, but it was having the opposite effect on her. Her mind was adrift.

The wind's roar grew louder around us. Angry rain changed to sleet as I watched a thin visible strip of window blur under a new layer of ice that seemed to be enveloping the house. I wondered if it was possible to suffocate under a coating of ice. The temperature had dropped dramatically in less than an hour. Perhaps we would just freeze in a perfect house-shaped form, neatly preserved until the next thaw, when we'd be discovered intact like woolly mammoths of the Pleistocene age. My heart began to race and, despite the cold air in our kitchen, I was sweating through my shirt. My body seemed to be catching up with my mind, realizing that The Storm was upon us and we were trapped there together.

Weather events in the modern age test our faith in the almighty power of civilization. Sure, recent years had brought floods and earthquakes and fires of a terrifying new breadth and frequency, but still, Western technology had always prevailed. Until that storm, we could all trust that our electricity would eventually be restored and our delayed flights would run again. Even at the height of the disastrous events we'd already lived through before, many aspects of our lives chugged on obliviously. Our paychecks still appeared automatically in our bank accounts, utility bills still accrued and emails still bounced back and forth among us. Always, we believed then, we would trump nature. Remembering this fallacy is crucial for understanding why I did the reckless thing I did next.

"I have to get out," I said, pushing my chair back with a screech. I don't remember deciding this, only doing it.

"What? No. No one leaves," Pia said firmly.

I shook my head and began pulling on ski pants, boots, another sweater. By my reasoning, it was bad outside, but not so bad yet that the right gear couldn't protect me.

"I have to get out," I said again.

Pia jumped up in a weak attempt to stop me, which I was grateful for, but I wasn't acting: I needed to get the fuck out. All of a sudden, every minute that passed felt like time lost to The Storm. It was getting stronger, and soon—we didn't know how soon—it would force us to succumb, cowering inside in waiting. I needed one last breath of fresh air and human contact before that happened, and I was afraid that I would lose my nerve if I hesitated. I was going to Peg's house.

I pulled down the earflaps of my red trapper hat and nodded decisively at Pia. She had her hands on her hips and a puzzled look on her face, but she didn't protest further. As I left, the door slammed behind me, sucked back into place by a swirling gust of wind. I ignored the wave of panic that swept over me. Sleet was stinging the small strip of exposed skin around my eyes and testing the resistance of my winter layers. Visibility was almost nonexistent, just a wall of whirling black, but I reassured myself that Peg's house was only a few minutes' walk (under normal conditions) through the woods, a straight line if I watched my footing and followed the dim glow of her porch light. I was outside and there was no turning back.

Almost immediately, I tripped over a fallen branch and fell to my knees. My gloved hands sank wrist-deep in icy water, which seeped in toward my fingers and up my forearms. The water was deeper than I expected and hiding a messy bed of fallen branches, twigs and decomposing leaves. Already, parts of my body were soaked and freezing.

I stood back up and took slow, deliberate steps, holding my arms out in front to catch unexpected tree branches before they impaled me. On three occasions, a waterlogged foot fell so deep into the slush that I had to use my hands to yank it back out without toppling over entirely. My cheeks burned, but my still-dry midsection sweated as I huffed my way through the woods. The sleet was coming down hard and I figured that it would be a few inches deeper by the time I made the trip back. It wouldn't be fun, but it would be manageable if I had some time to dry off at Peg's first. The biggest challenge was trying not to fall over. A headlamp would have been smart. It seemed as if everything in the forest—every leaf and branch and rock—had come unattached over the course of the past few hours and was swirling in a cyclone around my head. If there was a word for whatever weather effect was occurring, I didn't know it.

Finally, I drew close enough to the light on Peg's porch to see her shadowy form moving around inside the cottage. There was no chance of her being anywhere else on that night, but I was still overcome with relief to know she was there.

"Ash, my goodness! What on earth are you doing?" Peg said as she opened the door and hustled me inside.

I began peeling off layers, starting with the top of my body and moving down.

"I just had to get out," I panted. It was alarming to hear my own frightened voice aloud. "I hope it's okay that I came. I just had to get out."

"Of course, of course," she said, running my wet gloves and hat to the woodstove in the living room, where they could bake on top.

Modesty seemed a luxury by then, so I opted to take off my jeans, leaving only a pair of wet navy long johns between my bare bottom half and Peg's kitchen. I was as close to comfort as I could reasonably get.

"Sorry." I shrugged with a smile.

Peg laughed a big wonderful laugh and waved her hand as though she hadn't noticed that I was in my underwear. She was wearing what appeared to be an old pair of men's sweatpants with the fading crest of a school on the lower left leg and a red flannel shirt that thinned at the elbows. She looked older and softer than I'd ever seen her.

"Something hot?" she asked.

"Sure. Um, coffee, I guess. I'm not going to sleep tonight anyhow."

I noticed that Peg's house looked spotless. The kitchen countertops were gleaming and the area rug in the living room showed the undisturbed tracks of a vacuum cleaner. It seemed an odd time to be tidy. The only item out of place was a large basket filled with dirty root vegetables sitting right in the middle of the kitchen, where we now stood. It was an impressive cornucopia of oranges, reds, browns and beiges, still wearing the drying earth from the ground from which they were pulled. Peg saw me looking.

"The remains of my autumn harvest," she said. "I thought I'd cut them all up and roast them today before the power goes out."

"You could feed a dozen people with that!"

"Well, there's just me—and now, you. They won't do any good rotting in the basement. C'mon, let's get started."

Peg filled the kitchen sink with warm water and we stood side by side, gently rubbing tubers clean and piling them in the dish rack, one after another. It felt good to have something specific to do with my hands. We didn't say much, which was just fine. In the background, I heard the low voices of an AM radio station providing an endless stream of detailed weather information. It was one long, breathless report in an unfeeling male voice: "…wintry mix…accumulations are expected to exceed several feet in just the next twenty-four hours… unprecedented wind speeds wreaking havoc on property and roads…watch for falling trees and large branches across the state if you must travel outside…the National Weather Service in Vermont has issued flood warnings for every county… the National Weather Service has issued additional winter storm warnings in every county…evacuations are beginning in Windham County, Bennington County, Rutland County

MEG LITTLE REILLY

and Windsor County…several weather-related deaths in the southern part of the state already reported…unprecedented…historic levels…"

I watched the sleet come down in front of us and realized that Peg hadn't boarded up her windows, but there was nothing to be done about it now. I could tell the speed at which The Storm was coming and wondered how long I would be away from my home. There was no plan or purpose for my visit, but I couldn't fathom going back to Pia just yet, even as the space between our two houses seemed to disappear into a blur of raging sleet.

Peg patted the final sweet potato clean and announced that we would be moving to the kitchen table for the chopping portion of our project. She gave me a cutting board and a sharp knife and showed me the size that she preferred for each variety. As I settled into my new assignment, she put a mug of steaming coffee beside me and gave my shoulder a light squeeze. We were both just pushing through the motions of normal, busy behavior, pretending to feel okay as the world closed in on us. I knew that Pia would come up in conversation only if I brought her up, which I almost never did around Peg.

"I can't stop thinking about August," I said.

"I know," Peg replied, unable to offer promises of his safety. "Keep a close watch on that boy, Ash."

I sliced a purple carrot slowly and pushed the disks aside with my knife.

"Also, Crow," I added. "I can't get him out of my mind."

Peg sat up in her chair: "I went to see him," she said as if it had been on the tip of her tongue all along. "I was thinking about him, too. I just thought I should see him one more time before The Storm."

"Really? When did you see him? Did you talk about the runoff plan?"

"No, I didn't bring it up." Peg took a dainty sip of coffee. "I still hate him for it, but it's too late now. I went to see him last night because I had to know if he was right about all this…all his preparations. His approach has seemed so wrong to me for so long, but as The Storm got closer…I just had to know if he was right and we were wrong."

"And?"

Peg shook her head and frowned. "I don't know," she said. "He told me that his ex-wife and their daughter needed a safe place to stay and she asked if they could stay with him. They live down in Putney. He was obviously conflicted about it when we talked—going on about how there aren't enough provisions in that hideaway of his for three people and it wasn't part of his plan. He never intended on sharing it, but he seems still to care for them. He was undecided when I left… I don't know what he ended up doing."

"That bunker was definitely only made for one man's survival."

"Yes, well, I guess he has to decide if his survival alone is enough."

I took a long sip of coffee.

"I didn't know he had an ex-wife or a daughter," I said.

"It's not his biological daughter," Peg explained, "but he raised her from a little girl and he makes no distinction. He's been good to her, I think. They divorced about seven years ago."

It was hard to imagine this family-man version of Crow, but I shouldn't have been surprised. All of us had taken long, winding roads to get to where The Storm found us. Certainly none of us wanted to be defined by our response to that moment. I thought about Pia back home, no doubt bustling around the house with her own preoccupations of survival. It wasn't right that I had gone, or that she had let me go so easily. We were really just cohabitants living parallel lives in the same space by then.

"I don't want to go back home," I confessed to Peg. "Back to Pia."

"I know," she said softly. "But where would you rather be?"

My answer came quickly, though I had never voiced it before. "With Maggie Chase. I don't have any idea whether she thinks the same about me, but I can't stop thinking about her... That's so bad."

I had forgotten about the potato in front of me and the knife in my hand. Peg didn't have any response just yet, so I went on.

"Maybe this is all The Storm. Pia's anxious and I'm feeling alone. I know I still love her. When this is all over and everyone is themselves again, maybe we can start to repair things. I don't trust that I know what I want right now. You should probably forget that I said that thing about Maggie. It's not real."

The wind howled outside and I was reminded that, with every additional minute I sat at Peg's table, my walk back home got more treacherous.

"Be careful about blaming everything on The Storm, Ash," she said. "It's the catalyst for a lot of this malcontent, but it's not the cause. If there's something rotten in your marriage, it won't leave with The Storm. Fix things between you and Pia, or don't, but don't explain your problems away with The Storm. You're not that cowardly."

It was alarming to hear the state of my relationship summarized so coldly, and embarrassing to be so transparent. I knew that everything she said was true, but I didn't have the energy for self-examination. The world was closing in on us and it wasn't clear that we would live through The Storm, let alone thrive on the other side. I didn't want to hear what Peg was saying, not then.

"I think all I have is survival right now," I said with a tinge of anger in my voice. Peg should have known this. "I'll have to worry about becoming a courageous person later, if there is a later."

"Yes, of course," she said quickly, recognizing my hurt feelings.

The conversation was over, and I felt stupid for sitting there in front of Peg's vegetables in my long underwear all of a sudden, so I started to get up. As I did, she let out a sigh and I remembered the purpose for my visit.

I sat back down and looked across the table. "Peg, why were you outside earlier?"

"No reason, exactly. Taking it all in. Saying goodbye."

"Goodbye to what?"

"To these woods," she said. "There's a lot of loss ahead, Ash. Nothing is going to be like it was before. Your generation will experience the brunt of these changes. You'll see."

It wasn't the answer I wanted. The sadness that I'd seen flashing behind Peg's eyes in recent weeks now seemed to weigh down her whole body.

"Peg, are you going to be okay here?"

She smiled slightly. "You mean, will I be okay all alone? Yes, I'll be okay. And thank you. This isn't the way I envisioned things unfolding, but I'll be okay."

"Why *are* you alone?" I asked gently.

She took a deep breath and paused for a moment. "This may sound strange, but I've never felt alone in my life, not even recently. I've been in love twice, with wonderful men who made me very happy. Ultimately, they wanted things that I didn't need—marriage and children, primarily—and we parted both times, but I have only great memories of those relationships. I've had a very full life thanks to my travels and my studies and all the friends I've made along the way. Most of all, wherever I was, I felt loved and protected by the natural world. I know it sounds strange and maybe even antisocial, but that's the truth. The woods have been my greatest love."

It was the kind of sentiment one might read in a book and laugh at it for its poetic naïveté, but Peg said it with such conviction that I didn't question her. She got something from nature that most of us could not, or would not, be open to receiving. It would have been fairer for her to have been born an animal, to live outside, without boundaries. She was wiser than most of us, but still not quite fit for this confined human life. Maybe, I considered for a fleeting moment, she *had* been one of those animals before, or would be in another life. All of a sudden, Peg's aloneness seemed bigger than my own.

"But these woods are changing." I nodded quietly. I understood what she was telling me: the most consistent thread of her life was vanishing.

"Yes," she said into the table. "Irreparably and permanently."

I wanted to hug her and tell her that this was just one storm, that it would end, but I knew that wasn't true. This storm would change our world forever and, more important, so would every weather event—dramatic and subtle—that came after it. A transformation had been set into motion years before that was bigger than my optimism or Peg's love. There was nothing to say.

In the silence we listened to the dim crank-radio voice coming from the other room: "Most of the state of Vermont has lost electrical power at this time, with the remaining northern parts expected to go dark in the next few hours. Emergency management is warning everyone to shelter in place for now and avoid travel of any kind. If you are in immediate danger, 911 operators are working around the clock, but response vehicles are in high demand and emergency shelters are filling up quickly. A priority is being placed on people in buildings that have collapsed under fallen trees, anyone near exposed electrical wires and areas at a high risk for both flooding and hypothermia cases. I repeat—all others are encouraged to stay where they are and conserve heat. This is just the start of what is expected to be a very long and destructive weather event..."

"You should go," Peg said.

I nodded and walked to the entryway to begin pulling on layers. Peg brought my wet gloves, hat, scarf and pants from the woodstove, which were hot, but still soggy. I dreaded going back outside, fighting through the sleet and then hunkering down with Pia and the worms. I wanted to stay there with Peg and eat roasted root vegetables for days.

Her phone rang while I was pulling on my mittens and Peg excused herself to answer it.

"Jesus!" I heard her say to the person on the line, but it sounded like "jay-sus" in her accent. She said it again and then something I couldn't hear and then hung up.

"August is missing," Peg said from the doorway. "He sneaked out of his foster home and they can't find him. There's a search team out now. That was a social worker. She apparently tried you at home."

"Oh my God, I gotta go," I said.

Peg nodded. "Get home first. Don't do anything crazy."

I yanked the door open to break through a layer of ice that had been forming around its perimeter, allowing a blast of wet air to spray inside. For a moment, I couldn't remember where I was supposed to be going or why I was standing there. Peg handed me my hat. *Get home, find August. Or do I go out looking for August now?* I had no idea where to start.

"Thank you, Peg. Good luck," I said.

"You, too, Ash." She gave my arm a little squeeze and then sealed the door behind me.

Visibility had somehow worsened and the ice balls falling from the sky were noticeably larger. They came down as if pitched by a furious god, aiming directly at the exposed patches of my face.

I stepped from Peg's porch into a foot of slush that was just the right mix of rain and ice to be more uncomfortable than either on their own. I couldn't think about the wet, numbing sensation that crept around my ankles and up my shins or the pain of my still-healing foot as I forced it to work. To consider any of the frightening variables around me would have made that short trip impossible. So I heaved one leg after the other, swinging my arms for momentum and pushing forward. Every few steps, I closed my eyes against the stinging ice-rain, which made it difficult to see even when they were open. "Don't stop, don't stop, keep walking," I chanted. My thighs were burning from the sheer athleticism each step required and my heavy breaths were almost audible amid the howling wind.

How long could August survive in this, I wondered. Not long. Even in the screaming weather chaos around me, I had to fight to keep the frightening images of August alone in those woods out of my brain. Just get home and call the police to find out what's going on.

I had nothing to guide my steps but the faintest porch light coming from our house, which blurred into spots and danced away from me as my eyes—or my mind—lost focus. I knew I was roughly halfway there when my groin smashed into the fallen tree trunk I had climbed over earlier that night that crossed the path. It had a slick casing of ice around it by then and I realized our whole world was being enveloped in the same deadly cast.

I hoisted my weaker leg up and over the trunk, straddling it momentarily before putting all my weight down on the other side as I attempted to dismount. At that moment, my throbbing foot slipped on something beneath the slush, causing my knee to crumple and my entire body to fall on top of the useless limb. I put my arms out to prevent myself from submerging into the water entirely, which left my face exposed to a sharp branch that stabbed directly into my right cheek, just below the eye. The pain was acute, but the panic that burst from my heart and raced through my veins was worse. At first, I thought I had been blinded. I squeezed my eyes tight and imagined having to crawl the rest of the way, my face in the icy stew below. When I finally attempted to open each eye, blindness was ruled out, but my face was too numb to gauge what exactly had happened and how fast I might be losing blood.

I pulled myself up and forged on, each step more frantic and inefficient than the previous one. I had to get home before I died of hypothermia or blood loss or cardiac arrest—any of which seemed possible to my panicked mind. All of a sudden, I became aware of the countless branches and rocks that threatened to take me down, swarming forest tentacles, eager to pull me apart as punishment for doubting nature's absolute power.

My hat had come loose and was wet; cold wind screamed into one ear, which I didn't attempt to correct because I was afraid to use my hands for anything other than steadying myself and clearing a safe path. Pull up, step long, push down. I talked myself through each labored step in the slush, working to ignore the fatigue, the cold and the terrifying numbness that had now reached my upper thighs. It seemed impossible

MEG LITTLE REILLY

that everything hadn't frozen entirely, given the low temperatures, but the speed at which it all moved—in no discernible direction—must have allowed it to persist as a liquid.

Finally, my left boot hit something hard and, as I considered freaking the fuck out again, I realized it was the first step of our front porch. The light glowed in front of me and I could make out the handle of our front door. I crawled up the stairs on hands and knees, relieved to surrender to the pain, and banged on the door three times until it cracked just enough for Pia to peek through.

"Oh my God!"

She dragged my dripping body inside and began tugging off layers as my limbs went from numb to freezing, and then back to a burning numbness that felt permanent and frightening. Eventually, I was naked, drying on the floor in the entryway. Pia threw a blanket around me and we both massaged my moist, pink body to restore circulation. When I began to feel like a living human again, Pia ran to get her first-aid supplies to patch the shallow puncture wound and salve the aching bruises on my face.

"Have they found August?" I asked.

Pia nodded. "His parents have him. The cops just called. He walked all three miles back here a few hours ago—before it got really bad outside—so I guess they're going to just let him stay. They don't really have a choice at this point. Crazy."

"Jesus." I shook my head, intensely relieved to know that August was alive. It wasn't good that he would be trapped inside with his awful parents for the storm. But he was found, and that was good.

Pia didn't ask right away about how Peg was or what I'd done at her house or why I'd felt so strongly about going. As the primary initiator of erratic behavior in our family, those weren't questions that would have occurred to her. My guess was she didn't really care by then either. And I was back now, so she could play the role of doting nurse until her own obsessions forced their way between us again.

When finally I was clothed and wrapped in blankets, Pia and I sat together at two ends of the couch sipping tea again quietly. I appreciated her attentiveness at that moment. I didn't have to convince her of how terrified I'd been; it was all over my battered face. And it thrilled her more than a little.

I took a deep breath in and exhaled loudly, letting my head fall back onto a pillow.

"So," she said, eyes wide. "Tell me everything."

TWENTY-TWO

WE WOKE UP the next morning to what sounded like an explosion in the guest room. I jumped out of bed and felt my numb toes hit our icy floors. The power had gone out hours before and, even with four blankets and a winter hat, we had been shivering for a long time. I ran to the next room and found that a fat branch of a large tree had gone straight through the boarded-up window, sending wet, shattered glass in every direction. Sleet was coming in at an alarming rate and the temperature in the room was just high enough to melt it into massive puddles on the hardwood floor.

"It's bad! Put some shoes on—we need to fix this *now*!" I yelled to the bedroom, but Pia was already behind me.

"I'll go get a tarp," she said. "Let's just get the window covered."

For someone who had had as many tumblers of cabernet as she had the night before, she was impressively alert. But of course, these were her moments to shine.

I pulled rain boots on over my woolly socks and ran downstairs to search for duct tape. There were several rolls of varying widths for me to choose from, duct tape being one of the more obvious items in the prepper's tool kit. We met back upstairs at the broken window; with the hard, stinging sleet blowing in our faces, we coordinated our actions to hold the tarp in place over the opening and tape it to the wall. We went around and around the perimeter of the tarp and then just stretched the tape vertically and horizontally across the window. I slid an empty dresser across the room to stand in front of the flimsy setup. The dresser only covered the bottom half, but it kept the tarp from billowing too violently.

"Should we try to clean up? Mop or sweep or something?" I asked, looking down at the glass shards submerged in water around our feet and splayed across the bed that no one ever used.

"What good would that do?" Pia spat, ending our collaborative moment.

We shut the door to the guest room and jammed towels in the crack between the floor and the door in an effort to contain the cold air that was pouring into the rest of the house. The entire episode had lasted only about five minutes, but we were both heaving with exhaustion. As we walked away from the door, we realized that there were still hours and hours of frigid, powerless daylight ahead together.

"Let's just make coffee," I said, walking down the stairs.

The woodstove was cold to the touch as I threw split logs into its belly and fired it up. Thank God for this stove, I thought. There was nothing else to huddle around and nowhere to be comfortable in our house. On those cold mornings, the only difference between the indoors and the outside world was the absence of accumulation in our living room. The winter air was everywhere and we moved like ghosts enveloped in a cloud of our own condensing breath. When finally heat was detectable, we pushed our bodies as close to the stove as possible without catching on fire. Pia poured

MEG LITTLE REILLY

water into an old iron kettle that sat right on top of the stove and worked as efficiently as any modern appliance we owned. (Later, after The Storm had completed its punishment, that indestructible kettle would be one of the few items from our former life that remained intact.)

When she was warm enough, Pia went back to the kitchen and began pulling items from our cabinets, which overflowed with nonperishable goods. Canned beans and vegetables, pasta, rice, quinoa, wheat berry, peanut butter, almond butter, cashew butter, whole wheat flour, chickpea flour, rice flour, tamari sauce, olive oil, truffle oil… She was rearranging, creating a new system and order for the rationing of our sustenance. I didn't recognize it at that moment, but this would be her primary obsession for our remaining days in that cold, dark house. With no end to The Storm in sight and a finite amount of food in the house, Pia was devising a system for meals that would utilize the most immediately perishable of the nonperishable items while factoring questions of nutritional balance, digestion and—I hoped—taste.

"Can you leave the peanut butter out?" I yelled.

"No peanut butter yet," Pia said without looking up. "That's for later. You can use the cream cheese in the fridge. That will be bad by tomorrow."

I didn't want to argue, so I walked past her to pull a sweating tub of cream cheese from our powerless refrigerator and got to work on my disappointing breakfast. I watched two pieces of bread warm on the top of the woodstove, where my wet gloves normally rested, and tried to imagine other culinary possibilities for the days ahead. I wasn't particularly hungry, but this seemed a comfortingly simple project to focus on.

I returned to my post under the visible strip of window to observe the day's weather while I ate my toast. The wind was as strong as the day before, but the precipitation alternated between sleet and heavy, wet snow. It was trying to accumulate on the ground, but there was so much rushing water on the oversaturated earth that it sloshed around when it landed before melting into the mess. This was a troubling development. If the water levels continued to rise at that pace, I knew it wouldn't be long before it reached our doorsill and eventually even our windows.

I stood up and turned the radio on, hoping for cooler heads to inform me that my fears were unwarranted.

"What we know right now," started the familiar male voice of an NPR host, "is that all five boroughs in New York City are underwater. That includes Manhattan, which was evacuated two days ago. Unfortunately, not everyone is heeding these evacuation orders and there are a dozen confirmed dead as of this morning. That number will likely rise as temperatures continue to drop and rescue opportunities diminish. The next phase of this storm is snow, so things are about to get significantly more difficult."

The voice was hoarse and rushed. I could hear the sound of papers being shuffled and murmuring voices in the studio.

"We're getting new information now from Boston, as well," he went on. "I'm…I'm just going to provide the confirmed reports as we receive them, so please bear with us as we skip around a bit this morning. We're working hard to report on everything as it comes in. For now, we'll turn to our colleagues in Cape Cod, who are operating at low power thanks to a satellite feed from WGBH in Boston. They have a correspondent on the ground with the latest from The Storm. Let's go now to Roger Stearns in Barnstable. Roger, are you there?"

The sound went dead for a moment, clicked twice, then connected with a distant voice in the rain. "Yes, this is Roger.

I'm standing about three hundred feet from the shore, which is as close as I can get to the water without being knocked off my feet by the wind."

Roger on the cape in Barnstable was barely audible above the roaring ambient noise, but his terror was apparent.

"Roger, what can you see?"

"What I'm looking at now… I've never seen anything like this… What I'm looking at is a dark, almost black sky—at ten o'clock in the morning. There are low clouds moving quickly and the rain seems to be turning to snow. There isn't another soul on the beach and we can't stay much longer. It appears that most people have followed the governor's evacuation order. Yesterday, you could actually see the hurricane moving toward us from the southwest, and today the dark clouds are approaching from the north. When those two fronts meet—which could be very soon—the beach will be a deadly place. Already, you can see small boats that have gotten loose from the harbor and are being tossed around like toys in a bathtub. The vacation homes behind me all have broken windows and collapsed decks. And earlier I saw two cars floating down a flooded side road about a half mile away. This is no place for humans. And something seems to be…"

There was a pause and then a thunderous crash.

"Roger, what's going on now?"

"I can't hear anything… I'm going to have to sign off now!" Roger yelled. "The rain has turned to hail! As big as baseballs! I have to get back to the van…"

There was a loud commotion as a microphone smashed against something and the NPR switchboard turned back to the serene sounds of a dry man in a sound booth.

"Thank you, Roger, and stay safe," the voice said.

I looked back to find Pia standing only a few feet from me, listening to the radio with wide eyes.

"Whoa," I said.

Pia shook her head back and forth. "No, no, no, no, no. This just can't be happening," she said. "I need more time to start filtering the water. If the worst of it is already in Boston, it will be here by the end of the day! We aren't ready for this yet."

She went to the kitchen, but instead of beginning work on whatever water filtration project she had lined up, she poured chardonnay into a beige mug from her ten-year high school reunion and took a long gulp. Reunion Regatta & Clambake was written in delicate cursive on the side of the mug.

"We need to make good use of the daylight," she said, like some sort of pioneer wife.

"Fine, so what do you want me to do?" I asked. I was almost relieved to be put to work.

"We need more wood, Ash! You *know* that we need more wood and you're just stalling because it's a shitty job. Do it now, before the path to the shed is completely underwater."

I couldn't argue with any of those points, so I stormed to the front door and pulled on as much winter clothing as I could before going out to demonstrate that I wasn't afraid of a little weather.

Once outside, the sleet found its way under my thick collar, into my boots, through my gloves and around the edges of my hat so quickly that I may as well have walked out naked. It had been nearly twelve hours since my injurious trip to Peg's house, but the frigid wetness felt too familiar. I carried one armload after another into the house, each heavier and more waterlogged with each trip. I stacked them neatly against the wall for a while and then began dropping the piles in heaps around the living room. It was enough wood to keep us dry for a week, which I hoped would drive the point home to Pia that I was as committed to this survival shit as anyone.

After hauling the wood, I wanted nothing more than a hot shower, but when Pia reminded me that we needed to conserve the last of the hot water, I was forced to simply peel layer after wet layer off and jump quickly into a new set of warm, dry clothes. It was fine, for now, but what would happen when we ran out of dry clothes? How would anything dry now in the cold air? I decided to ration my clothes for the time being, doubling days on underwear and T-shirts. That reminded me that there were bigger indignities ahead as I had been avoiding a pending bowel movement for nearly two hours. (The water pressure would be enough to keep the toilet working for a while, but eventually the water tank, which was attached to our private well, would get too low.)

"Where do you think everyone went?" I asked Pia as I returned to the living room in dry clothes.

"What do you mean?" She didn't want to talk to me. She was busy.

But I had too many questions to stay quiet, so I went on. "They're evacuating entire cities—New York, Boston, everywhere—but where are they all going to go? The Storm's path covers the entire eastern seaboard. It's not like they can send them all to Ohio today."

Pia stopped moving for a moment and considered the question.

Before we'd arrived at an answer, the sound of another loud, sharp crackle sent us running to the kitchen. Everything looked the same.

"Over here!" Pia yelled, pointing to a window above the sink.

The enormous maple that stood only a few feet from our house—the one that we could touch and smell as we washed dishes in the summer—had split about six feet up from its ancient trunk and fallen to a ninety-degree angle beside the house. We could see little else around its wreckage of broken branches. The center of the trunk was hollow in places, apparently dead for a long time. This was the sort of thing I should have anticipated as a homeowner, but I was still learning such skills. The Storm hadn't given me time to get smart about country living. Large branches of the fallen tree were sinking into the accumulating puddles, joining sloughed-off bark and decomposing leaves. The north side of our house would look different without this great shade, I lamented. But of course, everything was going to look different.

"I don't think anyone takes them anywhere," Pia said as she returned to her food-labeling project at the table.

"What?"

"All those people who've been evacuated from the cities," she said. "I think the government just tells them that they have to leave, and then they're on their own. You just get in your car and drive for as far as you can until The Storm catches you... If you have a car."

This seemed too grim a possibility to consider at the moment, but Pia's theory would prove largely right. People of means and foresight left the cities early on their own—before the ice and snow made roads impassable. They fled to second homes, family members' houses and the couches of distant friends and relatives. But the majority of urban dwellers sat for hours in bottlenecks of traffic, finally driving as far west as they could get before fatigue overtook them. There were stories of entire highways filling with water or snow as drivers sat immobilized for hours, praying for the precipitation to end. On Route 76 in Pennsylvania, an old couple was found dead in their car near Harrisburg after the heat stopped and the temperature dropped. And two college students who had abandoned their truck on Interstate 80 and attempted to walk the rest of the way to Cleveland were crushed when a flooded bus tipped over onto them. We knew none of this then, as we bickered in our cold house.

"They probably have some system for getting people out," I said weakly.

We spent the rest of that wet day alternately drinking coffee and wine. (Alcohol was apparently the exception to Pia's inflexible food rationing system.) I fed the fire regularly and we dragged the kitchen table into the living room, which had become the only habitable part of the house. Pia talked nervously to herself a lot. She talked aloud through her meal plans, methods for staying warm through the night and an emergency bathroom strategy that involved a hole in the back deck and suspended tarp above. I spoke only when one of her ideas warranted discussion.

"We'll need to seal off the upstairs to retain the heat," Pia said knowingly.

"But the downstairs is going to flood eventually," I interjected. "Shouldn't we be moving this operation upstairs instead?"

"Sure," she said sarcastically. "That would actually save us a lot of hassle because we'll die of hypothermia before things really get bad."

We hated everything: the relentless cold, the smell of our ripening bodies beneath layers of dirty clothes, the knowledge that it was every household for itself at that point. Most of all, we hated the boredom. Hour after long hour went by with little to do but argue and stare out the window. We drank to stay warm and pass the time, but it only made us more morose.

The hailstorm that we'd heard reported from Cape Cod reached us that evening, rapping on the house like an angry lunatic demanding to be let in. By then, in my drunken haze, I could drift fuzzily into a childlike trance and watch the enormous ice balls outside with wonder. I didn't know nature was capable of creating such a weapon. I wanted to hold one in my hand, maybe keep it in our freezer for a while and take it out in the summer to impress August. I sat at the window, thinking these hazy thoughts and intermittently snapping back to reality, suddenly aware of the immeasurable damage the ice balls were invariably imposing on homes, businesses, cars, livestock, infrastructure…people. What was the world going to look like when we all got out of this, I wondered. Would we get out of this?

We fell into bed around eight, simultaneously disliking one another and grateful for the body warmth that each provided. With a winter hat, woolly socks and a heap of blankets, sleep was more comfortable than the alternative.

I dreamed that I was in a deep, rushing creek that came up to my waist. I was struggling to get out of the frigid water but couldn't move because my feet were stuck. The wildlife around me was frantic, too—birds, fish, chipmunks and a fox. Some were on the shore and some were flapping in the water with me, all rushing to get away from the creek. I made eye contact with a fox on the shore who looked terrified. I wanted to ask him for help and for some explanation of what was going on, but I couldn't find my voice. Suddenly, I thought I felt a fish chewing on my arm. I woke to find that it was Pia pinching me over and over.

"The hail stopped," she whispered, careful not to provoke the weather gods.

I took a moment to realign myself with reality. My hat had slipped off in the night and my ears were freezing, but my feet felt sweaty under two sock layers. All was quiet; the sleet must have stopped.

"I'm going to pee," she said.

The tone of her voice still sounded like she blamed me for The Storm, but I felt too hopeful to care.

I walked to the window and looked out the strip of exposed space at the bottom. It was snowing. It must have been snowing for hours because it was already so deep that our car was nearly buried and the contours of August's house could barely be detected through the trees. Somehow, in the nine hours we'd been asleep, several feet of snow had fallen and the temperature had dropped enough to freeze the wet ground beneath it. As always, the snow gave me comfort. It was quiet and insulating and somehow gentler. Vermonters knew how to traverse snow, I reasoned, which meant that we wouldn't be left to die in our cold, lonely house.

I fired up the woodstove and filled the kettle for coffee.

"This is a good start," I said, determined to be optimistic.

"It's spooky, Ash," Pia corrected me.

She was walking around the living room in an ankle-length nightgown of the sort I imagined Laura Ingalls Wilder wore on the prairie. "You think we're all gonna go outside and have a snowball fight? We don't have any idea what's coming. I think this is the calm before The Storm. I think it gets worse from here."

"Well, then let's just kill ourselves now!" I snapped.

"Don't think I haven't considered it."

She wasn't being facetious. I thought then and still think today that Pia probably had an end-of-the-world suicide plan along with every other emergency plan jotted down in her tiny notebook. But I couldn't go there, not then. And I didn't have much evidence to suggest that life was going to get better; it wasn't an argument I was prepared to lose. So I watched the flames grow through the iron pattern in the front door of the woodstove and stayed silent.

When it was warm enough in the living room to step away

from the stove, I walked over to my post at the window. The snow would fall hard and fast for a few minutes and then appear to taper off, tossing aimless little flakes about before speeding up again. I craned my head around to see Peg's house, hoping to catch a glimpse of her puffing chimney, but there was no life coming from it. That didn't mean anything; she could be conserving wood. I could feel cold air seeping in through the old windows, but I held my face close, careful not to miss any movement that might be detected outside. I had a headache from all the wine we'd consumed the day before and the brisk air felt good on my lungs.

Pia turned the emergency radio on and we sat at opposite ends of the couch under two blankets, sipping French press coffee and clinging to every word the authorities fed us. States of emergency had been declared in every state in the Northeast and Mid-Atlantic, Congress was considering for the first time voting remotely on a bill in order to free up relief funds and army reservists from around the country were being called to assist FEMA operations. It was satisfying to hear these institutions validate our experience, our life, but we didn't expect much from their response. Congress, relief funds…these things had no proximity to us. It no longer mattered that we lived in America, or even Vermont. We lived at 6 Chimney Hill—population: 2. Our survival depended entirely upon the resources before us and our own grit. The US government wasn't going to rescue us; only we could do that.

I must have drifted off while we listened to the endless reports of mounting devastation because the next thing I heard was a *bang, bang, bang* on the door. I jumped to my feet and instinctively grabbed Pia in a protective hold. She shook me off and we walked to the front door.

"Ash! Ash! Ash! Let me in!" It was August, panicked and out of breath. "Ash, it's my dad!"

I jerked the door open, breaking the seal of ice that had hardened around it and letting a short wall of snow topple into the entrance of our house.

"August, what is it?"

"My dad got hit by a tree and he's bleeding!" August could barely get the words out. His face was flushed as he stared up at me, pleading for action.

"Oh God. Okay, I'm coming."

I was already tugging on snow boots and looking for my coat. I could feel Pia bustling around me doing the same.

In thirty seconds, we were running behind August along the snow-covered path that connected our homes. There was a thin trail where his legs had pushed through the snow, interrupted by imprints of his body falling over in various places. The snow was so deep that it was inside our boots with the first step and soaking through August's jeans up to his waist, but we were too distracted to feel it.

When we emerged from the trail, I could hear the muffled sound of August's mother talking on the far side of their tiny house. We ran toward the voice and found her kneeling in the snow beside her husband, who was slumped on his side. The snow around his head was crimson, though it was hard to tell precisely where the blood was coming from. I could see the contours of a small tree under fresh snow just above his head.

"He came out for more wood and this tree must have fallen on him!" she shrieked to us. "The lines are still down. Do you have cell phones?"

August's mother was crying and screaming all at once. She must have been out there for a while because her flannel pajamas were soaked and her lips were turning blue. I could tell by her slurred speech that she was on something and had to fight off my anger.

"I have one, Liz!" Pia exclaimed, pulling her phone from a coat pocket and dialing 911.

"Thank you, Pia."

"It's a recording saying that the networks are overloaded," she said. "I'll just keep calling."

"August can do that," I said, aware of the petrified look on his face. He needed something to focus on. "August, this is your job now. Can you handle it?"

He nodded and Pia passed him the phone. She ran into the house looking for something.

I knelt down beside John and put my face close to his. He was breathing and alive, though I had no way of knowing just how alive he was. Pia emerged from the house and wrapped a blanket around Liz. Her teeth were chattering now and the color was leaving her face. Snow collected on our shoulders.

"We can't leave him out here," Liz said. "He could die in this cold."

Oh God, he could die either way, I thought. This man could die before us…before August.

No. I vowed not to let that happen and felt a surge of something sharp rise in my throat that I chose to believe was not vomit, but courage.

"She's right," I said. "Let's move him inside."

"I don't think you're supposed to move people in this state," Pia said. The tone of her voice was kinder than anything I'd heard in a while. At that moment, all animosity between us was lost and we were a team working to save a human. "What if he has a spinal injury or something?"

"You're probably right, but what choice do we have?" I said. "If we move him, we might make things worse. But if we don't move him, he will definitely…not be okay."

Death was all around us, but no one wanted to say the word again, not with August standing there.

Everyone nodded and we each moved in to take a part of the limp body. I slid my arms under each shoulder and hoisted his torso while the women each took a leg. He was a middle-aged man of average height and only a small gut, so I was shocked by just how heavy he felt in our arms. August bustled around us, opening the screened porch door and then the interior one. We shuffled inside, right up to their wood-stove, and released his body gingerly onto the cold floor.

Pia ran around the house, pulling blankets from each bed and piling them high on August's father. She instructed his wife to crawl under the covers with him and speak continuously to let him know that she was close. This startled me in its tenderness and I will never forget how graceful she was in those terrifying moments.

I could see now where the blood was gushing from the side of his forehead, staining the blankets around them. I tore up a bedsheet and fastened a makeshift bandage around his head, which was soaked red within seconds, but it did seem to slow the bleeding. I raced through every medical memory in my past, searching for useful information.

"Let's elevate him," I said, remembering the time I'd split my left eyebrow open in a grammar school sledding accident.

Pia looked around and pointed to couch cushions that we could use to help prop up his top half.

Liz was still talking softly to him, whimpering, really. She spoke about the day August was born, vacations they had taken, moments in their past that sounded embarrassingly small to me but held some meaning in their little family.

"It's ringing!" August yelled, holding the phone out for someone to take it.

I jumped and grabbed the phone just as a distant female voice finished her greeting.

"Hi, thank God," I said into the receiver. "We're at 8 Chimney Hill in Isole. A tree fell on a man and he's losing a lot of blood from his head."

"Okay, stay calm while I ask you a few questions," the voice said.

"Can you send someone out here in this weather? You have to send someone!" I was yelling at the woman, afraid that I sounded as distant to her as she did to me.

"Sir, we do have a few emergency vehicles on the road at the moment. They can probably get to you, but it might take forty-five minutes to an hour."

"No, we need someone here sooner!" I yelled. I was relieved to hear that it was even possible to send someone, but I wanted to impress upon her the urgency of the situation.

"He's not conscious," I said, "and he has a head wound that's still gushing blood."

I looked at August, who was fighting back tears.

"Okay, sir," the tiny voice said. "If you can apply pressure to the wound and keep the body warm until they arrive, we will have someone there as soon as possible. Don't move him any more than you need to. May I have your name?"

I walked through a series of administrative questions with the small voice, which seemed designed to keep callers like me occupied until someone arrived to help. Finally, I told the voice that I was going to put her on hold and begged her not to hang up. We needed to keep the line for as long as the network would support it or Pia's phone would stay powered.

I set the phone down and joined the other three on the floor around the body. August's father stirred a little and we all gasped with hope. Then we lost him again. He seemed to be drifting in and out of consciousness.

"August," his mother said, "tell your father how much you love him."

Pia and I looked at August, who began to cry.

"He's going to be just fine, August," I said, unsure of whether his mother's assignment was a good idea. "Help is coming. But it might be nice for him to hear your voice right now."

August nodded and wiped tears from his dirty face with dirtier hands.

"Daddy, I love you because you have funny jokes and we went fishing that one time."

We all laughed and I blinked twice to keep the sting from my eyes. *Please don't die, please don't die, please don't die.* I hated this man for the father he'd been to August, but his death would be the final, cruelest act of neglect, and August didn't deserve that. I wanted him to live because August loved him and because he was a human trying to survive. We were all under assault in those hours of The Storm and we were all going to fight to survive. It required no thought at all.

We sat quietly, listening to August's mother whisper silly things into the ear of her distant husband for what felt like a long time. The direct heat of the woodstove and the pounding of adrenaline in our heads had an oddly soporific effect and I had to work to stay alert.

Finally, there were lights. We hadn't seen even a town plow go by in more than two days, so the faint glow of headlights through the bare trees grabbed each of us simultaneously. August and I ran to the window, praying the lights were for us. At first, it wasn't clear. The vehicle was most definitely not the rusting, outdated ambulance that sat outside Isole's quaint volunteer fire-and-rescue department all year. This was an SUV of some kind, riding high on enormous wheels that were webbed in fat chains. My heart thumped at the possibility that it had not been sent to save our dying man, but then it stopped and three people leaped out of the vehicle, running toward us. Within seconds, there was a pounding on the door and the deep voice of someone saying, "Rescue here."

They rushed past me as quickly as I opened the door and gently nudged Pia and Liz out of their way to check John's vital signs, asking us questions as they worked. I watched August watch the men and felt a pang of jealousy at their superhuman powers. I hadn't seen these men around Isole, so I assumed they were from a neighboring town. One was probably about twenty-six and beefy. He took cues from the oldest, who must have been his father because he looked like a rounder, worn-out version of the same man. The other guy was in his thirties, dark skinned and lean, with fast-moving hands that were preparing the limp body to be moved to a stretcher.

"We can't thank you enough," Pia said with the same awed look as August. "Where are you going to take him?"

"Saint J.," said the older man without looking up. "The roads to Burlington are too bad and he won't last until Hanover. We have what he needs in St. Johnsbury."

"Is he going to be okay?" I asked.

The three men hoisted the stretcher and paused for a moment to answer.

"We can't know for sure, but probably," the older man said. "You stopped the bleeding, which is very good. And there's no obvious sign of spinal injury. He's been unconscious for a long time, though, so he'll need to be evaluated for cognitive damage. But he'll live."

We all breathed a sigh of relief. It would sink in for each of us later that this was a mixed report. But, for now, we smiled to know he would live. At that moment, as if on cue,

August's father opened his eyes and looked around for a few seconds before closing them again. *Thank you*, I said to some god somewhere.

"We can take one more," the older man said as they hurried out the door.

Liz looked at me.

"You go," I said. "We'll take care of August. We'll find you both as soon as The Storm clears. Okay?"

She nodded and pulled August, who was crying now, to her breast.

"I love you, Auggie," she said, and then she released him to my arms.

"Everyone is going to be okay," I told him.

We watched August's mother run out awkwardly after the rescue team and her husband. They loaded the stretcher into the back of the vehicle and drove off slowly down something that used to resemble a road.

"I'm hungry," August said, wiping his eyes.

I forced a smile. "Good, we have lots of food at our place!"

Pia was moving around August's house by then, locking windows, killing the wood fire and collecting winter clothes for August. She didn't seem as interested in interacting with him, but I was grateful for her ability to anticipate such logistical tasks while I took care of him.

We walked back toward our home, which was more difficult than it had been earlier, since our path had been erased by a new foot of snow. My entire body ached with stressful fatigue. It was early in the afternoon, but the perpetual dimness made me sleepy. We stepped inside, three in a row, to find that the woodstove had died out and it was almost colder than the outdoors.

August and I built a new fire together, discussing which pieces of cut wood were best and how big we wanted the flames to be. My strategy was to keep August busy and stay as upbeat as possible. I gathered tea lights from Pia's stash and placed them around the living room in an attempt to create a warmer, more festive vibe than the usually somber mood of our house. Pia gave me a brief glance that I knew meant we weren't supposed to use candles during daylight hours—too wasteful—but I pretended not to see. I would have used all the candles we had just to keep August feeling safe while he stayed with us. And, of course, Pia had stockpiled so many candles, there was no danger of running out.

We made peanut butter and jelly sandwiches and boiled water on the stove for hot chocolate. Pia didn't bother fighting with me about the departure from the food chart she had created and let me take the lead with August, which I appreciated. She was awkward around him—maybe around all children. Had it always been this way or was this a new development?

Everyone looked a little different in the dim light of The Storm: August appeared more childlike and vulnerable to me than before, and Pia was noticeably less beautiful, haggard even. Still, we were married and there was a working rhythm to even our disdainful days. She poured bourbon into my hot chocolate and the sweet burn was a gift as it slid down my throat. I wanted to drink three more mugs and sleep until the earth returned to its former self.

Instead of sleep, we played Scrabble. It wasn't a good game for a seven-year-old competing with adults, but recreational options at our house were limited, so we experimented with teams and rules. In round three, August declared that he was going to be the decider on all words, which meant that any word he didn't recognize would be rejected. We eventually agreed on a three-letter word maximum, which seemed to level the playing field and ensured a few wins on his part.

MEG LITTLE REILLY

When the game devolved into lining the chips up like dominoes, Pia called it quits and positioned herself horizontally on the couch. I refreshed everyone's hot chocolates and brought two sleeves of saltines to the table. August stuffed them into his mouth, one after another, and blew cracker dust at me while explaining why Chutes and Ladders is the best game ever invented. Then he stopped and looked around, apparently remembering why he was there.

"Do you think my dad's going to die?"

"No, buddy. I don't," I said. "He's going to be fine. You heard what those rescue guys said."

"Yeah." He nodded. "Because I really like my dad. I don't like his ponytail, but he's real nice."

We both ate more crackers.

"Are you gonna have a kid?" August asked.

I glanced at Pia on the couch, who was asleep or pretending to be.

"I don't know, buddy. We'll see."

August shrugged, already bored with the conversation. "Okay."

We ate more crackers and played Go Fish until dinner, which was organic macaroni and cheese from a box made with water boiled on the woodstove. Daylight disappeared quickly and, although it was only seven o'clock, we were all ready for bed by the time the last macaroni had been eaten. So we left our warm living room for the frigid upstairs. There would be no tooth brushing or face washing or pajama changes. Such civilities were a waste of energy and resources to us by then. Instead, we went straight to bed, peeling back cover after cover and eager for sleep to take us before we had time to think about the day's events.

I hadn't given any consideration to the sleeping arrangements for the night. How seven-year-olds sleep was a mystery to me, but August left no room for deliberation. He crawled in between Pia and me and made himself right at home. Maybe this was a perfectly normal way for a child to sleep or a symptom of his boundaryless home life, or maybe it was a response to the frightful things he'd seen that day. I liked it either way. I could smell his unwashed hair beneath my nose when he tossed around to find just the right position, and he made no acknowledgment of the light kicks his socked feet delivered with each movement. When August finally settled and his breath began to slow, I felt a small, sticky hand reach for mine. He squeezed tight and held on for as long as his sleepy muscles would allow.

TWENTY-THREE

THE SNOW CONTINUED for two more days. There were no breaks in the precipitation or lighter phases to give us hope. It just fell fast, constantly, until we were barricaded inside by nearly six feet of it.

We tried at first to make the most of the snow. August and I went outside to build an igloo and burrowed a tunnel through the dense bottom layer that went for a few feet before we lost interest and left the dead end. Eventually, there was just too much and the permanent chill in our bodies dictated that each day be spent close to the woodstove. After our last outside adventure, we surrendered to the suffocating wall of snow that was building up around the house and sealed off the front door with duct tape in an attempt to preserve heat.

Without power or phones, our only connection to the outside world was the news that crackled through our crank radio. There seemed no bounds to the crisis. Up and down the coast, people were dying in their homes of hypothermia, dehydration and whatever struck first when their medications ran out. Every now and then, we'd hear the first few sentences of a death so macabre that I would lunge at the radio and turn it off before August was exposed to the details; we heard enough to know that some people were resorting to desperate and hopeless measures. Rescue crews were working around the clock and supplies were being flown in from everywhere, but even with the support of the rest of the world, these efforts were no match for The Storm.

I turned the radio off whenever I had the chance, but it was a constant source of tension between Pia and me. She wanted to take it all in, to live in the chaos and feed on its energy. She sat on a small wooden chair parked beside the radio in the corner, with a wool blanket around her shoulders, and listened intently for hours. Sometimes, she took out her little notebook to memorialize thoughts that remain unknown to me, but mostly she just sat. When I insisted on turning the radio off, she'd storm to the kitchen for more wine or recline on the couch with a magazine. Almost no words were exchanged between us by then.

The boredom was the worst for August. He scanned our small bookshelf repeatedly and opened kitchen cabinets, hoping that something interesting would finally appear to him, but nothing did. At my urging, we built a fort out of sheets and pillows, which was fun at first—we brought nature magazines and snacks inside—but it was too cold to hang out in for more than a few minutes, so we eventually let it collapse. Occasionally I would see August's face fall, suddenly aware of his parents' absence and the uncertainty of his father's future. I did my best to distract him and offer comfort in small ways, but it never felt like enough. Pia wasn't burdened by any such obligation.

On the afternoon of the third day of The Storm's blizzard phase, our nerves got the better of us. Pia found half a pack of cigarettes in an old coat and smoked them all through the broken window in the guest room. August began tearing pages out of an enormous book of poetry that I didn't know we had and throwing the balled-up sheets across the living room into a basket. I didn't bother dissuading him. Instead, I watched each ball arc over my head and bounce somewhere in the general proximity of its target. When he got one in, he'd do a little dance with a karate-style kick at the woodstove. I think he was trying to provoke me, to make something happen in that quiet, gloomy space, but I couldn't muster much beyond a high five. Finally, the sun began to set and we made a dinner of canned beans and salsa on rice cakes, followed by handfuls of chocolate chips. With nothing left to do, we retired early to the bedroom. It was the only place warm enough to spend the night, so we were all in there together.

Sleep had ceased to feel restorative by then. Our muscles were restless and our nerves couldn't turn off. With no idea how many more cold nights we would need to endure, our captivity was beginning to feel like a life sentence.

In the blurry moment before my eyes opened the next morning, I imagined that we would all pad downstairs and make pancakes with blueberries and maple syrup before going out to play in the snow. But then I remembered where we were and all that had happened. August and Pia slept quietly beside me, closer to each other than either would have chosen. I liked having them both there in bed with me—warm and safe and shielded from the elements. They weren't bonding with each other as I would have liked, but we were all together, which was something.

It was probably six o'clock in the morning; there was no way of knowing from our boarded-up bedroom. I crawled out of bed and squinted through the exposed crack at the bottom of the window. At some point during the night, the snow shifted to rain and the temperature had risen noticeably. I had pulled my socks off in my sleep and was surprised to find that my toes felt warm for the first time in days. Was it possible that The Storm was breaking?

The Storm *was* breaking, according to the all-knowing voices coming from the radio. Pia and August woke up a few minutes after me, and soon we were all huddled around the woodstove, drinking hot things and listening to the latest storm report.

"The hurricane portion of this weather event has moved out to the Atlantic and been downgraded to a tropical storm," the deep radio voice said. "And the nor'easter has dissipated as well, leaving the East Coast to dig out from the mess it left behind."

"So what happens now, John?" an NPR host asked the expert. "Are we out of the woods?"

"We are most definitely not out of the woods. The worst thing that anyone can do now is get a false sense of safety from this warming air. This is where the real damage starts up north. Some regions got as much as eight feet of snow. That's going to melt, fast. And it has nowhere to go because the ground is already saturated and our water systems are overflowing. We're about to experience the worst flooding North America has ever seen. Roadways, homes, cars, schools—everything will be underwater. People need to get to safe, high ground and stay there. In some cases, that means evacuating your homes. I know FEMA is working with states to set up another round of rescue operations all the way up the coast, so listen to your local news for evacuation instructions and points of safety. It's going to take months to get power working in some areas. And the cost to our economy will be in the hundreds of billions of dollars. There may be no recovering from some of the damage ahead."

August's eyes were like saucers and I knew that we should

MEG LITTLE REILLY

minimize the bad news he was exposed to. I turned down the radio dial and shot Pia a glance that said "don't fight this."

Without the chatter, a new noise could be heard outside: moving water. In addition to the light rain, there was a constant drip coming off the roof, and another that sounded like it was upstairs in our cordoned-off guest room. There was also the low hum of rushing water, like a stream running all around us. Snow was melting everywhere and searching for a place to go.

August pulled off his fleece and announced that it was getting hot before going to the window to peer through the lookout space.

"Can we pee off the back porch, Ash?"

"Yeah, if we can get out onto the porch," I said. "Put your boots on."

We went outside to feel the warming air on parts of our body that hadn't been exposed to oxygen in days. August smiled as he added to a rushing stream that snaked through the deep snow in our backyard. He hadn't asked about his parents yet, but I knew I needed to be prepared with an answer. The truth was that I had no idea when we would be able to leave the house or where they were. Landlines would be dead for weeks and, even if we could get through to someone on a cell phone, Pia's phone had long since run out of power. What were others in Isole doing at that moment, I wondered. I decided to walk to Peg's house when things dried up for some guidance.

Things didn't dry up. As the morning hours passed, the water sounds amplified and closed in on us. The temperature had changed so dramatically in twenty-four hours that we were down to our long underwear and let the woodstove die out intermittently to cool the downstairs. All the ice that had formed in the guest room was melting through the ceiling now, collecting in a pot on the kitchen table. And the wet smell of worms had returned after days of icy reprieve. (Whether they were dead or alive in that box, I didn't have the courage to find out.) Worst of all was the scene outside. Snow was melting at an alarming pace, transforming into pools and rivers, sliding off the roof and dissolving into anything that was already liquid. We were located halfway up a gradual, sloping hill, so it looked as if it was coming down from August's house and moving toward Peg's, but in some places the water seemed to just swirl around in circles. The creek that bordered our back-yard overflowed first and then grew into a large, amorphous lake with no perimeter. We were in a houseboat.

There was no way to know if the runoff plan we'd been fighting for would have prevented the flooding and saved our town, but I burned with anger when I thought about Crow as I watched the water accumulate; maybe this could have…maybe been prevented. I didn't let myself linger on that thought; there was too much before us to worry about. That chance was behind us.

The three of us rattled around downstairs all day as we had for many days already. We were bored and angry, but relieved to have a weather change, something that suggested we were nearing the end of our captivity. We played Go Fish and gin rummy. August and I melted chocolate chips in a pot on the woodstove and called it fondue. For a while, it felt like the mood had lifted. We were hopeful, but we shouldn't have been.

In early afternoon, I walked to the front door to check the status of the flooding. I stood in my boots on the outside doormat and watched as the water rose up, up, up over the edge of the front porch. It was less than two feet from our front door with no sign of stopping. *Jesus Christ, it's here,* I

MEG LITTLE REILLY

thought. It would only be a matter of time before the water got to the door and then filled the downstairs. I felt sick all of a sudden. We were way beyond card games and peeing off the back porch. This was a level of survival I was not prepared to consider. I was most certainly not prepared to keep another small human alive in it. *Get it together,* I said to myself. Get it together. I didn't want to scare August any more than was necessary.

"Holy shit!" Pia yelled from behind me when she saw the encroaching water.

August ran up behind me.

"Everyone inside," I announced. "We're moving this party upstairs!"

No one was fooled by my forced lightheartedness. Pia spun around and began filling a giant metal pot with food that would require no preparation (crackers, condensed milk, beans, tuna). I asked August to gather up all his warm clothes and hold on to them while I slid boxes of candles, water tablets, batteries and matches to the foot of the stairs. Thank God for Pia's prepper boxes. I threw the hand-crank radio on top of the stack, so grateful for that one small connection to the rest of the world.

"Are we going to drown, Ash?" August asked, his arms overflowing with dirty boy clothes.

"No, buddy. We're not going to drown. Things are going to get really wet and we're going to have to move upstairs— but it will be like we're just camping out up there for a while. Did you bring the cards?"

"Got them," he said with great importance.

Please don't let this kid's parents die, I prayed to no one from inside my own head. *Please don't die.* This was a moment for prayer, but I had no experience with such an exercise. I wasn't even sure whom I thought I was praying to, but *not* praying seemed reckless.

"Enough talking. Let's get upstairs!" Pia yelled. She was too frantic and preoccupied with the moment to concern herself with the impressions of the terrified seven-year-old in her presence. But she was right, too; the water was coming in and we were out of time.

I prompted August to go first while I hoisted two heavy boxes, one on top of the other, and followed him up the stairs. I could hear Pia at my heels with a rattling pot of canned goods and whatever else she deemed essential. We hurried upstairs and set our haul down at the top. I made two more trips for water jugs and then assembled a makeshift wall around the foot of the stairs using two armchairs, knowing full well that it wouldn't do much. Before running back upstairs for the final time, I saw the water. It crept beneath the front door and spread menacingly across our floor. The pace at which the water was rising seemed impossible, supernatural even, but it was real. At that rate, I knew it would be upstairs by nightfall. What then?

I joined the other two in our bedroom and suggested with false cheer that August build another blanket fort, which he ignored. He was hovering around Pia, who was on her knees, fiddling with the radio. I crawled into bed and listened to the loud, choppy sounds of static as she redirected the antennae and walked around searching for the elusive connection. Eventually, August joined me and we flipped through old issues of *Scientific American* together from under the covers. Our eyes tried to read, but we couldn't see past the fear to the pages in front of us. There was little point in pretending to be occupied or calm. We were waiting for the water.

Pia set up a makeshift kitchen area in the corner of the bedroom and prepared dry tuna salad on saltines, which none

MEG LITTLE REILLY

of us ate. I opened the windows and, after much wrestling, managed to tear away the sheet of plywood that stood between us and the outside. It was a relief to experience daylight again, but that privilege also came with the ability to watch water rise up around our leaky ark. August couldn't pull himself away from the window and I was out of ideas for keeping him busy.

Eventually, he broke down. With his back to us, I could see August's small body heaving and convulsing with each sob until finally he stopped trying to conceal his tears and he ran to the bed to curl up in a ball beside me. His cries grew louder and shuddered through his whole body. I looked at Pia with searching eyes, but she was distracted and unmoved. This wasn't her thing, not anymore. I fought tears of my own and rubbed August's back with a firm hand until, after what felt like a very long time, his body released. Sleep washed over him quickly and he went deeper and deeper into safety. I envied his escape and lay down beside him, trying desperately and unsuccessfully to join him.

The next hour passed like a coma—I was alive, but incapable of moving and only faintly aware of my surroundings. I could hear the occasional tinkering of Pia around me, but I made no effort to see what she was doing. I couldn't even investigate the rising water levels downstairs, though I knew they were close because the incessant sounds of sloshing water grew louder with each minute. It was as if I was dying very, very slowly. And it wouldn't have been a terrible way to go, given the options at that moment. That's how my paralyzed brain reasoned—moving back and forth between hope and utter despair, alternately fantasizing about our escape and considering accepting my own death.

It was sometime in the late afternoon when I saw the lights outside the window. That was enough to jolt me out of my state and onto my feet. When I pressed my face against the cool glass, I could see there was a massive machine parked on our road. A tank maybe? Was that possible? Pia, who had been writing in her notebook on the floor, stood up and stared out the window. She ran to the radio and tried again to connect with the outside world while I tugged my rain boots on.

"Let's just go!" I whisper-screamed at her. I didn't want to startle August, who had begun to wake up. "This might be our only chance to get August out alive. We have to go NOW."

"That could be anyone, Ash!" she yelled back. "You probably can't get to them anyhow!"

It was true that I didn't know who was out there or why, but what choice did we have? Even if it was a daredevil attempting his own escape or a crazed marauder, was that worse than staying in our house to drown or freeze or starve? August deserved this chance and I would have done anything at all to keep him alive.

"I'll get the old canoe from the shed. I can swim to it if I have to. Quick, let's wave our flashlights out at them to let them know people are here."

Pia didn't move.

"You get him dressed while I get the canoe!" I yelled as I opened the bedroom door.

The water had begun to creep up the stairs and I hesitated for only a moment before running toward it. It was about six feet deep on the main floor of the house. My boots went in first, reminding me that clothing was useless—a hindrance, really—for the challenge. Next, my long johns and torso went under. It was cold and disgustingly dark, but I was moving too quickly to observe much more. With a frantic sort of doggie paddle, I could keep my head above the water, which was

MEG LITTLE REILLY

about two feet from the ceiling, and move toward the open front door. Flotsam bobbed all around me—household items that I recognized and invisible objects that crashed against my body as I fought through the underwater maze.

The claustrophobic pool inside my house finally spat me through the front door and outside, where the water levels were lower but the rain posed a new obstacle. Nothing around me looked as it had before. It was like a nightmare, dark and surreal, with haunting flashes of familiar objects appearing out of context. I was still floating, though I could feel my toes graze the porch now and then. The outline of August's house was in the right place, but many of the trees between us had fallen, revealing parts of the horizon I'd never noticed before. Our car was the same color and shape, though it had drifted into the woods and was resting at an odd angle against a tree. I saw all of this in an instant, aware of the precious passing time.

I took an enormous breath and yelled as loud as I possibly could to the vehicle parked in the road: *"We're coming!"*

The vehicle flashed its lights through the rain and I felt confident that, good or evil, the driver was acknowledging me. I pulled myself along the side of the house and paddled the ten feet it took to get to our shed. Inside, tools and toys floated around. Most of its contents had been left by the previous owners and I hardly remembered what was there. Mercifully, the canoe was floating within an arm's length of the entrance with two oars in its dry belly. I yanked it toward me and pulled it awkwardly back toward the house in a hybrid walk-swim. As I approached the house, I saw the ladder I had been using days before and threw that into the canoe.

I parked the canoe on the front porch and let it bounce back and forth between the house and the porch beams while

I positioned the ladder beneath the bedroom window. The ladder moved around unnervingly until I got to the fourth rung and I was out of the water entirely.

Before climbing up, I looked back toward the vehicle on the road again and yelled one more time. *"Stay there! We're coming now!"*

This time, there was no flash of lights and I knew we didn't have much time.

A blast of wind hit my right side as I balanced on the ladder and worked to ignore the terrifying cold that had taken hold of my body. I was growing weak to it and suspected that hypothermia might not be far behind. I climbed to the top of the ladder and banged on the window for Pia to open it.

August was inside, dressed for a blustering day as I had been before the cesspool pulled my boots and coat from my shivering body.

"We gotta go now!" I yelled from outside the window. "August, I need you to climb down this, buddy, quickly and carefully. Can you do that?"

August nodded with a forced brave face. I took two steps down and made room for his small body above me.

With my arms on either side of August on the ladder, I yelled again, "Okay, Pia, now you! There's no time left. Just leave everything."

"I'm not coming," she said from inside the bedroom. She sounded apologetic, but sure.

"What?" I gasped. "No, Pia, we can't do this now! Just come out here. I've got you."

"Ash, I'm not coming. I need to see this through."

"What are you talking about? Get down here! You're going to die!"

"Maybe," she said with a strange buzz in her voice. "But

I think I'm prepared. I don't want to leave the house. I want to stay here and *experience this.*"

I knew that was it. She needed the chaos; it fed her. Pia had been more alive in those final days in our flooding house than I'd seen her in months, and she wasn't eager for The Storm to end, even if it killed her.

Just then, the tank in the road made a honking noise and I realized how much time we were wasting.

"We have to go, Pia! August and I have to go. We have to find his parents… I love you, you know."

"I know," she said.

And that was it.

I rushed August down the ladder and yelled as loud as I could to the mystery driver in the road, *"Wait for us!"*

As we climbed into the canoe, I could think only of getting August out to the road. I had never felt anything close to the feeling I had for that boy at that moment. I would have sacrificed my life if I knew it would keep him alive. There was nothing else I needed. The sick, sad emptiness of leaving my wife alone in that house would come later, but in that instant, my only thought was to save August.

PART THREE

The flowers will bloom, when we are gone,
As fresh and sweet as now,
And droop in beauty o'er the clay
That wraps our mouldered brow.

The stately trees will rear aloft
Their leafy heads as high,
The gladsome breeze that through them steals
Will not our requiem sigh.

Those beauteous hills of green, o'er which
Our youthful feet have trod,
Will still remain the same when we
Are slumbering 'neath the sod.

—"When We Are Gone" by Mrs. A. D. Hemenway of Ludlow, Vermont.
First published in 1860.

TWENTY-FOUR

THE MOMENT OUR shivering bodies felt the hard metal of the tank, we left isolation behind for a new, communal existence. August and I had been saved. At the urging of the governor, Vermont's Army Mountain Warfare School had deployed all of its resources to help people stranded in rural pockets of the state, with a priority placed on flood zones, which was why a tank drove down our impassable road on that day. Two soldiers and three civilian volunteers were manning the vehicle. They had been driving around the hardest-hit areas of the Northeast Kingdom all day, picking up the unprepared and unlucky.

I don't remember all the details of how it ended, but I know that we were both hoisted onto the tank and wrapped in blankets. We huddled together on a long seat with a middle-aged couple who lived two miles up the road. An elderly woman joined us later and we all said very little, understanding only that we would be deposited at the nearest emergency location with the other storm refugees. From the fuzzy radios the soldiers spoke into, we caught glimpses of what was out there: destroyed roads and houses, many people waiting to be rescued from treacherous conditions, some deaths. I did the only thing within my power while we rode to the emergency shelter: I held August tight, assuring him that we would be okay.

We *were* okay. When the tank finally stopped, we were at the high school, only a few miles from my home. It was the same place we'd played basketball with Maggie weeks before, but now it housed two hundred dislocated people. It was barely recognizable to me from the outside. The entire parking lot was submerged in water and large chunks of broken pavement floated along the surface like icebergs. A blue Ford Focus that had flipped upside down leaned precariously against the far end of the building. The only signs of human life were on the flat rooftop, where volunteers in waders and masks used chain saws to cut a massive fallen telephone pole into segments small enough to roll off the side of the building.

When I realized where I was, I felt dizzy again, as though the earth was spinning faster than before and its contents swirling around me. Nothing looked as it once had. Where houses should have been, there were only piles of debris. The roads were torn up and empty, aside from the occasional out-of-place object that had been deposited on them (a mangled child's swing set, a dead cow) and the military tanks that crept slowly above it all. Most disturbing—and this was what made it seem so foreign—was that the cozy forest walls that insulated our hamlet on either side of the valley appeared to have been shorn bare. I could see straight across town and right up to the bald head of the mountains. Most of the trees had been pulled down by wind or uprooted by flooding, regardless of size or age. They seemed to fall in patterns, with one cluster leaning to the east and an adjacent group pointing toward the south. It told the messy, ruthless story of how The Storm had moved through—a story that had no forest survivors. August saw it all, too, and his body quivered beside me. I clung tightly to his hand as we were led into the makeshift school shelter. As the only familiar thing in August's young life at that moment, I wasn't going to let him go.

Inside, dozens of people stood around in groups, some crying or silently hugging. A young woman with a sympathetic smile directed us to two empty cots at the far end of the room and handed me a paper bag filled with ill-fitting donated clothes that smelled like someone else's attic. She explained that the sandbags and the cinder blocks saved the school and then hurried off to greet another group of refugees. We changed into the dry clothes and burrowed under the blankets for a while, working to bring our body temperatures back up to normal. Medical professionals were bustling around the room, but our chill seemed too small to warrant their attention as others were bruised and bloody. We were content to just lie there and watch; safety and warmth were enough.

Eventually, a line started to form at the other end of the gymnasium and we followed the crowd. With the other terrified faces, we waited patiently for soup as it was ladled into disposable bowls. I was so grateful for the nourishment, and for everything we'd been given in the period after our rescue. We were still in shock then; I could barely speak. The only thing that remains clear to me is the profound gratitude I felt to the strangers who kept us alive that day—people who had no doubt suffered losses along with the rest of us. Sometimes, today, I'll remember a flash of someone's face from that shelter or I'll catch the smell of soup-kitchen food as it floats by, knocking the wind out of my chest for a moment.

If it's possible to feel gratitude in your body like a fever, that's what I felt as we stood in line for lentil barley soup.

"Lost your house?" an older man asked us from behind.

I turned around. His head was bald and smooth and he had soft creases around his eyes.

"Ah, I think so," I sputtered. "I don't know. Couldn't stay there."

"Yup. I understand." He nodded. "Well, you and your son are going to be fine now. You've got all you need right here."

The older man gave August a light squeeze on the shoulder, sensing his fragility. We didn't correct him about our relationship; there was no reason to. I felt August hold my hand a little tighter and wondered how his own parents felt to be so far away from their child. They didn't deserve him, but I prayed that they were still alive. I needed to find someone at the shelter with information about what had become of everyone. I needed to track down Pia, too.

With our full bowls and plastic spoons, we joined a group of people talking quietly on the floor nearby and began to make friends.

In the days that followed, we created a sort of community among ourselves in the high school shelter, with enough small gestures of privacy and politeness to maintain a sense of civility in a living arrangement that would have seemed uncivilized before. We had food, electric generators, a roof and clothing, which was so much more than the people we saw on TV and heard the rescue crews discuss in hushed voices. We didn't see death immediately before us, but it was omnipresent—an inevitability on the other side of those cinder-block walls—and that fear kept us huddled closer.

There was the rash of deaths that occurred during The Storm from drowning, hypothermia, fallen trees and collapsed buildings. But what came after was more frightening.

People started dying from contaminated water and exposure to raw sewage lines. A violent gastrointestinal illness that originated at a pig farm in Pennsylvania spread rapidly, killing hundreds across the country in less than two days. There were stories of biohazardous materials leaking into rivers in upstate New York, which caused skin to dissolve on contact. Our bodies weren't armed for the waste and toxicity that had escaped our neat containment systems. It was killing us. And not just us—it was killing livestock and crops, fish and birds.

All of these stories made our survival feel more precarious—and filled me with guilt and anxiety. I tried to focus on my self-assigned job of shielding August from the horror, but my mind was always on Pia. I'd left her there. She may have died and that would be my fault. I went over those final moments over and over in my mind, working to convince myself that there was nothing else to be done. She refused to come with me. Could I have wrestled her out of the house? Perhaps, but certainly not down a ladder from a second-story window. Would August have lived if we'd stayed there with her? I was sure at that moment that his survival depended upon our escape, which still seemed true, but provided no comfort. I spoke silently to that higher power that I barely believed existed, praying for her to be alive.

Still, though I spent those days trying to see through a thick fog of guilt, I never wished that she was here with us. I wanted her to be alive, elsewhere, while I tended to August and worked to understand the new world we lived in. It would have felt like relief to have her gone, if only I'd known she was safe. This semi-relief feeling was worse than longing or heartbreak because it only compounded my guilt. What could be more callous than relief at such a time, I wondered. Did it take the deadliest storm in earth's history to provide me with a cowardly escape from my wife? I hated myself intensely.

The kindness of the people around me was a welcome, if undeserved, antidote to my self-loathing. Some of the people in the shelter we already knew. Bill, from the Subcommittee, was there for a brief period with his wife and two children while they waited for his road to become passable again. And a woman I recognized as a cashier at the food co-op was friendly to us. Others came from nearby rural towns: Irasburg, Derby, Glover. Sometimes people would arrive from other shelters that had exceeded capacity, or someone from a nearby cot would disappear after a family member made room in their home. It was a changing community, but a community nonetheless.

Most of our days were spent watching CNN as the destruction elsewhere was chronicled. An entire portion of the country had been decimated in the first forty-eight hours of The Storm and tens or maybe hundreds of thousands of people were missing—many of whom would never be located. Lawmakers in Washington had activated every emergency aid tool at their disposal and the international response was impressive, but so much more was needed. The Storm looked different from emergencies of the past. The devastation was too grand, too expensive and too lasting for easy solutions. With Manhattan, Boston, Philadelphia and Washington obliterated, it was hard to find hope in the news. Even the polished, smiling correspondents on cable had a difficult time maintaining composure in the face of that reality. There was little attention paid to the more rural and forgotten corners of our country that had been washed away, which was fine with us in the Northeast Kingdom. Staying under the radar was a way of life and source of pride for Vermonters; The Storm didn't change that.

As soon as we had enough generators in the shelter and the internet connection was restored (one of the only in the region), we lined up at the aging high school computers to check emails and message boards for signs of life from our family members. It took four days to find August's parents, who had been moved to a shelter an hour away after their hospital was evacuated. When we finally connected by phone, we all cried for our own reasons. August's father would need physical therapy, but he was going to be okay. As soon as we heard their voices over the phone line, I found myself thanking that unnamed god I'd been speaking with; it seemed ungrateful not to.

I'm never going to know why the universe decided to save August's father, but I felt indebted to some divine power for the outcome. The expression on August's face at the sound of his mother's voice changed me forever. He heaved an enormous, primal sigh of relief at first, which changed quickly to unease at the realization that his fate was unknown. He wanted to melt at his mother's breast, secure in the knowledge that she would shield him from further atrocities. But she wasn't that kind of mother and they didn't have that kind of relationship. So August was relieved, but frightened and unsure now, too. I wanted to never give him up.

"I wish you could come," August said as I helped him onto the rescue tank that was to deliver him to his parents. He looked nervous.

"Me, too. But I have to stay here and find Pia."

He nodded. "Maybe, after I see my mom and dad, I can come back here to be with you?"

"Maybe," I said. I didn't want to overpromise. I had no idea what was possible. The world had been overturned and I was at that moment without a wife or even a home. I had no idea what options still existed for either of us. "I'm going to find you as soon as I can." This I knew to be true.

I helped buckle August into the massive tank, possibly the

same one that had rescued us a week before, and gave him a hug that lasted long enough to make him squirm. I would miss his small body, his clammy hands that reached for mine at night, the way his dirty hair matted around his pink face when he woke up in the morning. I felt a love for August that was unlike any other variety of love I'd ever experienced and I ached to give him up. *He isn't yours*, I thought. But then, whose was he?

The tank pulled away and I waved until it was long, long gone.

I wasn't just sad to be without August. With him gone, I was left alone with my panic over what had become of Pia.

I spent another two weeks at that shelter. Mornings were devoted to looking for my wife and the rest of my family online while intermittently reading heartbreaking news of the tragedies that others had endured during The Storm. My parents and siblings were all okay. Their homes had suffered various levels of damage and I suspected that my parents weren't being honest about just how bad their living situation was, but I didn't have anything to offer them, so I didn't press for details. I couldn't even visit, not without working roads or access to a car.

One afternoon, after exceeding my allotted time at the shared computer, I found Pia on a live storm chat board. She had posted her full name and location and, just as I'd hoped, was looking for me. My heart beat quickly as I saw her name and the little icon beside it that flashed to indicate she was online.

Pia, it's me, Ash! I typed frantically.

Oh, thank God, Ash, she replied. Where are you?

We rushed through the details of our location and state of health, desperate to know that the other was safe. She explained that she had stayed through the final days of The

MEG LITTLE REILLY

Storm while the first floor of our house filled with water and then everything in our life washed away. Learning all this in text that scrolled across a very public screen was strange, inappropriately casual and distant, but there was no other way.

Pia: I was dehydrated and in the early stages of pneumonia when they found me, so my memory is a little foggy. I think a rescue crew carried me out, but I'm not sure how they knew I was there.

Me: It was me! I told everyone you were there, Pia. I was terrified for you. Are you okay now?

Pia: Yes, they took me to a pop-up medical site in Shelburne, which is where I am now. It took a while to recover, but I'm okay. It was scary. There were all these people with terrible injuries. Some of them died, Ash.

Me: I don't know what to say. I'm so, so sorry.

Pia: Thanks. I'm fine now. I've met some interesting people here, too. It's not as bad as it sounds.

Me: I'm just glad you're okay.

Our conversation continued like that for a while: Pia reported on the tragedies she'd seen and I stumbled along in the typed equivalent of speechlessness. I was sad for her, sorry for the responsibility I took for her experience, confused about what I was supposed to say. She didn't ask much about what had happened to August and me; I didn't expect her to. Finally, we had to go. Computer time was strictly enforced and I had already spent too much time at the one in front of me. I was unsure of how to conclude such a discussion and relieved to be rushed off without time to consider it. *I love you and I'll find you tomorrow* was how I signed off. She said something similar and that was it. We needed to make a plan for how to find each other, figure out our lives, but it would not happen on that day.

Once I knew Pia was alive, I could breathe again. The choking sensation that had been strangling me for weeks loosened around my neck, and I began to believe that life would go on. But how, I couldn't fathom. It was difficult to imagine a poststorm world in which Pia and I returned to one another—almost as difficult to imagine a world in which we were apart. Still, something changed when I left her in The Storm—or she chose not to join me. (Which had it been?) There was a lot of death around us in those days and we couldn't yet tell the difference between temporary changes and permanent endings. Whether our marriage could be saved after all that had happened was unclear.

I roamed around the cinder-block high school that had become my communal home like a zombie after that, watching others as they worked to stay upbeat and plan for the rest of their rearranged lives.

During lunch the next day, it was announced that Interstate 89 had almost dried out and road crews were hoping to open parts of it up within a few days, which elicited a round of tepid applause. Most people had nowhere to go, but it was the first hopeful thing we'd heard in a while.

The day after that, the bathrooms on the east side of the shelter clogged up and the entire wing had to be cordoned off.

Salt packets and napkins ran out in the cafeteria.

An old man died in his sleep.

These were the details of our lives: large and small, meaningful and minute. We responded to everything with equal

MEG LITTLE REILLY

attention because our physical and mental survival depended on both. We pondered the existential challenges of this new, devastated world while praying to God that the coffee supply didn't run out. In a different life, I would have thought it a humiliating existence, but coffee takes on a new flavor when it's the greatest available pleasure.

Pia and I chatted online every day for a week until finally the main road between her shelter and mine was scheduled to reopen. She said she could get a ride to Isole with the next delivery of supplies, which was two days away. I was thrilled. The promise of holding my wife again was the most hopeful news I'd received since August left. All of a sudden, the doubt and confusion I'd been feeling with our distance faded. I was sure that seeing her, smelling her, feeling her, would be curative; our bodies would remind our hearts why we needed each other.

TWENTY-FIVE

ROAD IMPROVEMENTS TURNED out to be more complicated and time-consuming than state officials anticipated, so Pia's arrival was delayed by several days. This was nerve-racking for me personally, but it also heightened tensions at the shelter because it delayed the delivery of supplies. We had learned to live without things like paper towels, but the absence of toilet paper, tampons and Advil was taking its toll. One afternoon a fistfight among three restless teenage boys broke out in one of the hallways and, though I was among the adults who helped break the guys up, part of me envied their freedom to express the frustration we were all suppressing. The living arrangement couldn't last much longer.

After the fight, the adults at the shelter agreed on the need to open the doors and allow for more exposure to the outside. Up to that point, the flooding had been so deep and polluted that no one went through the heavy doors of the high school unless they were accompanied by rescue workers. But the sun had been out for days and anyone with a pair of boots could wade through the muck by then, so it was time to get some air.

I was among the first to get outside. I borrowed a pair of too-large wellies from the man who slept three cots down and just roamed for a while under the direct sun. The water was ankle deep with a dark, oily reflective quality from all the filth it held. We were told that it was mostly farm waste runoff, but we knew better. It smelled like chemicals we couldn't identify and human sewage when the wind blew from the east. Livestock were decomposing in it—maybe people, too; we weren't ready to consider that. Still, the sun was hot on my face, I had two working feet and it felt good to be outside.

I roamed around the high school grounds for two hours on that day, down the main road to a gas station that had been abandoned and back across the underwater baseball field. A total of five trucks had passed in the time I was out, each creeping slowly through the poisonous pool and stuffed with people whose desperation was clear from afar. I couldn't have guessed where they were going; it seemed unlikely that there was anywhere to escape *to*. I suppose they were in search of the people they'd lost in The Storm, other desperate people in equally bad places.

When I finally went back inside, a volunteer directed me to the locker room to shower and change immediately—a precaution we all agreed upon before opening the doors. I took a threadbare pink towel from a bin and made my way down an empty hall. As I turned the corner for the men's room, a small, hurried body nearly crashed into me. It was Maggie.

"Ash!" she yelled and threw her arms around me in a quick hug. "I wondered if you would be here! I'm so glad you're okay."

I felt a surge of relief and excitement; it was like a dream to see her standing there. In all my anxiety about Pia, I'd been working to *not* think of Maggie. I had decided that I didn't deserve to miss Maggie or to wonder what could become of us. I had almost convinced myself that she wasn't real at all—and then there she was, standing in front of me. Her hair was pulled back into a messy ponytail and she had a smear of dirt above her left eye. There were new freckles on her face, as though she had been outside while the rest of us turned gray indoors.

"Maggie! What are you doing here? Are you staying here?"

"No... Sort of." She stuffed a package of bandages into the back pocket of her jeans and straightened her T-shirt, which said Central Vermont Slalom Finals 2009 in fading blue letters across the breast. "I was here for the first few days—down on the other end by the theater—until I could get to my parents' house. I'm just volunteering now. How about you? Did you lose your house?"

"I think so. I don't know, really," I sputtered. It seemed as though years had passed since we had last seen each other, and bringing her up to speed on all that had happened was too daunting.

"Is Pia here, too?"

"No, she's in Shelburne. We're going to see each other soon."

"Of course." Maggie nodded. "I'm glad she's okay."

We looked silently at each other, considering who we were supposed to be at that moment. I wanted more than anything to hold on to her, but I couldn't allow it. It wasn't just her that I wanted either. I wanted to feel more of what she had reawakened in me. After weeks of moving anonymously and robotically through my days in the shelter, seeing her reminded me that I was *known* by someone, was more than a ghost in Isole. I wanted to see Peg and Salty, too, to hear their stories about how the rest of the town had fared. Seeing Maggie reminded me of my place in Isole. It was my home.

"Do you have a car that can get around in this?" I asked Maggie tentatively.

"I do!" She seemed eager to change the subject. "My dad's truck gets me here. There are only a few open roads, but it's enough. Do you want to go somewhere?"

"Can we get to our road? I want to see my house. And August and Peg. Have you been back?"

Maggie shook her head. "Our road is still underwater. I think it will be another few days before it dries out. Is there anywhere else you want to go?"

Somehow, I knew the answer to this question immediately.

"Yeah, can you take me to see my friend Crow?"

She smiled. "I know Crow. Everyone knows Crow. Sure!"

Maggie didn't ask why we needed to see Crow. She knew that I'd been lobbying locals for the dredging project, so maybe that explained the odd request. Mostly, I think she was happy to do something away from that place, which had developed sharper edges in the previous few days. And maybe she was content to just go somewhere with me.

On a normal day, in our previous lives, the drive up to Crow's hill would have taken about fifteen minutes from the high school. But on that day, it took over an hour. We crept slowly through the still-flooded main streets, leaving a spray of ugly liquid in our wake until we reached the foot of the small, unrecognizable mountain our truck would need to climb. Fallen trees blocked the most direct route, so we tried another back road that state crews appeared to have cleared. Wide patches of trees around us had fallen during The Storm, which made the face of the mountain look like the aftermath of a horror movie up close. Road crews had cut and cleared a narrow passage up the road, barely wide enough for our truck, and we prayed not to meet any oncoming adventurers as we drove.

We could barely breathe as we took in the devastation around us. Houses that had been tucked cozily into that forest for decades lay flat among the trees that once protected them. There were colorful remnants of the lives spent there— clothes, toys, furniture—peeking through fallen walls and piles of crumbled brick chimneys. Because we were slightly higher in elevation by then, we had left the flooding and entered a drier phase of desperation, where The Storm's destruction could be viewed unobstructed, baking in the afternoon sun. (It was still March, but the weather had stopped tracking with the seasons.)

The possibility that Crow might not be alive came to me slowly as I worked to understand what I was looking at. No one on that hill would have survived if they attempted to ride The Storm out there. Was his shelter that strong? It was one of those regions that I'd heard about on the news and over quiet conversations about the "missing."

Maggie made a choking sound and I saw that she was crying as she held tight to the large leather wheel of the truck. The tears streamed down her face and dripped from her chin to her fading jeans, but she made hardly a sound. I wanted to reach across and touch her hair, but I didn't. I just sat there in the passenger seat feeling it, too. I would have cried if I could, but I was so hollowed out by my own loss and regret by then that crying seemed too much effort.

About a half mile from Crow's driveway, the cleared path that we had been following stopped abruptly. There was a massive pickup truck parked off to the side by a fat tree stump and a chain saw. Apparently, that was where the road crew's work had stopped. We had no other options but to leave our own truck in the middle of the road and walk the rest of the way.

We climbed out and began walking. I led the way with Maggie close behind. She had stopped crying by then. I could hear the crunch of her hiking boots as we focused our heads down on the mess of branches and uneven earth beneath us.

"There's a tree farm on the other side of this mountain," she said from behind me. "My family and I used to go every year in early December to tag our Christmas tree. Always a balsam; it had to be a balsam. Then we'd go back a few weeks later when it was ready and my dad would cut it down with this dull handsaw that he insisted on using. I think it had been my grandfather's."

We took a few more silent steps and I drifted into my own winter memories. Collecting evergreen boughs in the woods for my mother. Dragging new sleds up ancient hills…

"And now it's all gone," I said. "We get so attached to these rituals and places. It feels like it matters…but maybe it doesn't."

"What?" Maggie stopped abruptly and looked up at me as I turned around to face her. Her arms hung limp at her sides. "You don't believe that nihilist bullshit, Ash." I had hurt her. "You're devastated by the loss of these *places*. I can see it all over you. I love that about you. You just saved a seven-year-old boy you barely know, so don't tell me none of this matters… Jesus."

She began walking again and passed me on the left. Was she angry with me? I wanted to tell her that she was right, that those woods mattered more to me than almost anything and I was sick over what had become of them. But instead I said, "I know August really well."

It was a relief to arrive at Crow's driveway and turn our attention back to the task at hand. We had to climb over several fallen trees and used our hands to fight through the bramble to get to the opening where his humble house sat. Because his home was located at the top of a hill and out in the open, it appeared to have fared better than many of its neighbors at lower elevations. I searched for signs of life as we made our way to the front door, but I saw nothing. Electricity was still out and phone lines were down for hundreds of miles. If there was anyone there, I imagined it to be the most isolating kind of existence.

Maggie stood silently behind me as I knocked on the door. One light set of knocks, and then a harder round. No one came. We shuffled our feet and looked up at the sun, which was lower now as it was close to four, but still warm on our skin. I considered checking in with the vague deity I'd been talking to in those days but couldn't summon the focus. After another minute, I stepped away from the door and began walking around back with Maggie in tow.

As we turned the corner around the back of the house, I saw Crow's large, intimidating German shepherd sleeping in the shade. He lifted his head but didn't bother with us. Next to him sat a rusty lawn chair that was fully reclined with its back to us.

"What do you want?" a young female voice said from the chair.

Someone was there, but it wasn't Crow. I jogged a few steps and looked down to see a girl of maybe sixteen lounging in the chair with her eyes closed and an old magazine draped over her stomach. It looked as if she had been sunbathing, but she wore tight jeans and a black T-shirt with the name of a band I'd never heard of. She was frightfully skinny and pale, with visible blue veins that snaked around her bare ankles. Her toenails were splotched with chipping black paint.

"Is Crow here?" I said. "I'm a friend of his."

"What kind of friend?" she asked, with no apparent interest in opening her eyes or engaging further with me.

"A friend from…his meetings and from town. A regular friend. So he's alive?"

The girl snorted and opened her eyes. "Yeah, he's alive. He's in there."

She pointed to the shed that housed Crow's bunker. I nodded and motioned for Maggie to follow. With the worry of Crow's whereabouts behind me, I was free to indulge my curiosity about how his little shelter had endured The Storm. I walked quickly toward it and swung the large wooden door open.

The thin metal door behind it was closed, but not locked, so I gave two light knocks and then stuck my head in. Crow was sitting on the couch beside a pile of old photos. The interior of the room looked untouched by The Storm. Everything was more or less where I remembered it to be, but with a few lived-in additions. A cup of old coffee sat on the tiny kitchen table with lumps of souring milk floating at the top. There was an armload of dirty clothes pushed into a corner.

Crow was staring forward at nothing in particular. He took a noticeably long time to look up and acknowledge our presence but smiled slightly when finally registering me.

"Ash. How are you, man?"

"I'm okay," I said, moving a step forward to lean against the wall that the little bed folded into. "I wanted to make sure you were all right…and to see how things were going up here. You know my friend Maggie."

Crow smiled a little wider, but his body remained wilted. "Nice to see you, honey."

"This place looks great, Crow!" I went on. "It's, like, the only place in town that looks the same after The Storm. You were right about all this, you know?"

"Nah." Crow shook his head and looked at the floor. "I wasn't right about shit."

Something was very wrong.

"What do you mean? What happened?"

Crow took a deep breath and leaned back into the sagging couch.

"That girl out there?" He pointed through the metal walls. "She's my daughter. Smartest thing you'll ever meet. She lost her mom in The Storm—my ex-wife. I could have saved her, but I didn't. Now I'm alive and she's dead. For what?"

His eyes were searching into space again, glassy and vacant. We were barely there to him.

"Crow, tell us what happened," Maggie said softly from my side. I could feel her body slide down effortlessly into a cross-legged position on the floor, where she would sit while we waited for his story.

Eventually, Crow spoke again, relaying all of the painful and confusing memories of the previous weeks. His ex-wife and daughter wanted to hitch a ride up from Putney before The Storm struck, but he told them initially that there was no room. After the first day of The Storm, he realized that he'd made a mistake and changed his mind. Crow wanted them there with him in his little shelter. They worked out a plan to meet in White River Junction, where Crow would pick them up and take them back north. But when Crow got to their meeting spot, only his daughter was there, injured and in shock. The van they had been riding in with a group of travelers had been struck by a tree on I-91 and most of the people in it died instantly. His ex-wife was one of them.

It seemed a miracle to me that Crow and his daughter managed to get back up to the Northeast Kingdom unharmed at that stage of The Storm, but I didn't point this out. He was in the deepest throes of grief at that moment.

And now he was a single parent to a teenage girl he'd hardly seen in recent years. Crow's bunker was unscathed, but his new life was unrecognizable to him.

We stayed in the cramped space for a cup of tea and so many heart-wrenching silences. Crow cried on and off. Maggie held him awkwardly at times while I watched. I had never been so close to this kind of grief—violent, preventable, complicated death. It felt something like the time Pia convinced me to do a guided meditation in a sweat lodge when we were vacationing in Sedona. I remember my body transitioning from uncomfortable to unbearable in that hut and then to a heady sort of lightness where I detached entirely from my own selfish senses. I lost all awareness of my own grief and guilt while we were in there with Crow. It was clarifying, but I couldn't endure it for long.

Eventually, Crow stopped talking entirely and we sat in silence for a while. I didn't know how long we should stay or what one was supposed to do in such a situation, but it was getting dark and we were nervous about the drive home. We had to go. So Maggie hugged Crow's limp body and I promised to visit again soon. We left him there, in the indestructible little shelter that couldn't protect him from much at all.

Our walk back to the truck seemed so much longer than the walk there, accompanied by only the sound of our boots on the forest wreckage, which was deafening in my pounding head. I couldn't account for what we'd just learned. Crow had invested everything in the promise of his own survival—which he'd achieved—and it had ruined his life. But hadn't August's parents and the nice man who died in the shelter that week and all the families of the missing had their lives ruined, too? All the nonpreppers who had put family first had been punished by The Storm with the same wrath. If there was a lesson in all this, I couldn't find it. There was no order or reason behind the destruction and that was almost as frightening as the destruction itself.

Maggie had gained some distance ahead as I got lost in my thoughts, and I could see her climb into the driver side of the red truck through the darkening air. She had been crying again and her face looked pale even from that distance. What had she said to me on our walk to Crow's? *I love that about you.* She wasn't really talking about me, but my attachment to the land. Still, she had said the word. And, more important, she saw this in me because it was in her, too. We knew so little about one another, but it had been clear from the moment we met that we shared this fundamental trait. We were ourselves in those woods…the way they used to be.

I opened the passenger-side door and slid in, but I didn't bother closing it behind me. As I looked at her hopeful face, her soft reddish hair that fell around her shoulders and her small, strong body that sat behind the wheel, I felt a surge of something wild and alive. I reached around with one arm and pulled her toward me. We kissed desperately and clumsily on the giant bench seat of her dad's truck. Her body was warm and we both wore the ripe stink of people who no longer enjoyed daily showers. It surprised me how much I liked it.

She went for the zipper on my jeans first, and then we rearranged our positioning, with her lying flat on her back and my knees searching for somewhere to go. It was awkward and cramped, but there was no stopping, not for either of us, as we clawed gently at one another's bodies, working to move aside our grubby clothes just enough to make contact. A mosquito bit my lower back. I considered swatting it away, but just then…we found each other. Past zippers and layers and all that anger. We pressed tightly together, making sounds that were most at home in those haunting woods. I hadn't had sex in what seemed like a lifetime, but that wasn't why it felt so necessary, so essential to our survival. All the fear and confusion and loneliness of the previous weeks was unleashed between us and, if not fully exorcised, forgotten for the briefest moment.

No explanation or justification exists for why I betrayed Pia in the truck that day, but I believe that a decisive action of some kind was needed then to prompt me to start making choices about my poststorm life. Without that nudge, I would have just dried up with the rest of the wreckage. It was a complicating, terrifying and irreversible action that jolted me back into my life.

TWENTY-SIX

IT WOULD BE three more days before the supply truck that transported Pia could get over the mountain from her valley to mine. I spent that time away from Maggie in an attempt to clear my mind of her and minimize further temptation, but the memory of our indiscretion in the truck played on a constant loop behind my eyes. I saw flashes of her bare skin while I ate breakfast in the cafeteria and smelled our un-washed entwined bodies in the malodorous shifting winds from the open windows. That moment followed me every-where as both a thrilling memory and a new layer of guilt.

I had only one discussion with Maggie in those three days, to ask if I could borrow her dad's truck. Most of the roads in Isole had dried out and I couldn't wait any longer to see what had become of my house. She was happy to lend it and asked no questions about why I wanted to go alone. Every-one around us was slowly reacquainting with their former lives—seeing their wrecked homes or, worse, identifying the bodies—and it was understood that we each had to do this in our own way.

The drive home was solemn and surreal as I took in the

changes to the Northeast Kingdom landscape—a landscape I expected never to change. The Atkins family's sugar house had vanished from where it normally sat and half of their home was collapsed. Half a mile up, a rusty green Chrysler sedan blocked the entrance to the Pinaults' farm. Beside it, the hand-painted sign advertising a new litter of bunnies lay unreadable and cracked. And the centuries-old stone walls that snaked around the properties, delineating lines of ownership from generations past were toppled over, finally beat by something stronger than themselves.

Most haunting was the total absence of human life. Where had everyone gone, I wondered. Certainly, some people had left before The Storm. And others were stuck indefinitely in rescue shelters like myself. Still, that didn't seem to account for everyone. It wasn't just that I saw no one; it was that I saw no signs of anyone even passing through. There were no ditches marked with the wheels of stuck, spinning trucks. There wasn't even the occasional crushed Bud Light can from the bored teenagers that drove around at night. There was nothing.

I pulled the truck off to the side of the road at the entrance to our driveway, which was predictably impassable. As I worked my way on foot through the messy path, I noticed that all the trees to my left had fallen in exactly the same direction, while most to the right remained upright. More cruel evidence, I thought, of nature's random and meaningless punishment. Stop looking for order where there is none.

It was April and unseasonably warm, which was beginning to seem seasonal. Buds were appearing on the trees that still stood, but the sound of birds was noticeably absent. All I could hear was the ubiquitous hum of mosquitoes, which I didn't know then would follow us indefinitely thereafter. The mosquitoes on our new earth are fast and resilient. By the time you try to slap one, it's already grown fat with blood and is on its way to another donor. I was grateful for the protection that my long sleeves and pants provided as I walked toward the house, despite the sweat that was collecting underneath.

The first sight I caught of it was like a punch in the gut. It was mostly upright, but a massive fallen maple tree lay right through the center, its branches splayed out wildly. The windows were all broken and debris from the wreckage was scattered around the yard, baking in the sun. In case there was any question of whether I could return to this life, it was an inarguable sign that everything behind me was condemned to the past. Move forward, it said.

I crept through the house, awed by the destruction and inexplicably frightened to touch anything. It was like a nightmare I still hoped to awake from. The flooding had bizarrely rearranged all the furniture in our living room and drained color from the tattered fabrics. Upstairs, a wasp's nest sat comfortably at the foot of our bed, stopping me at the doorway. I was most startled to find that the antique fixtures that used to gleam in both bathrooms had disappeared; someone had taken them. It wasn't that I wanted them back for any material or sentimental reason, but it was the first evidence of the desperation many would find themselves in after The Storm. I didn't know then that stripped and looted homes would soon become commonplace across the country. Those were the earliest signs of our new economy.

When there was nothing left to see, I sat empty-handed on the collapsing porch one final time. I thought I would find more artifacts of my former life there—faded pictures in broken frames, mementos from noteworthy events—but there were none. I had never noticed it before, but Pia and I stopped building a life together when we moved into that house. Moving to Vermont was the realization of all our shared dreams, and once it became real, the longing for it disappeared and we didn't know how to define our existence anymore. Our future was blank.

Eventually, I walked down the path that separated our land from August's badly-damaged-but-still-standing little house. He wasn't there, but it appeared that his family had returned, so I left a note on the door, promising to come back soon. Knowing that August was alive was the greatest comfort I had. It wasn't enough, but it was something; a wish fulfilled (or a prayer answered) and an antidote to the hopeless confusion that occasionally overtook me.

I didn't visit Peg's house that afternoon. I don't know what kept me from walking through the woods—the woods that had almost killed me weeks earlier and now looked so flaccid and powerless—but I couldn't do it. I hadn't yet heard from or anything about Peg, and a part of me knew that the news wouldn't be good. Instead, I squinted through the jumble of fallen trees at her house, straining to imagine her drinking a cup of coffee at her kitchen table, and continued walking to my truck. I knew that she wasn't in there.

"Did you go to Peg's house?" Maggie asked when I handed her the keys an hour later.

I shook my head.

She searched my eyes. "Sit down."

We were standing in the crowded gymnasium that still served as a sort of recreational space for the wards of the shelter. A ring of women were knitting to my left while younger children darted around playing tag.

Space was whatever we made of it there, so Maggie and I sat on the floor, her compact form cross-legged and me hunched forward around my bent knees. My body felt stiff and cumbersome.

"What is it?" I sighed.

"I just got news of this while you were out," she started. "We don't really know much…"

"It's Peg?"

"Yes. Salty came by. He wanted to tell you personally. They found her body."

I dropped my head, unsure of whether I would throw up or burst into tears at the news. Instead, I was overcome by a dizzying ring in my ears. I watched the floor spin.

"Ash, I'm so sorry. I know you had grown close."

I could barely hear Maggie through the ringing, which continued for another minute before I could get any words out.

"She was outside? Alone in the woods?" I asked.

"Yes, how did you know? She was about a half mile from her house. No one really knows how exactly The Storm got her, but it was too late by the time she was found."

"I know what happened," I whispered.

"What?"

"I know what happened," I said again, more loudly this time. "The Storm didn't *get* her—she went to it. She asked for this."

"Why would she do that?"

"Peg couldn't stay to see what life looked like after The Storm, how it would devastate the environment. It would have been too much for her. She knew how bad things would be and that there would be nothing left for her here."

Maggie looked baffled but didn't argue with me.

I stretched out onto one side and pressed my cheek into the cool, dirty floor. Eventually, I felt Maggie beside me, close but not quite touching me. She began talking in a low, soothing voice that I thought probably worked well with the young children she taught. I closed my eyes and drifted between awareness and a sleepy haze while she spoke. She told stories about small, sweet moments she'd had with Peg, bumping into her at the coffee shop, occasionally riding her beautiful horses. I couldn't comprehend the finality of Peg's departure. I needed her there, in that new life, to help me make sense of things with her peculiar spirituality that I was beginning to understand.

When Maggie ran out of things to say about Peg, she reported on all that she'd learned from Salty's visit. He knew which roads were still bad, which local buildings would have to be demolished and who was leaving town for good. I didn't move or make a sound, but I think Maggie knew that I appreciated her efforts to steady me. And Salty was okay, which was good news. It sounded as if he was busier than ever, working to rebuild our devastated town and stay hopeful for everyone else's sake. His oldest daughter, who had been planning on coming back to Isole after college, had apparently decided to move to San Francisco instead. Maggie noted that this seemed to make Salty very sad, but it was probably the right thing to do; opportunities would be scarce in the Northeast Kingdom for a while. And on and on. Maggie stayed with me until I drifted to sleep there on the floor of the busy gymnasium.

TWENTY-SEVEN

Meet me at Mountain Roasters at 10:00 a.m.

THOSE WERE THE email instructions I received from Pia on the morning of our planned reunion. I had expected to meet her at the shelter and was oddly excited about showing her the life I'd been living in those weeks, to fold our separate experiences together again. But something had changed with her ride and now she wanted to meet downtown.

Exactly three establishments had reopened in Isole since The Storm and the coffee shop was one of them. I had heard from others who'd taken the shuttle bus into town that the coffee tasted odd (there was something strange about the water, despite the state's insistence on its safety) and you could pay only in cash, but the muffins were as good as ever. So I dressed as lightly as possible, in anticipation of a hot day, and decided to walk the two miles into downtown to meet Pia that morning. I had five borrowed dollars in my pocket.

I don't know what I envisioned for our meeting, but I was optimistic and entirely open-minded about it. Despite all that had happened between us, and the magnetic pull I felt toward

Maggie, I still considered a fresh start with my wife. I was sure that if she told me she wanted me, I would go. Repairs would need to be made and some bad habits broken, but if Pia wanted to do it again and better, that seemed reasonable to me as I walked along the side of the road, considering the possibilities for how our reunion would unfold.

At the end of my walk, it was a relief to step out of the hot sun and into the dark, aromatic cave of Mountain Roasters. There was one empty table near the front window, so I took a dog-eared copy of the previous day's *Burlington Free Press* and sat down to wait for Pia. I didn't have the patience to read the articles. Instead, I kept one eye on the door and scanned the national headlines, surprised by how little I knew about what The Storm had done to the rest of the world: Asian Markets Plummet after Storm's Wrath, New York City Transpo Continues Indefinite Closure, Unexplained Smog Plume Grows Over Youngstown… It was all too large to comprehend. The physical, economic and institutional collapse that The Storm had created seemed endless. This rattled me. I had no intention of leaving Isole but had been comforted by a vague belief that there was somewhere better to escape to, which was apparently not the case.

"Sometimes it's better not to know," I heard Pia say from behind me.

I jumped up from my chair and threw my arms around her. She seemed thinner and smaller than before; her embrace was weaker.

"I missed you," I said.

She let me hold her for another fraction of a second before gently pushing back and taking a chair across from me at our small table. I sat down as well, grinning widely for the first time in weeks.

"I missed you, too." She nodded, not exactly smiling.

"How was your ride? How do you feel? Do you want some tea or something?" I rushed through each word, unsure of where to start.

Pia shook her head. "No, no, I'm fine. I just wanted to talk, really."

"Okay, great. Let's talk, then." I took her fidgeting hands in mine and held them still. It wasn't clear whether she liked it or not, but I couldn't stop. I felt strange sitting across a table that seemed too large in a room filled with strangers.

Pia took a long breath before speaking. Apparently, we weren't going to spend any time chatting about small things. "Ash, we need to get out of here," she announced.

"Out of the coffee shop?"

"No, out of Isole," she said. "You didn't think we'd stay after this, did you? There's nothing left here."

"I don't think there's anything left anywhere."

"There's more…if we go far." Pia wasn't discussing this; she was telling me. "Remember Benny, my friend from college? His parents have a huge condo in Boulder. Some of us are going out there."

"Some of *us*? Who else are you talking to? This decision has already been made?" I felt the familiar choking sensation return to my throat. "But this is our home. I love it here."

"You don't love it here," Pia corrected. "You're comfortable and it's familiar, and that's what you like."

I shook my head. "It's more than that. I feel invested in Isole. August is here. August is here."

Pia rolled her eyes. "You can't stay."

She pulled out a tube of lip gloss and circled it around and around her lips with great concentration, as though it was the most important task in the world at that moment. She wasn't listening to me. Pia had made up her mind and was sure that I would follow her.

"Why do you want me to come?" I asked.

Pia looked startled. "Because you're my husband, obviously."

"That's not a good reason, Pia. It sounds like the right reason, but it's not. The right reasons are you love me and can't live without me, and you care about what happens to me. Any of those would have been the right reason."

She waved her hand, as if I was being overly dramatic and wasting her time. And with that gesture, I felt a stirring deep in my stomach. It started as a rumble and then shuddered through my entire body like a small earthquake. I realized that I felt nothing for the person sitting across from me anymore. There was the weight of a shared history, but nothing that pulled us closer in the present. There would be no fresh starts between us, not ever. This was the end. And just as I wasn't powerful enough to mend things between us, I realized that I wasn't powerful enough to be solely responsible for what was broken either. With that realization and the little earthquake that passed through my body, all the guilt and shame that I'd been carrying around since the day I left Pia in The Storm fell away.

It became instantly clear to me that this line in the sand before us was a gift—maybe the only gift—of The Storm. And I refused to feel guilty about that. The Storm had blasted wide-open all the small fractures that previously existed in our community and society at large—and our relationship was no different. I decided then to learn from the destruction and move on. I would rebuild something stronger, on a sounder foundation for an uncertain future.

I stood up from the table with tears in my eyes, paused for a moment to steady myself and walked out. Leaving that coffee shop without Pia meant leaving behind the last real thing that had been mine before The Storm. I had nothing now. But it was a bountiful nothing; I'd gained a big, hopeful unwritten future with that nothingness. It felt right.

TWENTY-EIGHT

AMERICANS TEND TO shine in the aftermath of disaster, coming together to reboot and rebuild. We promise to remake our great cities—this time bigger and better—as a demonstration of our will. Our leaders talk about the endurance of the American spirit and an unwillingness to accept defeat. This time was no different. The people in power assured us that America's resolve could never be broken. We were driving toward success! But that same relentless push to build and grow, grow, grow was what created this problem—not Americans alone, but we had a disproportionately large role in the overheating of our angry planet. For as long as growth defines success, won't this continue, we wondered to ourselves.

In the smallest, subtlest ways, I could sense a change in the people around me after The Storm. There was a hesitation to rebuild as big and bloated as we had before. Instead of rushing to erect grand, defiant houses where the old ones had been decimated, more modest dwellings were built. Demand for consumer goods dropped across the country—and stayed low—despite all that had been lost. And states spent their dwindling resources slowly, on roads and bridges at the expense of grand symbols like football stadiums and shopping malls. There's an immediate cost to this, of course. Low consumer spending has kept the economy at a sluggish pace and new jobs are scarce. But this slower, more deliberate recovery feels safer somehow. It's moving in the right direction and there's no risk of its reversal.

Like a shared religion, we've embraced simplicity with a renewed fervor in the Northeast Kingdom. The hard lines that divided us in the months before The Storm are dissolving again and we're returning to our roots, believing in the people we know and the things we make. Even Rodney Riggins realized soon after The Storm that his message held no power here anymore. The last I heard, he had a new congregation in South Carolina and a Riggins-branded line of prepper bugout kits. He left no lasting mark on our community.

Like a lot of people, I live closer to town now, within walking distance of the food co-op and the library. My small, sparse apartment is one of four in a large house just off Main Street. It's private, but not so private that we can't glean a lot about each other's lives through the walls. I share a car with a few other people in the building in a loose agreement that works surprisingly well for the time being. On Saturdays, I get together with a bunch of locals to repair a network of hiking trails that the state has no money to fix. We figure it will take about a year of Saturday hikes to restore the trail between Isole and Newport. It's a long time, but it will be done right and hold up better in the next storm.

I share all of this new life with August as his legal foster parent. As a single guy, it's unconventional, but most conventions are useless now and the rules have bent. Bev The Social Worker helped expedite the process once I got settled, and it has been as transformational as The Storm itself. August and I have settled into a comfortable routine, moving in a small footprint around our little town, but filling it up completely. School, work, cooking, hiking, reading, sleeping. Apparently, I needed these things as much as August. We're both better than we've ever been. Most important, August is himself—building forts and talking to birds and resisting reality at every turn. I'm going to fight reality off for him as long as I can. He'll grow out of the stories in his head eventually, but I won't let that happen a day sooner than he's ready to part with them.

Work dried up for my design firm as swiftly as The Storm's waters and we were forced to shut down. I worry about the few staff members who had kids and wish I could have done more to help them. For me, the end was a blessing. I volunteered to help the Vermont Tourism Board with some of their public outreach efforts in the wake of The Storm, and they eventually hired me as a part-time web designer. The pay is minimal, but so are my expenses. And it works for August.

I like this life. Maggie and August and I spend nearly every day together with Badger always a few feet away. She picks us up in the afternoon when school is out and I've finished my work for the day, and we drive back up to her house to chip away at repairs. Her home was badly damaged by The Storm, but it's salvageable. We cleared the yard of debris first, then pumped the water from the root cellar, refinished the wood floors and rebuilt the deck. It will look prettier than ever after the interior and exterior painting is done, which should be another month or so. August and I will move in when the repairs are all made and the divorce is final, which I'm looking forward to but not rushing. Like so many things in our new life, we're building slowly and sustainably.

My body is changing now, too. I'm using my hands, my arms, my back to build this new life, doing things I didn't know I could do. I feel physically exhausted at the end of the day and I sleep deeply each night. On a recent trip to visit my parents—who I see more often now—my father joked about the primitive work that has displaced many of my old digital tasks. He didn't say more, but I saw pride in his eyes. There's so much of him in me. It took too long for me to recognize my father's greatness. My father—the tough, rural, lawyer–outdoorsman–civic leader that I find myself striving to emulate most days. I don't say this out loud, but he knows. We chop and stack wood together with August in tow. I ask for his advice on our home repairs. That's enough for us.

Back at Maggie's house, we laugh through the hard work. She holds the wood in place while I pound a hammer into our new bookshelves and we debate which finish to use. I have to remind her to slow down and listen to her body now that she's pregnant. We're having a baby! What a strange, un-expected reminder of nature's resilience that is. An irrational vote of confidence in the future's brightness, despite so much evidence to the contrary. Months before, there was only me. Even in marriage, there was really only ever just me. And now I'm on the eve of having two children and a perfect, peculiar family. At the end of the day, I rest my hand on the paint-splattered clothes that stretch across her growing belly and marvel at how full life is today. She's growing—we're growing—in the most surprisingly wonderful ways.

TWENTY-NINE

THE LANDSCAPE OF the Northeast Kingdom was defined a few million years ago by the Ice Age. Glacial advances and recessions created its fields and forests and the melting water carved its dramatic mountains and waterways. And before anything could grow again, the vast, lifeless desert of ice had to cede to a warmer new climate.

It's not so different now. The Storm and flooding wiped out most of the life around us. The sophisticated network of wildlife and botany that lived here for hundreds of years has been evicted. What's left this time are the humans and the insects. The insects fared best of all in the poststorm world.

I want to believe it will regenerate, that another epic cycle of life is beginning today. I want to know that two hundred years from now, Isole's graveyard of trees will be home to *new* old-growth forests, where elder pines provide shade to eager saplings and low-lying shrubs; that the woodland homes for native wildlife will be restored and their lanes of travel bustling again. Most of all, I want to believe that the instinctive rituals of every species will still adjust predictably with the shift of each season. The black bear must be able to rely on the cold and the scarcity of food as a signal to rest for winter. In this fantasy, the forest still suffers traumas—there will be wildfires and early frosts—but only as prescribed by nature for regenerative purposes, routine ailments to build up immunity. I want to again believe in nature's invincibility.

None of this will happen, I know. The planet we live on now is fundamentally different from the one that spawned the forests I fell in love with. Everything is changing. Something will grow here; that's already begun. But it will be different. I wonder often how these changes will transform the culture of the Northeast Kingdom, a place that has defined itself in relationship to nature.

Amid all the loss of The Storm—my marriage, everything I own and the identity of my community—the loss I feel most deeply is that of the natural world. My Vermont woods not only look fundamentally different, they *feel* different. It's as if the composition of the atmosphere has changed just noticeably enough to make me aware of my breath.

We are animals from the past in a future habitat.

★ ★ ★ ★ ★

ACKNOWLEDGMENTS

None of this would have been possible without my tireless agent, John Silbersack, and my brilliant editor, Kathy Sagan. Both of you took a chance on me and I'm so grateful.

With all my heart, I wish to thank my parents, Anne and Joseph Little, for showing me the woods and passing along your sense of adventure, awe and gratitude. You gave me idealism, and I promise to pass it along to my children. Thank you to my children, Josephine and Annabelle.

I have the love of my life, Daniel Reilly, to thank for so much. You never once questioned the probability of this endeavor or the wisdom of waking up at four in the morning to write fiction before going to work at the White House. For your encouragement and humor and everything else, I thank you.

And finally, thank you to the women and men working to address climate change and alleviate the human rights, economic and racial injustices suffered under it. We're all behind you.

WE
ARE
UNPREPARED

MEG LITTLE REILLY

Reader's Guide

MIRA®

1. Ash and Pia are chasing a romanticized idea of a more simple and sustainable life. Is this relatable to you, or do you consider it a misguided or perhaps even a privileged fantasy?

2. Do you think Ash and Pia would have made it as a couple in Vermont even if the superstorm had not happened? Why?

3. Which of the characters in *We Are Unprepared* do you consider to be "normal," and which do you think of as "crazy"? Can extreme circumstances make sane people insane?

4. Which of the characters in the novel would you most behave like in these circumstances?

5. If you were facing the same weather disaster, would you align with the civic-minded mayor and Ash, or the prepper group and Pia?

6. Once the storm hits, civil society falls apart quickly, and the death toll begins to mount. Does this seem like

hyperbole to you? Do you think local, state and federal governments are this unprepared for a superstorm?

7. Is it noble or selfish for Ash to want to adopt August? Does the lack of choices in a rural, devastated place change this calculation?

8. Fear drives characters in this story to religion, alcohol and guns. What other vices and comforts do we all turn to in anxious times?

9. Does the superstorm seem plausible here? Do you consider it science fiction or an inevitability in our future?

10. No explicit assertion is made in the novel that the changing weather patterns are caused by human behavior, though it's certainly implied. Do you perceive this story to be about man-made climate change or about chance? How might those different positions affect your opinion of the book?

11. In your own life, what aspect of the natural world do you feel most protective of? Is there a place or an experience that you want to shield from the effects of climate change?

12. Do you believe successive generations will have a different relationship to the natural world?

13. Do you believe fiction and art can influence public attitudes about climate change?

What is your debut novel, *We Are Unprepared*, about?

We Are Unprepared *is a psychological thriller about how we live together in a time of fear. As a historic superstorm draws closer, fear threatens to unravel a marriage, a community and the entire East Coast. It explores how the consequences of climate change can hold us in a state of anxiety and paranoia.*

Your novel tackles some big issues, and yet at its core it is a domestic novel about marriage. Can you talk a little about what you hope to convey?

I initially conceived this novel as a story about fear in three tiers: the societal level, the community level and the domestic level. I wanted to go deep into the effects that sustained fear would have on our psyche and our relationships. As I did that, it became clear that the story would have to focus on a marriage. I just kept peeling back the layers, and eventually it took me to an intimate place. I accidentally wrote a story about climate change in our bedrooms.

I hope, first, that this is a story you can't put down, and second, that it's scary enough to be motivating. Fiction can do what hard science can't by using fantasy and speculation to paint a picture vivid enough to make the human suffering feel real. When it feels real enough, we will all demand bolder climate policy from our elected officials.

What inspired you to write a story set against the backdrop of an approaching megastorm?

Catastrophic weather events are the only time climate change has an immediate and hugely tangible effect on individual American lives...for now, at least. It's the one time when we can't look away. I wanted to explore what life would be like with the sustained and omnipresent threat of a storm forecast—which many places in the world live with already. It is a test of the characters' sanity and civility, which are far more tenuous than we like to think.

Politics taught me that it's impossible to effect change if people don't feel a sense of urgency and proximity to a problem. This is a major drag on climate progress. The science is in and it's incontrovertible, but we're not sufficiently energized about it. Well, a megastorm is urgent and immediate. It's motivating.

There's also an efficiency to my storytelling that comes directly from my experience in the White House. In political communications, you have mere seconds to capture the public's attention, so I tend to get right to it.

Are you a weather junkie? How did you research the environmental issues at play in the novel?

Like any kid who grows up in the country, I'm a weather watcher. To research this storm, I studied the biggest storms of the past decade. I wanted to create a weather event more powerful than anything we'd ever seen, but not far from the realm of possibility. So I looked at all the worst-case-scenario forecasts for those past storms and I made them just a few degrees worse. I tried to follow the science. My imagined storm doesn't require much suspension of disbelief.

The novel is set in a landlocked state. We tend to think of hurricanes as being coastal. Could the events of the novel really happen in Vermont?

Superstorms can and do devastate landlocked states now in our new reality. Part of what makes this story so terrifying for me is that it takes place in a region that we once considered safe from coastal storms. I'm not sure I knew what a hurricane was as a child in Vermont. Then in 2011, Hurricane Irene cost the state almost three hundred million dollars worth of infrastructure damage. I remember fighting back tears at my desk at the White House as I watched footage of my hometown on CNN that day.

Why did you choose Vermont as the setting?

In many ways, this story is a love letter—or an elegy—to the woods I grew up in. I was always going to write about Vermont. I know the Northeast Kingdom intimately. Most of my greatest memories are at its lakes and mountains and trails. And now we take our daughters there. Its name is befitting; the Northeast Kingdom is an enchanting place.

Ash and Pia move to the country to capture their idea of a more perfect life. But, as the novel's title implies, they are unprepared. Do you think they are foolish to pursue this dream?

Ash and Pia are motivated by fundamentally good principles: they want to redefine what success and fulfillment look like. They aren't alone in this; so many young professionals are rejecting the old standards of materialism and overconsumption, which is a great change. But I did poke some fun at all of us for the often-romanticized notion of what it means to live authentically. It can veer quickly into a parody of twee privilege.

Pia falls in with a group of people who call themselves "preppers." Does such a group really exist?

Preppers are real. There is a robust online community of people who identify as preppers, sharing ideas about how to be prepared and self-reliant in the case of emergency. It would be easy to dismiss them as a paranoid fringe, but I think that's a mistake. At their best, preppers have a healthy distrust of institutions, and they challenge our assumptions about what's possible. I'm still utterly unprepared, but I loved delving into this world.

One of the more intriguing characters in the novel is a boy named August. What role does he play in the events that unfold?

I love August. His character embodies my own anxiety about the disappearance of nature in children's lives. I don't mean a respect for nature, which I think kids are being raised with now, but an opportunity to be truly wild and of nature. I spent a lot of my early years in the woods, and it was such a gift. This isn't just an increasingly rare experience; it has always been out of reach for kids who grow up in urban poverty or minority kids who've felt unwelcome in our national forests and trails. I was heavily influenced by the work of Richard Louv's Last Child in the Woods, and I see now that it informed the character. I hope my readers fall in love with August and recognize the critical role that nature plays in his otherwise challenging life.

Vermont has a reputation for being a state full of dogged individualists. Does that reputation play out in the novel? Could this story have been set anywhere else as effectively?

Vermonters are rugged and self-reliant, but they also come from a long tradition of civic engagement, which makes Vermont a unique place. Town Meeting Day, for example, is still central to municipal decision-making, and I think it's such a beautiful democratic exercise. *The community story line in We Are Unprepared couldn't have taken place in any other state.*

What writers have influenced your work?

I could never name them all:... Barbara Kingsolver, Margaret Atwood, Donna Tartt, Mary Karr, Meg Wolitzer. I'm also a superfan of fellow Vermonter Bill McKibben.

Now that you've had your debut novel published, what's next?

Writing novels is all I want to do these days. I'm going to keep doing this for as long as the universe lets me. Right now I'm in the process of editing my next novel. It's also a fast, suspenseful story with big issues at its core and a strong sense of place, but the similarities to my first book end there. It's set in the Shenandoah Valley—another place that's dear to my heart. Stay tuned!